To Diane,
   Merry Ch
Gt. Barrier Is, Ne

Rosalie Bay,
Gt Barrier Is.
New Zealand
28-11-15.

Aisling's Cloud

Aisling's Cloud

DON E. McGREGOR

All characters in this book are fictional, except for major historical figures.

A catalogue record for this book is available
from The National Library of New Zealand

ISBN 978-0-9941140-8-2

Published February 2015
by Copy Press Books, Nelson, New Zealand
Copy Press Books, 141 Pascoe St, Annesbrook, Nelson, New Zealand

© Copyright Don McGregor, 2015

The right of Don McGregor to be identified as the author of this work in terms of section 96 of the Copyright Act 1994 is hereby asserted.

All rights reserved.

Except for the purpose of fair reviewing, no part of this publication may be reproduced or transmitted in any form or by any means, electronic or mechanical, including photocopying, recording or any information storage and retrieval system, without prior written permission from the publisher.

Printed by The Copy Press, Nelson, New Zealand.
www.copypress.co.nz

1

Sky

We are all clouds, floating in a limitless sky of uncaring time; some of us brightly light the heavens; towering, translucently bold entities, but most of us just exist unremarkable in the background; grey vapour stealing colour from the mother blue for some years; before fading forgotten…to be replaced by many like creatures; or so me rather fanciful and ancient Celtic heart tells me. Clouds rule and shape me, moulding my misty consciousness, always have done; but perhaps they're just a hazy mantle obscuring reality and distorting my perception of the vast sky that has been my life...

At times me old mind matches the curving whirls and whorls of ancient Irish jewellery design: bending, writhing and twisting, but dully gleaming nonetheless! Some memories in there loom proud, like ageless standing stones left by unknown folk on a western headland, defying the wild oceanic winds and eternity herself; but there I go digressing, yet *again*….

Bog skint we were in those far-off days; poverty a drab uniform almost everyone I knew wore; but ah, life had zest and zing! We saw a new world we could construct ourselves, tradition and oppression could be effortlessly and stylishly vaulted over. If convention had the temerity to object, we felt we could easily elbow her aside. The world we knew *would* change! Oh, such a staunch lot we fancied ourselves to be! Money was of course lacking, but accordingly, we were masters of improvisation.

Ireland was mellow then and had an easy pace of life, the air and colours of the land soft; people uncomplicated and open, humour abounded and simple pleasures sufficed. Yes, the loathsome British were there, damn them; but they to a great extent we ignored and made fun of them behind their backs, sometimes even to their faces when they couldn't understand our brogues, wit or native tongue that they'd tried for so long to stamp out. It was only later that they really hardened and grew vicious…

Then again, the real maelstrom none of us saw coming our way lurked hidden, buried within ourselves, us Irish: but that's another tempest laden sky…

Of course Mother Church towered above us back then, poking her many steepled nose into all our affairs, but here too, we were adept at sliding past the ever-present watchful priests, with oh so *innocent* looks on our faces… to hell with eternal damnation! That was a problem to be dealt with when the time came. Mind you, we still attended mass and the sacraments; we weren't stupid! Confession was where we sinned by omission; not revealing all we'd been up to, of course. But I ask you; who really does care, before one's deathbed? Ah, arrogant little buggers we were, for sure….

A hand-me-down child I was. My mother Siobahn had died of consumption when I was four years old. She was a maternal warm creature, who always sang as she worked, or so the tiny remnant wisps of memory tell me. Anyway, that's how she remains in my heart. Her sudden absence from my existence and her funeral are indistinct to me now, although low grey skies cried forlornly that day. Apparently, soon after me birth my father, a sailor, had disappeared over the horizon in time-honoured fashion and nothing was ever heard of him. What he looked like, I never found out because all the family photographs had been lost when my mother died…not even a wedding photo survived, or so I was told. Her and me Pa mayn't have even been married! I once heard my aunt and uncle talking about him: "Sure, he was a drunken ne're-do-well black sheep; an irresponsible *bastard* if ever there was one!"

So me mum's sister Auntie Biddy and her husband Uncle Bryan raised me with their three children who were older than I; Mary, Padraig and Connell. They tried to make me welcome, especially Mary, but I didn't quite fit, although I now think that was entirely my fault. I just sort of felt different; perhaps it had been me mum's death…and my late arrival in their world. I was just stoic about it all, rather than disturbed; I soldiered on through life quietly.

Aunt and Uncle were always scrupulously fair with us kids; she loving to all of us and he firm. I think my uncle liked me 'specially, 'cos I'd listen to his stories of Ireland's tortuous past, a subject he was very passionate about. He blamed his lack of education and low station in life on British oppression. His own kids showed little interest in this history. There were six books on the subject in the house and I learnt to read on these with help from my Uncle Bryan, his much loved Jack Russell dog Shamus always on his lap, under the crucifix and photos of Ireland's freedom fighting heroes from the past, hanging above us on our dull brown parlour wall.

He also managed to acquire some second-hand Fenian pamphlets and newspapers every week which we would discuss. He was a shop assistant in a small department store, not far from our shabby digs that were located in a grey Dublin lane. Things could have been much worse; there was an ocean of real poverty around us.

I must have been close to six or so when the dark cloud of death again loomed large in my life. Padraig had been larking around near the canal with his mates and had fallen off the embankment into the water; not an unusual occurrence! The laughter, shrieks of scorn and derision had suddenly died away when he didn't reappear, as was normal. Only a few tiny bubbles on the slimy grey surface could be seen… then nothing.

A muddy, unmoving and strangely limp body was retrieved hours later. Oddly enough, I still clearly remember the stench of the muck on his clothes. Urgh! In his coffin his surprisingly small white face was restful. He'd apparently knocked himself out on something hard under the water; there was a definite swelling bump on his forehead. Much screaming and crying went on at the funeral. Me aunt was bereft with grief. As she wept uncontrollably I tried to console her by hugging her. The pressure of her voluminous soft breasts I found strangely comforting and exciting. Although I was only young at the time, I was surprised at how my embrace helped calm her. I remembered something a priest had said in church one day and repeated it. "Don't worry Auntie Biddy, God has very very 'sterious ways!" This comment brought on even more tears of grief …and tighter hugging. My Uncle's face was wooden, as closed as a locked cathedral door during a riot. Mary and Connell wept and clung to him. Padraig the oldest son had been the dominant personality amongst us kids; yet now he was gone…

That night, just before I drifted off to sleep, wondering what life would be like without him, I heard my aunt discussing my comment with her husband through the thin wall: "A funny little fish that one; but there's a brain in there somewhere all right. How Siobhan would love to have heard that comment!" Then the weeping started again…

2

Song

Music is the lens through which I view life; tones and tunes massage my every waking moment; sometimes I am even unaware of their lilt… but ever-present they are. Mother has been heard to say that I was singing in the womb, and even though I profess disgust and embarrassment at the comment, I secretly think it apt.

In another way I was not like the other girls, I knew; as all my life I'd felt different and yes, *above* or at least apart from everyone else in some way, not really so much arrogance on my part as the quiet acceptance of an obvious reality. When and where the notion started I'm not sure; it had *always* been there as far as I could remember. No, it wasn't the wealth, although I cannot deny that made the idea seem less absurd. Impoverished it would still have inevitably blossomed, I was certain….

We had shifted to the Big House and estate when I was just a toddler; for me it was all just a normal pleasant backdrop. Only as I became older did I really understand how privileged my background was.

Mother believed that Father started it all, from when I was two, by calling me Princess and it just sort of stuck. He and I were really close, though my younger brother Rory seemed to miss out on his affections. He was curt, demanding and abrupt with the lad. Even at a young age I would firmly and gravely tell my father off for this neglect… and he would listen with an admiring twinkle in his eye; "Ye'd be right Princess Aisling…indeed!" Not that he changed his behaviour. I quickly learned that I could do no wrong. My warm kind mother grew close to Rory, trying to fill in the void, but though my brother still tried hard to impress our father, he never really succeeded. I decided my younger brother was not as strong or as wise as me, so I was always protective of him.

I was only six when I found an ancient Celtic lap harp buried in a pile of dusty old furniture while exploring the dark attics one rainy day. It was covered in a grimy sheet. Under the dust I could see the glint of gold. After a long careful clean, it proved beautiful; gleaming varnish and gilt; it enchanted me. Fit for an Irish princess, I secretly thought!

I loved to gently pluck a string and listen as the long soft note caressed the room and gently faded. Pleased with my interest, Father had it properly tuned. My first self-taught tune, plucked simply with one hand opened a world of delight for me. I was determined to teach myself how to play the instrument well.

I attended the local Catholic primary school attached to a time-worn church that looked out over a tidal estuary framed by low hills, peppered with villages, cottages and the occasional ancient ruin. I noticed that all the other village kids treated me just a bit differently, following the lead of the nuns…and more rarely the parish priest who fussed a bit too much over me. At first I tried to stop this, but it was useless, the special treatment continued.

I always joined in the playground games with tomboyish enthusiasm, yet my difference remained. I had no close friends at all though I suppose I was popular in a general sort of way. I did invite one or two girls to visit my home as I did theirs, but even when young I realized this was a mistake. Comparisons were invariably made; we were obviously so much better off than everyone else. Yet I was friendly and natural with their parents and families. I was desperate to not appear stuck up. Much to my father's disgust, I would prefer to dress simply rather than stand out. Anyway, I knew my manner and the way I carried myself was what really mattered in the scheme of things, so here too he acquiesced to my opinion.

Perhaps it was the way we travelled to mass each Sunday in a car. Almost everyone else walked to the church, I knew. We arrived when everyone was already there, underlining the difference. Gradually, I realized my father rather excessively enjoyed impressing people, in any situation. Even at a young age, I found this more than a little demeaning and embarrassing. When I would tell him off for it, that admiring twinkle would appear: "Ah, yes ye'd be right yet again, Princess Aisling!" But he didn't really change this behaviour, and gradually I began to think of him as a little weak.

The highpoint of any service for me was the hymns that would soar and echo in the old church, I would quietly sing along with melting harmonies which came easy to me.

Part of my inflated self concept did not allow me to fail at school; so academically, I really worked hard, and won prizes every year. Music was of course my best subject.

At the end of the year prize giving assembly when I was eleven, I heard a parent whisper to her neighbour: "Well, with the amount of money her father is always acoughin' up for the school and parish, of course the young colleen'd be awinning prizes, left right and centre!"

I spun around and glared at them. They looked away, quite mortified that I'd heard the comment. I was shocked and infuriated. After going up on stage and accepting the prize from the priest, with the standard curtsey, I turned and addressed the whole gathering. I spoke clearly and firmly, looking specifically at the two mothers who had made the comment.

"I would like to point out to everyone here today, that my father and family did *not* buy this prize for me, or any others I have won over the years. I have *worked* extremely hard to win them all." With that, I turned and walked proudly down to my seat in a stunned, silent gathering. Even the priest and Mother Superior looked at a loss as to what to say! A young colleen addressing an assembly like that! Well… I must have carried it off though; no one laughed or was scornful. Eventually they ignored this unprecedented announcement and carried on with the ceremony, as if nothing had happened. My mother was terribly embarrassed, but my father twinkled at me afterwards. "Ah, me Princess Aisling, ye'd be after telling them; that's for sure." I realized that I had pleased him in several ways. I'd comported myself with regal dignity, spoken politely but firmly, and I had also unwittingly reminded the locals he supported the parish and school in a big way!

I grew to be not particularly devout. The way I saw it, in Ireland religion was the background music in the chamber of the nation's life: it was ever present, occasionally admired, but most of the time just accepted as a backdrop, important yes, but….

Two things weakened its hold on my consciousness: the church seemed to relegate women to a second class citizenship, the priests and male hierarchy were always ranked much higher than the nuns, who had to defer to them. I didn't think that fair at all!

The second event occurred when I was preparing for that big Irish Catholic milestone, my confirmation. We kids were being coached through the ceremony by Father Mullins our new parish priest at the time. He seemed to me a rather tired and glum fellow, tall, middle aged, thin and wrinkly, who looked at me more than he should have done, with unsmiling eyes, making me feel uncomfortable inside. Was my young mind imagining it or was it just part of that special treatment I habitually received?

At one stage he beckoned me over too him, and withdrew me into the sacristy, a quiet cool and solemn place, that I'd never visited before. It was dark, but near the small red lace curtained window, church vessels on a white linen tablecloth gleamed, the little chamber smelt of incense and wine. Next door in the church itself the muffled tones of my classmates could be heard.

The priest sat down, his eyes still on me, and unnecessarily put his arm around me and before I knew it, his other hand was up my skirt stroking my leg, while talking about the coming ceremony as if nothing untoward was happening. Knowing this was wrong, I knocked his hand away, stepped back and drew myself up and glared at him. Initially he tried to poker face his way through the situation as my young eyes bored into his. Then fear showed as he realized even his exalted position was not going to work -in this instance. I was too strong willed and my family was *the* powerful force in our community and I, and he, knew it!

Strange how even at a young age I could read people…

Father Mullins looked away and mumbled something about rejoining the others. I spun round and walked out, very angry at this confrontation. After a few minutes, the priest rejoined our class and pointedly ignored me from then on.

I thought about what had happened, what should or could I do about it? In my mind there was a faint waft of guilt on my part, had I helped bring this on in some way? I couldn't talk about it to the other girls; such things could not be mentioned or discussed. But I wondered if any of them had received similar treatment. Possibly, I decided, and they wouldn't have known how to deal with it. But I watched the priest closely from then on, and he was aware of it!

I considered telling my mother, but decided not to as she hated any upset and became easily stressed. As well, I also felt she respected the church too much to do anything about it.

I instead decided to confide in Sister Loyola, a cheerful, popular nun who liked us kids. I broached the subject when no one else could hear. Her reaction astounded me; this nice lady told me in no uncertain terms that I must have imagined it, and it was even vile and rude to bring such a topic up. Father Mullins, an ordained Catholic priest, could not possibly behave in such a lewd fashion! It was just my imagination, or was a complete fabrication and so on….; *I* seemed to be the guilty party. I was angry…. how *dare* she refuse to believe me!

I looked at her, seeing a frightened weak lady who didn't dare confront the power of the church she was a part of. God and his organization didn't seem to care much for females or children as far as I was able to work out. Sister Loyola's reaction however, did make me decide to keep it to myself; I would not tell my family.

I was aware that Father Mullins now hated me, but would quickly look away when I gave him my "princess glare" as my father called it. I had power over the priest and knew it!

We all had to go to weekly confession, I couldn't avoid going; it would have been remarked on. But I was *not* going to confess to *that* man! Instead I spent my time in the confessional lecturing *him* about his behaviour, changing the usual words to: "Bless you father for *you* have sinned....!" He said not a word, but through the grill I could hear his laboured, stressed breathing and even heard him grind his teeth once. I revelled in the fact that he didn't know how to deal with me!

A few weeks afterwards he left our parish, being transferred to one at the other end of the country, in Donegal. He was replaced by a wonderful young priest, much loved by us kids and the whole parish. I rather fancied Father Mullins was leaving because of my continued pressure; such a fanciful, wilful creature I was! But then....?

The new priest Father O'Shea would sometimes even join in the rough and tumble sports in the playground, and was always cheerful, supportive and fun. Sister Loyola seemed much more relaxed with him around; she looked at me thoughtfully from time to time, not forgetting my approach to her. One day she more or less even apologised to me, for the way she'd reacted at the time, almost hinting that it had been an ongoing problem with the former priest, but she'd had no choice in the matter. All men had drives that we women must...er, contain. Though I liked her, again I judged her to be weak and wondered if Father Mullins was carrying on in the same way in his new posting...

I was always a good reader, unlike my brother Rory who initially struggled with the skill. Because I had few friends, I read voraciously, especially history, and secretly about powerful Irish princesses of old. Yes, I could proudly identify with them all right! My reading encouraged me to practice my harp playing, I made great progress!

One day on our way back from Sunday mass, Father took us a different route through an area of rocky poor land some miles away from our home, to an old abandoned church next to a strange empty looking graveyard. There were no grand grave monuments here, just small stones with names crudely scratched on them. At one end of the space was big pile of earth; a mass grave of famine victims. No one had been left strong enough to dig individual graves; the great hunger had taken away so many. A single low rock had inscribed on it:

R.I.P.
May 1846
63 souls.

but not a personal single name!

My father was blinking back tears as he looked around the plots. "Some of our folk are here Princess," he gestured at the big mound with a sweep of his arm.

A small grave apart to one side against the far wall, did have a name crudely scratched on a stone that had been pressed into the tiny mound:

Nora Kinnane 15 years.
16 Oct 1846

In my mind lapped a sad ethereal tune, a soaring penny whistle and harp faintly playing a haunting traditional air, bringing tears to my eyes. This grave had a profound effect on me; here was a relative of mine, who'd lived just sixty or so years ago, a girl not much older than me who had died in circumstances I could not even begin to understand. Two siblings, Katie and Tom, both younger, had been buried together in one plot at slightly later dates; so perhaps she had given up her food to keep them alive longer I surmised. She would have been a distant relation of mine and I wondered what she'd been like…

On our way home, a mile or so from the graves, Father took us to two small tree lined fields, where on one a shed sized rectangle of rocks marked the foundations of a tiny dwelling. The ground was damp and soft and my church shoes were soon covered with brown mud. Mother and Rory stayed behind in the car.

Father shook his head sadly, "Our old family home Princess Aisling, me father escaped the hunger, but only just. But don't ask me how. His whole family perished. When we left this place the house was destroyed by the English landlord before squatters could move in, as happened throughout Ireland. Some poor Irish folk were actually evicted and thrown out on the street with their pathetic belongings while starving. Larger farms were more efficient, the rent from small holdings didn't generate enough money for the bastards to *waste* in England!"

"Yes, wealth is the key Aisling, at all costs, to staying above disaster. The *key*, remember that, daughter." For the first time my father looked old to me; his wrinkled face intense and eyes tearful with emotion. Our visit had been a kind of personal sharing that somehow brought us even closer together.

On the silent trip back to our home that sad background music stayed persistently with me. I resolved to research the history of the great famine in Ireland.

The more I studied the Great Hunger, the more upset and intense I became. How could God have let such horror happen to poor people? This was another nail in the coffin of my religious belief.

As we swept into our drive and up to the Big House, I suddenly wondered about the family who had lived here for centuries before us: how had they treated their tenants? Was my family benefitting from their cruelty in any way?

Through this visit to my ancestral home, without knowing it at the time, I had gained a secret, lifetime close friend.

Nora abruptly appeared in the darkness of my room that evening. She never introduced herself, but I instinctively *knew!* She was quite clear in my mind; a very thin face with large worried dark blue eyes, tousled, black hair, dressed in a ragged shawl and coarse homespun skirt with bare feet. She was accompanied by that faint, wistful and ethereal music.

Her voice was lilting. "Y' comin' t' see me t'day was a big surprise Aisling; may t' good God be ablessin' y' now, f' visiting a starvin' cottage colleen like mesel'! T' years can't keep 's apart, *now!*"

Before I had a chance to answer her, she was gone.

She'd visit me from time to time, especially at important moments in my life, always seeming so real…

3

Sky

Smelly grey coal smoke burst in plumes from the four funnels and poured out across the slate coloured dirty waters. The monstrous black ship was so large there was no dock big enough to accommodate her, so she was anchored well out in the harbour, which made her appear a bit smaller to us here on the pier. Her raked masts and funnels made her look fast, even when anchored!

Smaller boats were running back and forth to her. This was one of my key memories as a teenager on my first train trip away from smoky grey Dublin. Special inexpensive excursion trips had been laid on by the train company and we had just been able to afford the outing. Thousands had lined the Queenstown/Cobh waterfront with us to witness the spectacle.

My aunt had called it "the grandest ship in all the world." Although owned by the English White Star Shipping Line, the great vessel had been built here in Ireland, up north in Belfast and we were all inordinately proud of that fact. Above me a flag with a big white star on it was fluttering. I distinctly remember the odd sound of its rope slapping noisily against the metal pole in the blustery wind.

We looked enviously at the people going out to the ship on the steam tenders that passed us. We would have loved to visit her.

We ate the thick sandwiches Auntie Biddy had made us and tried to ignore the smell of freshly baked cakes from the bakeries along the waterfront near us; we couldn't afford them.

Uncle Bryan had stayed behind, missing out on this outing entirely. I'd been upset about that and had offered to stay behind in his place. He'd appreciated my thoughtfulness, but told me that we didn't have enough in the kitty for a second adult fare. Mary and Connell hadn't thought to offer to give up such a rare treat.

But the highpoint of the day for me was a rather strange, distinct little cloud that appeared almost magically above the thin blue strata of coal smoke, from one little steamboat running out to the great ship. I'd never seen a cloud like it; it had an unusual reddish brown tint to it, almost a light auburn colour. Was it my imagination or did it move more slowly than the others across the sky? For some unaccountable reason it raised my spirits; I felt suddenly uplifted and cheerful, everyone noticed the change in me. It was all rather odd…

But we were cold, tired and hungry by the time the big ship had crept out to sea and had grown smaller, taking a distant relative of mine with her, a stoker, my aunt's favourite cousin. We returned to Dublin on our same day excursion train. I again marvelled at how fast we travelled and even the third class compartment seemed comfortable to me as the world slid past. I was seeing other places for the first time that I'd only heard about. We stopped briefly at Cork, and some other smaller towns, arriving back in Dublin at night.

A few days later it was discovered that the big ship had sunk, taking our relation and so many with her. Aunt Biddy was so upset at his passing. Life was sad at times…

For some reason this event seemed to me a monument in my grey existence. Yet that cheering little cloud persistently stayed in my thoughts…

4
Song

My uncle and auntie were going to America, and we were going to Queenstown to see them off. Actually, of course, we were really going to have a look at the wonder of the age, the *Titanic*, the largest, most luxurious ship afloat. My father did business with the builders of this leviathan, Harland and Wolff up in Belfast and we were going to have a special tour of the vessel.

I was in a grumpy mood on the car ride north. That morning, Rory had broken a piece of my favourite miniature crockery from my doll's house while clowning around. Although I was now twelve, I still admired the expensive birthday gift from a few years back. It had a little sign, "Princess Aisling's Manor" on its front wall. Even Father's attempts to cheer me up had little effect. I sullenly looked out at the passing countryside. Mother just put up with my mood by ignoring it.

The port of Queenstown was in a festive mood when we arrived, the waterfront was crowded with people everywhere, flags and bright bunting were flapping in the breeze.

We boarded a White Star Line tender; passengers and mailbags were loaded and with a puff of white steam we began our trip out to the ship. As we glided past a crowded pier a sudden burst of beautiful music erupted in my mind; from nowhere it seemed to me, and a spurt of unbridled joy came upon me. Where had this sudden change come from?

I didn't tell anyone, but Father noticed the abrupt change in me; "Ah Princess, y're a sparkling gem when y're smiling, y'know!" Even the fact that he'd embarrassingly said it in front of others didn't upset me as much as it should have done. It was all a mystery to me….

The ship was unbelievably large as we pulled alongside; the black hull towered above us and neat rows of portholes curved off far into the distance, both ways. We had to climb a steep gangway up to a door in the hull, I snagged my skirt on a railing at one stage, but the little tear was almost invisible. The vessel was luxurious and crowded with people and bustle. I loved the sweeping staircases with the round domed skylights above, the glistening chandeliers, the rich varnished panelling and ornaments, the pot plants, the restaurants and the grand decks lined with deckchairs. There was even a swimming pool, gymnasium and a Turkish bath aboard! We were shown my aunt and uncle's first class cabin, which was just perfect. All of us wished we were travelling on her and were very envious of the passengers we met.

"Sometime family… we must do it!" Father twinkled at us as we had afternoon tea with delicious cream cakes in the Café Parisien, complete with French waiters, and comfortable wicker chairs. We briefly met Captain Smith who presented Rory with a model of the ship and Mother and me with cups and saucers engraved with the ship's logo! He was such a nice man, but very busy.

After just an hour and a half on board we made our back to the waterfront. The music that had stayed quietly with me on board swelled again as the tender we were on passed that crowded jetty. But it gradually faded as we drove south to our home. It was all extremely puzzling.…

A few days later, we heard the astounding news about the Titanic sinking, the great loss of life. After an anxious wait of two days we eventually learnt our relations had survived.

How could such a large, beautiful creation have, just like that, been wiped off the face of the earth? We wondered how many other people we had met or seen, had died. Initially, there was some confusion as to who had survived, but in a few weeks we learnt that some first class passengers, especially men, had died. The loss of life in second and especially third class passengers was appalling. Nice Captain Smith was being held accountable in part for the disaster the newspapers told us.…but he had died in the sinking. Big inquiries into the disaster were going to be held on both sides of the Atlantic.

It was the second time it happened. As I lay in the darkness awaiting sleep a bright picture appeared in my mind; the thin face of Nora came to me that evening, her face particularly grim, eyes impatient, her lilt a little sharp.

"Aisling, Y'll be amemberin' the poorer folk aboard, many o' them Irish, like our'selfs, not jus' t' high'n mighty! *Cream cakes!* How c'd ye now? Well, I *ask* ye!"

She faded into an indignant, hungry blackness, leaving me feeling guilty with my wealth, but excited at this second, surprising but private, personal contact…..

We were all upset by the sinking. My Titanic cup and saucer reminded me of that memorable day but now saddened me, yet a remnant of that music that had surprised me that day on the White Star tender would slink back and console me from time to time…..

5

Sky

 To be quite honest, y'know, there's always been a permanent dismaying haze throughout the sky that is my life. It's disappointing; a bit like when you climb a mountain on a perfect day, expending all that effort, just to be greeted at the summit by an indistinct horizon in all directions.

In my mind I've always been a towering, broad shouldered, curly haired Irish lad, witty and well armed with devilish charm, a devastating twinkle in the eye and a nimble way with me words. It was therefore painful coming to terms with the scrawny shy figure that daily confronted me in my mirror; the thin, plain face, the weak light blue eyes framed in cheap round rimmed glasses, the sparse untidy thatch of hair that unenthusiastically crowned my uneven skull. To that accursed mirror I silently abused the God of Looks. In life I coped with my predicament by being quiet but sounding intelligent when I did open my mouth, which wasn't often. I was aware that some of the heroes of my land had also suffered from my affliction and it hadn't stopped *them*. I'd worked out even in my teenage years that appearing clever could compensate for the deficit of my appearance, so I really worked hard at it.

My poor background wasn't allowed to get in the way; I quietly educated myself with an enduring passion, becoming a free public library dweller, spending hours soaking up our tumultuous past and reading the histories of other nations who had shrugged off the yoke of colonialism. Uncle Bryan approved, although our discussions in the dingy parlour were often heated. These were the only times I really let myself go and freely expressed my innermost opinions.

Oh yes, another component of me makeup; Aunt Biddy nailed it when she once said to a neighbour, "Pigheaded little bugger, once 'e gets 'is stubborn up; watchout!" That I am for sure; always have been; in fact got worse as I went along through life …

As I studied the unfairness of our long history my spirit became aflame with hatred and cold determination for our enemies, but this blazing fire was unseen by others. I rather liked it that way; a core of my soul relished secrecy with a strange natural intensity. I might look nondescript, but there was a ruthless Celtic storm brewing in there somewhere, secreted in a deceptive, featureless overcast of dull grey.... at other times I imagined myself an invisible night cloud, skulking above in the mysterious darkness, but real nonetheless, affecting all, a harbinger of change, obscuring the stars with my blackness. There I go yet *again*; -talk about rambling on...!

Lonely I was though; aching for closeness and love that eluded me; that looks thing again affecting me confidence, I suppose; but here too, little did I know what a gleeful torrent the gods of fate would pour on me...

Song

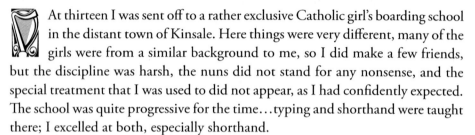At thirteen I was sent off to a rather exclusive Catholic girl's boarding school in the distant town of Kinsale. Here things were very different, many of the girls were from a similar background to me, so I did make a few friends, but the discipline was harsh, the nuns did not stand for any nonsense, and the special treatment that I was used to did not appear, as I had confidently expected. The school was quite progressive for the time…typing and shorthand were taught there; I excelled at both, especially shorthand.

At school I learnt how to read music, and continued to sing and play my harp developing my skill and confidence. I began to perform in public with two other girls.

I worked hard and passed all my school exams with flying colours over the years. By the time I was sixteen, I felt confident that I had worked out my world to a great extent.

The most significant and powerful creatures in my world were men. My father and uncles, the parish priest, the policemen, the military authorities, the mayor and local dignitaries who ruled our district were all men. The one real exception was the Mother Superior, our headmistress who was a woman to be reckoned with, but usually, she had to work in with males who held power.

Only as I grew older another aspect entered my life's equation; the goddess of looks had smiled on me; my long auburn hair, large green eyes, creamy face and slim but curvy figure always caused a stir, especially with the males in my world. Men, those supposedly all powerful figures, became weak and just folded when confronted with an attractive woman, I discovered. It was strange, I reasoned, that the more distant and less interested I appeared, the harder they tried to impress me. It was an effortless form of power I had over them, *stupid* creatures! Physically stronger than women but quite unaware as to how simply they could be manipulated by us, the fairer sex.

I didn't smile as much as the other girls, who seemed to do so all the time; being pretty they thought it. I rather primly considered that I didn't need to. It was that trying too hard thing again, I suppose....

Nora appeared before I fell asleep. "Hoighty-toighty nonsense Aisling! So y' fancy y'sel a bit o' a *looker*, wd ye now? It'll go t' y' head if ye don't watch out! Y' sh'd be agettin' more fat on ye bones, y' too *skinny* m' friend." Abruptly she faded.

Nora made being slim almost a capital offence! She did help keep me grounded, however... well, at least sometimes I felt so.

At one level I did become interested in boys, but the ones I met were never as self confident as I was, which caused me to quickly lose interest. My parents made sure I was quietly pursued by one or two eligible young men from quite well to do families; but while blessed with looks, my family's great wealth was a handicap I felt. I didn't want to be desired for that, thank you!

There was a secret part of my heart that hungered for a close emotional relationship, slight shadows and tones of loneliness would seep in occasionally, but I would overwhelm these with energy and activity, and of course music. Could there ever be a prince for me out there somewhere? I wondered from time to time...

I practiced my shorthand and typing by occasionally helping Father with his paperwork, learning a lot about the family businesses as I did so, but he thought it beneath my position in life to work in such a way. Yet the war had accelerated the trend of women working, as the men were needed for the front.

Before the conflict started to bite and I left girlhood behind, I had decided that Ireland must become a free and independent state. I joined the Cumann na mBan, the women's arm of the nationalist movement. My father looked on this as a temporary indulgence.

Nora approved however, a hint of a smile on her face. "Y'll b' doin a bit for poor ole Ireland, Aisling, gettin' ye feet back in the mud...well, a'least a lil bit; gd' fr ye, it'll be!"

I answered her. "I hope so Nora, but the women's group only has a supporting role..."

"Better n' nuffin' I'd be athinkin' ! Might be 'portant one day."

I started to learn the Irish language as a first step and eventually became quite fluent. Secretly I obtained some Fenian papers such as *Irish Freedom* which I read avidly, soaking up the ideas presented there, identifying with the nationalists. I introduced all this to Rory, who loved the idea of being a rebel. At an early age, he joined the Irish Republican Brotherhood or IRB as it was known then, not telling our somewhat pro-establishment Father…..

Nora seemed to approve. "Y' could be adoin' worse Aisling! T'ings in my day wuz *so* hard, we wuz starving yet goo' food was bein' exported left right 'n centre t' England from ole Ireland, many shiploads daily; 'twas a crime I'm athinkin'. Yes, we should b' arulin' our own land…*G'd* on y' girl! "

She made me smile…

Sky

The clock always ticked comfortably on the varnished wall above the orderly rows of volumes. The leather scented dark library was a silent second home for me, a refuge from the noisy teeming tenement in a poorer part of the city we called home. The hard wooden seats I hardly noticed; the ideas, stories and worlds I visited there submerged mere physical discomfit. I never took a book out of the free library, knowing that I'd be leaving a record of my tastes if I did; another way the Brits could nail us, I fervently and rather fancifully imagined.

One day while I was perusing an old Fenian tome a visitor disturbed me. He was chatting up the women librarians none too quietly in a West Cork brogue; they were obviously charmed by him. I would love to have had the nerve to do the same. Afterwards he came down the room towards me. He was all I wasn't. Average height, so taller than me, twenty or so; strong framed with brown eyes and curly hair, quite dapper in a smart suit that was almost English in style; but there was an air of importance about him, a restless confidence and energy. He grabbed some volumes off a shelf in my favourite section and sat down opposite me. There we sat reading for an hour or so. He read quickly, the pages impatiently turned with a snap. I surreptitiously glanced at him from time to time. He started and caught my eye on one of these occasions, looked at the volumes in front of me and nodded in approval, but said nothing. Eventually he arose and returned some works to the shelves, selected another from the Russian history section on his way back to his seat. I could see he had incorrectly replaced some books; after all I knew the Irish History shelves by heart, having read everything there several times.

I cannot abide inaccuracy in such matters, petty as that may be. I stood up and went and rectified the problem. I turned back into an angry suited wall confronting me. Quite unheard, the fellow was now standing directly in front of me, glaring down. I was intensely aware of my threadbare clothes and short meagre stature… but I was *not* going to be browbeaten, and defiantly stood my ground, waiting for him to speak. Oh yes, 'me stubborn' was up all right! I tried to keep the quaking fear I was feeling out of my eyes. Surely he would see my wildly beating heart emphatically shaking my thin body.

"So ye tink I got it wrong, eh?" He reached over and checked the volumes on the shelf and started. His face was annoyed. "Be Jaysus, you're right… now isn't that a thing? It's not like me to cock things up like that." (It certainly wasn't, in the seven or so years I knew him, I never saw him once make such a mistake, despite always being under great pressure. Indeed eventually, his very life and ours depended on his unfailing accuracy.)

'Well boy, so what do you tink's Ireland's problem eh? Lack of courage, huh?" He demanded, waving airily at the books on the table in front of me. I was surprised to be asked for my opinion, even though he was probably just deflecting me away from his embarrassment. I thought and looked carefully around the reading room before answering in a low voice: "Informers, too *much* courage, but not enough thought or cunning… just like the 1905 Russian revolt, you'll also no doubt have been alookin' at…" I glanced down at the volume he'd just selected…my cheeky but hushed voice trailed away uncertainly.

He stared at me for an age, his face inscrutable. I'd been right though, he was surprised I'd latched on to his game so effortlessly. "What's yer name then?" I lied, effortlessly making up one on the spot.

His eyes locked onto mine and he shook his head doubtfully. "Nah, ye're a *weedy* specimen! A *Weed* I tell ya. *That's* the name I'd give you."

A fury built up within me, but before I could attack him he added: "*But* there's some real Irish *balls* in there lad." And he grabbed my genitals through my clothes and tweaked them none too gently before he suddenly turned and left. "Me name's Mick by the way, boy," he called back and was gone, before I could gather my wits. He'd left the Russian history volume on the desk, unopened, I noticed.

The compliment had actually offset my painful nether regions and his hurtful honesty about my appearance. It had redeemed my shame a tad. If I'd known at the time who he was, or rather more accurately, the person he would become, I'd have glowed with pride.

Unknown to me a towering cloud had visited the rather empty space my life had become, foretelling of a distant deluge that would envelope us all in its boundless clutches… well, that's the way I see it now; sounds pretentious, doesn't it? Ah, there I go, yet *again*…. –sorry!

8

Song

When the war in Europe suddenly started, my world changed in many ways. The family's businesses prospered dramatically. Several of the local boys of good family who had come to parties at our house, joined up, and had become officers in the British army in the fight against the Germans, somehow hoping that their actions would lead to eventual home rule for Ireland; thousands of Irishmen did so. The fools! The sheer growing flood of casualties was their only reward.

I wanted to do my bit for home rule and put some feelers out in the movement. Living in our peaceful country backwater would achieve little, I decided.

Dublin was the place to be, but how could I get to live there? My father almost smothered me, his only daughter, with excessive care. Even my "going redhead", as he called my explosive outbursts of temper, didn't work in this case. My mother, although worried about me, sensed my need for a more meaningful existence and sided with me, but to no avail.

But a way presented itself to me; a musical scholarship to Trinity College, for which I worked extremely hard, sat some exams and a practical harp test and passed with flying colours.

Although worried about me being alone in the big sinful city, Father eventually relented with pride, as I was going to be the first member of the entire family to go to university; although he did upset me by suggesting that it was perhaps easier to do so now because so many men were away at the war. But I was so elated at escaping the nest that I refused to get annoyed! I could hear joyful tunes in my head. He arranged for me to stay with some family friends who had a lovely house in the leafy south of the city.

Dublin was smoky and noisy, a world of great buildings, parks, people and never ending hurly-burly. Life soon took on an established pattern; I settled into my studies, worked hard and began to enjoy student life; feeling special, yet part of an old tradition as the university was hundreds of years old. I put quiet feelers out seeking a way to help in the fight for Irish freedom, without much luck to begin with.

Eight months after me, my brother Rory had rebelled and had come to the city, ostensibly to work. What really made my blood boil was the fact that our father almost approved of Rory's attempt at independence; why should boys be treated so differently to girls? It wasn't fair!!

Actually my brother was involved in the movement and things were afoot. He was seldom discreet and told me of a possible coming rebellion. There was much drilling of the uniformed volunteers on the streets, some with mock wooden rifles, which made the rumours seem rather fanciful.... Rory insisted there were several thousand real rifles and much ammunition in the area.

During Easter 1916, I travelled back south to my home, Rory refused to join me for the holiday weekend; saying he was too busy.

It was rather soothing to return to my home; Mother was especially pleased to see me. The clean air and general peace of the countryside was a tonic to a pressured city dweller.

As I was returning to Dublin I heard the electrifying news, at a railway station on the way. There had been a large rebellion in the city, centred on the GPO in Sackville Street. Hundreds of men were apparently involved I was told. I worried about Rory; he was bound to be part of it.

The city had strange tense air to it, when I got back. I walked towards the city centre but wasn't allowed to cross the river. There was a group of British Army soldiers sheltering behind a makeshift barricade on the bridge not allowing anyone to pass. I managed to see in the distance an Irish flag fluttering proudly in the light breeze above the large building which gave me a bit of a lift. Only sporadic shots were being fired at that time. I left and apprehensively headed back to my accommodation. That evening I could hear rifle shots from a range of northerly directions; apparently a number of actions were being taken around the city. At first the most intense one being in the Mount St. Bridge/Northumberland Rd. area by the Grand Canal where the British suffered their largest number of casualties.

I was disgusted to discover that Trinity College was being used as a staging post for British Government troops. It was closed to students because of the rebellion. Travel became very risky, there was so much sniping; bullets were flying everywhere and there were many civilians killed.

Things were only sporadic for several days while the British brought up reinforcements and weaponry, including their field guns, and a gunboat, the *Helga,* started shelling the GPO from the river on Thursday. The crump of shells exploding could be heard. I stayed home, frantic with worry for my brother. I wondered where in the city he was fighting.

Another aspect of the whole business disturbed me. Confusion seemed to reign; the rebels were so poorly armed against a well equipped enemy, even one fighting a major war elsewhere at the time. I had heard of the "blood sacrifice" notion, which I thought was pointless and stupid. Would Rory be part of that? I couldn't find out anything for days.

Meanwhile law and order broke down in many parts of the city, and widespread looting and arson committed by the impoverished occurred, flames lit the night sky. Communication to my home broke down.

In the tenements Dublin's desperate poor had gained when the unemployed had enlisted in the British army, the "separation money" sent back by fathers and sons kept families alive. That was now seen to be put at risk by this rebellion…. and many of the poor bitterly opposed the rebels. Abstract ideas of freedom and sovereignty meant little; food on the table for hungry mouths was what really counted! Nora would no doubt have quite a bit to say about that…

The surviving rebels surrendered on the Saturday, and the city fell eerily silent, after six days of gunfire and explosions.

At last I could venture out to try and find my brother.

The scenes that greeted me were shocking, rubble, broken glass and bodies littered the bloodied streets, damaged and destroyed buildings were everywhere, many still smouldering ruins. Our beautiful city was transformed.

Armed British soldiers were still occupying roadblocks. Asking around, I eventually found out where the surviving rebels were being held, outside the Rotunda hospital. It took me so long to get there through the debris littered streets that I only had a few minutes to look through the lines of dispirited, exhausted fighters, wearing grubby tattered uniforms, many who were wounded,.

And then I found him! Rory gave me a weak grin; white teeth in a blackened face. When he saw me in the crowd of onlookers, he signalled to me that he was quite unhurt. I couldn't get close to him; the guards were not allowing anyone to approach.

I was in a rage as he was marched off to prison in Britain with the other rebels; for how many years; who knew? Such a waste! I'd heard that the leaders of the revolt were being executed… but it seemed the rank and file might escape that fate.

As I watched in a crowd of onlookers, many cursing and jeering the rebels, something really strange and completely unexpected happened. Into my mind came a deluge of beautiful music, completely suppressing my deep bitterness at the scene I was witnessing….a sudden abrupt softening of my mood. I was astounded at this explosion of feeling and music quite unrelated to the situation I was witnessing.

The crowd milled around as three soldiers dived in and extracted a young man standing behind me, whom they thought might be a supporter of the rebels. They made him join the line though he was protesting his innocence. In the melee I was carried along by the onlookers, and then the euphoric feeling faded as abruptly as it had arrived. It was to be some eighteen months before I was able to work out the cause…

I quickly returned to my lodgings through the wreckage strewn streets to get a message to my parents.

My father thought the revolution a stupid mistake at best. His Dublin business premises had been damaged and trade had stopped temporarily… that was for him a far more important consideration. Strange, how his views were aligned with the impoverished tenement dwellers……

Late that night Nora was mysterious when I asked her about the sudden feeling and music, but her big eyes smiled mischeviously, her voice smug… "S'appened b'fore t'ye, will y'be 'membering Lass? T'music'll change y'life, I'll be athinkin'… but only if y' let it!" She vanished.

What the hell had she meant?

9
Sky

I was seventeen when the Great War began; suddenly it seemed to us. There was much argument in the community; it was a typical Irish mess! Many of us felt it was good that Britain was occupied with a major conflict. The sad thing for us nationalists was that the conflict wasn't being fought on British soil but away on the continent. The Brits themselves should have felt the real consequences of their warlike ways. We thought perhaps Ireland would now be left more alone, but we were wrong. The British, fearing insurrection at just such a time, clamped down, not without reason as it turned out. However, perversely, many of my countrymen joined up to fight for the King, some for the money, others for adventure; anyway, the war was widely expected to be over by Christmas.

It wasn't. It dragged on interminably, year after year, with an ever-increasing casualty toll, in the tens of thousands. For Ireland there was a general fear that conscription would be applied in the country. But in the end, despite passing a law to do so, even the British realised that this might be too inflammatory a move, so they only just held off introducing it.

At eighteen I'd scored myself a permanent clerical job at a brewery that I found easy. Not drinking much had probably clinched it; anyhow I really looked the type. In my glass booth in the loading bay, I had to carefully record output and every single barrel that left the high brick building and to whom it had been sold. It was an important position to hold, and I proved to be good at it. The lorries and drays pulled in and out around the clock. All things considered the money wasn't too bad, but the strange thing was my hours. On my shift I'd start at midnight and finish at nine in the morning. I became used to padding around Dublin on my way to work in the dark, misty streets at night dodging the drunks. Since I didn't seem to need much sleep, it sort of felt like a full time holiday to me. My days were free: the libraries remained my natural haunt. I'd only sleep in the early evening.

During my third week at my new job it happened again: this time it was the *Lusitania* sinking off the coast of Cork, torpedoed by a German U-boat. Again the terrible loss of life…1400 or so souls; the British had learnt little from the *Titanic* it seemed to us. I would have been glad but again there were many Irish aboard her; as a race we seem to die rather well…

I didn't mix much with my fellow workers; I had to be in my booth almost all the time. But when I did join them I affected a boring demeanour, for which I took a lot of ribbing; I didn't mind. It was that secrecy thing again, I s'pose. Appearing dull had become second nature to me. When you don't say much, and keep to yourself, it's surprising how people tend to confide in you or talk quite openly when you're nearby. I'd hear snippets now and then and could piece these together. Sometimes the pauses and lowered voices aroused my interest and pointed me in the right direction.

Throughout 1915 things on the nationalist front simmered away; rumours abounded but nothing much happened.

I'd have loved to join the Irish Republican Brotherhood as they were called then, but I had that inordinate fear of informers. From my reading I knew the British were adept at using them; centuries of Irish history were littered with their foul deeds that had nipped nationalism in the bud time and time again. I went a few times to some nationalist hangouts, pubs mainly, but the loud mouthed drunken boasting and indiscreet bravado put me off. No wonder the Brits had us nailed! Anyway, even at this young age I'd worked out that a conventional rebellion could never work. I felt the Boers in South Africa had shown us the way. Guerrilla warfare had quite flummoxed the British to begin with; that was how to beat them! Hit and run, melting back into the landscape, small clouds in a sky of clouds, merging innocently back into the general population sky until the enemy relaxed; then sneak out and strike again. Direct conflict would be yet another disaster, yet this was what seemed to be in the offing as 1916 dawned. The rumours swelled and grew. The war was not going well for Britain at the time; casualties were mounting, so to us nationalists it seemed an opportune time to move.

On my way to the library from work on Easter Monday morning I noticed that the streets seemed strangely empty of people, although there were a few extra British soldiers sprinkled about here and there.

As I walked down Sackville St, (now called O'Connell) past the Central Post Office building, I was suddenly showered with glass when all the windows were smashed out from the inside. An old woman wearing a black shawl limping beside me gave the perpetrators a piece of her mind waving her walking stick at them in fury; but they just laughed at her. After removing shards of glass from my hair and clothes, I looked up to do the same, and saw framed in a window that man from the library, this time wearing a smart uniform of some kind and brandishing a pistol. His companions, as far as I could see, were dressed in an untidy assortment of outfits. He recognized me.

"Why, it's *Weed* again! We're declaring a Republic boy! Wanta join us?"

This all seemed patently stupid to me; against the might of the British Empire it was just an ill-judged venture at best or total suicidal stupidity at worst. Shaking my head I called up to him: "Haven't you remembered what I told you? Less courage and more cunning's what's really needed." It was the bravest act of my life to that time. His face hardened as I turned and walked nonchalantly away, very aware that I could be shot at any moment. Damn him! I still remembered my humiliation at the library.

But nothing happened. Hours later widespread firing started. British army reinforcements began to arrive. But aside from a few odd shots they didn't engage directly with the rebels, they just put a cordon around the occupied buildings and then eventually used artillery and rifles, sniping and lobbing shells from a safe distance. There were many civilian casualties as bullets ricocheted wildly around. Even the local Irish turned against the revolutionaries. It was a disaster on every front, even more so than I'd predicted. Not that I felt smug about it; it was such a waste of true Irish blood and goodwill for the cause of freedom for our home isle.

Every day now I travelled to and from work by a safer route. But the din of the battle could be heard everywhere in the city, especially the British heavy guns. Rumours shot around that the Brits would use the newfangled poison gas on the GPO; but in the end, thank God, they didn't.

Six days later the city was uncannily silent. The revolt was over. On my way home from work I went past the area again curious to see what remained. The damage to buildings in the area was substantial; some had been completely destroyed. Few buildings had escaped being pock-marked by bullets. Piles of bricks and smashed masonry made progress difficult.

The surviving revolutionaries who'd surrendered were being marched off to prison by heavily armed British soldiers; several rebels to be executed. Passers-bye were screaming abuse at the captives. I learnt afterwards that over two hundred and sixty civilians had been killed while only sixty-two rebels had perished. The Crown had lost one hundred and forty men in total. Some of these had been Irishmen who'd been fighting in France but had been brought back to quell the revolt.

As the captured rebels were marching away I saw Mick again. He glanced at me, nodded ruefully and shrugged. His face was dirty, unshaven and exhausted, his smart uniform now in tatters. I kept a fixed face as the British were watching the onlookers for any sign of supporters in the crowd. These they'd dive in after and arrest on the spot, taking them away. He seemed to realise this and looked away.

It was then I saw *her* the first time; a face crying with such rage her auburn ringlets were quivering, her green sky like eyes awash with pain and anger.

I was transfixed; the important history I'd been witnessing faded into insignificance. The wrecked buildings, rubble and crowds just sort of melted away; the world seemed to hush.

She was the most exquisite creature I'd ever set eyes on. Slim figure but slightly taller than I was; of course she just *had* to be. I again cursed my stature. But still my eyes couldn't leave her… I got the impression that she knew one of the rebels being marched off.

Suddenly the crowd milled around as a nearby bystander was arrested and in the melee I somehow lost sight of her. I rudely pushed through the throng in several directions looking desperately for the young woman; but nothing. She was gone though her face was engraved in my mind however.

For several months afterward I daily returned from work that way in the hopes of glimpsing her.… I never gave up hope of seeing the woman again, however, as is my nature. The creature had been a brief shimmering cascade of dazzling light momentarily glowing, but my life returned to the habitual, sombre haze I was now so used to. She must have been from out of town, but represented a towering rampart of cloud lit by a crystal sun in a peerless infinity of blue sky from another horizon …or so I deemed this ..this … *visitation*. Yes, that's what I called it!

Raving again, I know you'll be athinking…but….

10

Song

 The door burst open and the intense brown eyes looked me up and down for a fraction of a second, a shade of poorly disguised disappointment crossed his face. I was not used to such a reaction from a man!

"Well yer'l be knowin' the shorthand I've been hearing; typin' too. True er -Aisling Kinnane?" he glanced at my name on a piece of paper.

My regal glare had no effect on the tallish man at all. I was annoyed with his brusque doubting tone.

"I do. That's why I'm here, as far as I know!" I snapped back at him.

He waved his hand at a desk where there was a pad and a pencil. Before I could touch them he was speaking rapidly but concisely.

"Mmph then! Take this down: To the chairman of the Longford Chapter of the Volunteer Committee: Dear sir, I am most dissatisfied with the amount of funds raised so far……..." Michael Collins dictated for two minutes. It was difficult for me to keep up, but I managed.

"Read it back to me, now."

I did, perfectly. Of course I cheated, using my memory for the first three lines when I hadn't had the pencil in my hand, but I rather spoilt the effect by not looking at my shorthand squiggles, when I quoted them! He gave me an impatient glance.

"Mmph! Type it out now, two copies, carbons in the desk drawer there." He pointed to a new black and silver Remington typewriter on a desk and dived into a collection of papers on a loaded tray on his desk and was soon immersed in a document. It was no act I decided. Everything he seemed to do was fast. There had been no please, greeting or social niceties at all; a complete lack of manners…

I'd *show* him! The typewriter exploded in a rattle of keys as I typed the fastest I'd ever. In two and a half minutes flat, it was finished, using standard letter form. I rudely shoved it on the papers he was reading.

"Done!" I said abruptly.

He read it quickly, and then looked up at me. He thought for a second, and seemed to come to a decision with a grin on his face as he signed it and put it into his Out tray.

"Now Miss Aisling, can ye' be keeping yer trap shut, for Ireland of course? I'm getting' into the spyin' business, fightin' the Brits at their own game, anything ye see or hear, must not be discussed with anyone, even that brother of yours, Rory. Can ye do it?"

"I can!" I answered firmly.

"Are y'r fit then colleen, mmm, ye're a bit tall for us. Put yer arms up!" he ordered, laughing as I indignantly glared at him. He lifted me up. He was strong.

"Not too heavy then, good! Y'now, the female bum's the thing; they've caused problems in the past! Y've a comely figure, but I'm rather more interested as to whether we c'n get y'r through a skylight if we're raided, long skirts an' all!"

Never had I been treated like this in my entire life! My irritation seemed to please him mightily. He grinned again.

"Start tomorrow eight-thirty sharp, come here! Though, we'll be workin' elsewhere."

As he turned and rushed out the door, I called after him:

"If, I can be *bothered* to turn up!"

"Ye'll be here lass, for poor old Ireland! Though not for *me* I'm a fancyin'!" He was gone, so annoyingly assured of himself and laughing at my attitude.

Of course he was right, it sounded like an exciting job for a girl to have. I did turn up, and on time.

Although quite a few years older than me, I always saw Michael Collins as a young man in a big hurry. Everything around him was always done at an explosive pace; while letters were being typed, he saw a stream of people or worked with one of the other girls. To begin with I doubted how important this 'Big Man' was in the scheme of things, but he grew in my mind over the months. His language and temper could be foul when things went awry, but usually not in front of us girls. To begin with most of the work was concerned with finance, but gradually the intelligence side took over almost completely. I found it exciting to be in on secrets, learning the many ways we gathered information about the Brits, and being well up to date on the current situation; great efforts were being made.

At that time our main intelligence office was cheekily situated close to the main entrance of the enemy's headquarters at Dublin Castle! Mick seldom went there, however.

Although he was being hunted high and low by the British, Mick was always smartly dressed and looked at ease. He could be charming, but used to infuriate me. He only saw women as holding supporting roles in his world; not to be taken too seriously. He should have been a romantic figure, but in fact, he didn't seem much interested in women at all, at least from what I could make out.

One day I got to see a bit of how he lived, and the pressure he was continually under. We were walking together from one of our offices to another where a typist was absent, having fallen ill. The places were close together at times. We usually situated them in busy thoroughfares so all the coming and goings of people would not stand out. It was a cool sunny day; the birds were singing cheerfully, the sky was blue. I was enjoying being outside.

Mick was thinking intensely about something and hadn't spoken a word to me as we walked along. Suddenly, he swore.

"BeJaysus, not *again*!"

There was a checkpoint stopping everyone in the street; about five Tans, rifles and pistols at the ready and two policemen in all. Mick wrapped his strong arms around me, spun me round, kissed me on my cheek, breathing in my ear: "Take me pistol Aisling, quick!" He bumped his side against me; I could feel it in his coat pocket!

Out of the soldiers' sight, I took the gun out and stuffed it down the front of my coat; it was bulky and heavy. I was praying it wouldn't fall right through! We then walked hand in hand casually towards the barrier that had been rigged up. My heart was thumping. Like all men, the soldiers would eye my bust, and might notice the unnatural bulge of the weapon, so I lifted up my handbag, let go of Mick's hand and reached into it, pulling out a handkerchief and sneezed into it as we approached. Mick put his arm around me again, this time consolingly.

"Look here, Gentlemen, what's going on?" His accent was crisp and educated English, immediately putting the Tans at a disadvantage; his west Cork accent had disappeared completely! He presented his papers that I knew were forged by our side. I reached into my bag and took my genuine student pass out. The documents were only glanced at. My heart was wildly thumping so much that I was actually worried that it would dislodge the pistol!

"After terrorists, sir." The respectful tone was working class. Mick was frisked in a very cursory way.

Then my boss said something absolutely unbelievable in the circumstances, in a thoroughly irritated tone.

"I suppose you're after that damned Collins fellow. For God's sake find him *quick*, will you? I'm sick of all this nonsense. Can't a fellow carry out his business without interruption?"

The officer in charge of the checkpoint grinned and looked pointedly at me. I flushed red.

"Yes sir, we're really trying. I wouldn't want to disturb your *business* too much!" The soldiers all grinned, and Mick laughed. My annoyance, as I strode off indignantly with my handbag holding the pistol in place caused even more mirth. Mick followed and caught up to me.

I was feeling weak and absolutely drained by the experience. We turned the corner and without any warning he took me in his arms again, crushing the pistol against my chest. He breathed in my ear: "Look behind carefully colleen, w'd ye be seein' anyone afollowing us now?" While he embraced me I looked back, no I decided. I extracted the weapon from my coat and gave it back to him hidden by my bag.

"C'mon, we're late!" was all he said as we headed off down the street.

Under the casual bravado, there was method in his madness. He was so apparently relaxed and casual under pressure; I almost thought he really enjoyed tempting fate. Being caught with a weapon on him would be a death sentence.

Women were not usually checked… they were not considered to be very important. That fact could be useful at times!

There was no thank you or comment to me from Michael Collins. Everyone had to do their bit as far as Mick was concerned, and that was that.

I did feel however, that his opinion of me became higher. My secretarial speed and competence helped, and I would stand up to him fearlessly, which seemed to appeal to him. Some of the other women would be upset by his rudeness, but I refused to be impressed! He was only a mere *man* after all….

11

Sky

It was in late 1917, over eighteen months since the rebellion when I met that library fellow again. He looked thinner and gaunt, prison had been hard but the Brits had eventually released most rebels after executing the ringleaders they'd identified. They'd missed Mick; although I judged there was a bit of egotistical embellishment in his later description of his time locked up, I found out eventually that he had become a real thorn in the side of his captors, but he'd been clever and sly enough to not annoy them *too* much, so he wasn't separated and persecuted. Before the war he'd lived and worked for the Post Office in England for some years and understood how the Brits thought and operated. I learnt from one or two others that in the prison camp he'd been in the forefront of most activities, but hadn't been overly popular with the other inmates; being seen as a tad overbearing and pushy, yet he'd been respected in the end for what he'd got done. When he'd been released he had a good network of friends and acquaintances in the independence movements to utilize later on. Even more was the fact that he had gained legitimacy; he was one of the original 1916 leading revolutionaries and had not been executed. Because of the clumsy, harsh treatment of the leaders by the British, the population now looked on the event and participants more favourably. Mick still had that confident air and energy about him. He was also very high in the Brotherhood it was rumoured….

Once I'd heard all this I approached him quietly when I happened to see him on his own one day; but only after I'd made sure we weren't being observed. I offered my help. His eyes looked at me. I gave him my real name: Aidan Duffey, this time and told him how and where I worked. Such openness was unusual for me, but I felt somehow I could trust him.

He spoke intensely in a low tone. "Mmm, I *knew* you were lying! Well *Weed*! We were both right y'know! We failed as you predicted, but the backlash from the general population after those martyrs were executed paid off, so I was right there;

it all sort of helped, not that we're free yet by any means. The silly bastards let us out of prison after only a few months… that was because of public pressure, that we'd really worked hard at. We were after givin' them hell in the media, especially overseas, which worked a treat; the American Irish got really hot and bothered 'bout it and leaned heavily on the US government! A lot of our friends work in the newspapers over there.

"Well, I could use a low key boy working in the background with me; I'm now in charge of the National Aid Fund, up to my ears in work. Intelligence is takin' over though. Long term, we're goin' to hit 'em much as you suggested, with an Irish crock load of cunning. Ye're hired *Weed*! Those informer comments of yours, I've never forgotten lad… we're going to return that treatment to the bastards *with interest!*" He gave me an address to come to.

The very next morning after my shift at the brewery I went carefully to the place. Spotting some people watching the entrance and the street I walked casually past with my cap pulled down. I stopped at a shop some distance on and looked back. As I did so I was touched on the shoulder by a young teenage girl. She smiled shyly, her twinkly brown eyes warm, brushing her unruly dark hair back she spoke in a low tone. "Weed, come, it's safe; they're our lookouts. Mick said you'd be wary! So relax now won't you? Oh, and four knocks; once only." Suddenly she was gone.

I went back to the dark quiet entrance and climbed the narrow creaky varnished stairs with a heavily beating heart. The very solid door unusually had a small peephole which darkened after my four knocks; someone was looking at me I felt, and then after scraping sounds of sliding bolts it creaked open in a sudden burst of light.

Standing there was *HER!* My heart jumped and stopped for what seemed like an age… I reeled and nearly collapsed back down the stairs in a cloud of shock! I'd given up all hope of ever seeing that *vision* again and here she was just a few feet away, her eyes more flawless than even I'd dreamed them to be, a soft feminine face, creamy skin with charming freckles framed in that cloud of auburn hair, shining gold in the light coming from behind her. She seemed even taller than I remembered, *damn it!* I somehow got the impression that she was from a wealthier background than me. Again I felt like a starving, penniless urchin looking in the window of an expensive, upmarket bakery. Her educated voice was feminine and low as she reached out to shake my hand. "Come in Weed, I'm one of the secretaries, Aisling. Mick's flat-out today; I'm to show you what we do here. But first, our escape route, everyone has to know where to go if there's a raid…"

The soft touch of her hand accelerated my heartbeat even further. Her name somehow fitted the creature; a sound of distant music… I struggled to get my emotions under control and eventually became aware of a small crowded room; eight people were in this hive of activity; typists clattering away, paper trays heaped, bookcases containing files; hardly my idea of a revolutionary headquarters!

Still, fate had led me to this dream again; surely it had to mean something? I just wanted to be near her…and now my work here would enable me to stay close!

12

Song

 It had been a busy morning; I'd already typed out six letters and was replacing an ink tape on my machine when there were the standard four knocks on the heavy reinforced door. Mick looked up at me.

"Aisling, open that will you? Weed, short guy with glasses, he'll be aworkin' here with us. Show'm around will you." Mick went back to his dictation with one of the other girls.

I checked through the peephole; yes, the description matched. I lifted the heavy crossbar, opened the several bolts and pushed open the heavy door. I saw the man in the gloom look at me, somehow in shock, for a second or two I thought he might fall backwards down the steep stairs! Behind his round owlish glasses his light blue eyes looked startled. I shook hands and introduced myself. He was short, round faced, rather working class in dress and appearance... spoke in a Dublin accent, not that he said much at all. Yet, I found him somehow a little interesting. For the life of me I couldn't work out why! I showed him around our setup, which seemed to surprise him greatly.

Soon he was sorting out some reports for Mick. While I typed a new batch of letters, I started to hum to myself happily, for some unaccountable reason. Where this change in mood came from, I couldn't work out.

Over the next few weeks I noticed that whenever Weed was around, music would creep inevitably into my mind, it would stop abruptly when he left my presence, which was ridiculous! He said very little, but I did once hear him speak in low emphatic tones to Mick. Bit unusually, he wasn't particularly respectful.

"Far too much paperwork around Mick, they'll clobber us with it if we're not careful. We must take steps to at least hide some files or destroy the really important documents when we're raided..."

Michael Collins briefly looked at him and snorted, shaking his head,

Saying nothing he turned to me as a somewhat upset Weed left. Mick began to dictate at a slower than usual rate, his mind elsewhere. Suddenly he stopped.

"Hold it, Aisling, we'll come back to that one… New one, to all the Intelligence Heads: We must try and cut down on the amount of paperwork we are producing.…" He then proceeded to write much as Weed had suggested, almost word for word! So our newcomer was obviously bright and his opinions were of value. I heard he worked a nightshift as a clerk of some kind at a brewery in the city. The next day I was dying to tell him that Mick had listened and done something about his suggestion, but would that be breaking my undertaking of secrecy? In the end, I kept it to myself…

Weed didn't start work with us till 10am after his nightshift, I started at 8.30. It was weird how my world was silent for that ninety or so minutes; I began to regard this as my waiting for music time! Another rather unsettling aspect was when I went shopping for some new shoes; I could only look at plain flat ones! Strange, not my style at all.…

I used to glance at him surreptitiously from time to time, I imagined he might similarly be looking at me; that music thing haunted me. His face was ugly and plain at best, and he was short.…. I just couldn't come to terms with what was going on. Irish princesses were always supposed to be impossible to please, after all, I told myself…

Then came the day when the music in my mind stopped dead, and Weed *was only a few yards from me!* Something was terribly wrong! I stopped work and went to the window.

Across the road, my brother Rory had been stopped at a checkpoint and was being held! Suddenly Weed was beside me… he took one look and exploded into action, grabbing Mick's coat off a hook by the door and diving off down the stairs. Mick came and stood beside me, as we saw Weed without his glasses, approach the soldiers and punch my brother in the mouth and then kick him when he fell onto the ground! Some words were said, and then Rory was somehow set free; he got out of there fast! Meanwhile, Weed gave out cigarettes lavishly, slapped the sergeant on the shoulder, and then with the troops laughing at something he'd said, and before he could be asked for papers himself, suddenly darted back across the road narrowly avoiding a tram, then disappeared from our view. The soldiers were laughing as they watched him go. How *had* he done all that?

Mick, looked at me briefly with a self-satisfied expression on his face, before going back to work. "I *knew* Weed'd be able t' look after himself! Now, where were we....?" he started dictating again.

Weed returned, and as he entered, the beautiful music swelled in my mind again. I went and thanked him sincerely for saving my brother with tears of gratitude in my eyes. He looked embarrassed, nodded and just got on with his work. Strangely, from then on, he somehow seemed taller to me...

13

Sky

Each day when I was at the office my awareness of Aisling was total. In the sky of my existence she represented a gleaming cloud. Even when busily working and looking elsewhere she dominated my being; I seemingly had no choice in the matter. I inwardly cursed this impossible emotional addiction…

One day a few months after starting work there, while I was conferring with Mick about some rather upsetting financial reports from Donegal, Aisling suddenly went to the window and looked out down on the street below. She suddenly froze in tension. Despite the fact that I had barely spoken to her, I ignored Mick and joined the young woman, intensely conscious of her nearness as I looked out.

Her wayward younger brother Rory had been stopped by two policemen and two big Black and Tan soldiers on the other side of the road. They were easily holding him. I glanced at the white terrified face beside me…

Suddenly I became a tower of decisiveness: oh yes, 'me stubborn' was up all right! Running to the door, I snatched a man's coat and cap off a peg, the kind I would never wear; my caution and secret nature would never leave me.

I clattered down the steps removing my glasses and putting them carefully in an inside pocket where I discovered a pack of cigarettes. I had no papers with me. I remembered they were in my coat, but anyway I would rather not present them if I could help it. With *her* watching it didn't matter: *nothing* mattered! I sprinted across the road narrowly missing a draughthorse and dray piled high with bales of wool.

Squinting desperately to see, I rushed up to the group and punched her brother in the face. His head bumped the Black and Tan who was restraining him. His lip was split and blood dripped down his grubby shirt. The teenager was stunned and didn't recognize me at all… or the thick northern accent I adopted.

"You -little *bastard;* wait till our Ma gets you. You'll be bleedin' history!" I kicked him onto the ground, where he tried to protect himself by curling up. The Black and Tans laughed, I was much shorter than my victim.

"Get home you little *shite*, before I *kill* you!!!" I moved threateningly in his direction, then turned to the group. "T'anks for baling the little horror up."

Rory stood up uncertainly and glared at me. For a second or two, I thought he might attack me, before suddenly realising this was a reprieve of sorts. He just scarpered; not back to our office, I was pleased to note since he wasn't always fast on the uptake…

The grizzled sergeant looked at me suspiciously. I remembered what the great Mick Collins himself had done on several occasions. Keeping my loathing out my eyes, I reached into my coat pocket and brought out the pack of cigarettes and shared them out lavishly, slapping the sergeant on the shoulder. My accent even thicker: "The whole God dammed country is full of little scum like that… Well, I pity you poor sods trying to sort out the mess!"

"That's the truth then, for sure." They seemed to relax as they lit up and one suddenly shot out: "Aren't you going to join us?"

Lying effortlessly once again, because I detest smoking, I answered: "Love to, but me colleen hates the smell of it! *Women!!*" they laughed as they commiserated with me. I found a second pack in one of the lower pockets and tossed it at them. I called back "T'anks men! Oh *NO! BeJaysus!* There's m' bloody sister – on the damned street *again! Christ what a family!!*" I could hear their guffaws of laughter as I sprinted off in front of a tram that was trundling along the street and went to a safe shop around the corner, where we had friends. On the way I'd glanced up at the window and saw an auburn smudge… *she* was still there watching me. Our boss was standing beside her.

At the shop, the coat and cap were wrapped up in brown paper and tied with string. I put my spectacles back on again.

Unseen, my legs were shaking. I had never in my whole life had been as brave or had taken such risks or for that matter had been so overtly social! I would never have done so without her watching me!

Then again, I had in effect 'Michael Collins'ed' my way through the situation; having watched him in action for several months it came dead easy to me. Elation was starting to wash over me; I'd got away with it! I of course did have papers and a proper occupation, but I didn't want to draw any attention to myself, I was more valuable to the cause as an unremarkable citizen…

Wearing my glasses now, and a borrowed cap, I carefully walked back to the office carrying the parcel. The soldiers were still there across the road stopping people. Before entering the office entrance, I checked casually but carefully to make sure I wasn't being followed or that there was anyone suspicious around. The British G men from our nemesis Dublin Castle were always a hovering menace; but no, all was clear, just our usual lookouts were in place.

The stairs seemed steep to me; I was exhausted by my efforts, also I had come from a full shift at the brewery to this, which I regarded as my *real* work. I undid the parcel and put the overcoat and cap back on the hook. It was only now that I realised that it was *his* coat; thinking about it, it had been too big for me.

"Weed! I'll have you pay for those fags, *two* packets, you little bugger! And, I'm not going to be able to wear that coat again for a long time, the bloody Brits might recognize it…Dammit!" Mick was a stickler for reimbursement and had a memory like an elephant when it came to petty cash. In a grudging tone with a slight look of respect he added, "Next time Boy, actually *think* before you rush in; *one* packet of fags would have done it! OK?"

I was aware she was standing behind him, pale face; large green eyes regarding me, flooded with gratitude; it *had* all been worth it! She came to me tears in her eyes. Her quiet thanks embarrassed me; I nodded, felt awkward and just got back to work. But why oh why had the Gods of fate made her so much taller than me? Her presence was a permanent reminder of my impairment. Yet, I loved and achingly longed for the creature, but of course hadn't the nerve to tell her…

14

Song

My mother was making one of her periodic shopping trips to Dublin, although I rather thought they were really "checking up on her only daughter" inspections. She'd briefly meet Rory too, but I'd be the main focus of her visit, I was sure. As usual, this uneven treatment would annoy me immensely. Still, it would be good to see her again. My father was spending more time in Belfast on business these days and only passed through the city briefly on his trips north.

My parents were not aware that I was working full time for the movement and only spending a few hours a day at Trinity, although I would get some study done each evening.

I informed Mick that I was going to be unavailable for a few days, when I told him why he grumped a bit, but uncharacteristically accepted it. He valued my work, but my being at Trinity College cover story was important… people must not know where I worked; after all our security had to be paramount.

As was usual with my religious mother, we would end up going to mass at a church somewhere. Today, I quite enjoyed this change of routine, away from the often extreme pressure of the office.

The church was cool; the soft coloured stained glass windows were somehow calming. The choir was singing exquisitely, the voices blending and flowing off the high vaulted ceiling, my mind was wandering… then my eyes settled on some marking stones set into the wall, commemorating some famous parishioners who had passed on. I wondered what it must feel like to die….. and then a flash of insight hit me. I *knew* someone who could tell me about dying; Nora! She had died… another thing was: what happened afterwards? Was there really a heaven one went to?

Come to think of it, my "young" friend was often telling me off, but when I really considered things, our exchanges had been very self-centred on my part. I had never directly asked Nora about *her* life and times, the books I'd read about the Famine might not be accurately telling the whole story! A growing sense of excitement and anticipation changed my mood. My mother noticed but she always thought me a bit moody at the best of times. Then she wondered if my church visit had brought me closer to God in some way…

I smiled at her, but said nothing in way of explanation; my young friend was my secret alone, no one knew about her. However, I couldn't wait to "see" Nora again, but when would she come? Her visits were intermittent at best; I couldn't summon her; she'd come in her own good time….

It was three days later Nora appeared to me at the end of the day, as usual just before sleep; but bright eyed. Did she know somehow what was coming?

"What's dying like Nora?"

The thin face took on a hint of pride at being asked… she *knew* something I didn't. The tattered teenager frowned as she concentrated on her words.

"Bit hard ter say, that y'd be unnerstandin'." She said knowledgeably. " I starved ter death, as did hunnards o' tousands in thos' bad days, but at t' time I was adoin' m' best ter help m' brothers an' sister, I was aworryin' for 'em *so* much. I wasn't afearful like, f' mesel', anyways."

Tears welled up and began to dribble down her prominent cheekbones at the memory. My heart went out to her; tears were coming to my eyes too…

"Course, that was after Jesus took me Ma n' Pa from us. Had to drag em' out o' t' cottage…. So *heavy*….even tho' theys wuz skin'n bone b' then; since they'd given us kids mos' o' t' little food we had. Tired 'n weak I wuz tho', an' very puzzled why God id bring this down on us; which of course I shouldn't be atinkin'! I wuz too weak t' even pray at t' end….

I wuz a good colleen tho', lovin' 'n 'bayin' me parents, always aworkin' hard, say'n m' prayers each night an getting ter church on Sunday, but that last Sabbath… it was *too* far ter go. I didn' 'ave enough food…w's hexhausted."

Hopeless tears welled up in her dark eyes.

"Wiv my weak lovin' arms round the little ones who 'ad d' fevers an'cramps, t' world jus' sorta gently faded and my achin' tummy stopped ahurtin'… and that was that. T' baby o' t' family Danny wuz still very much alive….when I's is leavin' life… somehows he survived and yous is 'ere 'cos o' that….

"Defs not t' end of it all ye know Aisling… it's a sort of cloud of music 'n peace that's tipped on ye…and t' world ye knew 'bout. Ye's gently ladled inter a sort 'o broth of time, an' back to t' folk ye knew! I's hard t' s'plain, really…"

"Nora, please tell me about your life, I really want to know…."

Her face took on a mischievous look, with a hint of pleasure showing.

"Well, I might be adoin' that fr ye Aisling…I'm jus' atinkin', yous haven't bin axsurely *seein'* anything now, 'ave ye? Nex' time we'll see what I c'n be adoin' about that! -Mus' go now!"

I was left alone in the darkness, chewing over every word Nora had said. The poor creature, caught in a harsh world she knew so little about. I was really desperate to find out what had happened to my distant relatives. What was that about 'seeing'?

Sleep was very slow coming to me, so I got up and quietly played sad, traditional tunes, that sort of matched my mind, on my harp, while thinking…..

15

Sky

 It was late for me, as I hurried home about 8pm. Dublin had a dark sullen air about her dark arteries which were vaguely lit here and there by grubby street lamps. It was Friday night so there were quite a few people about. The rubble and ruins of the as yet unrepaired buildings damaged by the Rising defiantly stood out. Rain wasn't far off I reckoned which was even more depressing. The low hanging clouds above were threatening. Less than four hours for sleep before I would have to start work at the brewery. I was knackered, the pressure and pace of the fight was getting to me and I was only a sideshow, a supporting act. God knew how Mick managed to cope with his leading rôle. He was being frantically sought by the enemy everywhere.

The Brits were all over the town this evening; scared, armed soldiers eyeing all passers by suspiciously, as well they might. They were always a target; khaki clad aliens despised by most of the populace.

I'd perfected the art of maintaining an empty, unremarkable face as I tiredly passed a checkpoint; just another worn out toiler returning home. Usually they'd ignore me after a cursory glance.

I was walking along Mary Lane when I saw the rotund shape of Kirsty O'Hanrahan making her way towards me. Fishwifely in appearance and demeanour, normally she led a charmed life. I'd met her once some weeks before when she'd briefly spoken to Mick. Tonight she was being followed by two dark figures but obviously knew it. She recognised me; as we passed each other, without moving her lips or looking at me she breathed. "There've got Jimmy O, and taken him to the Castle... tell Mick!" She shuffled along and was gone, followed by her overcoated, hard faced shadows. I kept my head down as they passed me.

Damn! No thought of sleep now; I was wide awake...this was *big*! Who'd Jimmy been in contact with? Who'd he know? I'm ashamed to admit that I thought over my own few contacts with him… no, he only knew me as Weed, not my real name, just a few brief phone calls rather than face to face contact; I should be OK. The G men always beat the shite out of anyone whom they fancied might know anything…

Jimmy O'Brien was a key informant for us on British intelligence; where he got his info from we didn't know, but he'd saved many of us on occasion by giving us time to vanish before the crashing steps on the stairs, the pounding on the door before it was splintered and booted in. A small man, full of nervous laughter and bonhomie but tough and wiry to his core…a true patriot! No, we'd have a few hours before they'd torture anything out of *him*.

Still I must rush. I returned to our secret Harcourt Street office by a different route, checking repeatedly the reflections in shop windows to see I wasn't being followed; all clear. I made the signal to the watcher in the upstairs window in the building opposite and ran up the stairs, fatigue forgotten. I expected to be told where Mick might be. Usually at this time he was at Vaughan's Hotel or one of the many other watering holes he frequented, although he tried to be a bit unpredictable in this.

When I burst through the door I was surprised to see Mick still there. He had his back to me in the room which smelt of whiskey fumes. He was pawing Aisling who was trying unsuccessfully to fend off his advances, her eyes were desperate but startled and relieved by my bursting into the room. Storm clouds of anger swelled inside me. Instantly I was madder than I'd ever been in my life…..

"Stop that!" I roared, and he spun round guiltily to face me. Before I'd even thought about it I charged at him, picked up a chair and smashed it on his skull. Blood dribbled down the side of his flushed guilty face. "Go home! Get out!" I ordered Aisling harshly, but she stayed, rushing to stand close behind me. Mick collapsed in surprise then erupted up and attacked me, eyes glaring. I stood my ground; with the love of my life behind me, *nothing* would have moved me, I would have killed him without thought and my eyes must have revealed that, for he suddenly stopped. Looking at me and then at her several times. I could hear her tense breathing behind me.

A look of realization dawned on his face. I knew what he was thinking; he'd thought that when I'd rescued her brother from the checkpoint at great risk, I'd been trying to impress *him*, but now he realised it was Aisling herself I'd done it for. He lowered his large fists, shame and embarrassment replacing the rage. He turned away and staggered towards his office. I was amazed. I had somehow won against the great Michael Collins! Then I remembered. Squabbles were one thing, but we had a war to win.

I called after him, "Mick, They got Jimmy O, they've taken him to the Castle, and Kirsty Hanrahan, who told me, is being followed by two Gs…"

His voice was suddenly hoarsely sober. "*Christ!* Take her home! I'll deal with it all. Get out of here yourselves, this office is a goner now, Jimmy knew about it. I'll tell you where the new one will be tomorrow in the usual way; I'll need to get the files out as we planned." We heard him pick up the phone and speak in quiet pressured tones in the coded way we used; after all the Brits could be listening. Mick would effortlessly recall Jimmy's contacts and get all of them to go to ground immediately; helpers would arrive in minutes…

I turned and looked at Aisling, my heart wild as usual with emotion. This time I was unable to disguise it from her. Her face and peerless eyes looked as they had when I'd unexpectedly got her younger brother out of the clutches at that British checkpoint some weeks ago. Aside from the heartfelt thanks she'd given me then, we hadn't spoke closely at all, an awkwardness clothed us, although I'd watched her secretly as we worked, and somehow I'd imagined she was similarly watching me closely, but that I put down, as usual, to my wishful imagination.

Now, she was crying and shivering, clutching her torn blouse around her. To hell with the height difference; in an instant I held her with a desperate power as she cried on my shoulder, my face immersed in her lightly scented hair. Then I unwillingly pulled away. "We must leave *now*, my Love… we could be trapped here any time! *Quick* get your coat."

I'd actually called her *My Love!*

We left at a rush, but I still checked with the watcher across the road before venturing out into the street and signalled danger to him as we merged with the late shoppers heading to South Dublin where she lived. On the way Aisling held my hand tightly, refusing to let go. Her touch was electric, and every time her slim body and especially her breast brushed against my arm it warmed and excited me. When I stopped on a bridge crossing the Liffey to check if we were being followed, she drew me to her again. The dark waters and smoke shrouded lights of the city enfolded us. A small barge puttered past beneath us.

"Forgive Mick," she whispered in my ear in a lilt that was music to me. "He's always a very demanding taskmaster, although if you stand up for yourself he likes you. In general, work excepted; with us secretaries and typists he is always a perfect gentleman. He invariably makes sure that we girls are escorted home safely if working late. Today, he lost two friends from Cork and that'd be after tipping him over the edge; he drank too much and came back to the office. The whole British army is looking for him… and he has to keep moving, never staying in one place two nights running. I know for a fact he sleeps very poorly, if at all, yet his workload grows. He *is* Ireland's struggle at the moment, holding the whole movement together in a way no one else can; especially since Dev went to Americkay. Promise me you won't be saying anything about what happened tonight to anyone. We must be protecting his reputation; *mine* too for that matter."

She was right on every count; I'd also been surprised at our boss's behaviour. I promised her. How could I ever deny her anything?

After looking into each other's eyes, we kissed for the first time. I floated skywards until my cheap owly glasses got in the way and fogged up, but it didn't matter, we laughed till we cried about that as I tried to clear them!

At a British checkpoint we had to present our papers. The corporal in charge looked admiringly at Aisling and then at me, comparing our heights. He had a 'how can an ugly little sod like you bag a creature like this?' look on his face as he grinned sardonically and said "Off you go *big* man." Grinning at his mates he smirked; they laughed.

For a second Aisling and I looked at each other and roared with laughter as well as we headed off. He'd unwittingly used Mick's nickname on *me!*

The sombre city streets were now to our minds magically glowing with warmth, the drizzled cobbles gleamed with soft light. We kept looking sideways at each other as we went along and smiled with our eyes. Of course we bumped into people because we weren't properly watching where we were going; this caused us to giggle again. The disparity in our heights made no difference at all…

Then, all too soon, we arrived at her digs, a rather grand Georgian house buried in oak and sycamore trees. I'd never ever visited such a place, even in my cloudy daydreaming; this was a very wealthy area.

She regretfully took her hand from mine, looked at me searchingly one more time and then seemed to make up her mind.

She huskily whispered: "Wait!" in my ear and taking a big key out of her handbag, opened the large impressive door and disappeared inside calling out loudly in Gaelic. The door closed behind her with a creak.

Suddenly I felt an impoverished poser in a place I didn't belong. What if the police stopped by? My clothes didn't fit this area in the slightest. I guiltily looked around, but it was all clear. The door creaked open and she was standing there beckoning me inside with hungry eyes. "It's all clear, follow me… *Love*," she whispered. My heart swelled with emotion as I climbed a grand staircase behind her.

She took me to her bedroom….of which I saw nothing. It was all like a dream; impeding clothes hastily discarded, velvety warm cream skin, the softness, the scent, overwhelming impatience from the both of us, the sultry heat of our closeness, the smell of her perfume, the creaking bed, an explosion of feeling, then suddenly the calm peace and restful quiet as we clung together, silent in the snug darkness where dull outside city sounds began to register briefly. Then it all began again when she kissed my ear and tickled it with her tongue…

Forty minutes before I was due to start work, utterly exhausted but radiantly happy, I regretfully left her. I couldn't resist a glance back and as I turned the corner I saw a car pull up and several people disembark and enter the house. Whew! It had been close. And now I was going to have to do mundane work for nine hours… but with a quiet mellow glow in my heart which made fatigue irrelevant. Then I had to find out how the movement had fared and where our new headquarters would be based. We always had several options available.…

16

Song

It had been a very long day for me, there had been a veritable flood of letters and reports to type out… and of course there was no music to ease my mind. I had even missed my evening lectures to get this work done. My first two years at Trinity College had been a great success, but, to my parent's disgust, I had wanted to devote more time to the nationalist republican cause, so I was only studying part time now. I'd eventually had to explain where I spent so much time each day… but had made out I was only typing at a low level in the movement; they had no idea I was right at the top!

Alone in the office I got the great pile of tasks done quite quickly and was just getting ready to leave when there was a heavy coded knock on the reinforced door. I checked through the peephole, it was Mick! I let him in. He was quite drunk, and staggering around, I was helping him to a chair when he started to try and grope me, I resisted but he was persistent, tearing my blouse with his large clumsy hands.

For the very first time in my life I was scared, my usual superior manner and willpower were not enough to deal with his greater strength. The door suddenly opened and there was Weed! Usually he was at home sleeping at this time. He took in the situation at a glance and exploded into action attacking Mick with a chair, ordering me to go. I wouldn't leave and stayed behind him as he stood his ground. An enraged drunken Mick stopped dead and looked at us… I suddenly felt close to the plainly dressed figure standing like an immovable, protective wall in front of me. And bizarrely, despite the perilous situation we were in, the music returned,

Mick turned away, somewhat ashamed… Weed told him about a crisis and he sobered up immediately, ordering us to leave.

Weed and I left together, and he called me "My Love". My heart leapt, and a conflagration of music erupted within me….

Making love had been shatteringly addictive; I'd had no idea that I had so much feeling and emotion within me. Ignoring that I might be discovered behaving in such a way; losing that most valuable of a woman's possessions, her reputation, I'd encouraged him shamelessly, which made it all seem even more delicious!

I was reckless starting things off; undressing myself by tearing my clothes off impatiently. Weed was too much of a gentleman to have done so. Of course I'd touched myself over the years and found some pleasure; but this was another universe of delight and excitement; being fondled and caressed by a strong man you loved, who loved you, was incredibly exciting. A brief burst of gasping pain then a cacophony of arousal that left me shaking and exhausted, a little sore but mellow and at peace…..

At the steps as he was regretfully leaving, he unexpectedly said in that low voice I was growing to love.

"Ah Aisling, ye'd be a lilting aria in the concert hall of life!" One more deep look —and he was gone…..leaving me stunned, what a poetic, beautiful compliment; indeed, yes…. fit for a princess. Tears of joy welled up in my eyes.

A minute after we parted, the people of the house returned. Whew…. so close a call! I checked out the window, no, they hadn't noticed. The dark figure I now openly loved was walking off tiredly on the other side of the street to his work at the brewery. He'd already been up twenty four hours without rest….

I could hear them downstairs although they were trying to be quiet. No one in this house knew where I worked and what I did. They thought I was a hardworking university student of music.

Not wanting to face anyone, I pretended to be asleep, but in my mind Nora appeared as I lay on my bed in the darkened room. Her thin face and large blue eyes gazed at me accusingly. She brushed her black locks off her face.

"T' saints save us Aisling! How could ye now? Tho' he's a grand man for sure, I c'n see…brave and tender, I'll give ye that; but the *sin* o' it all, an' t' *risk* ye 'r atakin'!"

Then as her face faded, tears appeared in the corner of her eyes revealing perhaps - a hint of envy? There was no history tonight…

I knew my friend had died of starvation as a fifteen year old over sixty years before. Despite the Famine, she still held a straightforward, unblemished view of Catholicism and the morality of another age…and it gave her some comfort. My heart went out to her, she'd never known physical love, and would now only do so through me. I drifted off into deep slumber…

17

Sky

 Michael Collins was a fascinating character, not that I would ever admit it to him! Visually he was always crystal clear to me… no haze ever obscured my view of him.

In an hour, I would see a hundred versions of the fellow; he could be an arrogant tyrant, a sympathetic understanding friend, pleading, cajoling, a bullying miser one moment, generous to a fault the next, argumentative, conciliatory, loud and open, sly and secretive, warm and encouraging, cold and distant, reckless and excessively cautious…gentle and callously brutal; untrustingly suspicious and occasionally extremely gullible; you name it; there was no end to the complexities of the fellow.

Part of the reason for this flood of difference was the sheer volume and the variety of business in his day and the different groups and personalities he had to deal with. His output was prodigious. Finance had been his primary focus, he was the movement's minister of it after all, and had also been in charge of several big funds in the last year or so. Irish Americans had donated millions to the cause. As the Brits had tried to limit our banking activities, the movement was also using gold to fund our activities and buy weapons around the world. Secretly buried stashes of the precious metal were shifted around to avoid discovery. Mick was meticulous when it came to any financial dealing; no matter how big or small.

Then there was his foul-mouthed cursing, occasional drunkenness and rough house brawling he sometimes seemed to use to let off steam, even breaking furniture at times; wrestling and biting opponents: "getting a bit of ear" he'd call it. Strangely, I seemed to be exempt from this; perhaps my small stature had something to do with it!

Mick rose early and worked hard at his money files first, then would come the never-ending torrent of people to be seen each day. Often he would meet these elsewhere, sometimes at pubs; keeping our office secret. I would tag along with an eye on things, especially outside threats, as a sort of distant minder, while he concentrated on his meeting. Most people didn't know I was attached to him; we both thought it more effective that way. The hotels' staff eventually worked it out though and started to treat me with a low key deference, which I rather enjoyed. If I didn't feel happy with the security situation or felt things were deteriorating I would secretly signal my boss and we would quickly withdraw, separately. He began to trust my judgement implicitly.

Normally a man in Mick's position would be accompanied by several heavies but this was always obvious and was what the Brits were looking for. Mick believed that the best way to hide was in effect to not hide at all! For years, he casually pedalled his shiny clean bicycle around Dublin wearing a smart suit as if he owned the place; for all the world a successful lawyer or businessman... The stupid British were looking for their notion of a stereotypical Irish Paddy terrorist... probably a taller one complete with attendant thug-like bodyguard, and, so they usually never gave him a second look. Perhaps even his nickname helped here; some years before, annoyed colleagues had sarcastically nicknamed him the '*Big* Man.' Although taller than me he was only of average height, five feet ten or so, I remember, but he did indeed eventually grow to be very big and even vital in importance to the freedom movement of Ireland.

Mick had decided early on in his captivity that the Movement needed an intelligence service, just like the British had; fighting fire with fire in effect. I rather fancied my earlier comments when we first met might have influenced him here!

But now our intelligence on what the Brits were up to was growing and taking up more and more of his time. He was establishing a network throughout the country, which flooded us with information. Sorting, sifting and making decisions on the snippets that poured his way from a myriad of informers and sympathizers throughout Ireland filled the rest of his days. Detecting nuances in the big picture and out-anticipating the enemy were his forté; while still somehow avoiding capture. He was decisive, firm and usually right. His memory was superb and he needed little sleep, which meant he packed a lot into each day.

He was a slippery bugger though; a genius for keeping things in compartments; people would only know so much in their area. But despite the fact I was there for only part of his working day, over time I was able to glean what was really going on. I rather fancied I might be the only one who actually *knew* what many rather suspected. He was clever enough to have close contacts in every one of the movement's factions.

Michael Collins could be an arch conservative, shaking his head at the excesses of some of the firebrands in the movement one moment, while all the time secretly encouraging and supporting the extremists when it suited him; keeping all wings: liberal, conservative, radicals, you name it; on his side was his game.... "Gotta hold 'em all Weed; gotta hold 'em all; not an easy task. Christ, the show's a hell of a mess, at best!" He once tiredly confided in me.

Every Irishman has a strong viewpoint, myself included, and somehow holding a movement together when the Brits were trying to destroy it was probably an impossibility, yet he managed somehow to succeed enough to muddle through, since, despite the large bounty on his head, he wasn't caught by the enemy. There were innumerable close calls however...

It happened a week or so after Aisling and I first made love. I'd arrived at the office after my shift in the brewery to find Mick chatting animatedly to a short nervy type I'd never seen before, dressed in plain clothes; a crooked tie, tweed jacket and cap. He was probably an arms dealer as every now and then Mick would lower his voice and it seemed as if heavy negotiations of some kind were under way. Mick was always desperately trying to obtain arms for our side and he held almost all the purse strings. The fact that the man had been vetted to come here meant that he should have been OK. But it was the fellow's face that upset me; it was sort of indistinct, so obscured by a misty lack of clarity that I actually took off my glasses and cleaned them, to no avail. Yet Aisling at the other end of the room looked crystal clear to me.

I know what you're athinkin now....yet *more* of this cloud nonsense; but for me it was real. At times Mick was much too trusting and could be taken in by the odd character. I intuitively didn't trust this fellow, but couldn't get a covert warning through to Mick, who was flooded with bonhomie and intent on closing the negotiation. I tried to stay unnoticed in the background while observing closely what was going on. Things were brought to a conclusion; a handshake sealed the deal, and as the guy made for the door Joe Flannigan came in. Mick had a small mirror near where the coats were hanging and I saw the visitor's tense face in it for a fraction of a second; a wisp of surprise showed. '*He's here too!*' was what he was thinking, I was sure. I waited as I heard him go down the stairs and close the outer door and then I quietly followed him, glancing back at Aisling for a second who realised that something was disturbing me; her eyes were puzzled.

"Weed! I want you to.... Where the hell are you going?" Mick was irate and raised his voice.... but I ignored him and ran quietly down the stairs.

It was a dark rather scruffy day, a crowded Dublin street greeted me, I snapped a glance each way and eventually saw our visitor heading south towards the river. I crossed over to the footpath on the other side of the road. He did look back several times, but only to his side and never spotted me. I eventually sauntered along opposite him, then a little ahead, only a road width away, but quite unseen. Suddenly he stopped, peered guiltily around, seemed satisfied it was all clear, then entered a small pub. I crossed the road and looked carefully in the window; there were only four patrons propping up the bar at this early hour. I saw him go up to the elderly barman who directed him back out to the lobby where there was a phone hidden in an alcove. I silently entered low through the open door not wanting to darken the light coming from behind, and crept up close to him as he took a piece of brown paper out of his pocket, glanced at the number scrawled there in pencil and spoke to the operator. I crept up behind him; he was speaking in an urgent low tone. "You wouldn't believe the busy setup; *Collins himself* was there all right, I spoke to him, and who do you think walked in just as I left?"

I threw a hasty glance around to make sure I was unobserved, felt for the heavy pistol in my coat pocket and withdrew it, raised it above my head, then smashed the butt down on his head with all my might; centuries of hatred were behind my effort; bone crunched almost like breaking eggshells, blood splattered everywhere as he collapsed onto the bare boards, a scarlet halo appeared around his head in blood; I'd killed him! I smashed it down two more times to make sure. He hadn't had time to make a sound. *All* informers, really traitors, deserved such treatment I reasoned…

I grabbed the piece of paper, stuffed it in my pocket, ripped the phone cord out of the wall, wiped the hand piece for fingerprints, and looked around. Blood had been splashed everywhere. Despite my loud wildly thumping heart and thunderous breathing all was quiet: no one had noticed. I checked through the pub window as I left; the early patrons of the bar were still there, a reassuringly normal scene. My clothes were splattered with blood… what if I was stopped by a British patrol or checkpoint? *Christ, I was now a murderer!* But, then again, I now also felt I was a *real* soldier of our movement …

I forced myself to be calm; where was there a toilet I could clean up in? I needed to wash all the blood off the gun. There was another pub I knew only a few yards away around a corner in the street; Mick had met some arms suppliers there some weeks back. It had a small toilet out the back, and down a small corridor there was a phone. Off this space a glass paned swing door looked onto a bar. First I needed to get a call to Mick. Our office was compromised, yet again! My Love was also at risk....

I spoke quietly trying to disguise my voice with the operator, the Brits listened in, we knew from some of our girls who worked at the exchange. Mind you, at Mick's instigation, we managed at times to listen into some of *their* calls too! Using our current code word and a cryptic sentence that revealed it was me, I got across that the office must be abandoned. *Now*! It was.

"Skin of our teeth Weed; we all got out the skylight, even the ladies, long dresses an' all… our closest call yet! The barricaded door gave us an extra minute and half. Lost some damned papers an' letters too. How the hell did you find out they were coming?"

I took him to one side and spoke softly so no one could overhear us. I shoved across the scrap of brown paper with the pencilled numbers on. "He was ringing this number on a pub's phone and telling them everything, about your presence too, but I stopped him."

Mick's grey face was strained. "Be Jaysus Weed, that's one of the new Gmen's secret numbers at the Castle!! I only got it meself two days ago. That little *fucker*; how'd you stop him?"

"You haven't heard yet? Hit the bugger with the butt of me pistol, 'ee didn't even see me. He's dead. Maybe they're keeping it quiet. Mmm, I wonder why? Perhaps they don't want other informants to know. Spread it around to their side as a warning. You'll hear the details eventually. Nobody saw me, thank God!"

Mick's relief was palpable. The phone rang. As usual he spoke in crisp pressured tones. After hanging up he came to me.

"T'was hell to pay boy….. The barman was an old friend of m'father. They had him on an old IRB list in records so they've given him a once over. He's lost an eye already, foreign *bastards*! They got to the place very quickly, through the phone number probably. The barman was only a poor harmless old sod. The other patrons too have copped it. Just luck really; -wrong place wrong time. They've done the pub over and all present… did you see any of ours there? Are ya absolutely certain no one saw you?"

I shook my head.

"Well, that's a relief…you're safe. Get home to sleep. Now I've got to get a new office operating quickly. We need more phone lines, we always have at least three."

"Careful Mick, the Brits would have noticed how many we have on their raids and could check all the triple phone customers… 'twould be a right giveaway, especially *new* ones after a raid; they could find us that way."

"Good point Weed, try and think of any other pattern that might help 'em nail us, eh?"

After this event, I felt I was totally trusted by the 'Big Man'.

18

Song

I always loved Sundays. If the weather allowed, Weed and I would meet at St Stephen's Green, one of Dublin's oldest and loveliest parks. I would be humming to myself as I made my way there from the south, knowing that Weed was coming to me from the north, usually crossing the river at the Sackville St Bridge.

I would always get there first and wait for that burst of music in my being, telling me he was near. I'd spot his determined figure, a little wary as he made sure he wasn't being followed and that we were not being watched. The plain face I loved would light up when he spotted me....then we'd hug and kiss each other, looking deeply into each other's eyes.

The trees and gardens, the little lake and the open spaces seemed far removed from the frantic bustle and the densely populated business premises and housing that surrounded this oasis. We'd feed the ducks and swans sometimes from our favourite seat in a quiet corner, and had made friends with some cheeky red squirrels who lived near there in the trees above us. We'd be at peace sitting close together, sometimes in warm silence, listening to the distant bells pealing out calls to the faithful to worship; Dublin has so many churches. This place seemed a peaceful world apart to us with none of the often frantic activity of our office.

But there had been a recent change in Weed.... I sensed that something big had happened to him; but he'd not mentioned it to me. I didn't pry; in our work for the movement we both had secrets. Still..... he seemed even more determined and grimmer than he had been, not with me though; I felt he needed me even more. The change I felt had first come about at the time of the big British raid. It had been Weed who had phoned a warning to Mick in the nick of time.... our closest call yet! I still had bruises from our escape! Afterwards, Weed and Mick had had a secret, intense conversation about something.

My parents were visiting Dublin and I wanted Weed to meet them for the first time, but the silly boy was not too keen. He was worried as to how my father might react to his comparative poverty; I mean, as if money really made a difference! He was only a clerk at a brewery… which wouldn't sound very impressive to my status and money obsessed father who was always trying to link me to men from well to do backgrounds of 'good' family. I was quite sure that once he met my love he would see the worth in Aidan's obvious character and intelligence. Anyway, I had always been able to get my way with father: a mere man after all.

But, there was a secret slight hint of doubt in my mind. When I'd briefly worked in his office, just before starting university, I'd discovered there were secret parts to my father's business activities. I'd discovered for the first time that he could be heavy with people on occasion, but usually not when I was around.

I looked above through the branches of the trees at the smoky Dublin sky and hoped that all would go well in a week's time….

19

Sky

 I'd not wanted to, yet here I was, scrubbed up and dressed in my best, going to meet my love's parents, who were in town on business and visiting their daughter.

Aisling, from her comparatively privileged background, couldn't understand my reservations about this event. But it was going to happen sometime, so I reasoned we might as well get it over and done with. She was the apple of her father's eye I gathered, as they were very close. I expected him to be suspiciously protective and hell; I'd already slept with his daughter three times, when the town house's owners had been away! In those far off days this was a really big deal; it could even have been almost grounds for murder! I was really going to need my neutral face routine to work overtime if I was to come through.

As I had arranged with Aisling, I read the address of the house from a piece of paper, walked past the place, then came back as if I had never been near it, but in the upstairs bedroom window I saw her smile at me. I walked up to the door and pushed the bell press. While waiting, I looked around and was disturbed to spot someone watching from a hundred yards away, there was another one at the opposite end of the thoroughfare, whom I hadn't spotted when I walked in. Then in the curtained window beside the door, I saw the reflection of a person in an upstairs window on the opposite side of the road.

The door opened and there was my beauty introducing me to her father Eammon Kinnane, whose rather cold face and very firm handgrip led me to believe that he was not overly impressed with what he was seeing. At least this current situation was an opening for me.

"Sir, you are being watched here, one at either end of the road, also I think there is possibly a third fellow in an upstairs window opposite…."

"Well, are we now? So you're athinking that then? Well I suppose it's good to see you're alert. We are; they're mine." His face wrinkled as he surveyed me quite directly with cold green eyes, eyeing my best clothes with doubt. He had reddish hair and a very solid frame. I instantly sensed somehow that he would be a bad person to get on the wrong side of. His manner was almost patrician in tone, though probably not university educated I surmised. My lack of such a background would be obvious to him. This was not going to be an easy evening….

Aisling's mother softened the situation by joining us, a tall woman with dark hair, grey warm eyes and a welcoming smile. I instantly liked her. "It is nice to finally meet you…we've heard so much about you. We must thank you for saving our wayward Rory. What did happen, by the way? What did you say to those soldiers at that checkpoint?"

I paused before answering, "I just went through a little bit of drama Mrs. Kinnane, which luckily, did the trick. Unfortunately, I had to strike him in the process and he's never forgiven me. Even innocent, if they'd arrested him, it would have been much worse."

"We're really glad you did, he is a headstrong lad at times…."

Aisling put her arm around her father. "I told you Dad, he really does look after me…" Her father ignored the comment.

The meal was served at a grand table, with spotless cream linen, and silver cutlery. There were even servants serving us quietly and efficiently. During the meal Mr. Kinnane fired quite a few questions about politics and the economy at me. I always paused and thought before answering, revealing that I was aware of a lot of our history. One or two mentions of Irish literature also came up; I could hold my own there too, all right; those hours spent in the library were paying off! He wanted to know my opinion on things financial and I quietly gave it. Knowing he was a very successful businessman, in the last few days I had looked up some of the latest figures on Irish economic activity and managed to casually pop the odd statistic and up to date opinion into the conversation. I discussed the gold standard knowledgeably. Aisling looked at me in some surprise… obviously I was doing quite well, -all things considered.

She was a bit cross with her father for subjecting me to such a blatant examination, but didn't feel able to intervene. I didn't really mind; in fact, as things went along with no stumbles or missteps, strangely enough, I was rather enjoying myself, without revealing that fact in any way. He certainly was a strong character, but why his own guards outside? It wasn't all quite adding up….

I ate little, using my very best manners. The fact I didn't drink was perhaps seen as a positive, although a rather unIrish way of approaching life. My work at the brewery was briefly discussed. The random thought came into my mind that he'd already had that checked out. I didn't try to embellish anything…

As regards my family, I was quite open and honest, and didn't try to pretend to be anything other than what we were. Aisling's mother eventually talked about her childhood which was closer to mine; I got the distinct impression that she had married up in the world.

Aisling looked at me with eyes that again stole my heart…

Her father said firmly as he eventually stood up. "Right you ladies, us men will b' havin' a chat alone in the front room, for a few minutes." Aisling's mum looked up at the ceiling and winked at me supportively; my Love though, looked worried and irritated at the same time… but again was unable to say anything.

The small parlour was immaculately furnished and quite warm as someone had thoughtfully lit a coal fire some time before. It glowed nearly white and the ornate tiled fire surround gave off great heat. At my home we could never afford to burn so much fuel at one time. Mr. Kinnane headed for a drinks table with some alacrity and poured himself a large port. He started to pour me one then looked at me raising his bushy red eyebrows in question. Again I refused, which seemed to annoy him a bit, which was at least a little revealing. By again not imbibing I was taking the high ground, in his mind anyway. In the end I accepted a small one, which I sipped sparingly.

He was formal: "Mr. Duffey, my daughter tells me you two are doing great things for Ireland. Would you agree with her? She is always so damned fanatical about things…"

I paused before answering. "I agree with Aisling; I sincerely believe we are sir."

"-And this Michael Collins fellow? I've heard he is a boorish lout at times and he has certainly got the British up in arms! How actually bright and important is he?"

His tone was almost *too* casual. I was immediately on my guard.

"Mmm, why do you say that? I've heard he works around the clock in lots of areas, dealing with all sides. But, he's important, although there are many other players as well." I deliberately left things a little vague. I thought rapidly. Had Aisling actually told him we were working daily with Mick? If she had, that really compromised our security. No one should know we were a direct link to the movement's core. Probably, however, this pushy businessman had other ways of finding out….

Those watchers flashed into my mind again, they worried me… this was more the behaviour a low level gangster would indulge in! Suddenly things clicked; he must have had Aisling followed for sure, but our movement's watchers would pick them up, no doubt thinking they were from the authorities at the Castle. Hell, he may have had us followed on those nights when we had made love at the house she stayed in! But no, he wouldn't be so reasonable to me now if he knew that. Because I looked so innocuous, he probably couldn't *conceive* of it; thank God!

For several minutes the questions kept coming. A lot of the time I was non-committal as I tried to work out what he was really after… and eventually it came to me. This fellow wasn't interested in the Irish political situation or freedom and independence at all; couldn't really care less! He only wanted to know how he could further his business interests, and take advantage of the situation, maximising his profits! He wanted predictable stability at all costs and didn't give a damn *who* was in power! That idea I found repulsive and shocking… surely this couldn't be the case!

His headstrong daughter and son however had become fired up on the Republican side, but no doubt he'd like and need to have contacts on the that side of the fence, just in case…

I was coming to the stunning realization that my love's father was a classic Irish two timer… betting on both sides! In our history there had been no shortage of the species.

From then on I was increasingly vague… which he noticed. Then Mr. Kinnane brought our session to an end, with a somewhat ritualistic invitation to visit their family country house…sometime. I couldn't really refuse, so made the right noises. We rejoined Aisling and her mother. My love looked at me searchingly and apologetically at the same time.

As afterwards I made my way through the dark streets to work. I reasoned it had not gone too badly. Her mother was a gem and a possible ally. But I would have to hold back on my opinion of her Father. Aisling and he were close after all. No, it had not been what I had expected at all…

20

Song

Exhausted by the strain of the evening I went to bed immediately after Weed left. I was cross with Father, for subjecting my love to such a barrage of intensive questions, but he'd come through with flying colours, even better than I'd ever dreamed or thought possible. He *was* clever I knew, but even I had been surprised. I had also found my father on this occasion to be completely beyond my control which was a rude surprise for me. Where my future was concerned he was quite inflexible and demanding. With Rory he wouldn't have been anywhere near as protective. It was that girl thing again…. it wasn't fair!

Nora appeared, a critical young face, large hard accusing eyes.

"Y' got y'r way, an' see what happened Aisling! Y'r Pa went completely 'is own way with t' boy. Showin' off y'r fancy, *hoity-toity* lifestyle to a poor Dublin lad… don' think he was that impressed! *Servants,* well I ask ye! Showed y'r up a bit tho', didn'ee, eh? Fancy ladi-dah foods; whatever was yous folk atinkin'? Ye're all fergettin' where y'r come from, girl!"

Tired, I was thoroughly irritated. Nora loved to use words like *hoity-toity*, and these days she always seemed to be telling me off.

Before I even thought, I retorted: "What the hell would *you* know about modern life? You died at only *fifteen* for God's sake, in much simpler times during the Great Hunger!"

The thin face recoiled as if slapped; the dark eyes became tearful as she looked at me, so directly. Pain, shame and sad frustration showed as she faded away.

Oh God! I had really hurt my closest friend….feeling tired and irritable, I had been really thoughtless. I couldn't bring her back to apologise, though I tried. We were an age and worlds apart but, when I really thought about it, we shared a common humanity. Nora had a knack of making things simple and straightforward. I needed her commonsense!

Over the years a small part of me had wondered if my visitor was just a figment of my imagination, but her insights were too random and profound for that to be the case. I could share my intimate thoughts and doubts with her, a friend who would never betray me, I knew. But now I had rudely upset her. *Damn!*

And this was not all; Mother had invited Aidan to our home and strangely enough, Father had agreed….but I felt he was up to something; probably trying to impress my love with our wealth; putting Aidan off; yes that would be it! I knew it wouldn't work; but at least it would mean we would be together again, as he saw where I came from.

… 21

Sky

My Uncle Bryan's cough had worsened. It'd always been there, during my whole life with them after me mother had died. Its raspy grating presence had been an ongoing background that somehow matched our rough impoverished apartment. But now it had taken on a more ominous life; one day I discovered him coughing blood into a grubby handkerchief; it was the dreaded consumption we all feared so much; after all, my mother had died of it. His sallow face and deep-set frightened eyes confirmed this diagnosis. That fighting spirit had been finally dampened down and was now strangely lacking. Even his ever loyal companion, Shamus the little old dog, looking up at him with worried loving eyes, couldn't lift his spirits.

One afternoon when I returned for my brief sleep I found him a shattered slumped figure, battered and broken; he'd lost his job; apparently his coughing at work had disturbed the customers and, just like that, he'd been let go. I'd helped the family as best as I could since I was earning reasonably good money at the brewery, but they cared for several elderly relatives and there were no cash reserves. By staying on with them I was contributing more. But things were now going to be more desperate. Since he'd always had strong Fenian leanings and had been a minor foot soldier in the struggle over the years, I resolved after thought to mention his case to Mick.

Michael Collin's real area of expertise was finance. We were all aware, that as well as all his intelligence work, he also controlled several reserves, one of which was the benevolent fund for the widows and dependents of the 1916 revolutionaries who were still looked after, although this took up less of his time these days. Mick wore many hats in effect which is why he was always so busy. How could I do it? I'd never asked for any favour or support in any way, and I didn't feel happy about the prospect, but my family was in a desperate situation.

I approached Mick at the end of my day when I was exhausted. Peering at me over some papers he was perusing with an emotionless face he merely snorted

"Hmph!" and turned away, called to one of the others, and rudely resumed his intelligence work, firing out a flood of orders on a current operation. I doubted if he had even heard a word I'd said!

I felt deflated and angry as I left, though warmed only by a last look from Aisling. Why did I work so hard for this belligerent tyrant? Even then I thought of how he was carrying on the fight and holding such a ragtag army together. Dev was in the US having gone himself in the end. He'd stayed on overseas for a surprisingly long time too, upsetting the Yanks as much as anything it seemed. But, despite that, millions of dollars were being raised for us there… so it hadn't been a complete waste of time.

When I got home about 5pm I collapsed on my bed and drifted off into a sullen sleep. I was awoken by loud laughter coming through the thin walls of the living room next door at about 10pm, an hour before my usual wakeup time.

Mick had come to see for himself, despite all his many activities. I learnt later that this was typical of the fellow; he never trusted anyone when it came to a claim for finance of any kind and always checked up on it personally when he could. Mick merely winked at me before pedalling off into the night on his smart bicycle, as usual looking a well heeled professional gentleman, oblivious to the curfew in place.

Uncle Bryan had regained some colour in his face and his deep-set black-circled eyes had regained a bit of their former sparkle. "What a man!" was all he could say. He'd heard of the famous Michael Collins and had been honoured that his home had been visited by this legend. "And you, -you little *bastard*, you didn't mention a word about where you were all day! Y'know I've always wondered what y'were up to. Well I'll be damned! Still, wise to keep ya trap shut; will me'self too. The Damned Brits have got a fortune on his head. To think you actually know him and he'd come here! Well I'll be…! Hell, I hope none of the neighbours saw the classy wheels parked outside. Still, it's cold, dark an' rainy tonight, so they won't have noticed. He's going to help us, we should get through. But it's late; how'll he dodge the curfew?"

"I wouldn't worry about that, Uncle," I murmured without elaborating. Three weeks before Mick had been stopped at a checkpoint on his bike. He'd cheerfully bluffed his way through, as usual. I'd been with him and had melted away into the shadows, despite the fact that as a nightshift worker I had papers that exempted me from the curfew.

Just before midnight I strode off to work in a positive frame of mind, Mick had listened after all; he did value my work for him. I would share this only with Aisling, but no one else…

Song

I thought it only fair, after all Weed had visited my family; so I should visit his. I knew his background was very different to mine; as Nora had often reminded me, but I loved him so much and wanted to know and understand his world. He hadn't been overly keen, but had eventually given in. "Just make sure y' not bein' followed Aisling." He was always so careful and security conscious. I did what he had asked me; yes I was sure I was clear.

So here I was wearing a plain, sensible dark skirt, blouse and coat, my flat heeled shoes, going to meet his Uncle and Aunt. I mentally told myself at all costs I must not seem to be "hoity-toity" to these people, as Nora called it. Although this had been my idea, I was actually a little nervous, which was an unusual sensation for me. Confidence was never a problem normally. Even the music in my mind was a little hesitant…

On my daily walk to the university or work through South Dublin, I thought I passed through some poor neighbourhoods; but as I turned the corner into the little dead-end lane where Weed's home was located, I realized that this area was *really* impoverished.

Noise was the most striking feature for me. Many people were living there, crammed into a very small area. Families were large, arguments were taking place in the cramped apartments. The raised voices must have been a common occurrence as no one seemed at all concerned. Such a commotion enveloped the place; urchins played in the street and colourful washing was flapping in the wind, drying on lines strung across the narrow thoroughfare. Cramped conditions meant privacy was probably a rare commodity. People were looking out the upstairs windows; I suddenly realized that I was the centre of attention; even some of the children had stopped playing and were staring at me with wide eyed interest. I smiled and tried to put on a friendly face. Obviously not many strange visitors came here. A cheeky round-faced nine year old, asked me, her accent strongly Dublin: "Who'd y'be acomin'to see Miss?"

I was so surprised at this familiarity, I made the mistake of answering. "Aidan Duffey at number 21."

In a fraction of a second, it seemed to me, I was surrounded by a group of kids chanting at the tops of there voices, the sound echoing off the buildings: "Oooooh, Aidan's got a *girlie! Aidan's got a GIRLIE!*" One toddler grabbed my skirt with her grubby little hands.

My face reddened as I made my way through them to the plain door.

People seemed to appear from nowhere out of doors and windows to see what all the fuss was about, the eyes curious…

It had all been so unexpected I was quite embarrassed, but Weed appeared and rescued me from the throng, by ushering me inside his home, and closing the door firmly behind him. "Sorry about that Aisling, but it's the way we're atendin' to be 'round here!" The tiny hallway was dark; a few family pictures adorned the walls. Some tiny narrow stairs led up to the bedrooms. There was the smell of home baking in the air. He took me into the small parlour and introduced me to his Uncle and Aunt.

Uncle Bryan looked old and ill; grey hair and pale wrinkly skin with dark rings around his eyes, his thin frame was draped in old clothes that were now a little too large for him. He twinkled at me admiringly. "A thousand welcomes to our little castle m'dear! Young Aidan here's kept you a bit of a secret….although f"all the saints in heaven, I can't understand why."

I blushed and mumbled "Thank you."

Grey haired Aunt Biddy had a kind face. She jabbed her husband playfully with her elbow, but it was plain to me she loved him; there was an easy warmth and bond between these two.

"Get away with ye husband! Talk of the blarney….I'll give *y'* the saints in heaven! S'lovely to have ye here Aisling, come, we women'll be agoin' off to the kitchen now…." She shut the parlour door behind us and took me off to a cubbyhole dominated by a small gas stove, on which a kettle was boiling. Everything was simple but spotless, the shelves nearly empty, I noticed. The gleaming utensils, pots and pans were simple and inexpensive.

The smell of recent baking there was delicious. She took out a teapot and a small tin caddy of tea, which she gave to me with a teaspoon, "four will be adoin' it, I think." She poured some milk into a little jug.

I put four teaspoons in the pot, and added the boiling water

As she removed a tray of five oat bran biscuits carefully from the oven she said in a low voice, looking at me with serious eyes: "Aidan's a wonderful man....we wouldn't b' getting by without the lad, quiet n' strong but kind as well! Me dead sister, 'is ma, would be so proud! He's very clever too... all self taught; the time 'ee spends in the public libraries! We were so pleased to hear he had a friend… he's always bin a bit of a loner. Mind you, once 'ee gets 'is stubborn' up; watch out!" She laughed, then put on a mysterious face "By th' way I've got a bit of a surprise f'r ye…. But first, where did you two meet?"

I nearly said at work and then remembered the secrecy thing. "At an office, Aunt Biddy."

She noticed my momentary hesitation, and gave me a secret smile….

"Ah they're all little boys really, y'know Aisling. They t'ink they can keep their secrets from we women…Hmmph; there's a lot goin' on these days I'm asure." She frowned and added grimly. "May t' good Lord be aprotectin' us all through it tho'; tis troubled times we'ra livin' in…"

I decided I did like Aunt Biddy, although I'd never in my life met anyone like her. She was warm, loyal and doing her best. We carried the pot of tea, a little jug of milk, cups saucers and biscuits through to the parlour. I noticed the crucifix and framed photos on the wall, some books on the mantelpiece of the small fireplace.

I thought of the way my father had treated Weed when he had met my parents for the first time. Here, in contrast, there had just been a warm welcome, no interrogation or mental hoops to jump through. I smiled at my love to let him know I was OK. He twinkled at me in relief…as he poured the tea for us.

Biddy went out of the room and came back reverently carrying a bulky object wrapped in a small grey woollen blanket.

She had an excited look on her face. "Aidan's not told us much about ye M'dear…..but he did mention ye can play one of these! I borrowed it fr' me friend." With a flourish she removed the blanket revealing a crude old lap harp. Obviously this basic instrument was a precious item in their world, so I made the appropriate noises. It was quite out of tune and roughly made, but had surprising good tone and held its notes well, once I had tuned it by ear, as best I could.

"Me Biddy here loves t'sing, she'ves the voice o' an angel Aisling, I love to hear her. Don't s'pose y'd wouldn't be aknowin' "Carrickfergis" now would ye?" Uncle Bryan asked.

"I play and sing it often," I replied and started the well known folksong.

Biddy sang beautifully, so I harmonised with her… somehow our two voices blended magically, with little effort from either of us. The room darkened and when I stopped and turned round, I saw many faces, young and old, peering in at us through the small window, listening avidly from a now quiet street. Weed looked at me, "Sorry Aisling….but we're goin' t' have to share you …"

Before I knew it I was sitting in a chair out in the lane playing the old harp; a battered guitar and pennywhistle materialized; jigs were played, and all ages were up and dancing, from toddlers to old timers! It was a sort of impromptu street party.

Aidan looked at me, winked and went and got up a young teenage girl who was blind and obviously wearing hand me down clothes. She smiled radiantly up at him when he asked her for a dance. Her strange whitish, vacant eyes glistened as the two of them whirled around. He protected her from the lively throng. Faster and faster went the music till I just had to stop. The harp's gut strings were stiff from lack of use and my fingers were nearly bleeding. A great fuss was made of me by everyone.

Aidan brought the blind girl Amy O'Driscoll to me. Strangely, the whole throng fell silent. Her delicate pale face was gaunt but had a haunting loveliness about it as she spoke. Everyone was listening intently… the background noises of the city could be heard again in the hush.

"Music fro' heaven Miss, so light an' catchy…can I see how y'r alookin' now?" I was surprised as her slim fingertips lightly brushed my forehead and traced the contours of my face, my lips and then my eyes, even my ears and hair. She touched my eyes a second time. "It'd be a beautiful Irish princess avisitin' us t'day, w' smiling eyes an' bewitchin' tunes!" She declared. There was a great outburst of cheering and laughter at her comment.

Amy leant in as if to kiss me and whispered in my ear; no-one could hear. "An ancient hungry friend 'll b' acomin' back t' ye again…. she was mad at ye, but today, *here,* y've impressed her….I'd be thinkin'. Another t'ing Aisling, in yer future y' mus' follow y *'heart* 'n not y' head" Her lips brushed my cheek and Amy turned and felt her way back to her seat, sad tears trickling down her cheeks, she dried them with her sleeve as she bowed her head. What had upset her I wondered?

I was surprised at the messages… the first part had to be Nora! If so, it was great news, I missed her so much. The second comment I was a bit puzzled by …

Aidan noticed my reaction, "She's a bit fey, is our Amy." he told me, "What was she awhisperin' to you?"

"A secret or two," I murmured without elaborating …and he smiled at me.

I told him "I'll go; you need to sleep before your nightshift, Love."

I said goodbye to everyone then went to the Amy and whispered in her ear before kissing her forehead. "I think the *real* Irish princess is living here and she's the only one who can *really* see…." Her face glowed at the compliments. Her hand touched my face lightly again, I squeezed it and left her.

What a visit! I was escorted to the end of the lane by the inhabitants, especially the kids who hugged me as I turned to go. Aidan squeezed my hand and pecked me on the cheek and was gone.

I returned to my different world, surprised at how much I'd enjoyed myself! I'd let myself go and relaxed more than I had, *ever*. The area was certainly deprived, but the raw warmth and the appreciation of simple pleasures had affected me. Wealth insulated us from each other by giving us more space and therefore making our world quieter…less frantic.. but…perhaps less warm in a human sense?

I felt even closer to Weed having seen where he came from. And he'd seen another side to me. Our love would grow from this; a thought that cheered me greatly.

As I boarded my tram to the south, that haunting air came to me. My ancient young friend would come back to me tonight, I was *sure*.

Nora's eyes gleamed in the darkness. "Well, there's hope afore y' yet Aisling! Weren't y' the one then, eh? They loved y' playin' an singin' girl….an not a *cream cake* in sight! S' th' *real* world, girl……." She disappeared. Nora *still* remembered my visit to the Titanic all those years ago.

I hadn't had a chance to answer her. Probably just as well! I must not upset her again. I fell into a deep, exhausted but content sleep.

23
Sky

I made my weary way around the corner of the street into our dingy cul-de-sac to my home. The neighbour's washing was on lines strung across the street in the cold northerly and as usual the local kids were out noisily playing. There was the smell of the evening meals cooking…I was hungry! The overcast sky above was layered with blue coal smoke.

It had been a hard nine hours at the brewery plus another frantic seven at our HQ for the movement. Big things were going on there since the arrival of the Black and Tans and the officers Auxies some months back. The situation had escalated greatly; there was an increasing cycle of attack and reprisal throughout Ireland.

In the newspaper I was carrying under my arm for my Uncle Bryan there was a headline report of the little town of Balbriggan to the north where in reaction to the shooting of a Head Constable of the RIC, nineteen houses, a factory and four pubs had been burnt down when the Tan troops in the area ran amok. Two republicans had been captured, bayoneted and executed.

Of course we Irish realised that any news in the dailies related to our country was almost always tampered with to serve the British Government, accordingly we were adept at reading between the lines. The authorities were very silly here, since damaging reports of what was *really* going on always appeared overseas first, we would hear of these; foreign correspondents, especially Americans, reported things with brutal honesty. In reality however, Republican papers and newsletters tended to slant things *our* way. So a position somewhere between the two sides probably gave an accurate picture.

So many rumours were always shooting around Dublin, Uncle Bryan would declare with amazement on his face. "Tis a wonder, y'know, it'd be a miracle of the Good Lord that there's actually enough room for people and vehicles to move around the city as well!"

My aunt greeted me with a hug as I opened the door. My cousin Connell had gone north to find work, and had only got a borderline job so far. He was making noises of emigrating overseas when he could scrape enough money together for a fare, probably to the US. Mary had just married and she and her husband were struggling to make a living down in Waterford.

Shamus the friendly little old dog rushed out with a quiet bark to greet me and get his customary pat, before going back to my uncle. No matter how tired I felt, my homecoming always cheered me up. I was still in the nest and had been the lucky one in that respect. I was able to and didn't mind supporting these two; after all they had taken me in as a kid and had treated me as their own. My income and a small contribution from the movement kept the home, two foster parents and two other elderly relatives going since my Uncle had lost his job. He now did some minor clerical tasks for the movement. Also my hard working Aunt Biddy took in washing and did a little sewing to help top up our income.

Her wrinkled face smiled at me warmly as she bustled about in the tiny kitchen getting my evening meal before I would go to sleep.

"Ah Aidan, may all the saints be apraisin' ye now. How would we even get by without ye?"

I grinned back at her; "You'd manage Auntie, God always looks after true angels!" She laughed at the compliment, "Get away with ye Aidan, ah, y'r' a right little charmer when ye want ter be!" She shooed me out of her domain.

I realised that my folk were certainly getting on a bit; the poverty had contributed to this decline. My coughing uncle was elderly before his time, although his spirit would still shine through on occasion. Today in the parlour was one of these times. He looked up from the newspaper at me over his reading glasses.

"The swine are getting worse, all these people out of their homes an' winter's acomin' on; have y' seen the photos here? Terrible business son... an' then, almost daily, throughout the country there's these *"shot while tryin to escape"* stories...." He dropped his voice so Aunty couldn't hear. "How are we *really* doin' at the moment?" Since Mick's surprise visit some months back he would often ask me this. Despite the sworn secrecy I adhered to I would give him a snippet of the situation from time to time. He would keep it to himself I knew.

"Holdin' our own Uncle ... their over the top brutality in response to us tells everyone we must be scorin' some real hits. Ulster however is a tricky one.... Not so good there."

My uncle stared at me thinking for a second.... Then he reread the article again while I ate my stew and praties. The parlour clock ticked, Shamus dozed on his master's lap.

"Y'know," uncle said rather cryptically, a grim smile on his face. "The British will be always 'avin trouble with their *vowels*....I reckon..... *A* a bit, an' *U* a lot!! See 'ow bright ye are boy...." He giggled at his own guile.

What the hell was he on about? I went off to sleep my usual five hours wondering....

I was walking home the next day when it popped into my mind... of course: British to Bratish....as in brat, was the "A", the "U" which would form *Brutish* was much more apt. This was all rather Irish, such twisting and playing with words! Well at least I'd solved it! I'd cheer him up when I got home by teasing him for his cleverness....

24

Song

 It was early evening and I was making my way back to my digs. I happened to look in an antique shop window and saw something that interested me; an old harp. I pushed open the door and entered, the little bell over my head announcing my arrival with a muted tingle.

The owner was a very old man, who suddenly popped out of a hidden alcove peering at me over his old fashioned round glasses, as he sized me up. He glanced down at a large silver pocket watch he'd withdrawn from his waistcoat pocket by a chain. His accent was quite sing song in tone. "I'm almost aclosin' now Madam, but I just may have enough time to sell ye a little treasure…..perhaps even a *big* one; f'r a very good price, mind ye!" He smiled, showing even white teeth, his grey moustache twitching, his brown eyes twinkling.

Weed had changed me in many ways. My family usually bought things through catalogues, or had others do our shopping for us. We always paid the price asked. Weed however, usually bargained strongly when buying anything in the city. At first I'd been embarrassed by this, but then the revelation came to me that the people we were dealing with loved a bargaining match; they really enjoyed a haggle and actually respected him for this, looking down on anyone who paid the full price without question! The allowance in my bank account was now building up steadily, since I wasn't wasting money on clothes and unnecessary items these days.

I tried not to sound too keen. I looked around and picked up an object or two casually. I then pretended to discover the lap harp. "Can I try this?" I asked.

"If you're careful Madam, that's a fairly precious piece… we think it might be quite ancient; maybe over a hundred years old. Perhaps even the great blind Tourlough O'Carolan himsel' played it." His mentioning Ireland's greatest harp player and composer who had died in 1738, was pushing it a bit! I was almost certain it wasn't that venerable.

I inspected the instrument; it very well might have been old as it was fairly crudely made. The sounds were mellow; the notes were pure and long lived. Although the strings were a little closer spaced than was normal, I found it easy to play some traditional airs on it.

The shop owner listened with his head tilted his eyes closed. "Ah, that'd be the very soul of the Irish!" he murmured. "And dare I be sayin' Madam, played beautifully on the symbol of the nation…." Then he shook himself as he realized that what he might have sounded a bit *too* nationalistic. He observed me closely, I smiled at him and he relaxed. My playing had actually brought tears to the corners of his eyes. He was a bit embarrassed I had noticed.

"How much do you want for it?" I asked, bracing myself.

"To a player such as yesel', twelve pounds ten shillings and it's yours. I couldna charge y' more; ye've a lovely touch m'dear."

It was not cheap but then again not excessive either. I wondered if I could get him to come down… "Oh,' I said, as if I found it a bit pricey. I thought for a few seconds. "I'll give you ten pounds for it …"

He looked a bit surprised that a lady such as myself was bargaining. I waited patiently as he thought about it. He eventually said, "if you play me a few pieces, you can have it for ten pounds ten shillings."

"Done!" I said rather pleased with myself, this whole exchange had been rather fun. Half an hour later I was carrying the heavy package back to my place…..

Weed's visit to my home would mean it would be a fortnight before I would be able to do what I had in mind with the instrument…

25

Sky

It had come around. After months of high tension, frantic effort and close calls, with very little sleep, I managed to get a few days off my work for the movement and from the brewery. So, finally I was going to visit Aisling's home. She had gone on ahead, two days before. Mick was away in England, arranging yet another jailbreak. I travelled south by train.

Kinsale was a quaint, busy town, its ancient houses draped over a collection of hills that framed an inlet and harbour. The waterfront was lined with fishing trawlers that were coming and going around the clock; the scent of fish was strong from the drying nets on the quay, two grey warships were anchored out in the stream. Hopeful seagulls called and wheeled in the cool salty breeze above the craft, outlined against white swelling clouds in a dark blue sky.

It was also unfortunately the site of an ancient great fort which had been used by the British for hundreds of years as their main base in the southeast; the place was full of their soldiers, the hotels accordingly did a roaring trade. I stayed a night with a local friend of the movement, out on the road leading to the King Charles Fort. I was surprised at how narrow the main access road to the fort was; could this be a vulnerability we could exploit? There were many roadblocks around the town, on bridges and at major intersections. Despite the presence of so many troops, the British weren't taking any chances.

As arranged, I was waiting in the town square to be picked up at nine a.m. I expected a cart or lorry of some kind to be sent, but was astonished when a large dark blue limousine, complete with uniformed chauffeur swept around the corner and stopped nearby. I stood back, wondering who would have been travelling in such a grand conveyance. When the resplendent driver saw me, the only person obviously waiting there, he came over to me, looking doubtfully at my clothes and small cheap suitcase. He quickly established who I was, and told me that I was to go with him. He formally held the door open for me, and I rather self-consciously, though trying hard to disguise my amazement, climbed into the vast luxurious interior of red velvet, soft leather and gleaming wood veneers. He closed the door with a quiet firm click behind me, put my luggage in the boot, then climbed into the driver's seat and we glided away. It seemed to be a very powerful machine.

I wondered if someone else was also being picked up, but no, the vehicle was just for me! Hell, cars were quite rare in those days and being poor I'd never ever travelled in one before; trams, trains and the odd lorry, yes, but a whole luxury vehicle to myself! For a second or two I thought it might be an English Rolls Royce, but no, the name *Hispano-Suiza* was engraved on the silver handle of a drinks cabinet mounted in front of me, below the glass partition that separated me from the driver. Through a glass door of the unit I could see bottles and the tumblers inside had been each engraved *H-S*. This limousine must have cost a fortune!

Checkpoints in this vehicle were no problem I noticed; the name Kinnane seemed to be almost a magic password… my papers were only apologetically glanced at, the Brit soldiers were quite deferential and the car was not searched even once! This just confirmed my suspicions that Eammon Kinnane was cosy with our occupiers.

Why hadn't Aisling come along with the vehicle to pick me up? As we wafted along, my mind began to calmly evaluate what was going on here; I must not be too impressed or swayed by the current situation; because her father would expect me to be overwhelmed and feel out of my depth and act accordingly in front of his beloved daughter. That of course was what he was trying to do; proving to me that they were from another, higher class in which I did not belong. I was certain he was trying to underline this. I bet to myself that somehow he had stopped Aisling from coming. I'd check with my love.

Well, I would *not* appear be impressed, hardly mention the car at all, and act as if every day I was being whisked and cosseted around the countryside in such splendour. How dare he think he could impress me with such a crude display of excess! I was more than a little annoyed and wondered if I could score a bit back at him; by giving the slight hint that the vehicle might be a bit over the top, perhaps trying a little *too* hard….bit embarrassing really! That might annoy him in a satisfying way for me. Then again, he was obviously not a person to cross, but dammit, I wasn't either! 'Me stubborn' was up, railing against his earlier treatment of me….

My trip to the south east and now this leg of my journey had been quite illuminating. I was surprised at how many properties I passed had gates, walls and entrances that had been made to impress… obviously every farmer who started to make some economic headway, indulged in the practice! It was beginning to seem to me to be a land of pretension….If this car was anything to go by the Kinnane entrance would be really substantial, I reasoned.

I looked out the windows at the sky clothing a green land of shallow sandy estuaries sprinkled with tiny hamlets for an omen as to how my visit might go. It was a sunny but hazy day here… a light southerly wind massaged the landscape. There was no omen in the sky that I could see…

Thirty minutes later we swept up to some impressive cast iron gates, flanked by tall sculptured pillars on either side. Lofty ivy-covered walls bordered the estate stretching off into the distance on both sides. Just inside there was a small ornate two storey gatehouse buried in large trees that flanked a long sweeping drive, which eventually led to the Big House; a small castle to me; far bigger than I had ever imagined. Lush green fields well stocked with sheep and cattle surrounded the Kinnane's home. Obviously many locals were employed on the property.

In the intervening months I had quietly investigated Aisling's family. I was very wary of her father and was careful to be low key about my research. I'd discovered that at the time of the great famine, the Kinnanes had been impoverished tenant farmers… and just like the multitudes they had died when caught by the crop failures.

Aisling's grandfather, Daniel Kinnane however, had been the only one in his immediate family to survive. In the eighteen sixties, as a married twenty year old at the time, he had scandalized the local community by changing his religion, but he'd survived a later hunger; the Anglicans were recruiting and they had food! A hard-nosed, survive at any cost attitude, seemed to cling to the family.

Obviously Danny'd had some ability and was industrious. The fellow had been well rewarded over the years and had progressed up the economic ladder in a steady way, acquiring some wealth eventually as a farm manager. He'd been able after a decade or so to buy a small farm or two, which his sons had developed. On his deathbed he'd reverted to Catholicism again and his family followed him. They had secretly been practicing the old religion all along…

But the Irish never forgot the apparent switching of sides. Oh no, the taint of self-serving betrayal lingered on; even today, sixty or so years later!

One of Daniel's three sons had gone into the retail business and had done really well. The second had bought properties in the surrounding townships and rented them out, reinvesting as he went along. The family accumulated wealth quite rapidly and by the turn of the century Daniel Kinnane's third son Eammon could afford to purchase a Big House and an estate that had been owned by a major English family for centuries. The oldest son of that family who'd inherited the estate at a young age had gambled most of their fortune away in England. He couldn't make the place profitable or afford its upkeep, and so it was sold at a rock bottom price. It had only been occupied by Aisling's family since the turn of the century, for twenty years or so.

But the Kinnanes were seen as upstarts I was sure, part of the nouveau riche; aping the hated English. They were respected, yes, for what they had achieved, but not quite accepted in a land of long memories….with an often bitter religious divide.

This was where the rather aggressive family approach to life had come from.

And here I was at the heart of the family patch, a simple Dublin lad from a poor area… in a place I didn't belong in the slightest. But I refused to be overawed by it all!

As we glided to a stop on the crunching gravel at the front of the house, Aisling, her father and mother were waiting for me. I waited until the chauffeur had opened the door for me before alighting, in keeping with my decision to not appear impressed and look at home in these circumstances.

Aisling's eyes were soft and welcoming; she'd missed me greatly as I had her. Her mother also warmly greeted me. I shook hands with Eammon Kinnane, and quietly thanked him for the ride. His grip was crushing, his eyes were cold and betrayed a trace of disappointment for a fraction of a second that I had not been impressed by the whole set up. Servants carried my bag to my large room on the top floor, well away from my Love.

I longed to be alone with her, but her parents or servants seemed to be constantly around, even when she showed me around the estate.

Aisling and I continually gave each longing looks, when we thought the others couldn't notice. But we never even got the chance to have a private talk together. I would have loved to have gone to her at night but the family kept a wolfhound just inside the front door during the hours of darkness; and although I got on quite well with the dog…I didn't want to push my luck!

My good relations with her mother continued, but I sensed a hint of well disguised antipathy from her father…

On the day of my departure Eammon Kinnane, took me aside alone to his office. I actually guessed what would happen, as he headed for his desk and elaborately withdrew a chequebook from the desk drawer, and selected an expensive fountain pen from a stand.

"Aidan Duffey, let's talk plainly……."

I rudely broke in; still smarting at his crude attempt to impress and overwhelm me with the limousine…he obviously thought I was a bit simple. I was not even going to give him the opportunity to buy me off! My words must be stinging; 'me stubborn' was really *percolating* away!

"Please stop *now* sir. I'll not be awanting to put you in the cringing and embarrassing position of having an offer, generous no doubt, refused. I'm not that type, your daughter has better judgement, which you should respect and recognize. However, I do thank you for your families' hospitality during this visit."

His face was red and boiling as I turned, opened the door and left him. I was feeling elated; I'd *got* him in several ways! I'd insulted the arrogant sod, had made him feel gauche and crude to even consider buying me off.

The ladies noticed the change in me when I rejoined them. Aisling was puzzled and looked at me quizzically. I tried to keep a neutral face.

On reflection however I had been very unwise; it was stupid to make such a powerful potential enemy. Then again, I might be comparatively poor, but I had my pride! Still, lecturing him as to how he should accept his daughter's view… not wise at all! My Aunt Biddy was right, that stubborn of mine gets away on me at times. I wouldn't be able to tell Aisling what had happened either.

Mr. Kinnane eventually emerged from his office, all very businesslike, face emotionless. Aisling was watching him closely; trying to glean what had gone on in the library…

My goodbye was formal, and, of course, yet again there was a reason why Aisling couldn't accompany to Kinsale to see me off. The car was needed "to travel elsewhere on business after I'd been dropped off."

My love was almost in tears as I left the grand house in the luxurious vehicle and swept off down the imposing drive. Looking back I could see the small group, Aisling and her mother waving goodbye. Somewhat apart was Mr. Kinnane glowering at the departing car, which depressed me greatly.

But I must now get back to my Dublin life; the brewery job and the intelligence work with Mick. I wondered what had happened during this last week. It was dangerous to be out of touch! I must make sure that our offices had not been discovered by the Brits and changed location yet again. I would first check with some contacts who would know…

Aisling herself would be returning to me in three days time…

26

Song

I sadly watched the blue Hispano drive off, the large tyres crunching the gravel noisily, waving goodbye to my gutsy love. I was awash with embarrassment and humiliation at how my father had tried to impress my friend in such a blatant and shallow way; Father just couldn't conceive that under his plain working class exterior, Aidan Duffey was subtle and sophisticated, far more so in fact than my dominating parent himself! It had not gone well; we'd longed to be together alone… but we'd had no chance at all to be. Our only touches during the whole visit had been a handshake on arrival and departure, and once we'd managed to touch feet under the table.

As the car disappeared Mother glanced at me sympathetically and consoled me, "What a nice man, Aisling!"

Father merely snorted and turned away; I was aware he disliked Aidan. I was infuriated with him, and ran off upstairs to my bedroom, slamming the door behind me, throwing myself face down on the bed crying. This was not my usual behaviour and certainly not princess-like! The visit had been partly my idea, after all. Again, I'd not taken the unfair daughter treatment into account enough; where I was concerned my father was now a tyrant, more or less *beyond* my control! That thought made me boil….

That evening Nora was sympathetic… "Come now Aisling, c'ld 'ave bin worse! Y' fellow 'as got class, I'll b' givin ye that, 'n I knows *ye* aint atryin' t' impress 'm. Your Pa needs unnerstandin' now, even if ee's a tad hembarrassin' a' times……. His world is harder than yours…….where d y' tink d' cakes 'n cars n' wealth come from, when all's said 'n done….eh?"

27

Sky

The cold eyes flicked over me; in an instant I felt I was evaluated and deemed unimportant in the scheme of things; filed in a memory, just in case, mind you, but then they resumed their restless roaming around the others present in our office. Yet the deliberate, intense and scholarly voice never faltered. From time to time I could actually get the gist of the discussion. He wanted Mick to change the way our war was being fought; but my boss was having none of it; for the first real time in our nation's history, Ireland was showing strong resistance to British oppression, and he would not mess with a winning formula, so that was that!

Dev, as Eamon de Valera was known by all and sundry in the movement always worried me. I sensed an all-enveloping cloud of unbridled calculation and ambition about him.

Tall, thin and rather academic in appearance, demeanour and speech; he was hard to know. He lacked a common touch as far as I could see. Mick, being younger, looked up to the only real leader of the 1916 revolt who'd survived the British firing squads. Since he'd been born in America of an American father, and the fact they had little on him in their records, the British had thought it wouldn't have gone down well with the Irish lobby in the US, their current war ally at that time, who would have exploited his martyrdom to the limit; so he'd escaped the fate of the rest. The Yanks knew all about freedom fighters against the British! Also he'd been one of the more successful military leaders of the whole damned 1916 mess. Yet….I was always wary when he was around.

Mick tended to look up to his older compatriot, and paid him more respect than I thought he deserved. Dev's greatest skill was bringing together disparate groups and controlling his cabinet of fractious ministers…

28

Song

It was a quarter to seven in the morning. As I had arranged, the taxi was waiting for me patiently, motor chugging, blue smoke coming out of its exhaust. I was pleased the driver hadn't tooted his klaxon in my somewhat select, quiet neighbourhood, disturbing everyone. Carrying my big bundle carefully, I climbed aboard. I should just have time to get this done and get to my work by eight thirty; Mick hated people being late.

The city seemed to be an early grey cauldron of activity. I'd not been out at this hour in Dublin before and as we made our way north over the dark sombre river, I was quite astonished at the number of people rushing off to work, when it was barely daylight. Their dull clothing, blank pale faces and the smoky atmosphere, all made the scene seem a bit depressing. The street lamps appeared weak and blinked off as the eastern sky lightened.

I got the driver to stop at the road a few yards from the end of Weed's lane. This meant I would have to carry my load a bit further, but I wanted my visit to be low key, unlike the last time! I paid him and asked him to wait for me…

The flats and houses were humming with noise and activity inside them as I made my way along the lane, weak lights shone here and there through the curtains. I made my way past the red door to Weed's place.

I met one resident leaving her home who recognized me, said hello briefly and was gone. The kids were all inside at this time; no washing was hanging on the lines strung over my head. I made my way to Amy's house and knocked on the door. There was a pause and then a frightened voice answered me.

"Who is it? What w'd ye b'wantin' a' this hour?"

"It's Aisling, I want to see you before I leave for work Amy!"

There was a surprised pause and then a series of locks and sliding bolts were undone and the varnished door opened with a creak.

The undernourished face in the curly black hair had an animated glow to it, the pale sightless eyes seemed again to look right through me. She was wearing several layers of what looked like hand me down clothing of unmatched colours. Amy's hands reached up and her light fingertips traced the contours of my face again. The voice was soft. "It *is* Aisling; y' must've come t'see *me!* Weed'll not b'back till this evenin'.., I'm thinkin'. Come in, come in! I'm not agettin' many visitors, ye understand…."

The air inside was cold, although there was the smell of the morning cooking embers in the flat. The rooms were furnished very cheaply and simply, but everything was absolutely spotless.

She read my mind, "Sorry it's cold here, me Ma works *so* hard, been gone 'bout an h'r already; but the factory pays her ver' little; what wiv the rent an all, things are tightish now! Can't waste t' coal. Me bein' blind doesn' help. *Wish* I could help her, t' poor dear. M'dad died durin' the war, an we both miss him…." She felt over to a sideboard, " Here's a photograph of him; me Ma cries a lot alookin' at it…I have t' use me memory; I c'ld see a bit in those days….but m'sight's got worse since."

We sat in the dark parlour. The poor creature spent her days only doing housework to occupy the long hours…in a cold empty flat. When I put the harp in its padded container down she reached out and curiously touched it. She was puzzled because the shape gave nothing away.

"Amy, I've a surprise for you! I think you will be able to help your Mum out with the finances in the future. Surprisingly, for once, being blind may be a real advantage! Several hundred years ago there was an Irish lad who caught smallpox and became blind. Because of that we know of him today……Turlough O'Carolan; he's really famous in Irish music. He took up harp playing, wrote many tunes and collected others as he travelled the country. Being blind gives you more time to practice and blind people have a heightened sense of hearing and touch; so many people say, and I know you sing beautifully. So here is a present for you!"

I unwrapped and opened the box and withdrew the lap harp. I took her hands and passed her fingers around the frame and over the strings…. The notes that were magically wafting through the chilly apartment were joined by sobs of joy from the teenager. "It's really f'r *me* Aisling? How'll I ever be thankin' ye? Me ma'll be awantin' t' meet y'…."

"You can thank me by becoming a great player and singer. I won't be able to help you much Amy, because I never have much time these days. You'll really have to teach yourself; which is what we all do in effect anyway! That's why everyone has a different style. I'll try and get back from time to time, though."

I then taught her to really listen to the notes as her finger ran along the strings; so she could tune it by ear. By touch I demonstrated how to use the little spanner provided to tighten or loosen the strings. I warned her that the small tool was easy to lose, and to be careful with it. Then I showed her how to pick out a melody with her right hand and some simple chords with her left hand to compliment them. I looked at my watch. I had to leave her… alone, practicing joyfully in the dark austere little room.

Amy just managed to drag herself away from the instrument to see me off. In the doorway her grateful face became solemn. "May the Lord, Mary n' Jaysus be rewardin' ye f'r bringin' such happiness t' me Aisling. But *please* b' amemorin', -*heart* not head."

I walked away listening to the bolts and locks re-securing her door, this must be a rough area. I would like to have at least knocked and said hello to Weed's aunt and uncle, but I was already late…

I felt happy and somehow fulfilled; doing something to help someone felt meaningful and in some way, made me a better person. Again that comment about heart and head…I must think about what that meant when I had time. I asked the taxi driver to speed up on the way back; but the traffic on the roads had increased…..

That evening Nora flounced cheerfully into my mind. "*Well!* Ther b' times Aisling, when I'm atinkin' y' might b' agettin through t' pearly gates *after all!*

Helpin' that poor child…clever choice o' gift too…that'll change her world f' t' better! Let's face it, yere related t' me, so I *spose* it mus' vencherly rub off on ya, a bit! Nex' time take her some *food*, y' silly rich girl; she needs it! Not too fancy like, 'cos that'd be ashowin' off! Oh, an' listen t' Amy….. *heart* firs' not y' head; y' get it?"

She faded away and was gone before I could answer her and beg her for another view of her old life. Sometimes her visits were too irritatingly brief!

29

Sky

I'd become aware that Mick Collins was playing a many sided game… but didn't hold it against him at all. I could understand the necessity for it. Irish politics were made up of so many colours, tints and shades; everyone was opinionated on every aspect of our struggle. To lead and actually survive in this maelstrom he essentially had to tell people what they wanted to hear….then proceed how he thought, while somehow holding things together. He couldn't afford to alienate too many, especially of the old guard.

The Brits had suddenly started to gain on us; there were more arrests of our people; these were major setbacks for the movement; we were losing our edge in effect. We still had good overall sources of intelligence, but something new was evading our net and betraying our movement. Mick was worried.

Frowning one day he actually confided in me. "The bastards have brought in some outsiders who are workin' outside the Castle, so we haven't got a finger on 'em. But because they're new here, they stand out, and I'm getting some tabs on them. We'll squash'm all Weed… an' that's a fact! We're gonna have to be as heavy as they are, which'll upset quite a few on our side, but a helluva lot more on *their* side. They'll overreact for sure, which might just help the cause!"

I knew, probably more than anyone, that Mick made sensible, well reasoned comments to the conservative side of the movement complaining about "those damned idiot hotheads I have to deal with" while actually planning mayhem; he was the *worst* hothead of the lot! He felt that a vital tipping point in the struggle was coming, and acted accordingly. Yet he always was looking ahead to the future. Even some in the IRB now the IRA still thought that political negotiation might eventually come to pass.

I happened to be nearby when the "Apostles" were inaugurated. Aisling's brother Rory was one. He was a bit older then although not much wiser. Since that time I'd hit him in the face to save him from a checkpoint, he'd perversely loathed my guts.

The initial bunch of twelve nondescript men, dressed in everyday clothes, was secretly armed to the teeth. It was partially Mick's idea; the Brits were killing our people, so we would assassinate theirs in a carefully targeted way; anywhere, anytime; "Dead simple Weed!" He'd laughed at the aptness of the comment.

I was in favour of the idea… we were involved in a war after all.

Coming back from the brewery one morning to start a day with the movement, thinking as always of my love, I walked along a busy Parnell Sreet. Dublin was showing her sunny side today and was sparkling. A mild, rather school masterly type dressed in a tweed suit was walking towards me, when I suddenly realized he was being followed by two of the apostles with caps pulled down in an attempt to conceal their faces. I noticed another one walking on the other side of the road; a backup or lookout; perhaps both. In front of everyone a pistol was pointed point- blank at the back of the target's head, it cracked and he reeled and crashed to concrete, blood and brain fragments showering the screaming and stunned passers-bye. Two more shots thudded into the crumpled body to make sure; then the Apostles ran for it, jumped on two waiting bicycles in an alleyway and pedalled off into the traffic. People milled around looking down at the corpse. It had all taken only a few seconds. Across the road the watcher stayed for a second or two, making sure the target was dead and then he melted away. I rapidly did the same; I didn't want to be caught up in the inevitable dragnet and random arrests that would follow.

Later that day when I told Mick what I'd seen; he had a grim satisfied look on his face. "One less Weed; that swine was responsible for the deaths of at least nine of our people, actually interrogated and tortured them himself too. Well, we'll really let the other side know that we are getting them, by publicizing it like mad. We allow some of their informants to carry on so they can feed false info back to the Castle; all part of the game Weed. Sort of thing *they've* done to us for years! On the receiving end themselves now; it'll put the wind up 'em proper!"

He paused; the brown eyes looked at me searchingly as if he was trying to glean what I really thought; covering himself he added: "I carefully research each target to make sure no mistakes are made. Any of their cops who pull out of the game and leave the country we leave alone, even when we might have a score to settle. That encourages others to quit. But listen, not a word to anyone that I know, OK? Mind you, we don't want to upset them *too* much, we don't want the whole damn British army here, we *would* lose the war if that happened. We don't want to get the killing to foul up possible future settlement talks with them either. Got to be rational about violence…… must actually *achieve* something, right?"

I nodded with my blank face that seemed to reassure him; he knew I could really keep a secret. Despite the fact he supported direct confrontation at times he was one of the few leaders of our movement who was really looking ahead, taking a long view. At that time I wasn't entirely convinced. Could we ever be able to negotiate with our enemy? But with hindsight Mick was spot on…

30

Song

 Amy answered my knock; through the door her voice betrayed excitement as well as pleasure at my second unannounced early morning visit. The various slide bolts and locks were undone with impatience and she reached out to touch my face as usual. She again was wearing a hodgepodge of clothes, with mismatched colours....

"Ah, Aisling, I've been awantin' ter see you an' show you what I've taught mesel'. I can acksherley play some tunes now! Come 'n listen!"

The flat was again chilly, but this time I was better prepared; I was carrying a paper sack of coal for my friend and a bag of raisin rock cakes still warm from the bakery....we shared a couple and then the blind girl put some aside for her mother. Nora's advice had been spot on! Amy had loved that special treat. She put the remaining three cakes carefully into an empty cake tin in the kitchen.

"Me ma really wants ter meet y' Aisling, t' thank you f'r the harp and now these gifts. Aidan always makes sure we are OK...even *he* didn't know you were agoin' t' get a harp fer me. He was so surprised when he saw it! I'm athinkin' he loves you a lot, cos he goes quiet when I mention yer name! Y'know, when y'blind, y' hear extra things… "

Then Amy carefully took the cover off her most precious possession. The instrument gleamed with hours of polishing. She caressed the wood lightly with her long slim fingers. "S'lovely an smooth now; I'm thinkin' it sounds better 'cos of it. I'll play f' ye now…"

The instrument was in tune. She was proud of how she'd learnt to do that; and rightfully so! The average player found that a very difficult task to do accurately by ear, without any aids. "I really try an listen t' the notes, jus like y' tol' me to!"

She played some simple tunes with a gentle, natural fluency. Her left handed chords were simple but fitted. On balance she'd made great progress…. I complimented her, and the pale eyes gleamed with pride and pleasure.

I showed her the ways in which notes could be bent, plucked differently, adding polish to a tune, then some more advanced chords using all her fingers. I introduced her to some fast jigs. The young woman picked up any new task very quickly, and promised to practice everything new that I'd shown her.

We sang two songs together. The unheated flat was warmed by our voices and the music.

"You will be performing soon Amy at the rate you are going! I'll see if I can find a place for you to start earning a few pennies. Teach yourself at least six tunes, practice them and learn the words of the songs by heart."

She gave me an excited smile. "Could you?" she breathed.

In no time it seemed, an hour had passed and I had to leave. She hugged me and kissed me on the cheek. "Bless y' Aisling!" tears of gratitude again ran down her pale cheeks, and I turned and left. The door closed and those locking sounds could be heard as I walked off down the lane.

I was late getting to work which upset Mick a bit. Finding a taxi in Weed's neighbourhood was hard; so I had to walk for a mile or so. People there couldn't afford to use them so there were none around. Next time I must find out from my love what number tram I should take…

That evening Nora smiled at me warmly. "Tol' ye now didn't I …eh? G'd honest plain *food*, went down a treat now, didn' it? I'ma almos' getting t' be a bit proud of ye… changin' a poor girl's life f' t' better….doin t' dacent thing! An' I knows y' atinkin' about t' clothes now too……mmm, but t' coal was a *great* idea. I'd b' doin' that again fo' sure…." She then spoke in apparent wonder. "Well, well, *well*, yous might acksherly become a nice person one day!"

Before I could answer she had infuriatingly disappeared. But I slept happily that evening.

Sky

The fine rain streaked and clung stubbornly to the sooty windows as the small train chugged determinedly to the south shaking and swaying. The lowered sky clung to the rounded hills and made the villages we stopped in seemed colourless, which rather matched the feeling in my heart; apart from Aisling for a whole seven days! It would seem a *decade* to me!

My annual holidays at the brewery had come round… one entire week. Of course this enabled me to work full time for the movement and be close to my Aisling. Our movement had made several important assassinations around the country. These had enraged the Brits so checkpoints were everywhere. On this trip I had already presented my papers four times, and I was only half way to Cobh.

Mick had contacts on every train throughout Ireland… sometimes several on one train, who were quite unaware of each other. In the years ahead this would be called a "need to know basis"; compartmentalised knowledge was safer if anyone was caught. Sometimes there were several versions of a report arriving at our intelligence centre, so nuances could be read. Every troop movement or the travel of any important target or person was noted and the details passed back to our HQ, normally within an hour or two. The railway network was the key to our system; the telephone and telegraph were too open for our liking and were only really used for extreme emergencies. Couriers carried messages, sensitive documents and money by rail throughout the country. Bundles of reports flowed in daily. As I've said often, Mick was busy all right; how he did it all, I don't know!

A crisis had occurred; our network had been broken by a flurry of arrests and we were very wary at the moment…but it was vital that we directly contact a chapter of the brothers down south. Mick had quietly selected me; I had no form, a legitimate job and had a relative of my mother's in the area, an old aunt I could visit as an excuse. Also I was not known in that area by even our own people. It was an honour to be picked for such an important mission.

So here I was sitting in a third class carriage with three young British soldiers wearing my neutral, vacant, thick Irish Mick face. I'd been instructed to be in this particular compartment because hidden under a seat facing the engine there would be a Mauser pistol waiting for me to pick up. The checkups at the Dublin station had been too stringent for me to carry one on with me, but intelligence told us things were much looser down south. Mick felt I should be armed this time; our secret organization was often scarred by infighting between various factions and I might need to protect myself. I'd arrived last, just before the train started its journey, so if the weapon was discovered I couldn't be blamed for it. I couldn't directly look down at it, but I knew it would definitely be there.

The Brit soldiers sneered and made fun of me at first, but since I didn't react in any way they soon got bored with that game and then pointedly ignored me. As we rattled along, while looking out the window as the countryside slid by, I idly listened to the soldiers' conversation, trying to gauge their mood. After a while this became less stilted as they relaxed. Things were not going too well for them at this moment it seemed. They obviously felt very much under threat in Ireland and couldn't wait to return to Blighty; uneducated working-class lads who understood little of the situation or environment they'd been ordered into; hadn't that always been the way, historically? Young, but brave enough and brutal when scared, no doubt.

As we neared Cobh, I wondered how I could get my hands on that hidden pistol. Perhaps I should just hold back respectfully and let them go first… grab it and quickly hide it in my jacket when they'd left the compartment, and then emerge after them seamlessly; yes, that should work.

Just as the train noisily braked to a stop in a cloud of cinders and steam, the young soldiers hastily got their gear ready but the youngest dropped his khaki pack from the high luggage rack. It burst open and spilled its contents all over the floor, his mates laughed at his misfortune as they opened the compartment door and stepped down onto the platform. I helped him as some items were close to where the pistol was supposed to be. Some coins he had missed I handed to him. He was grateful for my assistance and as he left I felt around under the seat; the firearm was there as had been arranged. Bending over I surreptitiously hid it in my jacket, then quickly disembarked from the carriage. I was stunned to see a major checkpoint at the end of the platform aggressively *stopping all locals*! Hell, so much for intelligence! I quickly caught up to the young squaddy I'd just helped. Improvising quickly, I warned him he was losing something from his bag; he stopped and gratefully readjusted things. I helped, very aware that we were under observation. Trying to be casual but with my heart wildly beating we approached the barrier. I had my papers ready but I had seen other citizens being thoroughly searched. The pistol weighed an awkward ton and to me seemed to bulge through my clothing. I was ready to explode into action and kill if necessary to escape this situation; if the weapon was discovered I was a goner anyway.

But my grateful soldier companion waved away the men at checkpoints with a "He's orright!" and in the end my papers were only glanced at and I was through. The soldiers were forming a platoon; they marched off; there obviously had been quite a crowd of them on board the train.

My heart was still thumping away as I walked out of the station, and after making sure I wasn't being followed, went around a corner and then up a road somewhat breathlessly, to our local contact, a shoemaker. He was pleased to see I had somehow evaded the dragnet. Really pure luck had got me through! Apparently local security had been suddenly increased as one of our factions had just assassinated a collaborator without telling "Head Office". This was always a problem for us; sometimes personal local scores were being settled under the guise of furthering our struggle against the enemy.

Song

Nora had only visited me briefly for some weeks now… we hadn't had time to have a meaningful conversation about her past. Usually, when she came, she was telling me off for my behaviour, which quite often she did *not* approve of. My lack of religious fervour puzzled and upset her.

I had cheated a bit and had borrowed some books from the library about the Great Famine. I had broadened my understanding of that terrible period of Irish history. After reading three volumes, I felt quite confident that I understood those times reasonably well.

Nora would have none of it. She somehow *knew* what I'd been up to. She sniffed, black locks indignantly shaking, her eyes scornful:

"*Books!* Ye can't be unnerstandin' unless ye feet 're in the mud, an' ye tummy's arumblin' and achin'…..an' there's har' work t' do, an people t'look after, then there's te worry o' t' little people aleavin' us….prob'ly to find food for themselves." Nora was always superstitious.

"Aisling, I'm agoin t' show you wha' it was really like!" Her gaunt face took on a look of fierce concentration. Suddenly a dull light grew around her, then, as her face faded away, the light changed into a scene.

It was a tiny cottage with a very low uneven thatched roof, a stubby smoking chimney, basic mud unpainted walls with two tiny windows either side of the front door. This humble structure was located in two compact fields. At the far end was a copse of trees, along one walled side was a rutted uneven dirt road that meandered off into the distant countryside.

Then I realized with a shock that I had seen the foundations of this building with my father on our way home from church that day, back when I'd been eleven years old. But there was one difference, there were no trees around the little fields; plants were growing right up to the perimeter walls.

This was a mild spring day; I could clearly smell the earth and wood smoke and the terrible stink of a ramshackle outside privy. The two undersized fields were crammed full of plants, mainly potatoes. Two bent figures were tending the plants with crude wooden implements. Three young children were carrying weeds to a reeking compost heap at a corner of the field. Near the dwelling was a vegetable garden that was neatly tended. I was so entranced with what I was seeing that I was startled when Nora's close voice spoke to me.

"Com' on Aisling…. Le's look inside…these wuz t' good times. Me home is where ye've been acomin' from, af'er all!"

The door was very low, the inside was gloomy and it took some seconds for my eyes to adjust. The two very small windows with some glass panels missing and the small open front door barely illuminated the inside which was only one room in effect. Its low ceiling of straw and dried clay floor sprinkled with rushes; seemed overwhelmingly cramped to my modern eyes. At one end were two beds, on which some coarse spun brown coloured blankets were folded and stacked. In the centre of the back wall there was a glowing hearth with a suspended metal pot simmering; the smell was delicious; a vegetable broth of some kind. There was a little stack of twigs and firewood and some small bricks of peat beside the stones of the hearth. " 'S my job; ver *himportant* t' keep t' fire agoin', but not *too* much, y' mind; mustn't waste fuel now…"

There were some stubby plank shelves in one corner nearby, a few earthenware plates and cups were stacked there, with a large metal bowl that was used as a basin to wash dishes and no doubt at times the baby in. On the mantle above the fire was a plain wooden cross, with some tiny flowers in a homemade flax basket. Nora noticed my interest, and proudly said: " T' good Lord blesses us 'ere, an' is wiv us always…. "

I didn't know how to tactfully answer that.

Some weeks ago when I'd first visited Weed's home, I'd thought it poor; but compared with this, his place was an absolute *palace!*

The family came in; tired and exhausted from a hard day's work outside. My presence didn't seem to register… they apparently couldn't see me at all.

Unasked, seven year old Nora tended the wants of her baby brother Danny, while her mother was busy getting a meal prepared. A little girl of five Katie, and a three year old boy Tom played on the floor with some bits of wood. Nora's father Joe Kinanne, a big framed man sat wearily on the only seat and looked at his family with pride.

His voice was low: "Nora, get t' rent tin, there's a good colleen…" Nora, while holding her baby brother with one arm, reached over and lifted a stone by the fire hearth, revealing a small secret compartment underneath. She withdrew a small rusty container and reverently handed it to her father. He patted her on the head and opened the lid. Everything seemed to stop as all present looked at the coins he'd tipped out onto the table.… I somehow got the impression this was an important evening ritual. He counted them out slowly and carefully. "Ah, all still there, praise t' Lord, an one penny f' t' church. T' lil folk didn't spirit 'em away. We should be amakin' t' rent dis month!" He grinned tiredly at his wife, "But notin' much over, Love… still, we might be agetting a bit more a' t' market on Thursday, Mother Mary awillin'."

The scene faded and Nora was gone too. My warm large bedroom was quiet but lacking in someway; human warmth had faded with the scene ….I suddenly missed Weed terribly.

The vision had impressed me in several ways: the building was so totally basic, cramped and poky, the smells of this world were pungent, but another, rather surprising aspect, was the slow, simple pace of life. Time crawled by in such a leisurely fashion for these folk, and there seemed to be little variation in these lives; but a predictable existence must have been comforting and restful…

I now understood why Nora had once sniffed accusingly at me, "Yous modren folk've got so many *things!* " It sounded like a major crime; she'd had so little in her short life, not even living space. I was suddenly embarrassed by my family's wealth…

I wanted to know what had happened to my friend. I hoped there would be further instalments to come.

In my dark room I lay thinking… until sleep reluctantly claimed me.

33

Sky

The village was quaint; a small collection of twenty or so cottages and outhouses, a tiny post office and police station nestled in a shallow valley, surrounded by the tiny land holdings of the inhabitants. Separated by stone walls some of the small green fields had trees on their boundaries. They seemed to gently stroke the cloud filled edge of the clean, unsmoky and vast sky. A shallow bubbling stream wound its way through this landscape. To me, a city-dweller, it was a perfect picture of placid rural peace.

I was enjoying the change of environment despite the fact I was a visitor and therefore stood out. My relatives made me really welcome; my mother had been a native of this village, but had gone to Dublin to find work; a common Irish story. She'd been very popular and her premature death had upset everyone. There were many children in the village, some working in the fields and younger ones playing on the road.

George O'Connor was the local policeman. A popular local man, his twinkly eyes and grizzled hair that peeked out from under his uniform's helmet, had ruled this sleepy backwater and the surrounding hamlets for years. He knew everyone in the area and very little escaped his eye. Normally, members of the Royal Irish Constabulary (RIC) were our sworn enemies, being the eyes and ears of Dublin Castle, and were seen as their lackeys, but George was one of Mick's key sources as to what the police in the south western areas were up to.

Disguising the fact that he knew of me, he'd picked me up on the road from Tralee's railway station and given me a ride out to the village. We'd both been very wary for a while as we very casually exchanged the password phrases that Mick had given me, worked into the conversation in a natural way. Once we had relaxed, he was pleased with the message I had brought, and we could discuss how things were going on both sides. The police were being targeted by the IRA out here in Kerry … forcing the authorities to close down small stations such as his; meaning the government was losing a key way of obtaining local intelligence about supporters of our movement. The government now tended to group the RIC Police Officers together in fortified houses and barracks. George expected to be shifted to one in a few weeks time, his immediate area having been quite peaceful for some years…

He frowned, but his eyes twinkled mischievously at me. "Y'know," he said, "this damned political nonsense is after getting me down. Now if I could only have a dacent bit of good old fashioned larceny and drunken mayhem to deal with, life would be much more enj….."

He halted in mid sentence, quickly passed me the reins, jumped down from the cart with surprising alacrity for such a big man, hurdled a wall and sprinted over to a haystack. He dived into the hay and emerged with a skinny ten year old boy with a red hair and a freckled face, who was promptly dragged back to the cart, protesting his innocence.

"*Smokin'*, y' little devil…. Wait'll ye dad hears about this! I'll be a seein' him t'night at the pub. Give me the fags an' matches. Ever heard about a haystack fire boy? People lose their houses an sometimes lives fr' that!"

The boy was shivering with fear. "I's sorry, an' I won' be adoin it agin' Constable…. I *really* promise!" His brown tearful eyes beseeched the policeman.

We pottered along the windy road for a quarter of a mile, the lad quietly sobbing. Then O'Connor stopped the horse with a tug on the reins. "Mmm, get out of my sight Jimmy O'Shea. Maybe this once I'll be overlookin' your evil…… but *next* time….." he warned.

"Oh thank ye Constable… I *really* won't be doin it agin'!" The lad climbed down and ran for it.

George O'Conner laughed with me once the lad was out of earshot. Then he looked serious. "The father's a violent drunkin' bastard… who'd kill the boy if he heard what he'd bin up to! He'll never b' hearin' about it fr' me! The poor little bugger, big family, six other kids…the mother gets beaten up sometimes too. Well, at least I'll be atinkin' the lad won't offend f' a while. Did it m'self once when I was a kid, but of course, that was different, I was clever enough to get away wi't it," he giggled to himself.

I judged this policeman was doing a good job, using his knowledge of the locals and showing sensible flexibility caring for his charges. I liked him.

"I'd get out of the policing game if I could; too many of us have been shot, but I'd lose me pension; an' there's no other work for me. Another couple of years more

I'll be doin' this job then I'll be retirin'!" This was not uncommon throughout the country, the police who were Irish were seen as traitors, propping up the British and often doing their dirty work for them, but some of them looked after people on our side and kept us posted as to what moves were being made against us.

He was also a bit of a philosopher. Later that evening in his cottage, George looked at me wearily over his wire rimmed reading glasses, and mumbled to me: "You'd be knowin' then that history massages this land; playfully and gently a' times then violently pummelling her at others. We Irish dwell in this reality cushioned by our fatalism, music, stubbornness and alcohol, and don't forget a whole tureen full o' humour…. But t'ings are goin' to be getting much harder, mark m' words!"

"Y' right there George…" I had to agree with him.

A week after I left him I heard he' been shot and killed by an IRA group. Mick was livid! "A good man Weed, he was vital to us in his area, these simple local groups bugger everything up for us at times…they couldn't conceive he might have been helping our side. In their simple eyes, *all* policemen are the enemy. But if we inform them whose helpin' us, someone talks an' the Brits find out!"

The village policeman's death had diluted my unbinding loyalty to the cause somewhat; things were almost never clear-cut in our struggle.

34

Song

Work had been frantic for some time now; I needed a break. Weed had gone south on a job for Mick, although to all intents and purposes he was having a little holiday as far as everyone else was concerned; but of course I knew what was really going on! Although it was going to be for only a week, I'd miss him terribly! I felt the need to fill the emptiness with a good deed, helping Amy would be beneficial to my state of mind, I reasoned.

I told Mick I needed at least a morning off, perhaps a little longer; it was for a good cause, I told him without elaborating. He'd paused in thought and had then agreed; telling me to not make a habit of it! Although I was just an unpaid volunteer I was not really free to come and go as I wanted, long regular hours at the office were the norm.

First thing that morning, I went and bought Amy a new skirt and blouse of traditional design with some simple jewellery. Thinking about the recipient, I made sure the fabrics were attractive to touch. I then went to a second hand store and bought a bundle of matching clothing for her. I hoped I'd guessed the right size; if wrong I would have the outfits altered to fit.

Mrs. Murphy's Tea Shoppe was a clean, popular little establishment near the centre of town on Parnell St. close to the square. I went and spoke to the proprietor. She was a bustling, good humoured, rather rotund lady. I asked her if she would allow my blind friend to play her harp and sing for an hour or so. She didn't mind, and had a place in the tearoom for her to play, but said that payment might be a problem as things were a bit slow at the moment. No problem I told her, secretly I would pay Amy, through her, if need be. It would mean so much for the young woman. I told the owner I would be back in an hour or so. She told me things were quiet in the shop then, before the lunchtime rush. It should be a perfect time for a debut performance…

It was nearly two weeks since I'd last visited Amy O'Driscoll. She was overjoyed to see me. "I've bin alearnin' *twelve songs 'n jigs* Aisling, an' I knows all t' words, *-really!*" Her face was alight with pride, her eyes sparkling. Weed's Aunt Biddy had helped her, as she loved to sing with her close neighbour Amy.

I told her what we were going to do that morning and she became very excited, but apprehensive too. As she changed into the skirt and top, I told her where we were going. She touched the fabrics of her new clothes reverently, "So nice'n silky…" She felt the simple pendant and brooch.

"I feel quite a grand lady in these, t' best clothes I've ever bin having!" she breathed. I combed her hair and clipped it back. She did look quite natural and beautiful…and was quite unaware of the fact, which added to her attractiveness. I did like her I decided; to me she was an older, living Nora but here with me in my time…. And even more importantly, she was a link to my beloved Weed.

We set out for the teashop in the taxi I'd kept waiting for me this time. Amy held my hand tightly as the vehicle set off. "I'se never bin in one o' thees noisy contraptions…much too 'spensive! Oh *dear me!* T'rate I'm agoin', I'll be a rich lady afore y' aknowin' it!" We laughed together. She had Nora's sense of humour at times…

As we alighted from the vehicle, a roaring truck full of heavily armed Tans shouting abuse at the general population terrified her as it passed by us. Even at this time of the day they seemed to be inebriated. The Brit's policy of terrorising the population was backfiring in general, sending the scandalized public to our nationalist side. Amy clutched my arm tightly until they'd gone. Of course, she'd spent most of her life locked up in her quiet, cold little apartment. The noise and bustle of this outside world would take some getting used to.

When we entered the tearooms she became very apprehensive, I thought it was because of the fact she would be performing; but no, what worried her most was being in a strange place she didn't know. Being blind meant you had to find out where things were placed so you could move without bumping objects; learning the layout was vital. After introducing her to Mrs. Murphy herself, I guided her to the corner and sat her down not far from a small glowing fire.

The cosy room was quite bright and cheerful, but the colourful chintz tablecloths, pot plants and bright blue curtained windows looking onto the street where Dublin's inhabitants were bustling about their business meant nothing at all to my friend. She did notice the scent of baking and teas and coffee though; " Mmmm, yummy smells here Aisling, 'S like bein' in heaven I'm athinkin' ! S'warm too!"

Only five tables were occupied; about fifteen customers in all. I'd warned Amy that people would probably talk during her songs which is what they came to such places to do after all, and that she should just ignore this and sing on anyway; softly might be best. I said I'd sing along with her on the first song. We were going to provide a pleasant backdrop for the customers.

One man stood out to me for some reason. He was sitting at a small table set back a bit; fairly tall, brown short hair, well dressed. He refused to make eye contact, and appeared furtive in manner, nervously glancing at his watch every few seconds. He seemed to be waiting for someone. The rest of the customers were more what one would expect at this time of the day; wives, friends meeting, two elderly couples. This shouldn't be a difficult audience I decided.

The change in temperature had put the harp out of tune, especially the high note strings and it took us a minute to sort that out. Then we sang our first song. Amy had really improved; her playing surprised me. She'd incorporated the little tips I'd given her a fortnight ago, and even better, had introduced some of her own. Her style was light, lively but she could bring feeling and aching sadness to some tunes and her lilting voice complimented this to perfection. I was proud of her, although she was almost entirely self-taught. Our first number was enthusiastically applauded, which embarrassed Amy a bit. I told her she was really doing well.

A newcomer entered, I glanced up and saw it was -*Mick*! Smart suit, nice coat and elegant hat: dapper as usual. He was surprised to see me but pointedly ignored me, looked around and then went to the nervous man. I took the hint and pretended not to know him. But out of the corner of my eye I watched them converse quietly and intensely for two minutes during Amy's second song. Then Mick quickly left... the customer seemed to be wanting him to stay longer, but my boss was having none of it. Out the door Mick bounded and disappeared into the noonday throng, walking towards Sackville St. at his usual rapid pace.

Three heavyset grim men wearing trenchcoats with hats pulled down burst into the shop, sized up the gathering and went to the nervous fellow. I was almost certain they were intelligence men from Dublin Castle from G section, our greatest enemy! Surreptitiously I watched proceedings. The customer pointed out the direction Mick had gone in. Two of them rushed off but came back empty handed after a couple of minutes.

Again Amy was soundly applauded; people outside the shop looked in to see what the fuss was about. More customers came in, mainly to hear the singing harp player. They were buying tea and cakes, and soon every table was occupied and even more arrivals sat at chairs along the counters. Some eventually were even standing, holding their cups awkwardly. Business was really picking up!

Nervously, in a charming Dublin accent, Amy introduced a jig, everyone tapped out the time.

After she'd finished to even more applause, I told Amy I would go and get something for us to drink. I wondered if I could hear what was being said by the G men. Things were so crowded I had to wait to pass their table, which gave me more time to listen. I only managed to catch:

"…… so next time you get a chance to meet the bastard, get word to us sooner, right? Y' really sure it was him?" The customer nodded.

The Brits had nearly captured Mick, here today! I was stunned; I must get word to him immediately.

I decided to tease Nora a bit! She'd probably be watching from the other side, because she always seemed to know what I had been up to each day. Along with a pot of tea, I bought three large *cream cakes*.…I couldn't wait to hear her no doubt snarky comment about that, next time she came to me. Amy loved the treat, although she did get a bit of cream and icing sugar on her face. She'd never had one before! We boxed one for her to take home to her mum.

Mrs. Murphy said everything was on the house.

There were sounds of disappointment as we left. A couple of listeners put coins on a table beside Amy. She had had lots of requests for favourite Irish airs, at times people had sung along. It had been almost too successful! The flustered owner rushed over to us and gave Amy five shillings! She wanted the young performer to come regularly; it would be a paying job for her. "Love to have you here dearie, makes my shop stand out! Oh yes, an' everyone *really* loves yer music!"

As I took Amy home after nearly an hour and a half of performing, I tried to think of a way for her to get to this work on a regular basis. I did have one idea; one of my fellow students was finding it hard to make ends meet and only had evening lectures; could I pay her to accompany Amy to and from the teashop daily? I wondered if she would be willing. She'd get on well with the girl I was sure. Yes, I would ask her.…

Amy burst into tears. "Such 'n exciting day Aisling, *and* I've made some money of me own too; a *whole* five shillin's; some extra coins too, me Ma'll be really be surprised, *an'* new clothes n' jewellery.… I can't be athankin' ye enough fer everything. Really! Please come and meet m' Ma sometime!" she sobbed.

Once inside her place I hugged her, and told her how surprised I had been at her great progress. She was a natural performer. I said I'd get back to her as soon as I could, perhaps this coming weekend, and I would meet her mother then. I told her again my work was important and it was difficult for me to get time off.

I left her happy, feeling very pleased with how things had turned out.

That afternoon when Mick returned to the office I pulled him aside and told him what I'd heard in the tearoom.

"I was athinkin' that fellow was a bit *too* nervous, I arrived early and got t' hell out of there when things didn't feel right. Another close call! He'll have to be dealt with. And only a minute in it, eh? I was surprised to see you there though."

I told him about Amy, he was pleased to hear what I'd been doing….

"Some folk don't have much luck in life…should help others when we can. Still you're really needed here." It was the nearest thing to a compliment I'd heard from Mick!

Nora was quite forthright when she arrived that evening. Her face and eyes were mischievous: "Y' 'spect me t' get all atitchy wiv y' now don't ye? Well at least *t' cream cakes* got t' the *right* people this time; for a *hoity-toity*, spoilt rich girl, y' shown a bit of promise today; I'se is sortin' y' out quite nicely, I'd be atinkin'…y'know, a' times, -y' almost *human!*" She exclaimed in apparent wonder.

I begged her: "Please show me more of your world Nora… I'm dying to find out more…."

"Maybe next time Aisling, I'm thinkin' ye do deserve a lil' reward these days…." She melted away with the hint of a mysterious smile on her face.

35

Song

 I did talk at an evening lecture to Marie Byrne about taking Amy with her harp to and from the teashop. She was quite keen as she needed the money, but the idea of helping someone in need appealed to her more. Marie was quite a religious woman, but warm and with a good sense of humour. My real problem was explaining why I couldn't do it myself, I tried to give the impression that I was doing vital work in the area of finance at an important firm in the city; the last thing I wanted to reveal was my political leanings and work for Irish independence. That must remain secret…

Weed was still away, so that Sunday afternoon I took Marie to meet Amy. In the lane I was mobbed again by the kids, but this time I rather enjoyed their attention; they now knew me.

After general introductions, Marie got to know Amy and they were discussing her harp. The two seemed to be getting on very well.

This was a chance for me to meet my blind friend's mother; we spoke alone in the kitchen. Mrs. O'Driscoll was old before her time; short with prematurely grey hair done up in a simple bun, dressed in a plain fawn work smock and looked worn out. But she was formal in manner and had an air of dignity about her. Her sad eyes revealed concern for her only child.

Her voice was low. "I must be thankin' you fer helping me daughter Miss Kinnane. You have brought excitement and confidence into her life. I have done everything I possibly could for m' daughter, but it has not bin easy since me husband passed on. Believe me, I am thankful; but …" She spoke carefully and I somehow got the impression that her gratitude was less than total. Perhaps there was even a bit of resentment there, because I was taking over her daughter's life, introducing her to another world. I'd got a bit carried away at doing my good works. In the past I would have been extremely annoyed at such an unfair and ungrateful attitude! I would have pointed out to her, in no uncertain terms, that

I had really been inconvenienced by the time I'd spent on Amy, not too mention the cost, which had added up over time. But to my mind came a young thin face with big dark blue eyes.... and Nora's phrase "spoilt, *hoity toity* rich girl!" floated into my head.

Before retorting with a sharp comment, I paused and tried to imagine how Amy's mum must feel, working twelve hours a day, six days a week in a grimy factory... and even then barely making ends meet. Her daughter was the most precious thing in her impoverished, limited life, and I'd waltzed into Amy's existence showering my wealth around..... well-meaning or not. What should I say?

"Mrs. O'Driscoll, your daughter loves you dearly, but worries a lot about your health and that you work too hard. She is getting older and wishes to take pressure off you by contributing herself towards the household income. Amy does have real talent and is cleverly teaching herself and will end up earning good money playing her harp and singing. She is very bright and learns very quickly; believe me, she is a natural performer. I am unable to spend much time with her myself... but once she gets herself established, perhaps in a year or so, she should be earning enough for you to be able to stop work altogether and be supported by her full time. I will help if there are any problems along the way."

We could hear Marie and Amy happily singing through the wall in the tiny parlour. Mrs. O'Driscoll looked away and there was an awkward silence between us for quite a long time. I wondered what she might be thinking.

She eventually turned towards me, sighed and looked at me with tears in her eyes; an impoverished working class mum doing her best.

Her voice was low, almost defeated: "Yes, Amy is getting' older an' should have an interestin' life, but I don' want ter lose her. Because o' th' blindness, we've bin *very* close, but what if something happens ter me? Yer probably right; she *should* really learn to be independent, I suppose. We have no other family to speak of here in Dublin."

Not being sure what to say I impulsively reached over and hugged her consolingly; she was surprised and resisted at first, but then eventually clung to me, shaking with silent tears. I was astonished at myself; usually distant and formal; human warmth was not really in my makeup; I never did that sort of thing. Irish Princesses were supposed to be reserved after all. Nora's influence again?

On my way back to my place through drizzly Dublin streets I thought about the visit. I had made an astounding revelation: doing good for others benefitted oneself more than the recipient. The act of giving in itself was a reward. My young famine victim friend was changing me…more than I was aware. She didn't come that evening; perhaps she thought I needed time to think over my new found conclusion…

36

Sky

I was walking back from work at the brewery along the river to our new office in a positive frame of mind. I'd been let off work two hours early, as the auditors had decided to have an unannounced annual stock take, and all sales had ceased for a day, so I wasn't needed. Even a noisy load of heavily armed Tans I saw in a lorry rushing off somewhere couldn't dampen my spirits.

The warm glow of my love for Aisling was a constant gentle background to my life, in a few minutes I would be with her again. My job was valued, I was helping gain freedom for my country and it was one of those rare perfect spring days in Dublin, a cool breeze had brought crystal skies, sun danced on new green leaves and even the grey river Liffey seemed to sparkle cheerfully; yes, life was good! I suddenly spotted that girl who had reassured me on my very first day in the movement. She'd grown up and filled out a lot since I'd last seen her.

Her face looked strained but rather relieved when she recognized me. Before approaching, she casually looked behind her and then around us. Something in her manner brought a sudden stab of concern that pricked my sense of contentment. There was not a trace of humour in her eyes, only fear showed. Her words came out at a rush: "Weed, Mick says you're to go to ground immediately, wouldn't say why, but get to Vaughans hotel, the little back room. Don't go through any checkpoints; the G men are onto you; for God's sake be careful. You're *not* to go back to work again *or* home either. Good luck!"

Her dark brown worried eyes looked up at me for a second, and then she was gone up a side road, a brave determined figure, her long dark hair and green skirt ruffled by the wind, her shoes clicking on the cobbles.

What the hell could have happened? I was always so careful; I prided myself on always being non-descript and in the background… how could I have been picked up? I had a legitimate job; the only real crime I'd committed was the elimination (I couldn't bring myself to label it as *murder* at that stage) of a traitor;

still even there I had very carefully removed all possible links to me. So what the hell could have happened? If I ever got caught for that I'd swing… but I was even more fearful of what they would do to me to look for information before that. Dublin Castle's G counter intelligence branch tortured and mutilated suspects as the bodies of several of our comrades and innocents who'd been arrested testified. Usually, they didn't even reach the hanging stage; the standard British line was they "were shot while trying to escape…"

Ahead of me a hundred yards away I could see a typical Brit roadblock on a bridge. One soldier there seemed to be looking my way. I casually turned up an alleyway out of his sight, and then ran for it, removing my telltale identifying spectacles as I sprinted. Whether or not I was chased, I don't know. Thank God I was on the north bank of the river and didn't have to cross over.

On my way to and from work each day I had explored all possible routes and options, just in case, and it was now really paying off! I checked the grubby windows above me; no one seemed to be around. I dodged left, down another darker alleyway past smelly rubbish bins that led onto a small backstreet. I knew the right turn led to an eventual dead end; that might hold up a pursuer. I turned left and reached the road. I briefly put my glasses back on to check; it was all clear.

A whole hour later, after a few close calls, I arrived at the back entrance to Vaughan's in Parnell Square. Dodging around the barrels in the beer scented alleyway, I quietly let myself into a small, almost hidden door tucked in a dark alcove that was always left unlocked. It was an escape route in an emergency as the hotel was often used as a meeting place by Mick. The place was frequently raided and watched by our enemy, but it somehow remained a favourite of our leader despite that. I stopped and listened, just the normal early morning noises could be heard.

Unnoticed by anyone I sneaked up the stairs to the room we sometimes used for meetings. It was empty. I sat down in the gloom with the curtains closed, the light off and waited. My mind was in turmoil, trying to work out what might have happened. Had I been betrayed by some informer? As far as most people knew in the movement I was just a minor part time worker.

My thoughts were interrupted by heavy steps coming up the carpeted stairs; sounded like Mick, but also someone else. I braced myself. Joe O'Reilly, Mick's main right hand man poked his head around the door, he was carrying a pistol and started when he finally saw me sitting silently in the darkness, "He's here Mick." He then withdrew and stayed on watch outside when Michael Collins entered. The 'Big Man' was very quick as always when dealing with business. His face was pale and very grim, an expression I'd only seen before when a mate of his had been killed.

"Thought you'd get here in one piece, good. Now, complete and utter cock-up Weed and that's the truth. Still it's done. This is as bad as it gets believe me....

"Sources in the castle tell us that when they raided our office after you got that bastard who fingered me, they only found a few papers… got most of them out, thanks to you. But then we had a second raid on our replacement office. Remember that scrap of brown paper you got off him, with the secret G men number on? The damned Brits found that and on it was a faint finger print in blood -yours. The Gman who gave it to the guy y' killed, recognized the note. Somehow that was left behind; perhaps it fell on the floor or something. The bastards have got some matchin' prints from documents y'd handled at work…

"Apparently, one of the Gs has a brain, quite a big one too; dangerous sod! There was so much blood at the scene of the killing that he thought the killer would need to clean up somewhere, because you apparently hadn't done that at the scene of the crime itself. He reasoned it would have to be somewhere close, so he looked around the neighbourhood for possible places you could have done that. He found a small toilet in a nearby hotel that had small traces of blood around it and in the rubbish basket a scrap of toilet paper with another bloody print on it; a matching one. No one saw you where you bumped that bastard off, but where you cleaned up he found someone; the barman, who heard the toilet flush.

"He looked through the glass swing door to see who'd been out the back. He not only saw you, worse still, he *recognised* you as a worker he'd seen several times at the brewery loading bay, when he'd picked up his supplies. That, plus the description he gave, meant you were nailed. But he won't be spilling beans to the other side again after we deal with him!" Mick and the movement responded heavily to anyone giving information to or aiding the Brits in any way, a key aspect to his own survival.

"This Gman is on my list; we warned him off a week ago, but he won't leave the country. He's very good and we'll have to eliminate the swine; a violent bastard too, tortured Billy Moran last month so bad he died."

"They haven't got my name though, have they?"

"They have, and even worse than that; they've got a photo of you!"

My heart sank further. "How the hell could they have done that? I've made sure that there's almost none around Mick."

"Well I've just heard a few minutes ago as I left to come here, that they have a good photo of you. Where from I can't find out; which surprises me! In my experience when there is a catastrophe with many negatives like this there is always someone in the background! Have you upset anyone powerful Weed?"

I looked at him numbly and nodded no. I couldn't think of anyone…

"Don't go to your home, that's an order! Another thing, don't try and contact Aisling, you might end up involving her directly too."

He reached down into his sock and bought out a scrap of paper. "Here's two safe house addresses around here, stay at the first one if you can, the second is a reserve if there is some problem. Instructions as to the hiding places and how to get into them, also the escape route for each one. For Christ sakes memorise all this, then destroy the paper, properly. You might need this. Look after it, we're short as always." He handed me a Walther pistol and a clip of ammunition. "Now, I must rush; lots to do. I'll send a message as to our next move, Cork and then Kerry might be best. Be bloody careful Weed…"

He was gone and I was alone, shattered; just like that my life was transformed! The heavy cold pistol was little consolation. I checked and found it was fully loaded with six bullets, the clip held a further twelve rounds.

My *family*…if the authorities were on to me they must go to my home looking for anything they could find on me. Despite Mick's order I had to go and warn my uncle and aunt immediately before the authorities arrived. My cousins had left home two years back. Could I get there quickly without being spotted?

37

Song

It was odd; when I arrived at the office Mick was his usual busy self for half an hour or so, but then a messenger came with a note for him. This woman often handled intelligence direct from The Castle I knew. She waited while my boss read the contents; he unusually stopped all his activity, and went to the window deep in thought for a few seconds, before snapping out a string of orders in a low voice, that I couldn't quite hear.

When he came to me he seemed distant somehow and didn't directly look at me as was usual. What could have happened? I felt a sudden feeling of concern; it couldn't be Weed could it? I looked at my watch; no, at this time he'd still be working at the brewery…

Mick took an extra pistol and clip of ammunition from a cabinet, and left at a rush, leaving me with nothing to do. It was all very strange….

I busied myself by sorting out and filing some returns, but my mind was wracked with worry. No, something wasn't right!

Mick came back to the office after an hour or so, he took me into a side room away from the other typists and clerks. After shutting the door he sighed and spoke quietly, his eyes glinting. "Aisling, things are goin' to get sticky for a while; f' you too. Weed has bin outed somehow, an' the Brits are lookin' for him everywhere… *an'* they've got a photo of him too, *dammit!* They're calling him a murderer, so this is very serious. I've hidden him for a while, so he should be OK. But it would be wise for you to keep y'distance, somewhat. The buggers seem to know that there possibly is a tallish girlfriend with long auburn hair in the picture… so you're bein' looked for too. They don't have a name or photo of ye, just a very general description like. Maisie here'll cut y'r hair off, *now*! Then get home quickly an' stay off the streets for a few days, avoid checkpoints altogether if you can. Y' got t' do it colleen, fer Weed *an'* the movement."

I was completely stunned. Weed was always so careful about security, and was always unremarkable in appearance and manner, that was one of the things I loved about him; unlike my father, he *never* tried to stand out in any way!

I loathed the idea of cutting off my long hair which was part of my essential persona I felt, but Mick was clearly very worried….really I had no choice. I unwillingly agreed to do so.

As the locks fell to the floor, I closed my eyes and thought of my love. Our lives were going to be so completely different now that he was on the run. When would I see him again? I picked up a few locks of my hair and put them in my purse. If I saw Weed again, I'd give him a one.

Another of the girls in the office had a pair of plain glass women's spectacles which she gave me. With my roughly cut short hairstyle covered by a headscarf and wearing these, I looked almost unrecognizable.

As I left, Mick told me the transformation was perfect and that he'd contact me at my place in the next few hours and let me know what was happening. As the heavy door closed and was locked behind me, I apprehensively went onto the street. My head and the back of my neck were freezing! I tightened my scarf. I passed safely through a checkpoint on the bridge and got home without incident.

My room seemed empty; but at least a haven from a threatening outside world; it was the place Weed and I had first made love, after all!

I mechanically sorted out my college notes, I must finish my degree course, but worry about my now outlaw love kept welling up…

Later Nora commiserated with me: "Well, there's a turn fer t' books. Life's a pot o' stew, y'know Aisling; no matter wha y'put inter it, a big bad lumpy surprise will be alandin' on y' spoon…. at times!"

Something had been on my mind. I was almost afraid to ask her. "Do you visit anyone else in this way Nora? Perhaps in another time?" I wanted to say that I thought her my closest friend but was afraid to be so direct.

"No, of course not, you *silly* girl! I can't and don't wanta! Y' music was bewichin' an lovely: it sort of writhed, wriggled an' wandered it's way back thru t' ages t' me; y' tunes plays w' time, I'm athinkin'. When I hears 'em, I'ma sorta floatin' in sadness like, me 'motions is gently fondled, 't others I wants to dance!" Her lean face was dreamy, her eyes rapturous for a second, then sincerity showed.

"We's friends Aisling, even thos' y' a bit hoi…. er *grand* for a little cottage colleen like mesel'. We *are* rellies after all." She frowned. "I'se is not s' good at 'lationships…. But I'm atinkin', I'm yer great aunt! An nex' time I take y' back, look a' my baby brother Danny, 'e's ackesherly y' *grandfather!* I'd better look after 'im extra careful now!" She giggled mischeviously. "Got t' make sure y' get 'ere, don't I?"

I laughed with her; she had a very Irish, down to earth sense of humour. I told her she was my best friend ever, and she cried. I wanted to hug her, but… the years, history and reality intervened.

Then she was gone and I was abruptly back in my world of war and emptiness…. How could I have laughed at such a time?

38

Sky

For speed I splashed out and took a tram home, my cap pulled down, I alighted with a crowd of passengers and got past a policeman without being noticed and turned into our little street. I was greeted by a great commotion. Passers-bye had stopped at the end of the lane and were watching the scene curiously. I stood hidden among them. What could I do? I was the direct cause of all this distress!

In my lane people were leaning out of their windows from the multi-storey buildings jeering and abusing a dozen well armed Tans and Auxies who were alighting from a lorry. Even the cheeky local urchins who'd been playing on the streets joined in with relish. The scornful, cursing voices echoed off the sooty brick walls along with the sound of the stomping boots of troops.

One Tan, livid with rage, fired a pistol at one of the upstairs windows, missing the onlooker but shattering the glass above her. For a second the jeering and insults ceased, the kids screamed and ran indoors to their homes. But then the racket all restarted with renewed vigour and bitterness.

I was too late! Our door was kicked in and troops poured through into my home. Two Tans armed with rifles stayed with the lorry. They didn't look down the street at us spectators; rather they were apprehensively eyeing the windows above them, from where small missiles rained down on them occasionally.

The windows of my home were smashed out with rifle butts; a cascade of glass tinkled into the street, followed by our meagre furniture breaking on impact, crockery, clothing, bedding, the old mantelpiece clock and lastly photos. Expensive family photos were often destroyed as a punishment, history and memories obliterated. This apparently was a standard routine imposed on suspected Fenians. They would have looked for any photos of me first, but with my usual innate caution I had secretly removed all these and stored them elsewhere, once I had started working for the movement. Uncle Bryan's simple pictures of the past heroes of Ireland's fight for freedom on the wall of the parlour would be a dead giveaway and fire the troops up further.

We were only poor folk, all the broken stuff meant a lot to us and would take us years to replace, if ever. But I was more concerned with my Uncle and Aunt. My sick old Uncle Bryan was roughly manhandled out of the door by two big Tans, blood streaming down his face. Shamus the loyal little old dog was bravely trying to protect his beloved master by attacking his tormenters. A big Auxie took a running kick and a tiny bundle of white and brown yelping fur somersaulted and arced through the air to crash into the tenement wall and fall down limp and silent in the gutter; a bloodied heap. Uncle Bryan erupted in rage at this treatment of his old friend, but was quickly subdued and also thrown on the ground. The big officer kicked the frail curled up figure brutally.

Only fifty feet or so away, I couldn't contain myself and although it was suicidal, I drew the pistol out, slid the safety catch off and aimed carefully and fired at the bully's big head, it exploded in cloud of blood, his body crashed into his fellow raiders as it fell. They all turned in horrified surprise. The crowd I was standing amongst screamed and scattered for cover leaving me standing alone. Crouching down in the middle of the road to make myself a smaller target, I shot two other soldiers in the body, before they could lower their rifles and take a pot-shot at me. I let off a third then a fourth, ducking, as with an almighty crash another one fired a Lee Enfield at me; the bullet whipped past, and the walls echoed with the big explosion, I fired again and I think I got that Tan in the right shoulder.

Lying on the ground Uncle Bryan recognised me and through the pain gave me a weak thumbs up, then deliberately pointed at his own head. His meaning was clear, he knew what awaited him in captivity from all the Fenian and IRB magazines we'd read. I'd spoken to some who had been lucky enough to survive although crippled by the treatment the Brits had doled out to them.

In a fraction of a second, thoughts flashed through my mind. It was strange that just a week ago, when my aunt had been out of the house, Uncle Bryan had told me in the quiet parlour how much he admired me and that I might have a chance to do something and die for Ireland; had this been a premonition? He would see his death as a patriotic act. He was frail and had consumption…he wouldn't live much longer anyway, as he'd told me at that time, while coughing blood into his handkerchief. Through tears, I fired my last bullet, closing my eyes at the last instant. Another round just missed me, as I took to my heels and sprinted for my life round the corner. In my mind was the ticking clock on a mantelpiece in the little parlour and those heated arguments, my uncle's gratey voice... My old mentor was dead and I was the person who had killed him! Hatred boiled anew in my soul for these senseless invaders and occupiers of my land, who'd forced me to do it.

After sprinting a block I turned a corner, and made myself saunter along normally, taking off my coat which I rolled up, lining outwards and removed my glasses to disguise myself a bit. I boarded a tram that had just stopped. With a clang of its bell it started back past the end of our cul-de-sac. Looking down, I could see that the remaining troops were searching for me, roughly questioning people on the street. Our house was already on fire, which put the whole neighbourhood in jeopardy.

Flames and smoke were beginning to pour from the door and windows. The bastards must have used petrol to aid combustion; as they often did. The remaining soldiers seemed to be searching the other houses. Retaliation for the death and wounding of their comrades would be swift and vicious for all, innocent or guilty. My uncle was almost certainly dead. I was less worried about my aunt Biddy, in those far off times women were treated more gently, which was why Mick often used them as messengers. However she would be imprisoned. I must let the 'Big Man' know, to see what he could do for her. She knew absolutely nothing of my extra- curricular activities.... And what had happened to blind Amy? The neighbours would remember her, but this whole business would be absolutely terrifying to her, unable to see what was happening; just a sudden, brutal cacophony of noise. A thought came to me; my Aisling would check and look after her...yes, she certainly would once she heard of the street raid.

The tram ambled on its way, stopping frequently. I hunched up and held my bundled coat tightly hoping the other passengers would not smell the cordite on my clothes; the scent was quite pungent and obvious to me.

By a roundabout route I carefully made my way to the safe house. There was a large woman sitting in her lounge knitting, who had hated pictures of the British King and Lloyd George the English prime minister displayed on the wall prominently. Probably a good idea, if we were raided! For a fraction of a second I wondered if I had the wrong address, but no, Mick would never make a mistake about something like this. She pointedly ignored me as I quietly climbed up the stairs to the hidden cubbyhole he had told me about, which we had constructed in the loft. I lay down on the bed in the darkness after reloading the pistol first; I had to be ready for anything...

I felt numb. The calm blue sky of my life had somehow instantly been replaced with a purple black hurricane of turmoil. I'd gone from being an unremarkable citizen with a regular job to a complete outcast, murderer and terrorist. Having possibly killed three Tans and Auxies and my own beloved uncle in broad daylight, in all probability I would now be the most wanted man in Dublin. I'd brought death and strife to my family and my neighbourhood. I was the direct cause of major loss to my chronically impoverished neighbours… how they must loath me! They'd of course recognized me; after all I'd lived there almost all my life. *And* this was all because I had disobeyed a specific order from Mick; I would have to face *him* now. And Aisling, could I somehow have put her at risk? How could I contact her now that I was on the run, being hunted high and low? Exhausted, I eventually drifted off into a restless sky of slumber.

39

Song

 I heard about the street battle that evening. Dublin was humming with news of the skirmish. This had never taken place in a housing area of the city before. Citizens had read of the damage in towns like Balbriggan, Cork and other places, photos of the destruction were bad enough, but seeing it at first hand was another matter. Burnt, destroyed homes, buildings and the affected, now homeless people, were there for everyone to see. Many of the city's inhabitants did go to have a look at the site.

The Brits were incensed, as they blundered around searching for the "terrorist" Aidan Duffey. They then stupidly tried to blame the Sinn Feiners for all the damage, but there too many witnesses who had seen their troops in action. Also we had photos that appeared in the overseas press disproving their claim. So that backfired completely. Our side made the apparently quiet, normal Weed into a towering, heroically Irish figure.

Mick eventually told me that the now widowed Aunt Biddy had been imprisoned, and he was making sure she was looked after. We had sympathisers and contacts throughout the prison system. She knew nothing after all, but our enemy thought it a good policy to arrest family members of suspects. Blind Amy was safe staying with some friends as her house had been quite badly damaged by the fire. The movement was already trying to finance a rebuild of the neighbourhood. Mick was involved on that side.

My heart was in a shambolic shape. Weed could easily have been killed…how could I possibly survive without him? It was something I hadn't really considered before.

The phone rang downstairs. I was home alone and answered it. Mick's voice spoke a few innocuous sentences, which I took to mean he would meet me at eleven tomorrow morning; he had something he wanted to show me. The call cheered me up; at least it was some contact from a major link to my love. As always, I wondered what he was up to…..

Nora joined me in my anxious, sleepless darkness that evening.
"Nuffin' I can b' asayin' t' ye, y' poor creature…..at least ye're lucky enough t' ave a true love t' lose…not that y' 'ave lost 'im of course!" She sounded wistful for a few seconds. Then, before I could answer her, she said decisively.
"Acheerin' up we're aneedin'….come on. I'll show yuz more o' m' good times…"

I found Nora's sympathy and friendship gave me strength, but I wanted to ponder and wallow in my worry for Weed and our current situation…. Perhaps that was *why* she was doing this…to stop me dwelling on the situation we'd landed in. But my friend from the past really had the wind in her sails, so I couldn't stop her showing me her world…….

It was market day, a change from the heavy toil in the fields, so excitement was in the air. The cottage was warm, the air fuggy; so many bodies in a cramped space. The fire had gone out, and her mother arose and worked at getting it alight again…she blew on some embers, a little flame, doubtfully flared at first, then grew. The youngsters were woken up.
    It was barely daylight when Nora's father sent her outside before breakfast. "T' tools Nora….make sure no one's apeepin' now!" Young Nora took a small piece of brown canvas. put a black shawl on her head and went outside into the chilly morning air. She went to the privy and relieved herself. "Not s' col' t'day Aisling…. Some days…..brrrr!" Nine year old Nora shivered and drew her shawl around her.
    The sky was just beginning to lighten in the east as she looked around, checking over the walls bordering the property on all sides, and only then gathered up the precious tools left leaning inside the door, a spade, shovel and hoe, all with metal blades and some small gardening tools. She wrapped these in canvas carefully and lowered them into a hollow in the ground at the back of the manure compost heap and covered them with rotting vegetation. The smell was powerful! As she washed her hands at the pump and shook them dry, her older voice came to me.
    "Them's safe, I'm abettin'…..svaluable fings, mus' look after em!
    T' family's dependin' on me!" She said to me proudly. She splashed cold water on her face and brushed back her hair with her hand.

We re-entered the dwelling again. Breakfast was a noisy affair, Nora helped feed the little ones who had grown since my last visit; Baby Danny was now a two year old toddler. Outside, her dad gathered the sacks of potatoes and vegetables and baskets they had filled the evening before, and put them by the front door. There were some small ones, obviously for the children to carry; everyone had to help. Mother washed and dressed the little ones and tidied their hair. Market day was obviously a big deal.

"S' not too far; jus' four miles or so….bags get heavy tho'. I'm ahopin' we get t' g'd prices t'day! We never knows; theys up n' down all t' time….

"Back in these days, t' grand folks in t' Big House wuz good, tough but fair, me Pa would call 'em. We'd see 'em at times; their two girls w'd even gives us a wave from theirs carriage sometimes! Not t' older boy tho' ; ee's a bit high an' mighty like." Nora's face then looked grim. "Hmmph! We still had t' make t *rent* tho'! T' land agent Mista Morrison was acollectin' that. We didn' like *him* at all!"

The door of the cottage was barred, and the family set out, mother carrying baby Danny on her hip, and a large heavy basket of vegetables on her back. Father Thomas, staggered along under the load of two massive sacks. He was the only one wearing footwear; everyone else was barefoot.

Nora's voice came in my ear, "T' roads is hard on our feet… Dad's got t'boots cos' o' t spade an' shovel, 's hard to dig without 'em."

Across the road on the other side was another small holding. It looked less tidy than the Kinnanes, although the cottage was bigger. "T' Sullivans lives there; we's neighbours. We always leaves early t'gets t' a good spot at t' mark't! Theys is always a bit late….." She sniffed.

We walked on, joining other families. In the end quite a stream of country folk were making their way towards the small town at this early hour. There was lots of good humoured banter between the families. The women and girls all wore shawls over their heads, the men and boys caps…., everyone carried sacks, packs, baskets or boxes. We were passed by a few horses and traps of the well to do and some actual landowners. As they grew abreast, those on foot, usually tenant farmers, would stand back off the road until the animals and conveyances had passed. These were looked at enviously by all. There seemed to be a strong divide between the classes.

The scene faded, and Nora appeared bubbling with enthusiasm.

" 'S 'citin' isn't it? Nex' time y'll see much more……" She disappeared, leaving me thinking.

But then I was jerked back to my present harsh world as I worried anew about my Weed…

40

Sky

For three days I stayed holed up in the hidden loft compartment. Mick had told me gleefully some weeks before that his sources had reported that the Brits had been regularly astounded by the ingenuity of our carpenters at constructing hiding places. Often these spaces had escaped detection during raids and were only found on subsequent inspections. This place was really well equipped; it had a cleverly disguised hidden entrance with a small electric lightbulb mounted on the steeply sloping ceiling. Outside across a hallway, there was a toilet and a tiny kitchenette that could be used. In the cupboard was some bread and items of food that seemed to be magically replenished as I ate it. That lady downstairs must have been silently replacing it while I slept.

Each night I lay alone in the darkness, listening to the muffled street noises below, ears alert for any sound of danger or pursuit.

My thoughts kept returning to Aisling; my heart ached for her, I was very tempted to leave my haven and go to her, but I'd put her at risk since I was now a wanted man and I'd disobeyed Mick once…. I gritted my teeth and stayed. My uncle's death also played constantly on my mind…, my aunt's and Amy's predicament also nagged away at me.

Tucked under the eaves of the house was a small slot in the outer wall plugged with a piece of wood that enabled me to look out unseen at the street below, and a tiny narrow band of sky.

The scene below was reassuringly normal although there were many more patrols of well-armed soldiers and police on the streets. Once a group of Auxies on a lorry stopped for a minute nearby, but then drove off, much to my relief.

On the third day, I saw Mick laugh and joke his way through a checkpoint at the end of the street. He was dressed smartly as was usual and walking arm in arm with a tall bespectacled shorthaired woman. He made his way towards my building and was passing it when he went out of my vision. I hoped he was coming to see me…to end my incarceration.

A few minutes later I heard the sound of his bounding steps up the stairs. Despite his lack of sleep, great workload and ongoing tensions he was always a cauldron of energy. Mick tapped the coded knock on the wall and I opened the secret door. He entered with a rush; as usual, there was no small talk.

"Good, you're here, thought you'd get away. *Another* great mess Weed!" His eyes were steely, but not as much as I would have expected. Surprisingly; there may even have been a hint of grim satisfaction in his manner.

"Sorry to tell you, yer uncle's dead, executed, shot through the forehead while he was lying on the road, the bastards! Great old guy, who had a big influence on you, I'd be thinking. The eyewitnesses don't quite agree, but considering what was going on I suppose that's to be expected."

Mick didn't know that I myself had killed my uncle and I wasn't going to tell anyone. I could never explain it anyway; such a terrible thing to have to do; it was a leaden weight on my heart.

"Three neighbours were also killed; seven homes burnt, destroyed belongings littered the street. Made for great pictures, we got it worldwide within hours! A major massacre in the capital is how everyone is portraying it. Stunned residents surveying the extensive damage, faces wracked with helplessness and shock; and all within Dublin itself too! A perfect example of British brutality, clearly there for the whole world to see, Weed. They're hopping mad, especially since they fell for an "anode" job, yet again. We had a "photographer" get caught, so they relaxed a bit and we managed to get the real one on the scene who was quite brilliant… we were so fast that we even got one snap of the bodies in the street before they could remove them, plus a few photos of a poor waif crying over her pathetic broken doll amongst the blackened ruins. There was also a bereft blind girl crying over a smashed and burnt harp.…"

That of course must be Amy… the poor kid!

I knew the authorities had banned the use of cameras in public unless a permit had been obtained for their use. They didn't want their activities to be recorded, thank you! Cameras were large bulky boxes in those days and rather hard to disguise. They were also very clumsy to use. I knew we had built some into small delivery carts to record the damage done by the Tans and RIC Auxies. Sometimes we even managed to capture the blurred photos of troops actually in action.

Mick continued in a smug satisfied tone: "The wind blew the flames into the next street and guess what? It set fire to that small Catholic Church: St. Cheswyns! So we got 'em for religious persecution too! We've hammered that like hell and it's gone down a treat; even the Pope has complained to the Brits about it, and the faithful around the world are all up in arms already, 'specially the Yanks. Of course the Brits are usually overtly very careful about the religious question. All round a wonderful PR coup for our side, from start to finish!

"And then there is you, according to eyewitnesses, you are a quiet law- abiding, hardworking citizen, who, confronted with your impoverished home being brutally set upon and your family physically assaulted, stood his ground and fought odds of twelve to one etc. etc. Only problem there is the pistol….. -how you came to have it. We're saying you desperately got it off a Tan on the way to the scene. Of course they're saying you are a terrorist all along, with another murder to your name, but it doesn't quite ring true to the average person; because of your mania for secrecy, no one knows the truth.

"You killed a couple of Tans and injured three, two of whom are very seriously wounded and according to my hospital sources, are unlikely to survive.

"Anyway, much as I know you'll hate it, you've become a symbol for Ireland, a brave lone Irishman fighting for his family and his country. Wonderful stuff! You're damned near as famous as me now, and wanted desperately by the swine, who are flailing around all over the place at the moment; they're tearing the town to pieces looking for you! That work photo is in all of their papers, *an'* they've put a two thousand pound reward on you; dead or alive. As a symbol for us, you're much too important to be caught now. Y'know too much about the movement as well… but I rather think you'd not spill the beans.

"We thought of getting you out of the country, but that has an element of the cut and run about it: not a good look. Also, I know you wouldn't want to go. Sorry, but you're going to have to wait here another three days or so. Then we might be able to sneak you out by a boat on one of the canals. The roads in and out of the city are impossible; roadblocks are absolutely everywhere, random searches of houses going on too, all very heavy, which sends more of the locals our way. We'll eventually get you south and west till things cool down, yes, Cork or Kerry it'll have to be, I'm athinkin'…

"By the way, the lady here in this house is a protestant, so this place should be safe. She's on our side. It's bloody hot out there Weed, believe me; impossible for you to move till things calm down! Right, here's some more ammo, just in case. If you get caught, y' may have to use the gun -on y'self. Oh yeah, your Aunt is in prison for a few days, but our folk there are really lookin' after her, an' your blind neighbour Amy and her mum, we got a place for them nearby, till their home is rebuilt. So don't worry 'bout them!" He snapped a glance at his silver pocket watch. "Hell, must go. Oh, and I have a little surprise for ye."

He let himself out the secret door and was gone. There were some quiet steps on the stairs and that short haired lady entered. It was Aisling!! She'd cut her wonderful hair off and when wearing plain lensed glasses, looked quite different. I gaped at her for a second before I desperately held her in my arms. "Why, Aisling?" I eventually managed to ask her.

Her green eyes, surveyed me searchingly. "They showed your photo to some of their troops and one soldier recognised you as the short guy with the tall girlfriend with long red hair. Remember when we crossed the bridge that night and that Tan called you 'Big Man'? Thank God Mick heard that they were looking for me, before I could be arrested. They have no photo or name, but my hair stands out too much, so I immediately had it cut it off, damn it! My head and neck are freezing cold without it! One of the secretaries in the office has done some hairdressing, and we did it in a rush. I'll get it styled in a short French fashion when I can. Still, it's for Ireland after all, people have done much worse! The owlish glasses complete the change don't they? They're hounding all tall women with long red or auburn hair around the city. There's quite a lot of them!" She smiled with her eyes then held me with her usual intensity. "My favourite terrorist and murderer," she whispered lovingly.

"Ah y'd still be the most gorgeous colleen in the country to me, even *bald* Love," I breathed in her ear… "Well, maybe not *completely* bald." She thumped me as we laughed quietly.

Again our bodies melted in a warm pool of frantic desire, cocooned in that dark cubbyhole under the eaves.… Afterwards, in tired closeness we silently listened to the subdued sounds of the curfew bound night-time city. She would have to stay; the curfew had been extended, and was being emphatically enforced.

The future however weighed upon us. I would have to go and our parting would leave each of us desolate and alone. That beautiful French saying I'd read somewhere came to my apprehensive mind: "Partir est mourir un peu…" which translated meant "to part is to die a little." In our case it would be, to die a *lot !*

Communication was going to be very difficult; brief letters at best as I moved from place to place, trying to avoid capture. My whereabouts would frequently change, so how would her letters get to me? My letters should get to her more easily as she would be staying in Dublin, as Aisling was determined to carry on working with Mick. We would have to arrange a fixed address using a safe name, a code of apparently innocuous sentences that carried meaning only for us.

The war we were waging seemed to envelope us in a universe of uncertainty… but for how much longer would or could this go on? Were we winning or just holding our own? The more brutal the British became the more recruits we gained… we were definitely winning on the propaganda front but we were always desperately short of weapons and ammunition, and militarily we were at times lacking in cohesion. Different groups unwittingly overlapped operations at times. Mick had told me the movement was doing OK, all things considered, although it was still a close run thing… and he should have known, having so many fingers in so many pies.

A restless tossing sleep came eventually to us.…

Morning found us quiet and tense, we delayed our parting as long as we could, but as the tall slim figure disappeared down the stairs, my spirits sank into a sea of desolation and emptiness. I cursed my predicament, but it was too late to go back, I must evade capture and survive at *all* costs.

Despite being ordered by Mick not to, Aisling came to me the two following nights: she lied outright to her parents and the people she was boarding with as to where she was.

Our togetherness was pressured and desperate, but total. On the second night she told me tomorrow was the day that I would be leaving Dublin. From her purse she took out a long scented lock of auburn hair, and silently gave it to me. I kissed it…

Uncle Bryan's funeral was to be held in two days time. I cried as I thought of the man who had been such a large part of my life, and even more upsetting, the secret fact that *I* had killed him!

Our eyes were tearful as we had a final embrace and she was gone; quiet steps fading down the stairs, leaving a raw pain-soaked void…

… 41

Song

My trip to work that morning after leaving Weed was a nightmare; the city folk rushed about their business grimly. The place was full of troops aggressively stopping and frisking people quite randomly, trucks lumbered past loaded with search parties on their way to suspected Republican hideouts.

I wore a blue scarf over my short hair and with the spectacles no one gave me a second glance. My altered appearance seemed to work a treat. But really it was Weed they were after. Despite my nerves, I arrived safely. My Love was the cause of all this city wide fuss…. and knowing where he was, gave me a smug sense of satisfaction. I hoped he could leave Dublin safely; but that barely seemed possible with so many searching high and low for him. However I felt he would make it; he was smart, resourceful and cunning…and anyway, we were just meant to be! But how long would it be before I'd see him again?

Here at my workplace, I buried myself in work. But the office was lacking in music for me; Weed had somehow taken it away with him…

It was probably the shock and stress caused by what had happened in the last few days, but after a couple of hour's hard effort, I felt quite nauseous and unsettled. I told a preoccupied Mick I was unwell and that I'd go home. Unusually, he agreed immediately, and that was that. He even told me to take at least a week off! Weed's situation had affected us all to a surprising degree. Perhaps it was just the fact that I had been linked to Weed, meant that I was putting everyone at risk. Yes, that might be it.

I went to one of our hairdressers who could keep quiet, and styled my short hair into an American fashion. I didn't want to, but while at it, I had it dyed a very dark brown. I was told the colour would only last a few months and then it would revert back to my usual auburn. A complete stranger looked back at me from the mirror; I couldn't believe it was me, especially when I put the spectacles on! I decided to buy some more stylish clothes, different to my usual garb, which would add to the transformation. I stopped in the park on the way back, but didn't sit in our usual seat, just in case.... I would have to have an explanation for my dramatically changed appearance for my parents who would be shocked; as would the people I stayed with here. Mmm, what would sound plausible?

I wanted to go to poor Amy but wasn't sure where she was living now. But I shouldn't draw attention to her. Anyone linked to Weed would under observation.

Aside from some close calls, I had taken little risk while working for the movement, unlike my love who often seemed to be in the thick of things. I decided I would risk going to Uncle Bryan's funeral; representing Weed in affect. Funerals of sympathizers to the cause were always watched by the authorities; hoping to pick up any known Fenians.

It turned out to be a big sombre affair with hundreds of mourners at the service. Because this death was thought to be caused by the British, attendance by the public was seen as a way of objecting to their presence in our country.

No-one recognized me at all, not even some of the children who had harassed me on my first visit to the lane. There were some Gmen present blatantly taking notes and observing proceedings; the *swine!*

I looked around and found Amy and her mother sitting to one side, Aunt Biddy looked tearful, old and distraught. Next to the widow on either side of her, were Weed's cousins Connell and Mary I presumed. They were consoling her quietly. The cheap coffin was bedecked with flowers... candles flickered fitfully. Unusually, there was a small lap harp not far from the casket. This was obviously going to be quite a big service.

The church was small and packed, and then I saw *him*. Michael Collins was in the congregation himself! I'd heard he often visited our people in gaol and in hospitals alone, blatantly ignoring the risk. The enemy would never conceive he would take such a gamble, so he continually got away with it!

Uncle Bryan's death symbolized our struggle against the oppressor; especially with the way we had used it in a major propaganda effort. Mick was casually looking around and at first ignored me but then he started when he saw through my disguise on a second look. My dark dyed hair, framing my face under my black headscarf and those severe glasses fooled everyone else.

At the end of the service Amy was guided to a seat near the harp and she played and sang Bryan's favourite song "Carrickfergus." Biddy and the whole congregation joined in, myself included. It was a touching moment, voices blending magically. Amy's confidence and skill were definitely growing rapidly…

Mick slipped away after having a quick word with Amy. I waited to get a chance to speak to Aunt Biddy who had just been released from prison yesterday.

She didn't recognize me until I spoke to her. "Aisling, you've made it here, I'm so touched, m' Bryan did like you so much… as I do." She hugged me, silent tears running down her face. M' husband was very ill, the TB was agettin' him anyway; but dyin' this way would have pleased 'im, surprisingly enough! But I'll miss t' silly bugger fo t'rest o' m'days." She dropped her voice to a whisper. "And Aidan?" she asked.

"He's in a safe hiding place Aunt Biddy; he was so upset to hear of his uncle's passing, and was especially worried about you and how you'll get on now financially. And he's sorry he brought all this upon you. He was beside himself about you being in prison, but was told the Movement would look after you. He'll contact you sometime when he is able."

"Not 'is fault, Aisling. T' Lord'll always have his way. Prison fr a few days was no problem, I knew nothing anyways…an' even *they* worked that out in t' end; but I'm glad t' be out, mind ye. Some of t' women there have been there for months!" she shivered at the very thought. "I might b'come a prison visitor to help them. Bryan would approve of the idea. I must go…thanks again." Immediately, Aunt Biddy was surrounded by other mourners.

I went over to Amy who was sitting alone playing her harp sadly. She was overjoyed when I spoke to her. "Please keep your voice down Amy for everyone's sake! They don't really know who I am, but they're looking for me…. I've had to change my appearance!" I stayed still as the soft light fingers again touched my face, and then they discovered my hair was short, and felt the glasses. She nodded her head.

"Very different, I'm athinkin'….same good person though!"

She then told me everything that had happened on the day of the attack, how frightening it had been on her own, trying to make sense of the cacophony of shrieks, screams, gunfire and breaking glass. She'd lain on the floor, facedown clutching her harp, being sprinkled with glass from her windows, desperately praying. Then the burning had started…. The pungent smoke… She'd been saved by a neighbour who'd remembered her and got her out at the very last minute; unlocking the front door had taken an age! But she'd left the harp behind… "I cried most fo' *that* Aisling… twas like burnin' m' future!" she added poetically.

But after that the Movement had helped all the survivors. "That nice man who seems s' powerful, got me a new harp; almost as good as y'r one Aisling!" she added loyally. "He was 'ere just a minute ago…"

Yes, hardheaded Mick had a soft side…..

"I'm sorry me Ma couldn't come today; the factory wouldn't give her time off."

"I'm sorry too. Have you been back to the tearooms Amy? We must get you performing again. Old Bryan was listening to you today playing his favourite tune so beautifully, I'm sure! He was such a nice man. Aidan is so upset he can't be here….he loved his uncle and sends all his love to you all."

"He will be OK Aisling? Im'a worried for him so much! They're asayin' he's the most wanted man in Dublin, maybe even t' whole o' Ireland!"

"I'm worried too Amy, but he is very cunning and clever. But I feel so empty without him."

She reached out and held my hand consolingly, her face concentrating on things no one could see. Her voice was faint when she spoke again.

"Don' fret….a long life, in a big sky, Aidan'll be ahavin' I'm sure…" Her face showed a hint of a smile, then she came back to me. "You must be careful too…." We were interrupted by the priest who took the girl to introduce her to some mourners who had loved her playing.

I went home thoughtfully. Aidan would have a long life according to my friend. Should I have asked her about mine? Did I really want to know? And anyway, was she truly able to see into the future? I was certain that if I asked her, that "Heart not head" comment would no doubt come my way, yet again.

Regardless, I must get Amy performing again… I would contact the teashop.

Nora was solemn that evening and had messages for me. "Uncle Bryan is amissin' Biddy *so much*, an' all o' ye. He's 'specially happy 'is cough is gone, and he's wiv a certain Shamus agin'. Tell Biddy, nex' time you're aseein' her."

She looked me up and down with a frown of disapproval. "But, my, you'll b' alookin' different! A bit *too* modren, I'm atinkin' !

"So, poor Aisling, ye shy o' y' love now, alone ye'll b' afeelin', I'ma sure t' music'll be afadin' f'r ye a tad. But y' still got y' ol' young friend here wiv ye… I'm still acarin' f'r ye. If I w's able, I'd b' ahuggin' ye, tight as a *tatie buyer's purse, at t'market!*"

The thin face with the big sad eyes smiled as it dimmed and a somehow, less lonely darkness returned.

Yes, she was an important friend to me. Her comments were warming, but I wasn't sure *she* wasn't the one needing a hug! I couldn't work out what kept us apart.

Was it time, wealth or circumstance…or seventy years of history? I was unable to decide…

42

Sky

That morning as I peered through the slot at the outside world I was startled by the sudden coded knock. It had been so quiet; I hadn't heard anyone come up the stairs. I jumped with surprise. My pistol was at the ready I slowly opened the secret door.

That young woman who had first warned me that I was being looked for was waiting outside, holding a bundle of clothes. She eyed the pistol warily then whispered, "Change into these, then come with me Weed, a boat is waiting for you…"

Although tense and worried, she was brave and I admired her. Mick was keeping the people who knew me to a minimum by using someone who had already had dealings with me; a typical example of his genius at intelligence work.

The clothes were those a coal delivery man would use, complete with a grubby cap. They stank horribly. After wrinkling her little nose rather charmingly the girl rubbed some coal on my face. She then surveyed me with satisfaction. "You'll be looking and smelling the part now then Weed! Take your glasses off. Follow me at a distance, let's hope there are no new roadblocks since I came; we should be able to miss them."

Somehow, I was almost sad to leave my safe little cubbyhole where Aisling and I had made love for the last time, probably for months, if not years. I followed the young woman quietly down the stairs. Once outside, I stayed back for a few seconds before following the determined figure at a distance. That lady was still in the parlour when we left, still pointedly ignoring our exit….

With my glasses off it was not easy to follow my slight guide as we zigzagged through roads and alleyways but after a tense half hour we- arrived at the bank of the Royal Canal, a narrow waterway which wended its way through the city to the west. The girl came back to me, "The blue empty coal barge, they are expecting you and will leave in a minute … good luck Weed!"

Emotionally I thanked her; she had risked everything for me. She just looked embarrassed. "What's your name?" I asked wanting to repay her in some way, perhaps later when peace came.

"Just Miss Ireland will do." A quick look around to see we weren't being observed, and with a twinkly look in her eyes, she shyly and impulsively pecked me on the cheek, giggled… and was gone. I was very surprised, such things didn't happen to me, ever!

On the blue boat was an old wrinkled couple. He was dressed in clothes much like the ones I was wearing and was gap toothed, she in a long black dress. There was a stale smell about them that made me flinch, even stronger than the clothes I was wearing. But they welcomed me with respect, "Ye'll be the one aren't ya Lad? Showed the cruel foreign bastards a bit of the ol' Irish eh? Good on ya!

"Now listen close, we'll be goin' under a few bridges, an' there's checkpoints on some of 'em; things might get a little hairy." He turned and went aft, to start the oily motor with a frantic whirl of the crank. It was soon quietly chugging, puffing blue smoke into the frosty morning air.

His wife's long white hair had been dusted with smudges of coal dust. It shook a bit as she spoke to me, but her alert eyes were a startling light blue. She reached over and surprised me by removing my hat. She messed up by hair adding a bit of coal dust. "Thanks to Mick, we have seen a copy of the photo they're using ta find ya; you were all neat an' proper like in it, so now ya do look different. Take the lead from us if we get inspected; you're our son…. right? Me husband will be a drunken ole fool, who'll give ya a hard time…I won't be much different. Just play along, OK? Act like a hard done by son, sick of his parents. Cough like hell too, make out ye're sick. Now here's a broom, best to be busy when they're acheckin' us. Normally they'll only be glancin' at us as we pass underneath an' leave us alone. Hide your pistol up under this little side deck, ammo too. Make sure ya can get to it quick like…."

I slid the safety catch off, mentally reminding myself to be careful when I retrieved the weapon, and then I did as I was told.

She gave me a shrewd look and smiled slyly. "The smell works a treat Weed, puts 'em off every time…sensitive little Brit nostrils… as does lots of coal dust… they don't want ta get their fancy uniforms all mucked up, now do they? Silly sods! Ya don't notice the pong after a while."

Her husband let go the mooring lines and pushed the boat off the wharf and went back and put it in gear. The craft began to glide smoothly along through the calm dark grey water, leaving little ripples behind us. It was a cool fine day with small puffy clouds in a sky that seemed large and free to me, after my confinement in the secret loft room; a good omen?

I was beginning to get the impression that these two were a regular major part of the Irish resistance supply chain, in and out of the city. They certainly seemed to know exactly what they were doing.

But I was disappointed with the vessel; it was just a dirty coal-blackened completely open boat with nowhere to hide. Its tiny chugging engine was mounted in a small box towards the back. A grimy tarpaulin was rolled up on one side. The whole boat was essentially just a hold for carrying coal. People on the other moored boats glanced at us as we made our way past. As I began sweeping the coal dust up, I fervently hoped that there were no informers around. But here Mick's intelligence outfit had been so successful at tracking them down and eliminating them, not to mention widely publicizing the fact, the Brits were now being starved of their traditional source. I should be OK on that score…

The city slid past us slowly. I grew tense as we approached the first bridge, Dorset St. In the corner of my eye as I swept industriously, I could see Khaki clad figures looking down at us. Nothing happened as we puttered along. Coming up on our left I could see the threatening dark walls of Mountjoy Prison, a large complex of multi-storeyed buildings where many of our people were imprisoned; some on hunger strikes. Some had been executed; young Kevin Barry was under a death sentence there today. That fate awaited me if I was caught. I shivered, as the distant guards on the walls idly watched us crawl past.

On the right hand or north side of the canal was a railway line, beyond which there was a busy road carrying quite a bit of traffic. From time to time freight trains would noisily pass us, their puffs of steam were being blown away by the breeze.

We approached the next big bridge at Phibsborough Rd. It was strange how different everything looked from this new perspective. I knew there was always a checkpoint located here. This time we were stopped. My heart beat wildly as we were boarded by Two Tans. I casually swept my way towards where the pistol was hidden, as I wanted to be able to grab it, if the balloon went up.

When I was a young we had a handicapped kid living in our lane, who had the somehow annoying habit of keeping his mouth open, all the time. I did the same here, with a dull look on my face changing my appearance even further, I hoped. I looked the Tan officer right in the face. He glanced away in distaste, and checked under the tarpaulin, finding nothing.

"Papers!" he barked wrinkling his nose at the odour on board. His offsider covered us with his rifle. I just carried on sweeping, the coal dust disturbed by my broom hanging in the air and annoying them both. The old woman looked irritated, but went to the back of the boat mumbling to herself and brought out an old black handbag. She opened it, rummaged around inside and eventually withdrew three grubby bits of paper. Her husband looked quite unconcerned, as he held the vessel against the landing. "Keep sweeping you little shite, or I'll boot ya bloody backside from here to Belfast!" he yelled at me as if this was an everyday occurrence.

I looked back at my "Father," my face contorted with loathing. The soldier grinned at me; all English knew the Irish fought like dogs. My dirty misshapen face would look very different from that photo.

"Leave the poor lad alone, ya silly ole bastard!" yelled his wife as she roughly gave the papers to the soldier.

I began to cough deeply, just as my uncle had done for years before his death. Some coal dust had got in my lungs too, so it wasn't that much of an act. I could feel there was a handkerchief in the pocket of the smelly trousers I'd been given, took it out and blew my nose loudly into it. The cloth was bloody!!

"You consumptive -Git! Why'd we get landed with a useless a son like you, eh?" Me 'dad' sought support from our visitors.

The British soldiers eyed the dirty bloodstained hanky with some horror and the one on board stepped back from me. Tuberculosis or consumption was thought to be infectious by many. The officer only gave the grimy papers a cursory glance and passed them back to the woman gingerly.

A passenger train leaving the city had chuffed up the track and stopped near us. Up on the bridge a whistle was blown, and the soldiers left us, climbing ashore quickly. They joined the platoon, formed up and surrounded the train, rifles at the ready. They were going to have a surprise second inspection, a few minutes after the main station one.

The old man pushed the boat away from the quay. "We timed it perfectly, Mick knew about the big extra check here today, but the trains aren't always on time...." His wife smiled and kissed him as she stuffed the papers back in the handbag.

"Hee hee!! S'fun really, we should all head even further west; to Hollywood: bloody filmstars, we're so good! Charlie Chaplin needs to watch out! That dumb look on ya dial was absolutely *priceless*!" the old boy chuckled to himself, smiling broadly...his gap teeth looking even more unsightly. We all grinned.

"But those papers," I asked. "How'd you come to have papers for me?"

The old woman giggled disarmingly. "We don't really, but we've used those on lots of 'sons' in the last year or so. Mick's forgery centre knocked 'em out for us, an' they're obviously pretty good. Thank God the stupid Brits rotate their troops so often; they don't notice our changing family!"

We puttered on our way at a steady walking pace to the west; we had escaped, but I was drowning in loss as I watched the spires, domes, the ever-smoking chimneys, buildings and trees of my home town fade away slowly behind us. My spirit was fading also, apart from my love Aisling ….

43

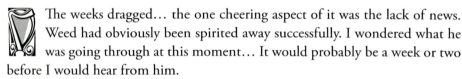ong

The weeks dragged… the one cheering aspect of it was the lack of news. Weed had obviously been spirited away successfully. I wondered what he was going through at this moment… It would probably be a week or two before I would hear from him.

Weed's absence did affect me; when I awoke each morning I would think of him, an upsetting thought which seemed to make me feel a bit ill. I did love him so much! I'd play my harp quietly while thinking of our wonderful times together.

I went into Trinity College and caught up on some work I'd neglected. My change of appearance was noted, but since I hadn't mixed much with the other students in the last year or so, no one was particularly interested; which suited me just fine. Somehow, it was hard to take university very seriously when I'd been out in the real world, helping obtain freedom for Ireland…

I met Marie Byrne again, who told me she was unexpectedly returning to her home in County Mayo. I would need to find someone else to take Amy to the teashop. What with the street battle and the loss of her house to fire my blind friend had been unable to sing and play at the venue.

I went back to our office, but Mick still thought I should keep my distance for a little longer… although there should be lots of work for me when I did come back. He told me Weed was safe as far as he knew, had headed west and joined one of our columns out there. I knew my love well; merely going to ground and hiding would never be an option for him.….

I decided to visit Amy, I needed personal human contact. First I went to the tearooms before catching a tram to Weed's neighbourhood. At first Mrs. Murphy didn't recognise me, but once she did, she was most emphatic; all her customers were asking for her harp playing singer, she was dying for Amy to come back! I told her I would try and arrange it.

I bought another paper sack of coal and some brown bran muffins to take with me.

The houses in Weed's lane were already being repaired. The workmen had started at the end first, so Amy and Biddy were already back in their rebuilt apartments, but the next ones were noisy hives of activity. Some of the young builders and labourers even wolf whistled at me! My changed appearance didn't make much difference, it seemed. I went over the lane to give them a piece of my mind, and they were so surprised, that in trying to get away from me, they tripped over some construction materials. The looks on their faces were priceless! This cheered me up no end; I was laughing to myself when I knocked on Amy's door.

It was still locked heavily. She was overjoyed at my visit and welcomed me in cheerfully. As usual, she touched my face, under my eyes and my forehead. Her face was calmly sympathetic, her light eyes glistened vacantly.

"Aisling, y' missin' y Aidan... I c'n tell. I do *too* y'know, and so does Biddy terribly...we must be helpin' her too."

Hell, there was a point, I was afraid that as Aunt Biddy's house was also Weed's old home, it would be watched by the authorities... so I hadn't visited her. I looked out Amy's front window, staying back behind the curtains in the shadows; since larger windows had been fitted and with the newly painted walls it was lighter and brighter than I remembered it, I had to be really careful. No one seemed to be watching, after all, weeks had passed since the raid and fire.

I told Amy I would go and try and get Biddy to come over.

Five minutes later Biddy was with us. Her face had aged, her eyes were sombre. "Aisling, it's so quiet without m' Bryan... I miss him s' much! They destroyed almost all the photos of him and the fire finished off the only others I had. Our relations have given me copies of some they had, though. But I think m' husband would have loved the new flat! I'm not busy enough, now m'house is sorted. But what has happened to Aidan; have y' any news?"

"Just that he's safe out west somewhere. He does send his love to you and was sorry he couldn't attend the funeral....of course, he misses his uncle Brian as well. As you can imagine, letters are a problem for us. It is harder for me to get one to him...because he's always on the move." I then told her Amy's message from the other side.... without saying where it came from...

"Yes, he'd be pleased t' get rid of his damned cough. "That I can understand. Y'know, the police are still visiting me, without warning from time to time and searchin' m' place looking for Aidan. Tell him, if y' can, to be really careful if he comes back t' Dublin."

Amy broke in, "He can stay with *me*....if he comes back. *I* don't get searched! Although I do get a bit scared when, I'm hearin' the cops at y'r' place Biddy! They're so damned noisy, 'specially at night! Even tho' of course my mum is here with me then."

Amy played her new harp and we all sang along. She was still making excellent progress and was definitely more confident and older somehow. I had a great idea about the tearooms; Biddy could take Amy there; that was such an elegant solution; why hadn't I thought of it before?

When I left them still singing more than an hour later, I felt more cheerful than I had for a long while. Being with the other two had been fun, socially I was too often alone now Weed was gone. Some music had even reappeared in my mind....

Yes, I must do this again. I arranged for Biddy to come with us to the tearooms in two days time. Weed's aunt was really looking forward to it.

That evening Nora was cheerful and pleased with me, her friendly face was animated. "Y' doin' t' gd work there Aisling… s' helpin' *you* too. Biddy's a gem now… she'll b' needin' y as well. S'good t' b' needed by others. Y' *have* t' keep atalkin' to people when y'r sad!"

Her face faded and a little market town appeared to me, white buildings, thatched and slate roofs, smoking chimneys; people, livestock and little stalls crowded the narrow streets, town and country folk mingled; it was a hive of noisy activity.

Some time must have passed, because Nora and her family looked much older; Baby Danny was a now a little snub nosed three year old, carrying a small sack though. Nora looked about eleven. Her mother Mary found a spot on a busy corner near a busking fiddler, put her baskets down, gathered the children's sacks around her and started selling potatoes and vegetables from her little garden to the passers-bye. Nora helped her, but kept a close eye on her younger brothers and sisters. Soon coins were clinking in her mother's little purse bag. Bargaining was the usual way of conducting business, but almost always with lots of humour and teasing…obviously the family had some regular customers, who liked buying from them. What did surprise me were the tiny sums involved. It shocked me that in total, the whole enterprise raised only a few shillings! This seemed very poor recompense for so much effort by everyone, yet Nora and her family were well pleased with the outcome.

The voice in my ear spoke knowledgeably, as if explaining something intricate to a child: "Y' see Aisling, we's got t' be very clever…some o' t' taties can't all come at t' same time, sames wit' t' veges: we's plant 'em so's theys come all year round… cos t' rent is owin' *every* month o' t' year!" Although still really only a child that challenge loomed large in her mind; non payment was an unspeakable horror hovering over the family….

She continued" 'Course, t' seasons mean there'll be one biggish crop this year an' m' dad'll b' aworkin' on sellin' that t'day! T' buyers'll pick that up at our farm in a horse n' cart. Gotta be good quality, tho'."

Her father Joe had gone off to meet the major potato buyers in the area. Strategically, they were based outside a Public house that was doing a frantic trade. Some of the farmers were already a bit sozzled!

Nora said proudly "But not *my* dad, he's always careful; keeps all the money for t' family!" She sniffed, "Not like our neighbour Michael Sullivan, 'ees a boozer! Wastes so much, 'is poor family, life gets a bit desperate for 'em a' times! Mind you, lotsa men do that; when mens get together, there's often trouble!"

This was an almost all male preserve… noise and humour here also cloaked the grim commerce taking place. Potatoes and some livestock were the major commodities dealt with, labour too at times. Pubs were sources of information as well as hubs of business and employment; alcohol eased the process.

The kids asked their Mother, "Can we Mum, please?" Apparently it was a regular market day routine…."All right then, but lookin' and smellin' only, right Nora? I'll have t' purse thank yer…."

Nora took her three siblings to a bakery with lots of goodies in the window, the heavenly scent had all four faces in rapture and they pressed their noses against the little windows. They all each said what they wanted to buy. Nora murmured the cream cakes would be her choice; but only if the family was rich….

They were disturbed by a fairly grand carriage that rattled past, everyone looked up; inside a rather arrogant, young male face with dark hair glanced out disdainfully through the curtained windows, sharp eyes taking in the scene outside.

Nora's voice in my head was surprised and scornful; "Wha's master Samuel doin' here? He's much too *ahoity- toity* for us simple folks; 'ee can spend our rents money tho'! Our landlord's only son, Aisling, don' like 'im much. They say the family pays some o' t buyers too, *an'* they own half the town! They's rich, olright!"

After a few hours of tiring toil, the family trudged wearily home this time with empty sacks, leaving the noise and bustle of the market town behind them. Her mother had made one or two simple purchases after bargaining hard and Nora carried these back home in her basket. Things had gone quite well on balance. Father felt the potato prices he had negotiated should have been higher; most of the family's crop would go to England but currently there was a glut on the market he'd been told, so prices were disappointingly low.

It was good to return to the quiet countryside and their own little corner of the world, the two little green fields and the low white cottage were a welcome sight; -home!

The scene and Nora dimmed away, and I tried to find a comfortable position to sleep. My back ached! I had been quite intrigued with that world, it helped me understand my friend and look at the modern world through different eyes….

44

Sky

 The substantial stone house looked solid enough, but its closed steel shutters with horizontal firing slots in them were the dead giveaway. It had a steeply sloping slate roof and several chimneys. Someone quite well heeled had built it last century, probably a landowner of some kind. In Ireland, land tended to be *the* source of wealth.

A rather forlorn Union Jack drooped from a flagpole out front. The building was some distance away from the village, and all its surrounding vegetation had been cut down and removed, including the stone wall in front. The outhouses had all been reinforced. Tracks over the ground leading to them revealed that at least one truck had passed and very deep scars on the soggy areas suggested the presence of a heavy armoured car.

This was a typical fort in the chain the British used to station their troops in disputed territory. Normally we would only be after the desperately needed weapons stored in the armoury racks and the rounds of ammunition for them, but we now also had designs on the vehicles. The war had changed and we were beginning to make serious progress, our ambitions were growing. We were starting to employ motorised, highly mobile columns, which gave us greater range and hitting power. All around the country we now had guerrilla units like this one, that usually had the support of the locals, striking hard then melting back into the population. The British retaliated even more harshly which helped further Irish recruitment. An end to this war of independence was coming.... we could sense it!

We'd crept up to within a hundred yards of the rear of the building to have a recce. Liam Casey ran a tight unit, I'd been impressed by the way he'd kept the lid on fiery young spirits, discipline was excellent and not a sound had been made as we approached within a hundred yards of the fort, hiding behind low stone walls and a copse of trees and bushes. Countless hours of exercises and training were paying off.

The guys gathered around him, Liam spoke quietly and decisively: "Right boys! Shouldn't be too hard, we'll bale the swine up in there and give 'em what oh. Flyin' Squads, hmmh, to be sure, we'll really get 'em *flying* all right!" there were some grim sniggers.

"We'll surround them, usual routine. Blue section, you'll take the rear, stay completely out of sight unless they break out and come this way; got it? Red you'll be behind the wall on the other side of the road at the front. Our visitor'll join you." He looked at me. "Yellow, this side, green the far side, your job'll be to pot 'em off if they try to get to the vehicles out back to escape. For the love of God make sure ya don't miss, lob a grenade if y'have to, but try and leave the vehicles intact. Don't forget that green section are in your firing line beyond the house. If you Greens stay level with the house, but not to the rear of it, that should keep y'r's safe. The two ladder men will be here with yellow, since there are not so many windows on this side. The Brits here don't seem to have any dogs, which is a blessing."

Just like in medieval times we'd climb up onto the roof and drop smoking firebrands down the chimney, but today petrol, a grenade or two and sometimes even gelignite was used to drive the enemy out of their havens. We'd then pick them off as they burst out the doors. If they blocked the chimney we would blow a hole in the slate roof, to drop things in. We had even scored a pump from a little dairy factory, a creamery, that could pump paraffin a surprising distance. This could squirt the flammable liquid into a building through any small hole we made in the outside walls or roof.

"After the raid you know where to go to regroup. If, however, things are really hot for you, head south, cross the river and climb up into the mountains. Don't go anywhere near our bases and caches until ya sure you've escaped pursuit.

"Withdraw now and keep your bloody heads down, we don't want to give notice of what's coming to them."

Young Declan wrinkled his brow and whispered. "What about the village? Can't we warn them? It's not their fault the enemy decided to have a base here. They'll really cop it, especially since the Brits are bound to lose troops." Everyone present was silent, they'd all been thinking the same thing; a brutal reprisal of death and destruction would descend on the innocent collection of ramshackle buildings: a pub, a tiny old church and six cottages buried in ancient oaks and sycamores.

Casey's face hardened, his tone annoyed. "We can't, someone'll warn 'em f'sure an' then you'll all be dead. This has to be a total surprise, ta succeed at all. We're in a war for chrissakes; there'll always be casualties...."

Everyone thought of his own home and village.

I wondered if this was typical; this operation would be towards the outer limit of our territory, did all our groups do the same, so avoiding causing damage to people our fighters actually knew? This also meant we participants would not be recognized by people who knew us…

Next morning early, as instructed, I joined my group the red section which sneaked to the front of the structure. It struck me as strange that the wall we were hiding behind on the other side of the road was intact; it was a perfect place to attack the fort from. Why was it still here? Surely the enemy would have removed it! As the early morning low sun began to rise, I noticed a faint mark on the soil and grass leading from the building across the dirt road to this wall. My suspicious nature was on fire, there was something odd about this; I didn't like it at all… *it could only be…*

I screamed out a loud warning to the members of my group to get away. For a fraction of second they looked at me before diving away across the ground that seemed to swell up in a massive flashing explosion which picked us up and helped us on our way, our eardrums hammered and ringing. I crashed to the ground a full thirty yards away.

By the time the five of us in Red section had picked ourselves up, shaken the dirt out of our eyes and noses, our hearing was starting to return; at first only distant sounding gunshots could be heard, then they rapidly became louder amidst the background ringing sound.

My shriek of warning had just saved us! But in the process I had taken away the element of surprise; on the other hand, they'd fired the mine off seconds after my warning…so the RIC must have realised they were under attack, anyway. Probably the cut telephone lines had let them know.

I checked, one of us had what looked like a broken arm; otherwise we appeared shocked, but OK. We were in the middle of a gun battle, and lacked cover now the wall was just rubble sprinkled on the ground. There was a crater where the mine had been planted. As best we could we took cover in this hollow. The whole attack had degenerated into a shambles, and when the signal was given, we withdrew, bullets whining around us.

My Red section was supposed to be covering the front door of the place, but the planted mine had put us out of action long enough for the RIC policemen to come out firing. One officer fired a Very Flare pistol into the air to summon help from the next barracks a few miles away. Large orange balls exploded in the sky above us. We'd cut the phone line, just before our attack. We wouldn't have much time now...

The police had one or two casualties on their side, picked off by the other teams and the house was well alight. There were two big gelignite explosions out the back; we'd destroyed the vehicles so they couldn't pursue us. *Damn!* We'd wanted those for ourselves *and* some of our best gear had been left behind...

We withdrew on foot, dispersing in different directions. My little group of three men headed to the southwest, where some low barren mountains blessed by white misty clouds promised refuge. We had quite a distance to go...

Looking back, we saw no signs of pursuit during the first hour of our retreat. The police we had attacked were probably fighting the fire, as we saw the smoke from the barracks die down. Then we saw trucks of other troops arrive. A half hour later there was a bigger burst of smoke but this time further down the road; they'd set the village alight! Several buildings were ablaze, we could easily see the flames from seven miles away. God knows what had happened to the completely innocent people there. We had been the cause of their misfortune, all for nothing. Our hatred for our enemy ground away at our decency....

Silent and morose we left the narrow windy road and set off cross-country. Trudging along with our heavy weapons I made my mind wander... my policeman friend George had been due to go into a barracks of this type.

I rammed that thought down and wondered how Aisling was getting on, alone in Dublin city. How I missed her softness in this hard life of violence....

45

Song

The music in my head had subsided to an empty murmur. Weed's sudden absence from my life took away all meaning. He was being sought everywhere by the authorities and although I should have been worried for him, I somehow still thought he would come through this unscathed as he was always resourceful and intelligent. I missed his quiet humour, gentle touch and warmth, but above all the meaning and future he'd given my life.

I sometimes walked on my way home through St Stephens Green, where I'd spent much time with him, but the park seemed barren now, the trees and lake less magical somehow. I missed him so much.

Once a week I would pour my loss and love into a coded short letter to him. I would use a different name each time and disguise everything, so only he would understand the contents. I would send it to a post office staffed with sympathizers to our cause. They'd slip it aside until someone picked it up....or would forward it on when instructed to do so.

About three weeks after he'd gone I received at a brief pencilled letter from him; mailed to an address here in Dublin. Reading between the lines he was out West and was surviving, but also was feeling desolate, and missing me terribly. My heart leapt with joy at our shared misery; he was there and forever mine! He promised to do his best to keep in touch. Music swelled within me again….

It was about this time something strange happened; a new tiny tune meandered into my being, somehow persistent, present, day and night, in a mild, sleepy sort of way; it puzzled me at first.

Even when I felt a bit off colour it was contently there. My lower back hurt a little…..then suddenly I realised, I'd missed my usually regular period! I couldn't be……..*I must be pregnant!*

At a library on my way home I checked the early symptoms of pregnancy in some medical books; yes I had them all. I shuddered; an unmarried mother in

Ireland was a shunned and sad creature. God what could I do? I must get a letter to Weed immediately!

Walking on my way home, I shivered as I passed a stark walled building that was somehow forbidding in appearance, despite a little gentle cream statue of the Virgin Mary recessed into the front wall. The doors of the place were heavy and always closed. There were no signs, saying what the building was, but at times during the day one could hear the unnaturally subdued voices of children playing, out of sight. The place was spoken of in hushed tones and threatening whispers; it was a home for unmarried mothers and their illegitimate children; a grim place of shame, blame and penance.......lost souls in a hypocritical, so-called Christian world!

I had always been arrogant and had imagined only silly working class girls got pregnant before marriage; I always saw myself as much too educated and clever, not to mention wealthy: above that sort of idiocy, but here I was! Tears welled up in my eyes.

What would Nora say? Oh God! How could I even face her?

The large eyes were stricken with worry and sympathy. "I'm athinkin'...wes shouldn't be apannikin' now, before we's knows for sure; right Aisling? You's rich, so find a doc to makes certain....yes, that's t' firs' fing to do. Get that letter off t' Weed now; he' sloyal an brave, so no problem there, 'ee'll be back ter y', in a *jiff!*

"But y'r folks, oh *deari-me!* There'll be a real *to do* with y'r Dad now. But y've got a few months up y'r sleeve t' get t'ings sorted. Anyhow, y'mus' sing to t' lil one; -mos' himportant that!" My sympathetic distant relative vanished.

There had been no lecture this time because this was a major change in my life. It should have been a time of unbridled delight, instead of the aching apprehension I was feeling.

Nora understood; she was a supportive friend, when I felt so alone with my secret....

46

Sky

I went outside the stone cottage into quiet peace, leaving behind me the murmured pressured voices in Irish discussing the next steps to be taken. Sheep dung and peat-smoke scented the yard. I checked, yes the guard was awake under cover in the small cowshed, peering down the track that joined the coastal road leading to Lauragh and on to Kenmare.

Aisling in my mind as always, I looked at the magnificent scene. Glowering grey stone mountains, monuments to time herself I fancied, framed a busy sky of startling white rushing ramparts of cloud buried in the azure heavens. The air was fresh and blowing steadily from the not too distant ocean, massaging the land with a time worn patience. The lake not far below seemed ancient, dark and mysterious, a remnant of the age of the glaciers. The other white cottages buried in trees around the lake edge seemed somehow at peace. The sun was sharper, the clarity of it all beguiled me, as usual; I wondered at how I'd been so unaware of Dublin's dirty coal smoke tinted air; here in the south one could see forever…

One day after the war Aisling and I would live in this magnificent place, I told myself; but such a notion was buried in the deep murky waters of uncertainty…

Here on my beloved Beara Peninsula war seemed so far away, but that was just an illusion; no part of Ireland was safe. The Brits might have fewer outposts here, but in isolated areas they could be more vicious, as they were under much less scrutiny. They were aware that way out here in Kerry more of the population was agin' them, and they were suspicious of everyone. The smaller population meant it was harder to hide and country folk tended to notice everything…

My position was a bit ambiguous, but the local IRA group respected me, because of my somewhat unwarranted fame. They would seek my advice at times in areas that they were expert in and of which I knew little, but my quiet thoughtful routine got me through somehow. There was one thing I had noticed during exercises that I felt could be improved: I suggested to the captain that when moving, the men disperse or spread out more, bunched up as they were they made a bigger, easier target to hit, especially if an enemy machinegun was involved. They listened, and improved dramatically in this area.

I had joined this fighting group of fifteen just a fortnight before. They were trying to unobtrusively drop me off at an isolated safe house somewhere in the region, but twice now the selected place had proved unsuitable as we'd been observed by locals. We were now temporarily holed up on this farm, until our squad would move east to attack another important British outpost on the coast at the port of Castletownbere.

While surveying the clouds towards the north rather dreamily, wishing Aisling was here with me to share the scene; my eyes were caught for a fraction of a second by two pinpoints of light, well below the road which led to the Healey Pass and on to Adrigole village on the other side of the mountains. Our intelligence had told us that the Brits kept strictly to the roads, rarely venturing cross-country up there. We'd also picked up from one of our people in the target port, that new regular troops might arrive by steamship soon, from Kinsale to the east. They must have landed and been deployed already! I turned my head away but kept my eyes on the spot and again the afternoon sun rewarded me with a brief double sparkle. It had to be binoculars and it was unlikely a local could afford such an expensive item. It must be the British and there would have to be quite a few of them spread out across the hillside, as I could see several fields of sheep across that slope were being disturbed by something, although it was miles away. I couldn't spot any advance scouts anywhere.

I pulled my cap down and had a pee against the wall, just the sort of thing the Brits would expect of the Irish, and then casually strolled back across the yard to the cottage.

"I think there may be troops coming down from the top road! Stay out of sight; they're miles away as yet." I called out to the squad's consternation. "Who has the best eyesight amongst your men?" I asked the platoon chief. A skinny rather awkward youth Thomas was selected.

"Stand back from the windows in the dark, so the guy with binoculars can't see you. Look at the fields just below the road, and tell us what you see."

The young man started counting. "Thirty-eight in total, though there might be one or two more. There are two pairs each lugging something heavy I think. They are lagging a bit behind the main group however."

The chief swore, "Bugger! Probably machineguns! We're completely outnumbered. Thomas, you stay watching, let me know if there is any change.

"Right we're leaving this place men, and there must be no sign whatsoever that we were here. At least this time we have an hour or so before they arrive. What the hell are they doing in this neck of the woods? I don't like it when they're unpredictable! They'll probably have road transport meeting them down here, so we must allow for that, maybe even some more soldiers in a lorry…

"Clancy, you, tidy the beds, Pat the kitchen, get rid of those dishes and cutlery, dry them carefully. Arms out the back door, leaning against the wall, out of sight from them, now!

"As for our sentry, why didn't he pick this up? Sneak down and warn him to come back to us here," he ordered me.

"It was only a fluke I happened to spot the flash of light, just happened to be looking the right way at the right time…pure luck," I explained to our chief.

He frowned at me. "Good reminder that we shouldn't have anything shiny on *us*, and that goes for your damned glasses too. Too many to tackle here, so we'll retreat. They're not moving as if they know we are right here at this moment, smells more like a fishing expedition to me."

Our jobs done, we all gathered together. "Tidy up our tracks as we leave. Here's what we're going to do, all crouch down and rather than go in the opposite direction to the South where we could be trapped at the end of the peninsula, we'll travel out of sight climbing to the east behind those walls. Got it? No one is to be seen, and keep your eyes peeled especially for a post on the ridge ahead. Try and not scare the sheep, which is nigh impossible. Thank God it'll be dark in an hour and a half!"

Michael O'Finney, who'd lived and fished on the nearby coast for most of his life, looked up at the tops and then towards the distant coastal inlet and headland. He unwittingly tilted his head on one side as he thought. He spoke authoritively: "Sure there'll be thick fogs here captain within an hour, especially on the high ground…"

"God, I hope y'r right man. That'll help us Mickey, gives us a slight edge, which we need!"

A quarter of an hour later, clutching our ragtag assortment of odd weapons, we crawled and crouched away out of sight behind the walls going in an easterly direction, a row of dark caps bobbing their way along. Fog did arrive in just forty or so minutes. We were then able to walk upright and move more swiftly up to the head of the valley, guided only by our precious captured British army compass, before turning north again climbing up the steep slope a bit beyond where I'd first spotted the Brits. I was amused by how much reliance we put on our enemy's gear and ideas. Almost every one of our guerrilla groups used the British Army Manual as its bible, its guide for military action!

Three wearying hours later, after climbing as fast as we could in the damp, cold dripping atmosphere, we reached just west of the Healey Pass. Knowing how the Brits would often have a pocket of troops in such a key strategic position, we strained our ears for any unusual sound, but heard nothing. Then we became aware of the faint whining, distant hum of a lorry climbing up the steep dirt road which went through a series of hairpins and switchbacks. It was a God-given opportunity for an ambush where surprise was always an essential element. A sudden attack in these conditions, night and fog, would be last thing they'd be thinking of and since they already had many troops in the area, they'd probably be quite relaxed. This vehicle should be more or less empty and since it was travelling so slow; it would be a perfect target. There was also lots of natural cover for us....

"Mickey, how long do you think the mist'll last?"

The young fisherman wrinkled his brow and thought for a second or two. "Dunno, Cap'n. Maybe till morning like, but not much longer, I'm athinking."

The dripping hard faces looked at their leader... some wanted a scrap...and felt it was a hell of an opportunity. Others were worn out and needed rest.

"Stay down, not a sound, let'em pass this time, and that's an order, though; *dammit!* I'll explain why afterwards," Keenan spoke firmly.

There was a quiet moan from a few men who relished some action, but then they did as they were told, sinking down into some damp sparse undergrowth and rock crevices some yards back from the road, blending in with the darkness. A little stream bubbled and chuckled as it meandered towards the road where a ditch carried it away downhill. We watched with our weapons ready, just in case. I slid the safety catch off my pistol and waited tensely...

The truck's weak headlights swept over us as the vehicle turned a last corner, but our fighters stayed frozen. The wall of noise seemed deafening in the fog as the lorry approached, then, just opposite us, it stopped! We sank even further down into the stunted clumps of grass.

Steam was pouring out of its radiator. A sour cursing cockney was driving the covered truck. " 'Oo the fuck gave us this junk? It's cold an' bloody foggy, yet -it still boiled! " He looked quickly around at the misty blackness and up at the dark rocky towering landscape and shivered. "*Christ*, I loath this God-forsaken shithole of a country with its bloody bog-dwelling gits, all trying to kill us!"

Our hidden fighters less than a hundred feet away smiled grimly to themselves. If only he knew how close he was to that fate….

His sergeant offsider glanced at his watch, put aside the map he had been reading and climbed down from the cab holding a tin with a wire handle. "C'mon, the lieutenant'll be the one to kill us if we don't get down to that valley. Open the bonnet, I'll get some water." He went to the stream and filled the tin.

There was a major commotion on the back of the truck. Hell, it was full of troops! "Can we get down Sarge?" several yelled out.

He walked to the back of the truck and called up over the tailgate. We could hear everything above the quiet noise of the still idling motor:

"Nope, we're behind time as it is, should be no more than half an hour till we get there. We gotta get there before the fog lifts, so we'll surprise the bastards! This group of fifteen bandits down in the valley won't expect so many of us, that's for sure. One of them is a real prize; he's a murderer from Dublin, one Aidan Duffey; after Collins, the most wanted criminal in the whole damned country! The little four eyed swine is to be left alive if possible. He was definitely with them when they arrived at the farmhouse. Come on, hurry up you two!" he bawled at the driver and his offsider.

Lying on the soggy ground, It took me a few seconds to realize that it was *me* he was referring to. I really must be infamous!

But how the hell did they know so much detail about our little group? It *had* to be an informer! They'd known we'd be staying at that farmhouse, so that when they returned the young couple who rented the place would already be suffering at the hands of troops who had come down the hill cross country on foot. Now, who had known I was with the group? Not many. We should be able to work it out by elimination. I glanced across at the granite face of our C.O.

There was an explosion of white steam and much cursing as the radiator cap was removed. The radiator was filled as the motor ticked over, the cap replaced, then the driver and his mate climbed back on board and the large vehicle slowly accelerated off down the incline into the mist. The sound of it faded away. Only the stream and light wind could be heard. We waited a little longer, then finally stood up, stiff and shivering; Christ it was cold!

There was an awkward silence as we stamped our feet and waved our arms in a vain attempt to keep warm and restore our circulation. Captain Keenan spoke:

"Good, boys, -excellent discipline, and hell, are we outnumbered here! Fret ye not, we'll get 'em in the long run… believe me.

"This peninsula is too small for a large action, with essentially only two roads in and out; we'd be easily trapped, and it seems the Brits have quite a lot of reinforcements to draw on; much wiser to hold off till we are further north. They shouldn't expect us to head that way. Well, we've certainly learnt a lot, they're on to us here in a big way. It *has* to be an informer; none of you bastards I hope." He looked around at the grim faces. "Let me know if you have any ideas about who it might be… C'mon we're on our way. You lead Rory. Weed, I want'a talk to you."

As we trudged off up the foggy mountains, he held back with me so we couldn't be overheard. "The damned Brits know you are here with us. Now I can't even trust my own men… which is humiliating! Believe it or not, *you* may be the reason why this whole area is crawling with 'em. When the silly Brit bastards get a bee in their bonnet, common sense doesn't apply, and you've become a major figurehead in their minds. They're out t'get ye at all costs! Mick Collin's propaganda has really been abuilding you up, because it's been great for the cause. He figures ya can look after y'self.

"Yeah, but it's too dangerous to keep you with us, so I'm goin' to drop you off, you must fare for yourself to a great extent. I'm a hoping y'not superstitious like! Now here's where y' to go, just follow these instructions. None of this lot are to know where it is, only one couple livin out here I trust, will know where you are. They'll help you a bit, but it's certainly goin' t' be a bit lonely like. Once y'gone, I'll hint t' the others that you've been taken away by fishing boat off to somewhere.

"Now stay with us till I give you a sign, then go where I told you…"

47

Song

 Looking back afterwards, I cannot believe how unlucky I was! Of all the months to travel, early November 1920 was about the worst I could have picked.

Terrence McSwiney, a popular Lord Mayor of Cork had finally died after a seventy four day hunger strike in Brixton prison; eighteen year old medical student Kevin Barry who had been captured during an IRA attack in Dublin, was executed at Mountjoy Prison on All Saints Day, the First of November. To do such a thing on an important religious day for the land was for all of us a shocker! These events triggered off reprisals throughout Ireland.

I left for the west on the second so I ended up travelling in the middle of this storm. Perhaps I was too self-centred, missing and worrying about Weed and my secret pregnancy to be fully aware how dangerous things had become.

As Nora had suggested, I decided to get a doctor to verify that I really was pregnant, although in my heart I was almost certain that was the case. Anyway, I needed to know if all was well with the new arrival, and what would lie ahead of me, as I knew very little about birth. Books only gave part of the answer…

I thought a woman doctor would be more understanding and perhaps discrete; the stigma of being an unmarried pregnant girl in Ireland was toweringly negative. I reasoned the doctor would have to be in an area where I wasn't known or be likely to come across me in normal life.

There were very few women doctors…but asking around might give rise to suspicion, I was fearful of being found out. I went to the library and found several female doctors in a medical list that used their full names so I could pick the females out by their Christian names. My father had businesses and contacts throughout Ireland, so I would have to avoid these somehow.

I found her; a Dr. Agnes Mason who practiced in the town of Tralee, the capital of County Kerry. At work, I checked a secret register of medical practitioners supportive of our cause; and there she was! She'd been a GP there for many years, so would be quite experienced.

My father had never mentioned the place... it should be all right. I decided to go ahead with my plan, although it was a long way to travel; the thought that I would be closer to Weed clinched it. I might even be able to contact him! When I got out there I'd put some discrete feelers around; and then there was also my personal, secret weapon, that flood of music when he was near me... If ever he was close, I would know!

Mick was away somewhere, so getting a few days off work was straight forward enough. I told the people I boarded with that I was visiting some friends in the west of the country for a few days. I went to my bank and withdrew enough money for my travels with a healthy reserve for emergencies; I would pay cash throughout my trip. I packed lightly and caught the morning train to Limerick in the west. From there I would take another to Tralee. It was quite a long way and I wouldn't arrive until early evening. Was it really necessary to take such lengths to be private? I asked myself. Yes, I shuddered at the alternative; being forever labelled as a scorned, fallen woman. I would use another name throughout my trip; Weed's heightened sense of security had rubbed off on me....

It was early winter and through the train carriage windows the morning frost covered fields gleamed in the wan sunlight...there was a cold beauty about the passing scene. Mist draped the valleys, low cloud crowned the hills and mountains. My morning sickness had flared up again, slight nausea engulfed me; I wondered where Weed might be at this very moment. I would have loved to be able to tell him my momentous news! My mind was quite restful as I mused on that quiet little tune in my head that *was* my unborn child, I was sure.

On arrival, I was rudely snatched from my reverie by the presence of many police, Tans and Auxies at the station and in the town. They appeared even more belligerent and active than usual for some reason; although they ignored me. Otherwise, Tralee seemed quite a pleasant little town. Before it got dark, I found a small boarding house and took a room there. I went to the doctor's surgery and arranged an appointment for the next morning.

My night was not very restful, as on the streets outside there were sporadic bursts of shouting and conflict, breaking glass and noisy vehicles, which only died down just before daybreak. I knew that Kerry was a very active area in the struggle but was surprised at this level of enemy activity.

That morning early I walked to the surgery braced for an ordeal. The bare trees, cold wind and misty rain did little to cheer me up. But once inside, the place was warm and cosy, a fire glowed in a tiny grate in the waiting room. I was obviously the first patient of the day.

Doctor Agnes Mason was older than I had expected. Grey hair, round face, perceptive twinkly eyes. My appearance surprised her; indeed with my dyed, styled short hair I did not look very Irish, which may have worked in my favour on my trip here, when I thought about it.

I had the sensation Doctor Agnes *knew* instantly why I'd come to her. She was sympathetic and supportive and after an examination told me I definitely was with child, but all was well, as far as she could tell at this early stage, I should have no problem physically. She asked me about the father.... I didn't tell her who he was, but since the doctor was on our side, I did mention he was on active service out west here somewhere and didn't know yet he was about to be a father. I wasn't sure how I could get word to him. She said she might be able to help.... contact wise. She wrote a name and address on a piece of paper and gave it to me. I quickly memorised the details and promptly destroyed it. The doc looked at me with surprise and respect.

Otherwise, she discussed my predicament in society and how I should cope with it. Did my parents know? I trusted her for some reason and told her of my difficulty. She surprised me by warning me against using the church in Ireland if things became desperate...*especially* institutions. She wouldn't elaborate why, although she mentioned she did work at one. I should go overseas, perhaps to France. She could tell I was quite well-heeled and that this alternative was within my means. I asked her if the whispered stories about homes for unmarried mothers were true…

She wouldn't answer directly; just lifting her arms in a gesture of hopelessness and sighing sadly. This did little to cheer me up.

Doctor Agnes told me to think about everything we had talked about and come back for one more visit the day after tomorrow to discuss anything further and ask her any questions I might have. I was tired and didn't fancy an immediate return to Dublin, so I agreed to do so.

I was pleased with the way things had gone; the doctor had been perfect, exactly what I had needed.

Outside things had deteriorated; apparently some policemen had just been kidnapped and two others had been recently shot so the authorities were in an aggressive mood.

Lorries and armoured cars were roaming around the streets of Tralee. I quickly walked back to my boarding house. Damn! I wouldn't be going out today to explore the town.

Then random firing started up, bullets began whining and whistling around, homes and businesses were hit. All shops and offices were forcibly closed. Troops terrorised the whole town, setting fire to houses and stores of suspected IRA and Sinn Fein sympathizers, assaulting and occasionally shooting innocent passers-bye on the streets.

I became quite frightened: was the owner of this boarding house a possible target I wondered? I had two of us to consider… my unborn child must be protected at all costs. I felt unarmed and vulnerable.

I expected things to die down… but if anything, the situation deteriorated further; the smell of burning buildings, and constant gunfire continued.

Since all businesses had been closed, food ran low, families were eventually starving, no one could buy eatables and larders were running out of supplies. The authorities would not allow farmers or merchants from the surrounding countryside to bring in food or enter the town; markets were banned. Troops systematically terrorised the populace.

If only Weed was here with me! He would have calmly and cleverly dealt with what was happening. I was in my room, lying on my bed feeling helpless and vulnerable; fretting about the situation I had landed myself into, when the front door of the boarding house banged open. For a second I experienced a stab of naked fear. Had the troops arrived to cause us harm? I gathered up my courage and went out into the hall, joining the landlady Mrs. O'Brien.

He was fat and loud, but obviously brave. Dressed in bright colours, with slicked down black hair, bulging tired grey eyes, Joe Hindman was a reporter for an American newspaper group who was also staying here.

He looked at us both. "Sheez, it's hairy out there! You gotta believe it! Yous gals aint goin' anywhere! Stay here inside; an' keep away from the windows. I'd put my mattress on the floor and sleep there if I was you. Man, they're absolutely crazy; never seen anythin' like it, even durin' the War!" He looked at Mrs. O"Brien. "I need a coffee…. Could ya get me one Maam?"

In the little kitchen we sat around the little table, the small range glowed, the kettle hummed as it boiled. Joe told us what was going on outside. This past Sunday, All Saints' Day, volleys of shots had been fired at worshipers emerging from the churches, men women or children, it made no difference. Today any person out walking could be randomly beaten up or even shot. Tans were lugging tins of petrol around and were setting fire to the property of known or suspected Sinn Fein or IRA supporters. Many plate glass windows in the town's shops had been smashed. He told us he'd learnt from a source inside the authorities that a food shortage was going to be used as a weapon against the people of the town, to try and get the two captured Tans back.

He looked around the kitchen and then at us, stroking his chin as he thought. "Yep this place should be a perfect base for me, Ladies; quiet and out of the way." A thought occurred to him and he frowned. "Y'r not in the IRA I hope?" We both shook our heads, and I looked particularly upset at the very notion!

"Good! Some of my foreign correspondent friends are based in the Grand Hotel and the RIC and Tans are payin' them too much attention, cramping their ability to move around. Wearing these bright outlandish American clothes *should* protect me, I hope!" His face betrayed doubt. "Yep, I should be much freer stayin' here. Now have y' got much food here Mrs O'Brien? They've put up posters announcing that *'All businesses, including bakeries, are going to be kept closed until further notice.'* I think this could go on for a week or so… ration y' food out, just in case Gals!"

He then retreated to his room. For a couple or hours a day we heard the quiet rattle of his typewriter…then he would go out daily and face the mayhem on the streets, getting stories and bringing us news as to how things were going. He had many very close calls, but bluffed his way through, by making out he was sympathetic to the Brit's cause. "Yep, close one today gals! Had t' lie me *butt* off to the thugs! *Oops!* Sorry ladies, y' don't talk like that over here, I know. Anyway, quite a few locals have copped it, I'm afraid…"

I couldn't leave the house and keep my appointment with the doctor. Day after day fear permeated our lives. Outside the arson, shooting, and restless truck patrols roaming throughout the town continued. Anyone fighting a fire was shot at.

I worried about everyone back in Dublin, who'd be wondering where I'd got to. I kept to myself in my room, lying on my bed fretting about my situation. The three of us in the boarding house did ration out what little food we had…and I felt permanently ravenous; my morning sickness disappeared. However the little tune was constant, so I knew my baby was growing, unfazed anyway.

Things finally calmed down a week later and it became safe to walk on the street. The "Sack of Tralee," as people were calling it, was over. Since the Crown forces had not allowed any citizens to clean up the damage the place was littered with glass, debris and burnt ruins. The pleasant little town was a scarred mess.

Everyone had emerged and were heading for the bakeries which had just opened; food was finally being delivered to shops in the town, shell shocked folk were lining up to buy. They looked around them bitterly and stonily ignored the cause of the destruction: the armed troops sullenly observing them.

I went to the doctor's surgery and was shocked to find it burned down. I asked where Doctor Mason was. I was sad to hear she'd been arrested and taken away for interrogation and imprisonment somewhere. I cursed to myself. She had been a supporter of our movement and I hoped the kind lady would come through safely. She would have been a great support for me… now I would have to find another practioner. Thank God I hadn't given her my real name and address! The Brits would check all her records, before destroying her surgery.

At the railway station I bought tickets for the next morning, to Dublin, via Cork this time. I would be leaving early. It was hard to keep a neutral face for the Tans on duty there; I loathed them!

Nora was in a rush when she appeared. "So y'definitely gonna be a mum…G'd! Tralee; well, there's a turn for t' books, 's not *really* a famine -when all's said n' done…not a *cream cake* 'n sight eh? Must 'ave bin grim!"

Her face grew serious. "*Real* hunger's not a joke, y' gotta believe me! T' shootin's a worry tho'….. I'm glad y' got thru m' friend. Y' right ter fight t' Brits. But b' careful when y'r' getting back t' Dublin…..t'ings'll be ahappenin' there *too* in a week or so… jes you look after that precious baby now." Her face blinked out.

I liked my friend… she was a warm constant in my life…her warning concerned me though, I must be careful.

But there was one regret; out west, I had not been able to contact my love… doing so in this environment would put him at risk, for sure.

As I was drifting off, for the very first real time, I detected a slight movement of the creature growing within me….

48

Sky

 Our platoon had headed north at first in these Caha Mountains but then turned west, descending down to the coast road by Tuoist. From here we'd travelled only at night, hiding in the hills and sleeping during the day. There was tremendous enemy activity on this road from Kenmare. Troops were heading south, they must have thought we were trapped somewhere well down the peninsula, still trying to carry out an attack on that eastern port.

We were cold and very tired, but even worse was a feeling of unveiled suspicion that permeated our group of fifteen, although Captain Keenan and I were exempt. After all, I'd spotted the advancing troops and had saved everyone. We could easily have all been killed; how had the British known exactly where we were, how many there were in our team and the fact that I was present? I was glad I would be leaving the group; the underlying tension was getting to everyone.

We approached the beautiful Cloonee Loughs area, jewel-like little lakes surrounded by a verdant growth of trees and bush sprouting by ancient rocks. There were isolated lights of a few farmhouses buried in the darkening countryside. At night, the waters seemed mysterious, the bushes rather threatening, especially when our passage disturbed a family of deer! They'd noisily erupted out of the dark ground and crashed off through the undergrowth. Our hearts all beat wildly, as we froze and waited… a distant dog at one of the houses briefly barked, but after that nothing happened, and we continued on our way.

Keenan came to the back of the file where I'd stayed as he'd instructed. He made sure no one in the group could hear us. "Weed, lucky for you this is *my* country! When we cross that bridge and turn that corner you'll leave us, double back the way we came …no goodbyes, just disappear as far as these men are concerned. If we do have a traitor in our group, he won't know exactly where you left us.

"Now, four turns back you'll go inland on a track to the left, forest to begin with and then rather poor open fields. Keep on several miles till you reach a small farmhouse on y'right. Make sure you can see a small stone circle to the right of it, then you'll know you've got to the correct place. An old couple'll be there, distant poor relations of mine. Tell them I sent you and say these words..." He gave me a strange phrase in Gaelic. I memorised it. "They'll give y' instuctions as to where to go from there. And Weed for God's sake be careful! The bastards are really trying t' catch ye...."

I thanked him. He was a good leader and a brave soldier who inspired his troops, yet maintained tight discipline, and could demonstrate sensible restraint at times. He realized the limitations of guerrilla warfare, but was as brave as a lion when it was necessary. He could think clearly under pressure. I must tell Mick about him. If only we had a lot more like him in our movement....

"For Ireland lad, her freedom'll come, believe me...an' soon I'll b' athinking." We shook hands and as he went back to the head of the column, I hung back a bit further, then in a dark patch stopped and waited in the shadows until I was alone. As fast and as carefully as I could, I retraced my steps and followed Keenan's instructions to the letter...

49

Song

Nora turned out to be correct; towards the end the month there was an explosion of Crown forces activity in response to a major operation on our side. The Brits had brought in some new secret intelligence operatives, working completely outside the Castle framework who had begun to successfully catch our people.

I had arrived back at work on the 11th of November. Mick rudely asked me where the hell I'd got to for a week. I had to tell him, using my 'visiting friends' excuse. When I told him I had been in Tralee, he understood why I had been absent for so long without communication. After a few dictations he asked me what had happened there. My story backed up what he'd heard.

I became aware that something really big was in the offing; activity seemed to grow to a fever pitch, during the next ten days. But I never found out what was going on….

Mick became really stressed. He told me to stay at home for a few days after the weekend…and to keep off the streets. He didn't elaborate why. Normally I would be independent and more or less ignore such advice; but my pregnancy made me feel more fragile and careful. After my Tralee experience I stocked up on extra food supplies, just in case….

That Sunday morning twelve British secret police operatives were assassinated on Bloody Sunday, the 21st November 1920. There were many more targets but some were missed; at one raid at the Gresham Hotel in Sackville Street, one nervy assassin turned a corner and shot his own reflection in a hall mirror, alerting his victim, who escaped!

One of the targets was killed at his home, not far from my digs. From my bedroom window I could see the aftermath: the ambulance taking the body away, the G men interviewing neighbours and violently searching nearby houses.

Such an attack so widespread and coordinated had never been thought possible by our enemy; nothing like this had ever happened before. Dublin Castle was besieged by panicking officers with their families in tow, frantically seeking shelter, now too afraid to live out in the community any more. In that way the operation was a great success, also after this event, many officers resigned and left Ireland for good.

But enraged, that afternoon some Auxies and Tans fired machine guns into a crowd of innocent civilian spectators of a game at Dublin's Croke Park, killing fourteen and injuring scores of others.

The capture and subsequent deaths of two of our best local leaders Dick McKee and Peadar Clancy was a body blow to us. The Brits bought in "Detention without Trial" and began rounding up hundreds of our people throughout Ireland who were on their lists. The whole damn thing turned out to be a national disaster; we'd been almost *too* successful! Life was going to be much more difficult for us for a while.

But I was untouched by the turmoil outside; quietly playing my harp and singing to my growing baby....

Nora was pleased that I had taken her advice and that her prediction of trouble had come to pass.

"G'd, Aisling, y'lookin' after t'baby proper like...an y'r singin' beautifully t' it, jus' like I was atellin' ye to! T' sore back an lots o' painful peein', an' findin' a comfortable sleepin' position; ain't fun tho', poor friend!

I'll b' takin' y'mind off t'ings a bit..."

Her face vanished and the inside of the cottage could be seen; Father Joe was reading a newspaper in a slow laboured fashion, a worried frown on his face. The kids looked much older yet again, Danny and Tom were playing on the floor with some wooden marbles, Katie and fourteen year old Nora, her face full and round, were doing some sewing, while their mother was cooking the evening meal. The smell from the bubbling cauldron was enticing, the fire warmed the small space, it felt cosy in here; there was really a sense of family present.

Father frowned. "S' big worry Mary....a big change f'r us, I hope not too drastic! Who'd b' athinkin' it, both the Master and Missus an' t' two girls at t' Big House gone! Such a terrible thing.... The ship foundered, I think that'd be sunk, ah, yes they mention wreckage here; it was on its way t' *France*...of all places! T' bodies recovered; why t' devil they were aneedin' t' go *there* I ask ye? I can't understand it at all!" He read on: "T' funeral's next market day: we sh'd be agoin' I think. We gonna b' dealin' with t' son Master Samuel now, which is a worry….. Hope he keeps t' Land Agent Morrison on…at least we's used t'dealin' wi't 'im."

Nora's concerned voice came into my head. " D' son wuz t' one we saw in t' carriage, 'member? I'se worried 'bout this…."

Her father read on silently for a minute and then shifted uneasily on his creaky wooden chair several times. "Wife, they's keep talkin' of Irish farms being too small an' not 'ficient enough!" He shivered. "They's jus' putting a few tenant families out on t' road, homeless! Says 'ere theys c'n legally do it….any 'provements made t' farms by t' tenants belong to t'landlord, 'cept in Ulster. T'saints protect us!"

He nodded his head and turned a page noisily. "Ooh, there's a story here abou' a new disease for t' taties… up north. A blight of some kind….only a few farms affected so far, praise t' Lord!"

He threw down the paper; three stories he'd read had upset him. He rose and angrily went outside banging the door. The kids looked up with anxious faces. Mother Mary sighed and shook her head as she picked up the newspaper and folding it carefully, placed it by the hearth kindling pile; nothing was wasted here. Her voice was soft and warm: "There's always things t' annoy us 'n life…. but *good* things ahappen too, sometimes I'll be athinkin'!" She gathered up her brood in her arms and hugged them soundly. They all giggled, and she returned to her tasks. "T' g'd Lord'll look after us!"

Nora was worried about her Dad, and went outside to join him. He was letting off steam with some frantic digging activity at the end of the field away from the cottage. Nora went to him, and put her arms around him tightly. They stayed like that till his anger subsided; nothing was said….

A large strong figure and a slip of a girl, a plainly dressed pocket of supportive love, facing a harsh world they had very little control over, both fearful of the future…..

The scene dimmed. As yet, they had no real idea of the true magnitude of the catastrophe in front of them… but then the thought crossed my mind….do any of us, at anytime, ever know what lies in the future for us?

Sky

It was so barren I could almost have been on the moon. Dark ominous peaks towered around me and the valley was so empty it had a stark beauty all its own, although somehow a sense of death could be felt. The captain's comment about superstition now made perfect sense; I was staying in a tiny abandoned famine village high in the mountains, which had been devoid of life since the eighteen forties when all the inhabitants had died. They must have been impoverished even before the potatoes failed, as the soil here was poor, the ground rocky.

I stayed in one broken down cottage, asking myself who its former inhabitants had been, and wondering if they dwelt there still in spirit; it had been their home after all. I couldn't imagine they'd had a landlord as this land was not really fertile enough to be worth owning. Perhaps they had just been squatters who'd climbed into the depths of the mountains to be independent, if so, I felt at one with them. I was poor and forced to be here as well.

The quiet of the place was unnerving to me, a city-dweller, at first, but eventually the sighing wind over the rocks and around the simple walls of the ancient dwellings, the occasional lonely birdcall, the burble of the little tarns, all became soothing to my mind. Aisling was there with me too in spirit, the memory of her laughter and warmth dwelt within me... her loving face came to me in the mist, the skies, clouds and my glowing little fire in the dark cottage ruin. I'd smell and kiss the auburn lock of her hair she'd given me and wished she was here sharing this existence with me. I spent hours wondering what was happening to her. How would her family feel about me now I had been labelled a murderer and terrorist by the authorities? Would they be trying to lessen her attachment to me?

During the long hours of the day, I'd read and reread the few letters she'd managed to get to me on my travels. They were well worn by now... I was always on the move, and was never sure where I would be next, which was far safer for me. It had been easier for me to get letters to her as we had arranged; I posted mine to a friend of hers, only using a nickname. The authorities would be trying to get to me via her I knew. But hopefully Mick would be on top of their tricks and would protect my Aisling. There was no way of sending a letter from this spot.

I didn't dare light a fire of any kind during the day in case the smoke was spotted. Even when the cloud came down I still kept that rule, as from time to time the sky would suddenly clear. Anyway, fuel for a fire to cook and keep warm was scarce, I had to roam this valley for miles each day to obtain enough, although I felt vulnerable when in the open. I kept my eyes on the tops for any sign of the enemy, but saw no one. I became really fit.

I had to live on the supplies I'd carried in my backpack, these I could renew once each week by sneaking back down at night to the stone circle house, where they'd leave some food out for me. After that first meeting, I never saw the old couple again.

I habitually looked out for any sign of approaching soldiers, although I saw no vestige of humanity at all in my isolated world. By my third week I had subconsciously learnt all the shapes of the rocks around my haven, and would be able to pick up any change telling me if anyone was coming, even in the dark, I rather fancied. My attitude was positive; at least I was safe in this place….

Song

 I hadn't heard anything from Weed for some weeks and felt a bit panicky. My child was growing apace and the father did not know; I needed his emotional support, *now*! I felt empty and alone. At work I asked Mick if he had any news.

"He's OK Aisling, we're apparently havin' a spot of bother with a column he was with out west, an' because he's so valuable to our side, he's holed up somewhere safe but very very isolated….though that means y' won't be hearin' from 'im for a while. Wouldn't fret though, he can look after 'imself; don't y' worry about that! If anythin' comes up. I'll let y' know."

That did cheer me up a little. Weed's life was risky and he had to be really careful. Around Dublin I was daily reminded of this by the now faded wanted posters displayed around the place with that rather poor photo of him the authorities had obtained from his workplace. In large black letters and numbers they stated the big reward being offered for his capture or information leading to it. In true stroppy Dubliner fashion however, most were defaced; beards, moustaches and spectacles had been added to the photos! Anyway, to a great extent other crises had occurred since and now new "terrorists" were also being sought…

I visited Amy and Biddy at the tearooms one day. Obviously things were going brilliantly, the audience was very animated and appreciative of Amy's singing and harp playing… she was getting quite a bit of money from tips, supplementing the money she received from Mrs. Murphy.

When she heard me speaking to Biddy, Amy looked up with pleasure. Once she'd finished her song and had acknowledged the applause of the audience with a modest dip of her head, she beckoned me over. Her voice was low and husky as Biddy went off to get us tea and cakes, leaving us alone.

"Aisling, 'slovely to hear you have come, I've bin aworried 'bout you!" Her gentle hands did their usual exploration of my face. "Y' upset, aren't you? Mainly

Aidan I'm aknowin'…" She frowned. "But something else is afrettin' you now, isn't it? You must be asharin' y' problems….they're like loads we have ter carry; always lighter shared!"

"Aidan's OK as far as I know… he's safe but in an isolated place…hundreds of miles away. I just miss him so much Amy! I'm sorry, I should see you more often. Next week I will bring lots of fresh songs for you to learn…" This exciting news would distract her I knew.

I didn't feel I could share my pregnancy with *anyone;* well, not until it had become so evident I had to. It would be Weed's and my secret alone.

Biddy returned and smilingly joined us with our refreshments; she was a lovely person, easy to be around. I mentally thanked Nora for dragging me out of my limited upper class circle of friends and aquaintances; these relationships were more warm and real to me now somehow.

While Amy told Weed's aunt about me bringing new material for her to perform, I had another thought; as a last ditch course of action, Biddy would almost certainly support me, give me a place to live after the baby arrived, if I was cast out by everyone else. Yes, she'd be loyal and brave enough to stand up to the local priest's pressure; especially since it was Aidan's child. She'd love to help care for the infant she could call a grandchild!

But I still couldn't bring myself to tell her or Amy……. -yet.

52

Sky

It was the gleaming orb in the sky that did it! One night when I glanced out of the stone ruin to check that all was clear, I was greeted by a large moon that had risen over the craggy tops while I'd been dozing. Its outer worldly grandeur was so bewitching; the barren high valley had been transformed into a gleaming kingdom of interplaying stark light and black shadow, shiny ebony rock and flowing crystal streams. Myriad unwinking stars dusted the heavens.

I actually cried, tears streamed down my cheeks, as for the first time, real loneliness welled up in me. If only I could have shared this with Aisling! Such magic would have drawn us even closer together, I reasoned, cementing our love with a haunting memory just we two would share forever. But I was here alone, with no recent news of her, and staying in this place would mean that lack would continue. I stayed up all that night till the moon had died and the sun had banished the stars with its incandescence.

I came to a decision, to hell with the British and safety! I'd head north to Kenmare and the one contact I'd heard of there, and get a letter off to Aisling. There might be one for me from her and possibly Mick had also sent one to me. It was already six weeks since I'd last received news from her.

Still I must be careful, if I was captured, the letters I had from her might put the girl at risk... likewise the lock of hair. I would *have* to burn the treasured letters that meant so much to me, but I would hide the hair in the lining of my clothing......that would be hard for anyone to find in a search. I would be taking a part of her with me and it might be lucky!

I reasoned to myself that, once I had left my refuge, the option of returning to this place would still be open to me; it would be risky, yes, but worth it; 'me stubborn' was up again...

It was good to have a plan of action after so many days of marking time! I left the next evening, leaving a message for the couple in the shed where I'd picked up the food, as I crept away, senses on edge. I retraced my steps down the valley, leaving open country through the little lush forests lit by an intermittent moon that was now overshadowed by racing clouds. I felt strong and fit and covered the ground quite quickly on the main road, not walking on the noisy shingle but silently on the grassy verge. All seemed quiet, the countryside was asleep. I braced myself when I got to the place where the column had disturbed those deer, but this time nothing happened. I reached the point where I had left the group, so from now on the territory would be new for me. I felt incredibly alert, strong and self reliant; in fact very pleased with myself, in so many ways it was easier to not have to worry about others…

It was early morning, the sky was showing the first hint of daylight, and I was beginning to tire a bit, thinking of finding somewhere to hole up for the day, when I suddenly smelt cigarette smoke! I froze and spotted, quite close, a British army checkpoint on a bridge! They'd placed one where the coast road was flanked by the little Cloonee lakes on the land side. I eased myself off the road and back into the undergrowth, watching the scene like a wild animal, senses heightened and wary. I could see from their silhouettes that two Tans armed with rifles were awake, there'd be others probably sleeping, in a nearby house. I slid the safety catch off my pistol. This event was a timely warning; I'd been feeling smug, and if one of the soldiers had not been lax and lit up, I'd have walked right into the trap. I *must* be careful, any slip up would be punished by death or worse, I knew too much about the movement, how it operated and its leaders. God knows what they'd do to me if I was caught alive. But still, my longing for contact with Aisling overcame my fears… I really had no choice in the matter and would risk *everything*!

I slid back into some bushes a hundred yards back from the road and curled up. I was feeling cold, hungry and tired, as the eastern sky began to lighten over the mountains. I dozed and napped during that day, watching the checkpoint when awake. How was I going to get around this obstacle? A long detour of many miles in the dark through swampy territory would be needed. I eventually dozed off, woken from time to time by passing carts and buggies, the usual traffic on this coastal thoroughfare.

But then I had a stroke of luck. Two lorries full of Brit soldiers approached and stopped at the checkpoint. I sank further into my cover; watching and listening. One of the vehicles may even had been the one we'd watched up at the pass.

I could just make out what was said as the officer loudly addressed the young men. "Right you lot, the group we are after have left this peninsular and have attacked our units to the north. We and they have suffered casualties. Now, we'll go north to reinforce our units to try and contain the rabble, and block them coming south again. Dismantle this checkpoint, get your gear and board the trucks, you only have two minutes, so *move*! "

The checkpoint men moved with alacrity and were soon climbing up onto the back of the trucks. With a noisy roar, they headed off down the road to Kenmare.

I couldn't believe my luck as I waited patiently until darkness fell. I must not be seen by any locals, yet get across this bridge before the moon rose again making secret progress impossible. I quickly achieved my aims as the road remained empty. There was bound to be a curfew in place in these parts. I went from shadow to shadow, making good time, still wary of secret roadblocks, but there were none. I was very hungry because I had finished all the food I'd been carrying, yet had to keep moving onward. In the back of my mind were those folk eighty years before in the famines who'd tried desperately to walk to food sources for their families, many hadn't made it. I wondered if anyone from my high refuge cottages had tried unsuccessfully to do so. I resolved to toughen up; things were much easier for me. I wasn't really starving in comparison; the road was no doubt in better condition nowadays too…

53

Sky

 I made good time, as only three hours later I had reached the little town. The pastel painted buildings glowing across the river in the moonlight almost seemed a metropolis to my eyes! I had been away from civilization for some weeks.

But first I had to cross the old suspension bridge, the chains of which were quietly creaking and groaning in the breeze. This continual sound should mask my movement…

Before crossing, I carefully searched for any military presence, as main roads and railway stations) in and out of towns were always monitored closely. I spotted them in the shadows just beyond the bridge, two soldiers who were sleeping on the job, their rifles pointing skyward askew. No doubt there would be support billeted close by. I crept across and past them unseen in the gloom on the other side of the road, and made my way to the safe address I had memorised. On the way there, by a church I found a letterbox. I took out my letter and with my pencil addressed it by moonlight and posted it. I hoped the stamp on it was the correct postage. The innocuous, rather English sounding name of Miss Emily Brown should slide past any Brit checks and eventually reach Aisling. Mick really had the Postal service sewn up; his people might even retrieve it for her. I had achieved my one big aim, and had let Aisling know I was still alive.

The contact place I was looking for was a bakery and very easy to find because the heavenly smell of bread wafted through the cool air enticing me in my hunger; also it was the only business lit up and operating at this early hour.

As I crept along I was very disturbed to notice that some houses had been damaged, broken windows had been boarded up, and many doors looked as if they had been kicked in. There were one or two bullet holes in some of the buildings. The damage looked recent to me. My sense of tension rose. In my jacket pocket I slid the safety catch off my pistol, ready to use it if necessary…

I approached the rear of the shop along a parallel residential street. A barking dog became a nuisance, in my mind waking the little town. I froze and waited but never saw the animal. No one appeared and it calmed down eventually. The rear door of the bakery was propped open, to let cool air in I presumed. *Two people were working inside.* Damn! I hadn't expected this; I only had one name memorised: Sean Quinn, but before I could withdraw, the baker wearing a grubby cream apron and carrying a flour bin came outside, saw me and with eyes wide in stunned surprise gave me a look of horror. He quickly checked up and down the street and then the windows of the surrounding houses before frantically waving me inside.

"Christ! It's Weed is it? Get in here *quick*, the bastards are everywhere!" I hastily entered. His wife, a short dark woman looked up at me, mouth open in surprise, fear in her wide dark eyes. She began to shiver with dread, even though the glowing coals of the ovens made the room really hot. The fire was roaring, and after creeping around in the early morning quiet hours, it seemed a noisy place to me. She obviously didn't want me there... and looked out the door desperately.

The bakers face was sour. "The town's been hammered by the swine; almost all our men have been arrested, the movement is destroyed here. Buggered if I can work out how *I'm* still free. I was sure they'd have something on me. It's actually *you* they are looking for; they seemed to have heard that you're in the area... there's an informer somewhere. That two thousand pounds reward they have on your head don't help! Sinead, get 'im a bag o food ready...." He ordered his wife. She hurriedly obeyed, putting two loaves and some small cakes in a brown paper bag.

I didn't like the sound of any of this. It seemed as though I'd been the direct cause of a lot of pain and suffering. "I'll get out now, before sunrise. Would you by any chance have any mail from Dublin for me? One from HQ and maybe also some personal ones for me too; they'll be addressed to a Peter O'Leary."

My heart leapt as the baker told me. "Yep, these were given to me by a brother a week ago, had 'em hidden in a flour bin, got through two searches, undiscovered." He handed me two floury envelopes, I quickly crammed them up my sleeve. *Success,* this risky trip had been worth it! I felt elated and turned to go, reaching out for the ...

Sinead suddenly screamed and dropped the bag, spilling its contents over the floury floor and onto the British army boots that had appeared unheard in the noise of the roaring fire. Her husband's face was smashed by the butt of a rifle, blood and teeth splattered the white floury floor, as he collapsed. His shrieking wife was punched in the face and collapsed. Before I could withdraw my pistol I was rammed against a wall, my legs were kicked from under me and I crashed to the floor. I doubled up as kicks rained down on me. My pistol and ammunition was extracted from my pockets. Since they were looking for weapons, they missed the letters and Aisling's lock of hair when they patted me down, which was a victory of sorts. They hoisted me up again. I was sore all over, but nothing was broken as far as I could feel. Four burly Tans restrained me.

A tired looking officer faced me. Dreaded Auxiliary uniform complete with tam'o shanter, medium height, brown hair, grey eyes, had a sense of entitlement about him, I dully noted. He inspected me from head to toe. Then compared me to a photo he took out of his wallet. His English accent was crisp: "So, hair's a lot longer, lost a bit of weight, but we finally got you, you dumb Mick! No doubt thought you were bloody clever, but actually you're as thick as two *Irish* planks. Thought you could sneak into town without us noticing! Private Jones, will you show this little four eyed murderer your particular skill?"

The cockney Tan grinned and began to bark, exactly like the dog I'd upset when I'd entered the town. So he'd warned everyone that I'd arrived!

"We heard you'd left your group some weeks ago…I had a hunch you could be still in the area, and might try to come here.

"You of course thought that the sentries guarding the bridge entrance were sleeping. Well the British army *never* sleeps! How do you think we came to have the greatest world empire ever seen, eh? We waited nearly three weeks for you to turn up, and then this morning we saw you sneak in! Didn't bag you right away, as we rather fancied you might come to this known Fenian, which is why we held off arresting this fanatic, waiting until you got here. You helped to absolutely confirm his guilt for us by coming to this bakery."

He ordered: "Arrest the baker and his wife but go easy on this four- eyed worm, Men. They want him very much alive in Dublin and undamaged, no more bruises, well not *too* many! They're going to have quite a few questions to ask him when he gets there and a show trial. Meanwhile, we'll deal with these two locals, interrogate them ourselves. Shielding an armed murderer from the law….you both have the death penalty of course to look forward to," he snarled threateningly at the hapless baker and his wife.

No one had mentioned the mailbox by the church, where I'd posted the letter… there were trees around it, so in the dark, they must have missed me. Aisling would at least know that I loved her still…

The Auxie officer turned towards the oven and reached out and warmed his hands. Suddenly, he made up his mind. "Bring Quinn here!" He ordered harshly. The baker could barely stand, his pulped face and broken teeth streamed blood which had dribbled down his cream apron, he was dazed and had to be hoisted up on to his feet by two burley soldiers.

"Two questions I want answered *Commander* Quinn, and quickly. Who are your contacts in Sneem and Cahersiveen? Where is that second arms stash located, including the twenty pounds of gelignite? Above all, where are the two Thompson machine guns? You see, we know all about your resources."

The Baker sagged in sullen bloodied silence. "Grab his left arm; we'll start with that one." The officer reached over suddenly and rammed his victim's left hand down hard on top of the stove and held it there for ten seconds. The man roared and screamed in pain, but the Tans restrained him roughly. When his hand was removed the skin bubbled up over his palm and his fingers had melted together. There was the bitter smell of burning flesh.

Sinead, blood pouring from her nose and split lip, her long hair dishevelled and grey with flour from lying on the floor, shrieked and struggled ineffectively with the soldier restraining her.

Most Auxies had been through years of conflict in the Great War and were quite desensitized to violence. This officer didn't appear particularly bothered as he looked at me and drawled: "Nasty business, but the way I see it, my men are being killed and wounded by you terrorists… so if a couple of Micks get damaged… we actually don't fucking care, understand?" He turned back to Quinn. "You're going to be executed soon anyway, so why put yourself through the pain? We won't be supplying any medical care; sadly our jails are a bit basic. Really, this is all quite unnecessary and messy, y'know. Now, your wife is watching.… -poor woman, quite shocking for her, I'm sure." he smirked. "Why not put her out of her misery by just telling me what I want to know, eh? Your right hand will be next, and then your *face* which'll be even uglier by the time we've finished. Contacts in Sneem and Cahersiveen and your arms dump, explosives and Tommy guns … … No? "

I was engulfed with complete hatred for these animals, but couldn't do anything, as I was being held with my arms pinned painfully behind my back. I looked at the officer, remembering the number 4125 on his epaulette, the three pips on his shoulder and his general appearance. We'd get this bastard if I had any chance of sending these details back to our guys in Dublin. I looked for any identifying marks on the Tans as well, what regiment were they from etc. But as was usual, their uniforms were varied and rather anonymous. However I noted there was a small badge with a snake engraved on it on their Tam-o-shanters.

The baker suddenly grunted and leant forward as if he was about to say something. The officer leant towards the bloodied face. "Yes?" He asked encouragingly.

"*Get the fuck out of Ireland, Englishmen! It's our country, not yours!*" roared Sean Quinn through his broken mouth. He tried to spit at the officer, but a loose upper tooth still hanging in his mouth got in the way somewhat. However, it was the bravest thing I'd ever seen up to that time. Or was it magnificent stupidity? I asked myself. Why enrage an enemy when you were completely helpless?

The officer lost his urbane manner. In a fit of temper, he grabbed Quinn's hair and jammed his bloodied face down on the stove top, and held it there for an even longer period this time. The shriek of pain from the victim was bone-chilling when the face was finally lifted up. There was the same stench, and I tried to close my eyes to not see the melted, blistering face….the nose and lips raw red and blackened but eventually I did open them and saw the damage. I'd never forget it …for the rest of my life.

Sinead screamed again, vomited and fainted as a door banged open. A line of three young wide-eyed children stood looking out at the scene in the bakery with horror. A six year old girl was holding a whimpering baby, a boy of about three stood beside her with his mouth open. A small nightied figure of about nine gestured the other kids to stay back. She ignored the situation, the Tans restraining her parents and me and hurled herself at her mother. "Me poor ma," she moaned as she kissed the unconscious Sinead. The little colleen looked up around at the soldiers and her brown sad eyes widened even further as she recognized that the bloodied, blistering mess being held by two Tans was her father. She frowned as if she couldn't believe that people could behave like this. All of the Brits were embarrassed by the child's straightforward open look, the officer most of all. No one tried to stop her. She went to her unconscious father and took his hand… unfortunately it was the burnt blistered one… as she wiped her hand on her fathers apron, she threw her arms around him, and said as a stream of tears wet her cheeks, "God bless you Daddy, I love you," she made the sign of the cross then again looked at the Tans and me shaking her head in disbelief as she walked, head held high, back to the group in the doorway.

"I've three little ones I'll be aneeding to look after now," she said quietly and she left the bloodstained bakery walking with quiet dignity, going out the door and up the stairs, taking the group of kids with her. The Quinn family obviously lived above the shop.

The little girl had transformed the situation; an accelerating frenzy of brutality had been stopped dead. There was more than a hint of shame and guilt in the air as the officer brusquely ordered his men out of the building. We were to be taken to an armed barracks. Several soldiers stuffed their pockets with loaves and goodies as they left the bakery.

The officer's voice was irritated. "You and you, guard the front and back doors. No one is to enter or leave, right? That includes those little brats. We're going to search the place from top to bottom again within the hour."

As we left the shop, the window above was lifted up, which shocked the soldiers for a second. They lifted up their rifles, but it was only the little girl again, with her younger sister, her brother and the baby, by her. She called down in Irish, "Dad, Ma, I'll tell them…don't worry! I'll look after the kids…"

Quinn and Sinead had regained consiousness in the cool night air, she whimpered, he said nothing, although every movement caused him to gasp in pain. I was unceremoniously dragged along. The mother began crying again. Sean called up painfully through his burnt lips, and the still dangling tooth also in Irish; his voice distorted and strange. "Remember us little Orla. Pray for us Sweetheart."

With four Tans looking after just me, there was no hope of escape. I looked up at the free, open early morning sky as is my way.… clouds tinged pale orange pink over the eastern hills, promising a fine Southern Ireland day.

All the noise and commotion had obviously woken the neighbourhood; sullen blank faces looked out at us as we passed. Kerry was a stronghold of the Republican movement; the British a loathed presence here.

We arrived at the fort which was only a block away from the bakery. The rising sun lit a limp Union Jack hanging from a white staff, the 'butcher's apron' we called it …that *obscenity!*

All the windows were shuttered with rifle firing slots in them, just like that fortified house we had attacked weeks ago. High walls surrounded the back, with armed sentries stationed at the corners. The place was very much on the alert; even at this early hour, Tans were everywhere. The baker was dragged off to a building at the corner of the yard. They took me and his wife to an administration block where I was thrown into a tiny windowless cell, lit only by a grill in the thick wooden door. Two guards were stationed outside. Obviously I was seen as a dangerous and particularly valuable individual, so they weren't taking any chances where I was concerned. I didn't see where Sinead was incarcerated....

54

Song

I awoke early that morning feeling that something was terribly wrong. The tiny soft tune was still there within me, so it wasn't the little one. That little person was growing daily I could feel, which was a relief. I was finding it harder to find a comfortable position to sleep, my back was beginning to ache every night now, and this had affected my slumber overall.

I got out of bed and went to my window and pulled back the drapes; it was chilly, the bare trees swayed in a light breeze, but the city was its usual bustling grey self; nothing out of the ordinary there...

I was puzzled; where did this feeling of unease creep in from? It had to be one of two things, work or my love Weed. Oh God, it couldn't be my love could it? Had my letter got to him yet? My heart quivered anxiously. I wondered; was this a bit too near the edge of sanity, responding so dramatically to mere emotional notions? But they felt so real and *definite* to me.

I pulled myself together, dressed, breakfasted and went to work. All seemed OK there, but when Mick arrived he was unusually distant and wouldn't make eye contact with me. He used the other girls in the typing pool for dictation and unusually I was given only minor administrative tasks. This upset me as I was sure I was his favourite shorthand typist. If Weed had been hurt I was sure he wouldn't react like this; no, I sensed there was something else in play here.... but for the life of me I couldn't work it out. And then a thought came to me; somehow, *Mick had discovered I was pregnant!* Oh God! But no, he wouldn't behave like this in that case.

The nagging worry stayed with me all day. As I left I was told to take some days off, I'd be contacted when I was needed; and that was that!

Nora commiserated with me that evening. "A poor thing ye'll be.....but a break f'r ye'll b' good for t' littlie, eh? A blessin' it could be....take it easy for a day or three! I'll shows yey wha' real hard times is....."

The cottage was dark, old embers in the tiny fire glowed faintly. A fitful moonlight peeked around the curtains. Everyone else was asleep, but Nora was awake listening to a wild wind blowing around her home. She was thinking of her father's main worry, the dreaded potato blight disease that had spread and reached as close as the next county, just fifty miles away. There seemed to be no way of fighting it, but her Dad had made them increase the size of their vegetable garden, just in case, at the expense of their main crop. Apparently other vegetables weren't affected so much by the scourge; but it would take weeks for this change to pay off. Strangely, the misfortune of other farmers had helped them; healthy taties were in short supply in Ireland and Great Britain and the price they were getting for theirs had soared!

Another gust hit the little building and moved the curtains inside. Nora couldn't sleep, her mind wandered. Master Samuel had visited all his tenants inspecting the farmlets with his land agent Mr. Morrison in tow. Their neighbours, the Sullivans had been warned about the condition of their place… they'd been given a lecture on efficiency; an impression was given that the new young landlord wanted larger farms on his estate!

Under her thick homespun blanket Nora shivered at the notion… her dad had been fearful about it all. Then apparently Master Samuel had gone off to England and hadn't been seen for some weeks…

She must not lie here and worry. It was always better to *do* something. She slid out from under her bedclothes, not wanting to disturb the quietly breathing figures around her. The strong winds outside would dislodge branches and twigs from the copse of trees at the end of their far field. By going now she would score them before any of the neighbours could! Nora wrapped her shawl around herself, picked up a large basket, eased the door open between gusts and closed it quietly behind her.

She looked up; a few stars winked at her, the moon was peeking through rushing clouds, it told her it was very early morning; just before sunrise; the wind was chilly. Many folk were superstitiously afraid of the dark, but Nora felt relaxed as she made her way to the end of their land. Her bare feet cool in the dew on the soft soil. The trees looked black and shadowy above her. Before she jumped over the fence, she paused and listened. There were mysterious rustlings and movements, but she felt there was no danger. She checked, the dirt road was empty both ways.

There were many branches down, which she gathered up and put over the rock wall. She filled the basket up with twigs, till it was brimming, then also lowered that carefully over the wall onto their land. She was doing a good job carrying out her responsibility for keeping the fire going! This new fuel would need drying though. She had a sudden thought, and felt like doing something daring!

All Nora's life she'd been fascinated by a small family of squirrels which lived here in a large tree. She'd seen them daily while working in the field below. She wondered where they slept; it was a strange, mad thing to do, but she decided to climb the tree to see! She was surprisingly quick and nimble. The eastern sky was just beginning to lighten as she climbed up the low branches.

Her voiced breathed in my ear…. "It was a bit silly, but I wuz havin' fun…'citing eh? I'se always wanted to climb dis tree…an check up on m' lil' furry friends!"

In the faint light I saw Nora find a hole in the trunk, near where she'd seen the squirrels in daytime. Ah, that was where they lived! They were sensibly sleeping. She looked around from this unusual vantage point, she was having fun!

Suddenly she froze and pressed herself hard against the trunk buried in the shadowed foliage. Down the dirt road, a dark silent figure was approaching, zig zagging from one side of the road to the other, arms moving strangely. It seemed to be wearing a black shawl over a hat…but it was a male she was certain. Nora was terrified. She would be seen by it if she tried to get down; glued to the trunk Nora watched in fascination. Who or what was this ghostly apparition? Was it a banshee of some kind? A devil or black spirit from ancient times revisiting her corner of a superstitious land? No normal human would be up at this ungodly hour; malicious evil must be abroad!

The furtive figure came closer, she saw what it was doing; it was throwing small objects over the walls on either side of the road…That was puzzling; what could they be, bad luck charms, or fairie dustballs of some kind?

The black shape passed her, threw some things onto the Sullivan's farm across the road and then lobbed two small objects on to Nora's family's fields; she took note of where they landed. Now the shape was moving silently away, in a strangely familiar way. As it shuffled off down the road she began to relax. Up in the dark of the tree she hadn't been spotted! The mysterious figure moved further away down the road, Nora shinned carefully down the trunk.

Suddenly her bitter intense voice came into my head, seething with rage:
"I sees 'im, I did…. wreckin' honest people's lives…… *in ter long run he killed us!*"

I saw Nora more clearly in the growing morning light as she climbed back over the low wall onto her property. She went over to where she thought one of the objects had landed; found it and picked it up. The stench of it nearly made her vomit! It was a small rotting potato... the second object was identical....

Leaving the firewood she rushed back and entered the cottage screaming, "Pa! Y've gotta see, wha' he done!"

Her father was rubbing sleep out of his eyes as he burst out of the little building. When Nora showed him the diseased potatoes his anger was explosive.... "Who in God's name 'id do such a thing?" he roared at her. Nora's mother and her siblings emerged in their bedclothes, bewildered by this early upset.

As he picked up the rotting taties it came to her: that walk...her brother had made fun of it! *It was Mr Morrison the landlord's rent collector!* Nora told her dad about her suspicions; she wasn't absolutely certain however.

"Master Samuel in t' Big House is after having a harder streak than his parents had. He don' want small farms, we're all aknowin' tha', but t' go this far? Surely not!" Her father shook his head in disbelief.

Her father asked her what she'd seen. He then went across the road to the Sullivans, waking them. The neighbouring farmers found the two rotten potatoes thrown onto their land and decided they had to burn them. Some of Nora's firewood was immediately put to good use; smoke and hot flames lit up the cottage. In everyone's mind was a question, would the potato sickness already be in their soil?

After that, the farmers went up and down the road, warning the tenants. They discovered that only holdings belonging to their Big House were affected; the properties beyond the boundary of their lands had not been infected.

There was only a suspicion, but anger amongst the tenants grew, as they argued amongst themselves as to what could be done. Really, they were helpless; they didn't want to upset their landlord or his Land Agent Mr. Morrison, and be evicted. Nora's father was surly for weeks afterwards. Every morning they checked their small fields carefully before starting the day's toil, to make sure no more attempts to spoil their land had taken place...

Nora's voice came to me again; "I shouldna done it... but I wuz *so* mad! Four days after t' bad tatie lobbing, Mr Morrison ee comes to get t' rent., We paid im a' t'door of t'cottage as usual."

Mr. Morrison was a grim faced man... serious and rather non committal.

His tweed jacket, white shirt and tie betrayed his elevated status in the scheme of things. He was carrying a brown leather satchel, containing the rent book, receipts and a purse. After counting the coins carefully and depositing them in the latter, he filled out a receipt, handing that to Nora's father, with a slight nod of thanks. Little was said during this solemn transaction. Nora's father was trying to control his temper; as yet we had only suspicions….

I then saw my young teenage friend escort the Land Agent to the gate politely. She spoke to him with mock sincerity: "I works *really* hard Missa Morrison; we's got t' make t' rent! I'se starts *so early* in t' mornin' sometimes, an' I sees strange t'ings then! Black shawls athrowin', either side o' t' road!" she added cryptically, with an innocent look on her face while looking up at the man intently. For a fraction of a second guilt and then fear flashed onto his visage, before his usual serious blank face returned.

Nora spoke to me again, her voice triumphant: "Ise *gottem,* he wuz guilty orright…. An' he knows *I know,* what 'ees bin up to! T' walk; twas 'im, Ise' sure!"

Morrison angrily left her at the gate and went across the road to the Sullivans. They didn't have the rent money, yet again. Mr Sullivan had felt so upset and powerless about what had happened, he'd drunk a blue glass bottle of cheap poteen, and was drunk. There was much loud arguing, while his family cowered around him. Nora felt sorry for Missus Sullivan and the kids… they were stressed and crying at the situation; they could only afford to pay part of the rent owing this month. Threats were made on both sides.

Anyway, apparently, the blight didn't arrive in the area for some weeks….the delay was probably caused by their prompt action within an hour or so of the attempted infection. But the first diseased plants appeared almost exactly where the two rotten potatoes had landed on their fields; somehow the soil had been tainted with the disease for it quickly spread across both fields. It affected almost their whole potato crop. The stench of it clung to their two small fields and the surrounding land.

The scene melted away and I was alone in the dark, disturbed by what I'd just seen. In my mind, such unfairness was why we were fighting for Irish independence…

55

Sky

I pressed my ear against the cold door of my cell and heard the officer order someone to send a coded message to Dublin Castle letting them know that they'd captured me. I was pleased; Mick would know I'd been captured as he usually obtained all important communications and knew the codes immediately they were being used!

"We'll get him to Mallow and on the train quickly before he can be rescued…" I heard no more as there was a distant scream from the baker; they were working on him again. He obviously wasn't giving away anything. I tried ineffectively to block out the chilling sound… his wife must also be hearing this too. *Christ!*

I could still hear his weakened intermittent cries of pain, when two and half hours later the door crashed open and with an escort of four plus a driver and a sergeant in charge, I was hustled up onto the back of an open lorry. I was trussed up and left lying flat on the deck while my guards sat on the benches on either side, rifles at the ready. My glasses were roughly taken off me. In this prone position I'd be down out of sight of anyone looking at the vehicle.

Lying on my side I was confronted with large polished British army boots, and smelly khaki socks, just a few inches in front of my nose as the truck bumped and swayed along the windy country roads. After a time one soldier got the bright idea of resting his feet on my body and the others soon followed his lead. Although heavy I didn't mind as I could now see a bit of the passing countryside and a distant strip of sky through a gap in the planking on one side of the vehicle as we puttered steadily along. I'd been tied up tightly and the tray of the truck was hard and uneven, so what with the weight of the boots on me, it only took a few minutes for me to be stiff and sore all over.

Really I was lucky, no broken bones or major damage so far. My mind brought back the fate of Sean and Sinead Quinn and their four children. Little Orla Quinn would stay in my mind; Ireland was saved if she was an example of the coming generations. Those poor kids must all be traumatized by what had happened in their home. Their father was going to die in agony anyway. And that Auxie officer had quite exact information as to what he was looking for; there must be an informer, who had also betrayed I was in the area. Not many people had known about me… yet he and the other soldiers up on the pass definitely knew of my presence here somehow; yes it just *had* to be.

Aisling as always was on my mind, I was certain that letter would get away safely….a thought that gave me a sense of some elation, although this small success had come at great cost to me; the price of 'me stubborn', I suppose… and there were still those letters in my sleeve; I mentally kicked myself. I'd completely forgotten those in the cell, what with the screams and uncertainty….

But now what was my future? I would hang of course, but I'd be tortured to high heaven first. I knew too much and had become a poster boy for the fight for freedom on our side and the Brits would like to score a great publicity victory with a big trial. My evasion from capture and not being brought to justice demonstrated abject failure on their part. They desperately needed a success as Mick was winning the international publicity battle, hands down. More atrocities were being committed by the British in a desperate attempt to regain control of the situation: we had to be winning!

Hell, the enemy weren't taking any risks; there were six different soldiers looking after me here; a driver and armed sergeant up front and four wary Tans, two on either side of me at the back. Everyone was on high alert and I knew why. Our brigades had become very adept at getting prisoners out of gaols, and ambushing those in transit, recapturing them, although I didn't have much hope on that score; the enemy had acted so quickly with me, our side wouldn't have had time arrange a rescue, I'd be thinking…. *Damn it!*

56

Song

Despite being told to stay away, I went to work anyway. Immediately I arrived at the office, Mick called me over, his face haggard and grim. "Have to tell you Aisling; Weed has been arrested by the Brits in Kenmare! So far they haven't touched him… obviously going to crow about his capture and put him on show here in Dublin…they need such a victory urgently!

Of course we'll be atryin' to get 'im out of their hands, but don't hold y' breath, our chances aren't good… he's so important they'll be takin' no chances; extra guards everywhere; secret unpredictable movements. It looks like they're bringing him back here to Dublin, already. Y' best bet is t' pray for the silly bugger, we had him in perfect safety, but he left it for some reason….. even *you* might be the cause! Though, he's a slippery sod, so I wouldn't write 'im off just yet!" Despite the positive words his face portrayed real worry.

I felt devastated and nearly passed out on the spot… my heart a twisted mess; the father of my unborn child's life was really in danger!

I left work, not being in any state to be effective. But I needed to be with people I knew….

I went to see Amy and Biddy; I didn't want to upset them, but they were going to find out sometime, anyway, I reasoned.

Amy was absolutely devastated, at first her thin face contorted in horror… then she went to that faraway place and calmed down, her pale eyes glistening. When she eventually spoke her voice was quiet and husky: "Aidan'll b' acomin' t' Dublin unharmed all right, but not quite t' way t' British would like! S' very quick n' 'noisy, an' a tad terrifyin'!"

Her face relaxed and became calm as she took my hand and squeezed it. How did she do it? Hope glided back into my mind; I strangely felt more at peace. Amy was often correct….she'd predicted Nora's return without even knowing about her existence. But what was that about "terrifying?"

Perhaps Weed had read my letter; if so, I *knew* nothing would stop him coming back to me once he got that news, But he would be a very well guarded prisoner of the Brits, I knew...

Biddy was also upset when she heard the terrible news, but again Amy calmed *her* down. The blind girl was so quietly emphatic...

She played her harp and the three us sang some ballads. I set out for my digs afterwards, thinking....

Nora was consoling, her face sympathetic. "Y' friend Amy sees far.... 'n time and distance, I'd be at'inkin! Right too, usually. Yous bein' upset aint helping y' littlie growin' in y' tum Aisling. Perhaps a look agin a' my times'l distrac' y' abit, eh? Only a week or two affer y' las' visit; things wuz awful, *an*' gettin' worse!"

The fields looked different; in general the plants growing appeared less healthy; the tips some of the plant's leaves had dark blotches on them. The blight was beginning to take hold; a sickening whiff of rotting potatoes was clinging to the property. All the family was working, frantically trying to rescue the untainted plants by digging out those that were infected, and burning them on a smoky bonfire. It already seemed a hopeless task....

Across the road, their neighbours place appeared empty, with similarly diseased plants. Strangely, the cottage door was firmly closed despite the warm weather. A thin column of smoke coming out of the squat chimney was the only sign of life. All the tenants had furtively discussed the news: the Sullivans were going to be *evicted!* Two days ago the notice had been delivered by the estate's Land Agent Mr. Morrison. The Sullivan family had nowhere to go and had barricaded themselves inside their cottage. With a diseased crop, rent was going to be impossible to pay.

Her shawl protecting her head and face from the sun, Nora was working on their plants, her back bent, when noise on the dirt road had her straighten upright. Coming down the road were horses, two wagons and uniformed figures wearing high dark blue domed helmets. Some were even carrying rifles as if they were expecting trouble. One cart had three large posts about twenty feet long lashed to its deck and a longer, more slender pole. She wondered what they could be for. The rest of her family joined her, watching this unprecedented activity across the road. Her father's fists were clenched with impotent rage...but he couldn't do anything to object; his own family's position was too precarious. Everyone felt tense and afraid, even young Danny, who clung to his mother blinking back tears.

It seemed to be a regular occurrence for the constables, who appeared bored by proceedings. Some lit up cigarettes and one a pipe while they stood by around the cottage. First there was the heavy knocking on the door, and shouted commands; from within came answering sounds of defiance, muted by the thick stone walls and thatched roof.

Since no progress was being made, orders were given. The three heavy poles were erected into a massive tripod close to the cottage, the men straining to assemble the tall structure with ropes. The longer piece of heavy timber with a steel tip on one end was suspended from this by chains; it was a battering ram!

Then with six of the men working hard, the terrible pounding began; the ram swung and crashed into the wall; at first only cracks appeared. Between the impacts screams of fear within could be heard, especially from the younger occupants. Each booming impact weakened the structure.

By now other tenants from the estate's farmlets down the road had come to sullenly stand and watch proceedings, a fate that could await any of them; nothing was said…

The thump of the ram pounded in Nora's head.

"Twas after givin' me a horrensous achin'," Nora's stressed voice said in my ear.

The constables readied themselves as the wall was finally breached; the rocks collapsed in a plume of dust inwards, forming a gaping hole. Two burly policemen disappeared inside.

One policeman at the rear of the building lit a brand of twigs, and casually lobbed this onto the thatched roof, for a second or two it smouldered, then crackling loudly, flames leapt upwards; a plume of smoke, a pungent smell of burning straw drifted around the holding, The door burst open, and the family exploded out of the cottage coughing and gasping. A violently struggling Mr Sullivan emerged, restrained by the two policemen who had entered the breach. There was much yelling and swearing abuse, then the mother and older children were allowed to go back into the building to quickly retrieve clothes, bedding and a few poor belongings. It took several trips and the little piles on the ground grew. Nora wanted to cross the road to help, but she had to avoid Mr. Morrison at all costs. He obviously hated and feared her since she'd revealed she knew what he had been up to that early morning. Her mother and father went over to help while she looked after her brothers and sister who were upset. The smoke stung their eyes, and caused them to cough when it wafted their way.

The flames grew and entering the broken cottage became impossible. There was an angry murmur in the small watching crowd that had gathered. The Sullivan family was forced out the gate and onto the road with their few possessions. They stood there in stunned horror as their world was systematically destroyed in front of them.

After half an hour the flames began to die down. Then the systematic destruction of the family home began as stone by stone it was levelled. "Such a waste it is!" Nora's dad grumbled. The Kinnanes tried to console their now evicted neighbours, who seemed to be completely shell-shocked despite the warning they had been given.

A horse and trap clip-clopped up the road. It contained the local parish priest. All the spectators and tenants stood back respectfully, the men removing their caps, the police kept their helmets on however I noticed. The gleaming vehicle stopped, the priest took in the whole scene, then glanced down at the Sullivans, nodding sadly. He blessed them making the sign of cross, merely stating: "Tis God's will my children!"

I was watching the scene intently and saw the priest then glance at Mr. Morrison, who gave him a slight nod of approval. Nora never noticed of course; she had far too much respect for the church and what it stood for. But from my privileged background, I knew cooperation when I saw it. This well-fed, black-habited –*lackey, was* legitimizing such brutal treatment and was calming down the situation to the estate's benefit! The priest then turned the trap and withdrew, not even offering a ride to the family in his empty buggy! Nora and her family couldn't conceive of blaming God's local representative… such an elevated personage could do no wrong as far as they were concerned. I was angry and feeling vicious about what I'd seen.

Wearily, sympathetic goodbyes were said by all as the Sullivans trudged slowly away from the land they had lived on and had farmed for years, awkwardly carrying their few possessions. Their home had been levelled; a low pile of rocks and a few charred beams was all that was left. Two constables stayed behind to make sure the tenants did not return.

The scene disappeared into darkness, and Nora's apologetic voice spoke.

"Wese wanta be ahelpin' them, but *our* rent was acomin' up soon! All scared wese were……wha' wit' d' crop an' all! Tings for us was lookin' afrightnen' too"

She left me. I idly wondered; had my family been unkind to our tenants? I didn't think so, but then my father's heaviness in his business dealings came to mind…

I was glad the little tune and growing person within me was unlikely to have such things happen in his or her lifetime.

Sky

 Strange, my life was now doomed, yet I was stubbornly enjoying the earthy scent of the trees and fields while I was able to, though spoilt a bit by the exhaust fumes; when it happened!

The truck slowed as we turned a tight bend in the road to cross over a small stone bridge when two loud shots rang out. The sergeant crashed backwards and the driver fell sideways out of his seat! Was I being rescued or was this just a random attack? The truck ambled to a stop, running off the road by itself into a shallow ditch as two of the four troopers stood on me and fired at the ambushers. I wriggled desperately and they lost their footing and fell; I had reasoned that this would cause them to miss their targets. One crashed down on top of me presumably dead and a pool of scarlet blood appeared in front of my face on the deck. I closed my eyes and braced myself as bullets flew around the truck, thudding into the frame and ricocheting all over the place. Well t'would be a better death than a British hangman's noose, I was thinking and again I saw my beautiful Aisling, warm and misty in my mind, love swelling in my soul, but then her image faded as the firing ceased. The truck motor was stopped and the silence seemed loud. I began to hear birds in the trees and bushes that lined the road.

Rough Irish voices asked "Is he there?" Another familiar warned: "Careful, make sure they're all dead first…. "

I called out, "I'm underneath the body on the back… tied up."

The body lying on me was roughly hoisted up. And I could look at my rescuers. It was Captain Keenan and his little brigade, although some faces were missing and there were some new members. "You okay Weed? Hell, we actually got ya! Y'd be a hell of a lucky Paddy me lad, that's for sure! Dublin telegraphed us and a girl got the message out here to us very quickly by telephone at where we were stayin', tellin' us that they'd be atakin' ya to the train at Mallow. Unfortunately there were four possible routes they could go, but our local boy Clarry here, felt they would use this quiet back route as you were important, so we took a punt and here we are! The odds were really against ya! We'd only arrived mere minutes before the ambush. What the *fuck* are y'doing leaving the safe place I sent y' to, eh?" However, he didn't look that annoyed; his column had had a great victory. He had obtained weapons and ammo, *and* a truck… and got away with it without suffering a single casualty or injury! While he spoke, two off his group checked carefully to make sure the Brits were really all dead. There was a sudden loud report as one, the driver, was found to be still just alive. He was executed; shot in the skull….

A sharp pocket knife was produced and my bonds were cut. I was bruised and stiff as I gratefully got down from the truck and stood up, looking around at the countryside, the low wall lined road, the trees and brambles, the rolling fields. I couldn't believe I was free again! All the Brits were now dead, their corpses grotesquely warped. My captors had taken my glasses off me when I'd been arrested and I wondered if one of these Brits might have them.

I answered Keenan rather vaguely, "I left it because there was somethin' I just had to do. Can you ask your men to look for my glasses? I'm dangerous without them."

Keenan frowned at me. "Mmm! Right, you lot! Quick, we've got to really move; bury the bodies behind the wall there, undress 'em first, the uniforms'll come in handy later, look for a pair of spectacles. O'Shannesy you get water from the stream, splash it around, I want no signs of blood anywhere, even on the grass verge, same wit' those tyremarks where the lorry drove off the road. This place must give no inkling of a skirmish at all. Tom you keep watch to the north, Clarry to the south, and don't forget to keep an eye out sideways, cross country too! We don' wanta be surprised! Liam gather up all the weapons and ammo and put 'em on the truck. We gotta get away from here, quick like!"

My glasses were found in the dead sergeant's uniform. He'd probably fallen on them, I tried to straighten the frames, and succeeded a bit. Although not perfect, I could more or less see clearly again!

Keenan turned to me. "Because of local reprisals Weed, we now have a policy of "disappearing" victims of our attacks if we can. Freaks 'em out no end when armed units just vanish!" He gestured towards a distant farmhouse and outbuildings. "The farmer here won't be happy, but he'll be dealt with, if need be. We're takin' the truck, so we'll eventually have our own 'flying squad' Weed."

Just an hour and a half later we were twenty miles away, having travelled along windy dirt tracks; the horse and wagon following behind us. The captured British Army truck was stored in a barn well off a narrow country road, the vehicle's tracks obliterated by long planks laid on the ground and the vehicle run over them, then the depressed grass raked up again; in a day there'd be no trace of its passing.

58

Song

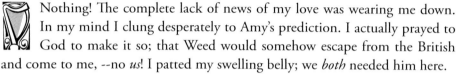 Nothing! The complete lack of news of my love was wearing me down. In my mind I clung desperately to Amy's prediction. I actually prayed to God to make it so; that Weed would somehow escape from the British and come to me, --no *us*! I patted my swelling belly; we *both* needed him here.

I didn't go into work as Mick had ordered. But I couldn't stay hemmed up in my digs; besides, walking would be good for me in my condition. Completely avoiding that grim home for unmarried mothers and their children, I naturally gravitated to the seat by the lake in St. Stephen's Green, but even the squirrels there seemed subdued to me today. Even the sky seemed neutral and colourless! After resting there for a while, I wandered through the noisy streets and eventually found myself at the church I had visited with my mother…I entered it and sat quietly in an empty pew, in the stained glass darkness, thinking about my life in general and my current predicament…

That was the place where I had made up my mind to ask Nora about her life; I was a much better person for what I had learned about her times. Although it had happened seventy or so years ago I was worried about what was going to happen to her next; it would be harrowing, for sure. That eviction of her neighbours had been shocking and reminded me why I was fighting for Ireland's freedom.

My back was sore when I finally made my way home. I passed a small hall where a choral group was singing beautiful harmonies; that cheered me up! Music was always a balm to me; the very key to my existence.

Nora was supportive in her usual indomitable way: "Wese close friends now Aisling, an' knows each other's secrets. Yous is always athinkin' that *Ise* is good f' ye…. But y' should be aknowin', *yous* is good f' me, too! Ise need ye! Yer like m' warm pile of *compost* in a garden o' time, or rather m' hexistence! I'm atellin' ye; very 'portant t' me ye are.... T'night, no history, no more upsets. Sleep f' t' littlie, -*Friend.*"

With a soft smile and sincere eyes she was gone, leaving me loving her tact, and smiling at her simile. My worries lessened in my mind within the shelter of her love and concern. I must tell her next time she came that she was my famine treasure; a glowing green Irish jewel from the past; she'd like that.

Considering my circumstances, I slept surprisingly well...

59

Sky

We rested nearby in an old empty farmhouse. I told my rescuers what had happened in Kenmare; the bakery raid, my capture, the brutality Sean Quinn and his family had suffered. I gave them a description of the officer and the Tans. Keenan promptly noted the details in a small black notebook. The mood was grim; this was why we were fighting for the freedom of our land, against these... *monsters!*

Captain Keenan then motioned me outside and we spoke privately. His face was hard and intense. He wanted to know the specific details of what the Brits had asked Quinn. I told him. "He said *twenty* pounds of gelignite, right? And *two* Tommy guns? We've *got* the traitorous bastard...and he of course knew about you being with us too! I separately told all my guys different arms figures, insisting that they each keep it to themselves." He withdrew a grubby piece of paper from his pocket; on it were pencilled initials and numbers.

"So much goin' on Weed, I wrote it down, didn't want to trust m' memory... it could be a death sentence after all. Christ I hate this war! He's popular with the others too. Fought well for us ..."

He handed me a Webley pistol, safety catch off, then grimly took his own handgun out of its holster and called into the building, his mild voice not matching his face. "O'Malley, could I be a'seein' you for a moment?"

The man emerged calmly, but his face changed when he saw the pistol in his captain's hand...and my one also ready. He knew we *knew*. Fear and guilt showed, as his body began to tremble. I thought he might try and make a run for it, but he worked out it was hopeless.

"The Brits had your arm's numbers and you knew Weed was with us. You put us all at risk, you *traitor*! But why, O'Malley, *why?*"

The emaciated middle-aged man looked for a second or two as if he might protest his innocence, but then his eyes sank down to the ground. "It was goin' to kill me family if I didn't, the kids had no food and I couldn't get a job to feed 'em; I was desperate. Even the church couldn't help; they had too many in need, they said. The Brits gave me money for information and paid it straight to me missus. Me wife was dying, starvin' herself t' try and feed m' little ones. Christ, I never wanted to…." His miserable, weak voice quavered and trailed off pathetically. He looked up. "I fought well for you, shot the driver today…"his voice was weak and hoarse.

Poverty and unemployment were widespread in Ireland at the time; many went very hungry, which in a land of such agricultural wealth was in itself criminal. His general appearance completely supported his story.

"How'd ya keep in contact with them?" Silence ensued, the sallow face turned even more pale and empty under his cap, his eyes cast down. The voices of the others conversing inside the building could be heard.

Keenan's movement was so sudden; it surprised even me, his pistol smashed sideways into O'Malley's thin face. A bloodied weal appeared from one ear to his nose…. He didn't make a sound…

Threateningly Keenan raised his pistol again, I kept mine steady, pointed at the man's temple.

The voice was just a hoarse whisper. "I leave 'em messages in certain places… or mail them notes too sometimes." He gave us a series of drop off points and the name and address he'd used for contact. His voice was miserable and hopeless in tone… he knew what was going to happen. O'Malley pleaded, "Listen, please tell my Maire an' the kids that I love 'em, don't tell what I done —please, the shame would be *too* much. Me kids'd b' treated like poison…." He made a frantic sign of the cross. "Jesus save me; I had no ch…"

An explosion, wide eyes, a scarlet circle on the cheap worn jacket, and a crumpled body on the ground…blood oozing into the barnyard mud. I noticed the darned elbow patches on the worn jacket, patched trousers and holes in the soles of his shoes.

The shot had the others in the group erupting out of the house, arms at the ready. The two sentries on watch also rushed back from their posts. There were looks of shock, disbelief and then anger when they realised the figure lying dead in the farmyard with blood streaming from a wound in his chest was O'Malley their comrade.

Captain Keenan was forceful; his face and eyes granite. "This bastard was informing on us to the British and has just admitted it. Any of you could have been killed by his actions. *He* was why we've been dogged by the enemy for weeks. They knew more or less where we would be, 'cos he told 'em. He broke his oath to the Brotherhood. But this is not to get out, right? As far as anyone is concerned, he died in action. You gonna have t' trust me, there are lives at stake…. Get it? This stays in our group or …. Now, you two, bury him outside the yard. Sentries get back to your posts, now!" Keenan went back into the house in a sour mood.

I stayed outside as the moody assembly mumbled about the execution. I looked sadly at the sky. Impoverished, hungry O'Malley was also a casualty of our war against the British. I believed what the man had said; he'd done it just to feed his family…times were hard and the war and instability had affected employment rates greatly. We didn't pay our soldiers as they were just volunteers. Now there was another family without a breadwinner. Keenan understood this I was certain, but he'd really had no choice… we had to come down hard on *any* disloyalty. I might have a word with Mick about the case; perhaps one of his funds might help the O'Malley family. He had done so once before in a similar case of betrayal in Dublin: "Not the damned kids' fault!" he'd exclaimed when someone had objected.

The sky and wan clouds did nothing to ease my mood, but then I felt the letters in my sleeve. Christ! I *still* hadn't read them. I'd forgotten completely! The last thirty six or so hours had been a rollercoaster of emotions and events; capture, torture sessions, sudden freedom again, and just now, an execution! I hadn't slept a wink for nearly two days and was weak with hunger. I took the envelopes that had so nearly cost me my life out of their hiding place…

One was obviously from Aisling; my fingers trembled as I opened the envelope. The letter was of course quite innocuous in tone; the British opened mail randomly all the time. My heart jumped as I read the coded words we'd arranged that told me she loved me. I checked the date on the Dublin postmark, only six days ago. My heart sang! But then I noticed something a bit odd… within the letter she'd mentioned the word pregnant twice and in the family way once.

She said Sally's florist business was surviving, just; though obtaining flowers and goods was a problem. Apparently when she'd asked for a loan at the bank there had been a "pregnant pause" at the meeting she'd attended. She talked about the mythical Emily being in the family way…then in a P.S. she said Sally's pregnancy was going well, but there might be social problems. Also her husband who was away overseas didn't know that there was a child on the way yet.

My fatigued brain finally clicked. *Aisling was pregnant…!* It was monumental news; I was to become a father! Then came the shattering thought; my love would be an unmarried mother, a fallen woman, a sad outcast in a land of puritanical excess where a so-called Christian church showed no pity, understanding or flexibility whatsoever. My heart spilled out to her. And then there was her father… *Jesus Christ and Mary*! Her parents didn't know yet; that'd be "social problems" she'd mentioned. I must go back to her in Dublin, despite the fact I was now an outcast, murderer and terrorist, being sought high and low by the authorities. But she needed me….

The comments about Sally's business, I took to refer to Mick and the movement, things there were marginal… but we were hanging in there, as usual short of arms. Well little change there. Out here in Kerry the locals were more upbeat as to how things were going.

After several minutes thought, I opened the other letter. From Mick this time, it was typically much more direct and brief. Translated, he was ordering me to stay away from Dublin at all costs. I was to remain in hiding. Things however were happening.…. I wondered what that might mean, sort of sounded big to me.

Still, really, I had no choice I *would* go back…

I pulled Keenan aside. "Letter from Mick Collins," I said and waved the envelope. "Must get back to Dublin as quickly as possible," giving the impression that I'd been ordered back. "Y' can't get me to the train tomorrow can you? Or any lorries going through?" I knew that Dublin's food and fuel were brought in daily from all parts of Ireland.

The Captain frowned. "Suicide, Weed, absolute suicide! They're acheckin' the trains at every station, the roadblocks are even worse in a way, they're completely random, as are the canals these days. You're too damned famous and they're looking for y' everywhere; that reward for y' capture dead or alive doesn't help…added to that, they've just caught you and now you've disappeared yet again, complete with six Tans! All hell is going to break out in this area for us now anyway because of that. Tomorrow we're heading southwest *fast*, up into the mountains again to try an' get out of it."

'Me stubborn' was up again. "I gotta go, even if I have to bloody well walk there!"

Keenan stroked his chin reflectively. "Well, there might just be one way…."

I slept like a log for a few hours, but the group were up and moving out well before dawn on a couple of horse drawn carts, leaving the lorry hidden under hay in the barn. This place was about six miles away from the route they were taking me on… it should escape detection. It was cold and grey outside. I was going to be dropped off, only Keenan knew where. We stopped at an isolated farmhouse that had a telephone and he made a call.

"Ye're lucky Weed, I'll give y' that. S' happens, timin's almost perfect. He's goin' that way in an hour or so, will avoid the Brits. Here's what y' to do ...." Keenan gave me some instructions out of the hearing of the others, finishing up with a warning to never divulge how I was travelling. Even his own people knew nothing about it.

I was sad to be leaving and thanked the group for my rescue, but the O'Malley execution had dampened morale badly. I watched them head off west on the horse and cart, as light appeared in the eastern sky; brave fighters for our cause, dressed only in everyday clothes, caps pulled down against the cold of daybreak.

I made my way to a large farm as per instructions....

60

Song

Two days had dragged past. Even Amy's dollop of settling calm and Nora's positivity were starting to wear off. My extreme anxiety was beginning to return again. Amy had been so certain, but there had been no news. Where the hell was Weed? However, the consoling soft tune of the growing child within me was still a pleasant backdrop.

The phone rang as I was preparing my breakfast; I recognized Mick's voice immediately. "Miss Kinnane, your package turned up but has been mislaid again; not sure how it happened… it's in perfect condition as far as we know; we definitely had it safe and sound in one of our offices, but now we seem to have completely mislaid it again! We're looking for it everywhere; I'll let you know as soon as we find it."

My heart leapt as I thanked him and hung up. Weed had somehow escaped again unhurt! My blind friend, God bless her, had been correct! Now he *would* return to Dublin, if the rest of her prediction came to pass.

I looked hopefully out the window, the low sky was dark and stormy, a strong wind was blowing, shaking the trees and whistling around the house. There was even the odd flash of lightning, garishly lighting the grey buildings. I even prayed yet again to God for my Love's safe return to me….

The skeletal face and dark eyes held an "I told you so" expression on them.

"Mmm, *well!* Ise s' happy f' ye! Y'd be after deservin' a bit o' g'd news like! He's acomin' back ter ye, f' sure…as *I* bin atellin' ye. Tho' Amy's really got t' goods, hasn't she now? A *fey* n' kindly colleen, if there ever was one! Tonigh' I wanta share wha' happened t' me….afer t' Sullivans was 'victed."

The scene appeared, the family working in their sorry looking fields. Across the road the Sullivan's place looked like a wasteland, a threat to Nora's family…

"M' dad could read!" Nora said proudly. "E read in an ol' newspaper we found a t' market, some weeks ago, that t' disease was 'fectin' tatie crops in Amerikay fir's, an' he wondered if it had been brought from there to Ireland wiv t' taties on t' ships…maybe t' Hengland firs'." Her voice changed as if she was speaking to someone who couldn't possibly understand: "Y' see Aisling, wese be relyin' *too* much on taties, but dis is t' only plant that b' growin' well enuff on poor soil, like most tenant farms has in this isle, n' can feed a family….an have enuf over t' sell for t' rent! Dad was atellin' me famines 'as bin 'ere in Ireland b'fore; -*scary!*"

My friend dug up an infected plant, clustered around the blackened roots there was only stinking mush. "Urgh!" She shook her head sadly.

"We's agoin' hungry already, Aisling. Ma's vege garden 'as just fed us but mos' o' er crop was sold a' t'markt t' pay t'rent dis month. We's all scared, an' dunno what'll ahappen t' us! We's g'd 'onest folk, always aprayin' t' the g'd Lord an' mother Mary….. but they don' seem t'be ahearin' us."

The family all looked more thin and emaciated than the last time I had seen them. Nora's face had become pinched and angular; her changed appearance shocked me. Everyone was moving more deliberately and slowly, conserving their energy; seemingly with little hope. I followed them as they wearily made their way into the cottage. There was the smell of cooking vegetables, the fire was only smouldering. Father and Mother seemed to be the most affected by the lack of food, her father collapsed into his chair, exhausted, his clothes seemed to hang on his wasted frame; Nora's pale mum nearly fainted and had to stop and hold onto the wall to steady herself, pausing for a time before preparing the tiny cauldron with a few vegetables steaming. She started as she glanced in the vessel, "Someone's taken some…..we have to share it out…" She looked at the children; Danny, now an eight year old, looked very guilty.

"Right Dan me lad, lettin' down t' family… we *'ave* t' share lad. Less f' ye t'night." His Dad mumbled. "If I'd t' energy, Mr.Belt id be aworkin', an' hard too!"

The boy ran outside crying…. Then he suddenly he poked his head back in the door. "*He's* here, *again!*" he called out. The family went to the window and peered out.

The estate's Land Agent Mr. Morrison looking well fed was walking along the road: smart jacket, breeches and boots. He peered over the wall at their fields, obviously unimpressed with what he was seeing. He came back to their gate. His voice was heavy: "Rent's due, end of the month Kinnane! You'll be after havin' it ready for me, or……" He airily gestured threateningly at the ruins of the Sullivan's cottage on the other side of the road, as he strolled off.

This was completely unnecessary psychological torment for starving people. My reading had told me that these rent collectors often actually were the landlords themselves. It was not uncommon for them to lease the land from the absentee owners and sublet it to tenants. They could be cruel and vindictive and their power was total. I wondered if this might be the case here. Nora had told me Master Samuel had been away in England for some months now. In southern Ireland tenants had no legal protection or rights at all; any improvements they had made to the property reverted to the landlord. Ulster in the north had some slightly fairer laws.

The food was ladled out, with all eyes watching ravenously. Danny, mother and father had the smallest portions…. Nora tried to give some of hers back to her parents.

"Y' gonna need it Nora, t' eldest mus' b' able t' l'k after t' young'uns… y'a g'd colleen. T'Lord bless ye!" Mother was emphatic.

Nora had a look of determination on her face….after eating the meagre offering, she stood up and mysteriously told her parents, "I'se got an idea t' 'elp us ……it's cruel b' I must be adoin' it while I'm strong enuff!"

My friend walked slowly out the front gate……and along the road to the little copse of trees at the end of their farm.

Her voice came to me, clearly: "Couldn't jum' t' wall Aisling, no' strong enuf now; but I'se 'ad t' do it! Fings is desperate! See, only *I'se* knows where dey are!"

First she picked up a few twigs and looked for any berries growing on the brambles. But there were none to be found; ragged, starving people passed on the road daily, trying to find nourishment anywhere; they missed nothing. Two plants were flourishing untouched however, one as tall as Nora with neat pretty clusters of flowers on it "S' hemlock Aisling, terribly poisonous, an' t' other's nightshade … nice lookin' berries on that one, bu' same thing….it'd kill ye in a *jiff…*"

Then in the twilight Nora rested, eyes closed while leaning against the trunk of a sycamore tree, tears of distress trickling silently down her thin cheeks. Finally, she started to quietly and carefully climb the tree with a thick sharp stick in her mouth. About twenty feet up she, she paused, then rammed the trunk violently with her stick several times, weeping out loud now. She dropped the stick and reached into the trunk…bringing out five bloodied little furry bodies without looking at them, and reverently wrapped them in her shawl. She lowered herself down to the ground, and walked back through the gate to the cottage, still sobbing.

Nora's distressed voice spoke in my ear. "Such a nice cute lil' family….they's was fun an' friendly…..but…." she sobbed uncontrollably and shook her head in abject resignation.

When she presented the contents of her shawl to the family there was much excitement. The squirrel's bodies were small, but represented *meat* to go with the few vegetables they would eke out.

"Mother o' Mary bless ye Nora! Yous an' angel fr' heaven, I'ma tellin' ye." Her mother hugged her. Her dad kissed her on the forehead and took out a knife and right there on the plain little table began to skin the creatures. Nora turned away, lay on her bed, with her head under her pillow, weeping, she didn't want to see or hear what was going on….

The picture faded, leaving me thoughtful. My poor friend, having to kill creatures she'd loved for years, to help feed her family. I now understood completely why food was so important to her. How much my family and modern folk had blithely wasted over the years… I felt mortified!

I was restlessly awake for some hours; thinking…

61

Sky

I avoided the Big House out front and went to a very large grassy field behind, which rather strangely had no animals grazing on it. There was a very big barn open at one end… and inside was… an *aeroplane*! I'd only seen one or two as small specks in the sky, never up close. It looked much larger than I thought it would.

I never saw him and jumped when a quiet crisp voice close to my ear said, "Right, you're the fellow wanting a lift to Dublin eh? No names either way OK? Safer for both of us!" I nodded.

"Good, help me wheel the machine out; careful where you push, they're quite light and fragile…here's okay. Now when we land near Dublin and I signal, you scarper… just vanish within seconds… no thank you or whatever, just go. Try an' make sure no one sees you, got it?"

He was twenty five or so, had a British twang in his no nonsense military accent. "Used to fly for the bastards during the War. Here in Ireland the authorities never think the Irish would ever use an aeroplane, so I help the movement out from time to time. *Never* mention this to *anyone*, the damned things are so rare in this country they'd track me down instantly.

"Now, you'll sit in the front cockpit, climb up. But put your feet here…it's strong enough…on this dark little path, remember to use it when you get off, otherwise you damage the wing, and then they'll know I had a passenger on board of some kind." He fastened a complicated system of heavy canvas straps that held me firmly to the machine and then showed me how to release them all by pulling a pin.

"It should take us only a couple of hours, weather's deteriorating at the far end though, could be a bit bumpy, but no problem. You set?" He gave me a soft leather helmet and a pair of goggles for my eyes, both a bit too big for me. The arms of my spectacles got in the way and hurt my ears at first.

I nodded again; I was in a bit of a daze. Trussed up I was terrified; everyone knew that aeroplanes were unbelievably expensive death-traps, but 'me stubborn' was up again; I *would* get to my love even if it killed me. I saw Aisling's beautiful face superimposed upon the lightening sky, and listened to the early morning farm noises. The flimsy machine quietly creaked a little as it rocked in the light easterly breeze. It smelt of castor oil and petrol.

The flyer adjusted something in his cockpit and then went to the front of the plane, and swung the propeller several times. There was a cough and a splutter and then the motor began to run evenly. Conversation was now impossible. He ran around the wing and climbed aboard. After waiting five minutes, he reached over and pulled a rope on either side jerking some blocks away from the wheels, then quickly dropped the lines. The plane began to rumble forward. The noise and vibration, the drumming of the tight fabric, the bumpy ride over the uneven ground; everything was so alien to me. We turned and faced the red eastern sky which was brightening rapidly, I couldn't see directly ahead as the nose of the plane was tilted upwards.

There was a shattering crescendo from the motor and the craft leapt forward, travelling faster and faster over the ground, the air rushing past with a roar. Suddenly I could see ahead as the tail came up. We were speeding directly for the low trees on the boundary of the field. The bumping got lighter and lighter then ceased as the plane left the ground, and began to climb. The ground seemed to sink away beneath us; the trees flashed past and were gone. We climbed in the cool morning air. In front of me were some dials, one was labelled airspeed, the needle was pointing at sixty miles per hour…this was the fastest I'd ever travelled in my life! The other gauge was an altimeter; it said we were already at five hundred feet. And as I watched it moving I realised we were climbing steadily. I began to get used to the infernal racket.

Occasionally the plane would buck up and down a little, I looked back at the pilot. He was quite unconcerned and gave me a thumbs up sign. So those were the bumps he'd talked about.

I looked outside, fascinated by how so much could be seen from this vantage point, although the lower wing of this biplane got in the way a bit. The world looked so different from up here. Down there on land it would be hard to hide from aeroplanes. I thought of my lonely, empty valley on the Beara Peninsula. There, I could have been spotted easily from one of these craft.

I saw below me, in front of the wing, a main road. And there was one of those fortified British barracks, again with the hated Union Jack flying quite clearly from the flagpole, three trucks parked out the back. Then the lower wing blocked the scene, until it re-emerged behind and then I got a different view of the place. In front they had placed a checkpoint on the thoroughfare; traffic was lined up on both sides of the road waiting for inspection; but in seconds, it seemed, it was all was gone behind us.

I felt a little smug. Up here I was avoiding all that nonsense, and what speed I was making towards my Aisling! Seventy five miles per hour the dial now told me, and we were fifteen hundred feet high above the ground.

As always the sky and clouds fascinated me. Up here the heavens seemed incredibly vast; occasionally there were small clouds below us, blocking our view of the neat patchwork of green open fields, their dark shadows moving over the country side. I was beginning to really enjoy my trip.

Looking to our right I could see some barren peaks; those would have to be the Wicklow Mountains to the south of Dublin. I tried to see ahead to our destination, but an evil looking dark line of purple cloud as solid as stone blocked my view, hiding the city under a soaring wall of cloud and a line of lashing rain beneath it. As I watched, I saw the odd flash of lightning under this barrier, only a few miles or so away.

As we got closer and closer to the edge of this cloud, the air became bumpier; we were lifted up and pressed down so violently that I couldn't believe the wings stayed on! I was terrified and was very glad of my safety harness now. The pilot had reduced height to fly in the gap under the cloud, and there, through the rain and hail which were beating a harsh tattoo on the wings and fuselage I finally could see the houses, churches, great buildings and factories, streets, trees rivers and canals of our capital. Somewhere down there was my Aisling! Then I recognized green Phoenix Park below us. The world tilted as we circled it, bouncing up and down in the eddies of air.

If conditions had been calmer I would have been fascinated at the scene. But I could see from the smoking chimneys below that a very strong wind was blowing. How would we get down in one piece?

The pilot straightened up and headed north; soon we reached the edge of the city, and fields and open country appeared again. We made a series of turns and the engine started to go quieter and we descended through the bumpy air, sinking eventually towards a field, which seemed to rush up and flash past us, our wheels touched and then we bounced over the uneven field, coming to a stop by trees that lined the boundary, the motor idling. The structure rocked in the strong gusty wind. I looked back, the Pilot signalled me to get out quick. But mouthed the word: "*Careful!*"

I pulled the pin on the harness removed my helmet and goggles, leaving them on the seat, and climbed stiffly out of the leather rimmed cockpit, down the little track on the wing and onto the ground. The wind from the propeller was freezing. I waved a thanks to my saviour and then dashed to the trees where I hid as the motor revved up and the craft slowly turned around and taxied back to a barn like building on the far side of the field. I didn't think anyone had seen me but I waited for some minutes, looking around me. This silence was a bit unnerving! Then with my cap pulled down against the wind and light showers, I made my way back to the city. It was beyond belief that I had come such a great distance in so short a time!

That evening I had safely entered the city on minor roads that I hoped shouldn't have checkpoints. It was Sunday and with my cap pulled down I walked warily along, avoiding contact with the people going to and from church and the children playing in the streets. After weeks alone and time in the countryside, the city's flood of people was unsettling to me although I spoke to no one. I had one bad moment, when I heard a truck coming around a corner and dived behind a wall till it had gone. A group of heavily armed soldiers motored past me; but they were going somewhere. I shivered as I felt the comforting weight and bulk of the pistol in my coat pocket. I was of course not up to date on our safe houses… but decided to risk going to that last one I had stayed at several months back.

Now when I thought about it, I was really in the frying pan. I was being looked for, people from my home neighbourhood and place of work knew me by sight and that bloody reward might prove too big a temptation to impoverished folk, and there were a lot of them about! And how was I going to contact Aisling?

I managed to get to the safe house; looked for any signs of change….but no, everything appeared just the same, I quietly opened the front door, the same woman sitting in the parlour again ignored me, the King and Lloyd George's pictures remained on the wall. I crept upstairs and entered the secret room. But before sleeping, I went to the little bathroom and in the mirror was horrified by the strange oily face looking back at me. There were big white circles around my eyes where the flying goggles had been! There was a tiny piece of soap on the basin so I made good use of it, drying myself on a dark towel. I cleaned the whole area to give no clue as to my presence and then shut myself in the cubbyhole. Hungry but worn out, I slept soundly under the eaves, where I had last made love to my Aisling a few months ago. My pistol was handy on the little dresser beside me.

How to contact the woman now was a problem; I wanted to be low key. The fewer people who knew I was back in town the better....but I was excited at the prospect of seeing her. But what were we going to do?

62

Song

 A sudden burst of ecstatic music grew in my mind, quite swamping that persistent little background tune that I knew was the creature growing within me.

I was excited; it could only mean one thing: *Weed had to be back in Dublin!* It was only three weeks or so since I had mailed that letter telling him that I was pregnant. Nora had been correct when she'd told me he'd be back as soon as he heard the news!

Where would he hide here in the city? Mick was strangely distant and preoccupied when I saw him and I never got a chance to speak to him properly. But a messenger did come and whisper something to him. My boss cursed in surprise. I thought I heard the address Weed had last hidden at being mentioned. Ah, that was it! It made perfect sense, when I thought about it, Weed had returned to the safe house he'd last used before leaving Dublin, hoping it had not been compromised since that time. My heart sang when I considered the risks he was taking just to be back with me; or should I say *us*? My baby bulge was growing daily, it was now almost impossible to hide.

I would go to him there, but wait until this evening. Mick would no doubt go fairly promptly. I must buy some food to take to Weed, now what else would he have missed while on the run?

63

Sky

 An hour after I woke, steps on the stairs disturbed me; the knock was firm. I checked through the tiny peephole; it was Mick, wearing his usual smart suit! Once I let him in, he was quick as always.

"What the hell'd you come back for Weed? I *specifically* told ya not to! And how in God's name did ya get from Mallow t' here s'quickly, without bein' picked up?"

"Can't say Mick, Sorry."

"Mmm, Well, there's not much I can do for y' at the moment….stay holed up here for a while, I s'pose. I'll get some papers sorted for y'… eventually. It'd be a disaster f'r our side if y' got caught, *again*. Anyway, I needed a word with y', face t' face.

"Now listen, this is a *shocker* f'sure! One of our eyes at The Castle has found an unsigned note on y' file. It's what started all your troubles; I *knew* it had to be something!

"We traced this informer's note back to the postmarked PO and had a big break; where it was dropped in the mail, one of our people remembered who'd posted it since the stupid bugger had used a large important looking business envelope, but unusually didn't want to register it. That stood out! The destination address rang alarm bells too, but it was sent on through, in case it was one of those test letters the Castle uses to nail our people from time to time.

"People tend to use one PO most of the time, but this man was a stranger so of course he stood out. It was posted by a wealthy gentleman who drove off in a large dark blue car. I've checked and found out that it was Aisling's father who dropped you in it, the stupid rich bastard! And *I* could have been caught through you!

"Aisling can't work with me any more. I personally think she's trustworthy but can't risk it. She's gotta go; you tell her; I won't be in Dublin for a few days.

"The note was only aimed at you and told 'em that you worked at the brewery, and that you were a dangerous secret Republican. He didn't know much detail, thank God!

"You'd keep ya trap shut, I know. I get the feelin' that Aisling may have confided in him, at least a bit. I'm aworkin' out what t' do about the mess. She's the best shorthand typist I've ever had, dammit! Does she need t'know that her father dropped y' in it? Then there's brother Rory. *Christ*, he's in on some of the worst bits of our fight! Has been discreet now, however, I must admit.

"I s'pose that bastard Kinnane didn't approve of a Dublin working class boy kicking around with his precious daughter. So there y' have it. Bloody *fuckin'* mess all round, Weed!"

I told Mick about the watchers Kinnane employed; a detail that seemed to interest him, and also the businessman's general heaviness. As well, I mentioned how he'd tried to get info out of me; the economic fence-sitting also annoyed Mick greatly.

"Lot's of *that* about Weed. But once we've actually won, they'll be our oh so *strongest* supporters." He took out his pocket watch and glanced at it, "Must go!" He shot off, leaving me alone with a mind of jumbled emotions.

So my love's father was responsible for my new nightmarish life, and indirectly the death of my uncle and neighbours! And now the bastard was about to find out his daughter was pregnant and unmarried! *Fuck me days!* What a scenario! Now what should I do?

This time I would do exactly as Mick ordered; I would stay here lying low until something could be sorted out....

I was disturbed about an hour later by a quiet coded knock on the secret door, the same code that we'd used when I was here months ago. My revolver ready, I released the latch and Aisling stood before me, with smiling loving eyes full of tears. Her hair was longer than when we'd last met, and was styled differently. She looked a bit tired but radiant to see me.

Ever practical, she was carrying a small shopping bag of food. My arms enveloped her, and we hugged in silent warmth. I drew her into the room and closed the door. We sat on the edge of the bed, my arms around her. We just looked at each other anxiously at first… then both smiled as we realized nothing had changed. The feelings that locked us together remained intact; no, they had in fact *increased* while we were apart.

"Love, how the hell did y' know I was here?"

Aisling's soft voice hadn't changed at all; her tone was music to me. "That lady downstairs got word to Mick, who by the way, is hopping mad that you've returned! He's really puzzled and can't work out how you got from Kerry to here so quickly, especially in one piece! Travel is murder at the moment; the Brits have really gone to town on the checkpoint front and there are lots of random arrests throughout the country.

"But I *knew* you'd come back to me once you got the news." She put my hand on her belly; I could feel a soft swelling bump, which made my emotions rise. "My parents don't know, my father would kill me and God knows what he'd do to you! He's really heavy when he gets going. Oh why did I have to be the only girl in the family? What should we do now?"

The mention of that bastard who had wrecked our world upset me; I found it really hard to control my face… and changed the subject by asking her what had happened at the office since. I needed to be up to date and inquired about the current political situation. Apparently, Mick was flat out, things were coming to a crescendo; as far as she could work out, we had reached our limit and couldn't continue much longer… but the Brits seemed to be similarly war-weary. Their floundering brutality and overreaction throughout the country had cost them; they were completely losing the propaganda battle on the world stage. "So they've put some peace feelers out; an Australian bishop was doing some intermediary work shuttling between the two camps. "Although I'm not supposed to know that. We've had lots of close calls and have changed our office many times since you left. If they caught Mick the whole game would be over…"

I listened avidly to all her news.

"But there is something else, and it is a bit strange." A frown crossed her face as she continued. "I may be imagining it, but Mick is behaving differently towards me. I thought he might have heard about me being pregnant. But no, there's something else… almost like there's a loss of trust of some kind, which really upsets me. I get the feeling he's pushing me sideways at the moment." Her face was puzzled and forlorn.

Yes, Aisling was upset all right, which was surely not good for our baby. I thought of a natural way to approach her stopping work.

"Aisling, stop working for the movement, *now*. We shouldn't risk this little person's wellbeing…." I touched her tummy. "Imagine what could happen if you had to escape through a skylight, or got roughed up by some raiding troops. Please don't take the risk! I'll be here in Dublin with you now; we must get married!

Oops, I haven't officially proposed yet! You might turn me down!" She smiled at me in a way that told me that was impossible. "We'll try and find a sympathetic priest somewhere to wed us. Anyway, your bulge is now too evident." I couldn't tell her about her damned father. I needed time to think about how I could break it to her: I wouldn't bring it up now……if ever.

But what could we personally do? My stepfather was dead; there were no close relations or friends favourable to the cause here I could call on. I couldn't put my Aunt Biddy at risk a second time. Our personal situation was overwhelming! I was still a wanted man throughout Ireland so how could I ever hope to make a living and support a family? Where could we go? And how much time did we have before we would be forced to act? I didn't have a clue as I listened to the quiet steps fading off down the stairs. I lay back in the darkness thinking….

64

Song

 I left my Aidan and descended to the street, the mind music faded as I joined the bustling outside world…the little one was moving weakly within me, reminding me of my perilous situation.

But things would all work themselves out now, for sure. It was wonderful to have my dearest Weed back with me. He looked older and leaner but seemed stronger in some way since I'd last seen him. Being on the run had made him harder and more cunning I sensed. Actually being caught had been a great shock for him; it should have been a death sentence. Thank God he'd been lucky and had escaped more or less unharmed. And he'd got back to Dublin so surprisingly quickly…

He'd come back to me, his Irish princess, regardless of risk. Loving me above all else; a fact that made me inwardly glow… that proximity music stayed with me.

My hair was longer now, the colour starting to return to its original shade, but styled in a modern, almost a flapper shape, so the troops on the street posed no problem. I felt they were no longer looking specifically for me these days, anyway. I must grow it longer again…

Not going into work tomorrow would be depressing; I was sure that important things were going on and that I'd be needed. What had happened? Why was I on the outer? But Weed was probably correct; I shouldn't take risks with our coming child…

I was tired, so I made my way back to the south of the city across the Liffey and through the tree lined streets to my lodgings, to rest. I was absolutely exhausted. The evening was fine now with puffy pink clouds in a blue sky; birds were calling and the air quite warm.

The two storey house I stayed in and where we had made love that very first time had an imposing private air about it…being surrounded by trees and somewhat back from the road. The sudden thought came to me; could I hide Weed here with me?

The daring prospect excited me greatly; we had to be together, and this would stop me having to make tiring, risky trips across town. The owners were often away. I worked through the possible problems that might arise. Getting him safely across the river to here would be nearly impossible; he and Mick were the most wanted men in Ireland! But there might be a possibility; what if Weed took a leaf out of his boss's book and dressed smartly for a change? With his glasses off he just might get away with it. Where could I get some dapper clothes that would fit him? Then the papers too…the movement must supply those.

I went to my room and sat at my harp and played a light Irish folk tune while thinking. I couldn't admit to myself that I was a fallen woman, again I felt myself much too clever to be a in such a position, a sad outcast. But I was and the mental pressure on me was crushing. My father would explode with anger when he found out I was pregnant and my mother would die of shame; I had let my family down, completely. Wealthy families had ways of dealing with this situation, but no, I would *never* be parted from my child! Weed and I must get married, no matter what!

The phone ringing interrupted my mental turmoil. It was my father.

"Aisling, Mother has caught the flu, it's bad; you're to come home immediately. Newbury has a car on its way to y'now. Train ticket's are booked; the driver'll have them. She's ailin' bad Princess, her temperature's very high, doesn't look good." His voice sounded strained. My parents were not particularly close I felt; Mother's piety and Father's hard headed approach to everything in life precluded closeness. She must be really bad.

I knew the 'Spanish flu' had killed many thousands throughout Ireland in the last two years… almost every family had been affected. It was subsiding a bit now, but occasional spikes would occur. The "black" flu' was the worst variant. I was fearful for my mother, who had always been a kind and warm presence in my life….

I hurriedly packed and went downstairs just as the car swept into the drive.

Newbury, father's Dublin manager was himself driving. He handed me the first class train ticket and we rushed off to the station.

The manager asked me, "Where's your brother Miss Kinnane? I can't find Rory anywhere in Dublin! But tell your father, that I'll keep trying."

I quite honestly said I didn't know, and thanked him for his efforts. Rory was doing full time secret work for the brotherhood here in the city, but what he actually did I didn't know; but I had my suspicions. He had become a closed door to me; which had to mean that he was up in his neck in something really serious; yet he'd always been closest to my mother, so he must hear what was happening.

Damn! I hadn't had a chance to get word to Weed that I was going to be away for a time. No, I couldn't send a note to his address; much too risky! It was a safe house after all. How long was I going to be away for? My love, alone holed up… longing for me and not knowing why I had disappeared. Then I thought of our intelligence system, almost certainly one of our people would notice me on the train, or in our car and report that back to HQ. Word would get through eventually to Weed, surely, and possibly Rory too…

Despite my misgivings about religion, I actually again prayed, this time for my mother's well being.

This might be a chance to tell my father of my condition, but even the mere thought of that upset me greatly. I couldn't imagine how great his rage would be when he found out.

I never really looked at the Big House as the car swept up to the main entrance; I jumped out, opened the front door and rushed up the curving staircase. Mother lay pale and a little delirious on her bed. But when I arrived her eyes lit up as I squeezed her hot hand. I told her I had been praying for her… and that she must get better.

I meant it; suddenly for the first real time in my life I needed and understood my mother; the secret unborn child growing within me needed a loving grandmother and even now, at this early stage of my pregnancy there was a shared experience. Unusually for me, I felt soft and vulnerable….

Her fevered brow was shiny with sweat and she was almost too exhausted to speak. I dipped a towel into the bowl on the bedside dresser and gently cooled her pale forehead with it. Her hand was limp when I held it. Her raspy speech was almost inaudible. "Darling Aisling, you *need* God; pray more… Rory?"

"We're trying to find him Mother; he may be away from Dublin. He's been so busy I haven't seen him for a week or so. Now rest Mother, I'll be here with you." After a burst of coughing, she drifted off to sleep.

There was a nurse in attendance so she was in good hands. As I went downstairs I heard my father arrive back and I went outside to greet him. He was obviously extremely upset and worried about Mother's condition. His lined face was grim and there were dark circles under his eyes and his voice was harsh. "Where the hell's Rory? We can't find him anywhere in the city. This damned Republican nonsense… it'll wreck the country, mark m'words! Anyway, what the hell is my son actually *doing* for a living?"

He spoke unusually firmly, his eyes like granite: "And *you*, young lady, are going back to your studies full time now… *or* you're coming back to live here, and that's that! As for the wanted terrorist criminal you were kicking around with…I even brought him here for you and *that* has tainted us all. The authorities got wind of your relationship with him, but I managed to play that down… it even affected some business I had with them! Thank God he's on the run, probably left the country. I knew he'd be trouble; not in our league at all. My daughter mixed up with a brewery worker! We'd be laughing stock if society found out!"

Normally I would have effortlessly stood up to him and ranted back, arguing forcefully; indeed I could see he was braced, expecting me to do so. But I was tired and the situation I was in was completely overwhelming me. He had hit on the very key to my life, so how could I ever break the news of my pregnancy to him now? God knows what he'd do if I informed him when he was in this state…

I simply looked at him silently and then turned away and walked back upstairs. I was aware that he was astounded by my lack of reaction. *Good*, as far as I was concerned!

We barely spoke for the next week; meals were awkward, silent affairs. Day and night otherwise, I stayed by my mothers side. She rallied, her temperature eased, and although still weak, she especially lit up when Rory finally arrived back for a three day stay. He was tougher, stronger and much more confident than the brother I had known in the past. He stood up to Father and disdained him, which amazed the old man…bullying sarcasm and cruel comments had no effect on his son now whatsoever. Like me, Rory just ignored our father's outbursts. Eammon Kinnane's children were now beyond his control, and he could sense it!

There was one bad moment for me. I'd just finished breakfast when I felt a wave of morning sickness nausea coming; before I could control it, I vomited. Father rushed to help me, absolutely terrified that I may have also caught the flu', as that could be a symptom of its onset. He touched my brow to feel my temperature, I pretended to be off colour and went to lie down on my bed for an hour or two… he checked on me several times. I made sure my baby bump was hidden by my bedclothes.

After that his tone was more conciliatory and we at least communicated a bit; discussing local news, but studiously avoiding any contentious and therefore important topics. A bit of our former closeness returned in the next two days.

Mother, had overcome the worst, and although still weak, even tried to get up at one stage. Her spirit returned, she was now aware of everything going on around her. Rory's return had been a big rallying point for her, but she was sad when he left. The local priest had visited several times during her sickness which also lifted her outlook.

It was time for me to return to Dublin, and Father said he would take me in the car to Cobh to catch the train. I knew that he would want to discuss my future as his tone had become a little more reasonable. Oh God, how could I handle this?

65

Sky

Day followed boring day in my dull hidey-hole, yet Aisling didn't turn up. Something must be wrong! I had nothing else to really think about, so I worried incessantly about her. What could have happened? Could she be sick? Perhaps there was a problem with the baby! Surely she'd get a message to me… no, on second thoughts, she wouldn't risk my safety by doing so. I must wait for her.

In the past, I would have cheerfully gone out regardless, but my capture out west had graphically reminded me how vulnerable I was; so far I'd been bloody lucky, but I shouldn't push it!

About five days after I'd arrived I heard some welcome steps on the stairs outside. Through the peephole I saw it was Joe O'Reilly, Mick's sidekick, carrying a parcel. I opened the door.

"Pleased t'see y still here Weed! Mick wasn't sure y'd b' doin' what he'd told y' to! Y' colleen bought y' supplies but here's some more food. Y'll have to stay here a bit longer… there's a hell of a lot goin' on at the moment! So hang in here for a while. Oh an' he said to tell y' that Aisling had t' go home…went by train; someone in the family's sick….the flu'….might be her mother. Anythin' special y' need? …I gotta go!" He went off down the stairs.

How the hell did Mick know that Aisling had visited me here and had bought me food? After some thought it came to me. Of course, it was the lady downstairs with the loyalist pictures on the wall, who always seemed to studiously ignore comings and goings, but missed absolutely nothing! She'd told them I'd come back, after all…

So that was why I hadn't heard from my Love. She hadn't risked my safety by contacting me; she knew that her travel home would be noted by someone in our network. The flu' worried me though; her mother had been kind to me. I hoped Aisling wouldn't catch it. Our unborn child's life was at stake as well!

Alone I spent hours trying to work out what we should do; how we could marry and live together...

Through that viewing slot I longingly looked at the people outside who could freely go where they wanted; that was a dream existence to me now. The narrow sliver of sky I could see was again unsatisfying. I missed its blue vastness and above all the ever-changing, misty creatures that dwelt in her depths or should that be heights?

I waited....

Song

There was awkwardness about us in the car as we left the house for the railway station at Cobh that stormy morning. Father leant forward and slid the glass partition closed with a snap so Gilbert, our chauffeur, couldn't hear what was being said in the back. Behind us I noticed our black Ford was accompanying us.

Not a word was spoken for a few miles, a fact that seemed to help accelerate my morning nausea. I decided to concentrate on the scenery in an attempt to control it. At the back of my mind was the thought that it was not like father to hold back but I could sense a big discussion in the offing. Unusually, he was thinking carefully about how he was going to approach things. In a way I was doing the same...

I doggedly looked at the little white capped waves on the estuary, the grey storm clouds topping the low hills, which I knew Weed would have loved.... the smoke from cottage chimneys being whipped away by the stiff breeze. My old school by the bridge looked so tiny to me now... the adjoining grey church somehow fitted the landscape; ah, memories in stone now. How time changes us, I mused.

Then I saw Katie O'Halloran, an old schoolmate working in her parent's house garden. I waved as we passed; she waved back rather unenthusiastically; reminding me of my hatred of this limousine of excess. A friendly wave could be interpreted as a "look how rich I am" act....

Father cleared his throat, his tearful green eyes regarded me gravely; "Princess Aisling, we must not be afightin' now." He touched my face lightly. "I'm glad y'r came back for Mother, and y'r did a good job acarin' for her... it was touch 'n go when y' arrived, y'know. I really believe ye made *the* big difference, brave too; the damned disease is catching as we all know. Yes, I'm not much good at such times...but you obviously are. Thanks for all your efforts Aisling."

I looked at him, in a way I'd been surprised how much he'd been affected by Mother's close call. My harsh attitude to him softened; he seemed vulnerable at the moment. I involuntarily reached out and squeezed his hand,

"Only did what a daughter should, Father…" I murmured.

My mind started to race. Was this sudden closeness between us a good time to tell him of my pregnancy? He was going to find out sometime anyway. He didn't seem to notice I was not myself, not as self assured, or as argumentative as usual. But I did love him, faults and all. He was my dad after all… but learning that his daughter was with child? God, how would he react? I could tell him by telephone, from a distance… but that was cowardly. I braced myself. I *would* tell him now!

The car slowed as we entered the narrow windy section of road at the top end of the bay, trees swayed, cows and sheep huddled sheltering from the wind by the hawthorn hedges. We entered a sharp turn.

My heart fluttered impulsively. "Father, there's something I must tell you… I am…"

Suddenly, I was thrown forward as our car abruptly stopped. Blocking the road was a green farm lorry, piled high with hay. Father wound down his window and yelled, "Move that *bloody* wagon out of the way, *now*! We've a train t' catch."

Out of the hedges on both side of the road emerged four men armed with pistols and rifles….they were all wearing caps pulled down and had handkerchiefs tied around their faces, just like the cowboys in the movies; I was too surprised to be fearful. I looked through the back window, the Ford was also being held at gunpoint. Our chauffeur was forced out of our car, frisked for weapons then held at gunpoint. One of the ambushers found a pistol in the glove box.

Another figure peered into the car, a pistol pointing at us; he seemed to recognise my father. "He's here men. Eammon Kinnane, get out *now!*" he ordered rudely, ignoring me completely. My father climbed slowly out of the car sounding suddenly very conciliatory. "Now lads, I don't have that much cash on me… hardly worth arobbin' now…still, I could manage sixty pounds or so…" He reached for his wallet…

"Typical!" The fellow with the pistol snorted. In a loud voice he proclaimed. "Eammon Kinnane, for informing the British Authorities by letter, on one Aidan Duffey, and thereby subsequently causing the deaths of several people, you are hearby condemned t' death by the Irish Republican Army. There is absolutely no doubt about your act. Have you anything to say?"

I felt as if I'd been smashed in the face, My mind raced frantically, yes, my father *would* do that... so it was *he* who had suddenly destroyed our world, turning my love into a fugitive....bitter hatred welled up in my heart, overwhelming everything in my mind...

My father's tone was even and calm, trying vainly to get control of this situation. "Boys,... boys, what's all this nonsense about, then? Me daughter here and m'son are in y'r movement... I'm on *your* side, all the way...." he lied.

That weakness again: he'd hated us being in the movement from the beginning, yet here he was, lying to save himself!

Father suddenly realised that nothing he was saying was working and changed tack; "Well, only a few words on a piece of paper, when all is said and done; nothin' really at all, gentlemen." He'd actually *admitted* his guilt!

The pistol was fired at point blank range, the car windows on that side splattered in scarlet, through the open door, tiny splashes landed on the glass door of the drinks cabinet and began to run down to the carpet as his body crashed to the ground. Three more shots were fired; two more to the head, one to the heart. Through the open car door I could see the bloodied heap of my dead father lying on the gravel road.

My first reaction was silent shock, then a whirlwind of thought and emotion pounded my mind. Father had been *executed* right in front of me! I should have been screaming with upset... but the reason for his execution and the suddenness of it all, happening at just the very moment when I was wound up about breaking the news of my out of wedlock pregnancy to him! I dived out of the car falling heavily onto my father's body....I looked up.

One man had a rifle trained on me unwaveringly, his eyes above his mask showed intense loathing during all this. He only left me when an order was shouted out, and then they all ran off around the corner, including the two from The Ford behind us. They'd taken the weapons from our bodyguards and had tied them up. I heard a motor start and a vehicle drive off. Gilbert came to me, stepping around the corpse. He was pale and shaking, barely coherent.

Trembling fear began to take hold of my body; the pain of my fall on top of my morning sickness, it was all too much. I had never had experience of mortal violence at close hand; my father was a bloodied crumpled heap on the dusty road, silenced forever by death. My mother was weak from illness... how was she going to take this news? She also was aware of Rory's and my involvement in the Republican cause, the very assassins of her husband! It was all overwhelming; too much for even a strong person to bear.

I crawled back up into the vehicle and collapsed in shock on the blood splattered velvet rear seat in the car, my stomach churning as a crippling pain suddenly stabbed my lower abdomen, my legs felt wet, and even more blood flooded the carpet; I realised the quiet melody that had become such a part of my life *was silent!* Uncontrolled tears ran down my cheeks before a black emptiness welcomed me....

67

Sky

 After weeks of boring hiding, the news was astounding! Aisling had heard the details first and came to me with shining eyes; the first time that I had seen her so animated since the loss of our unborn child and the death and funeral of her father some weeks back.

Dev and the Dail, the Irish parliament, had wanted a direct armed confrontation with the British, against Mick's advice. Guerrilla tactics were the way to proceed as far as the 'Big Man' was concerned. But Dev went ahead anyway; the Custom's House in Dublin was openly attacked and burned, with a high loss of life and many captured on our side; a disaster as Mick had predicted all along. However such a blatant attack on a major target in the capital of Ireland may have ended up tipping the balance. After claiming for years that they had things under control in the country, this demonstrated that the enemy's position was weak at best… a decision was made by the British Government to negotiate a settlement.

A truce had been signed with the Brits, and both sides would cease hostilities, starting at noon the 11th of July 1921. Our side had been very close to collapsing, but the other side had finally worked out they couldn't win unless they threw a whole army at Ireland. Still bleeding and bruised from the so called Great War, there was no public stomach in Great Britain for that course of action. The Dublin Castle administration had wanted to carry on the fight, but they'd been overruled by London.

Of course any ceasefire would be a messy affair, especially on our side where all the semi-independent groups would be hard to bring into line… but everyone was exhausted so eventually it held. The Tans and Auxies, the RIC and army, withdrew to their barracks; our side stopped all action and set about secretly rearming. The bitterness on both sides remained, yet the uneasy calm continued.

It was bizarre and eerie how the killing on both sides stopped. News of deaths around the country had been a daily occurrence for so long now; peace was almost unsettling…

I had been on the run, in hiding for many months. I couldn't believe it when Aisling told me that my name had been mentioned on the Truce document, along with Mick's, MacEoin and others, some of whom had been released from British prisons. We were granted immunity! It took me a while to get used to the idea of freedom of movement. I did worry however about someone taking photos of me; if the fight should start again…. I waited two days before cautiously leaving my safe house. The truce was holding well, in fact much better than expected.

That first time I went out in public Aisling laughed at the way I kept looking behind me, and peering ahead for danger; it had become a reflex way of life for me.

Dublin was in a happy mood. There were no troops around, and the populace seemed light-hearted; they'd embraced the Truce wholeheartedly and spoke as if the war was actually already over.

Aside from being with Aisling in an open setting, my greatest joy was seeing the vast sky above, the heavens seemed infinite, the clouds vast and monstrous looked at from outside. In my various hidey holes I'd only had slivers of the sky visible to me.

Aisling's hair had gone back to auburn and was growing longer again, which I found more attractive.

We walked hand in hand, across the river and down the busy narrow streets to our favourite seat in St. Stephen's Green Park. The trees were clothed in bright green summer leaves; and yes our busy friends the squirrels were still there, chattering away. The little lake glimmered in the warm sun.

We had much to discuss. What was I going to do now? I must find a job somewhere.

But there was a slight concerning niggle; a vague misty cloud in my mind. Aisling had changed; this had been less evident when we had only snatched moments together. Or was I just imagining it? She seemed to be more reserved with me than she had been. The loss of our unborn baby and her father's execution of course affected her greatly. I didn't know how to tactfully broach either of these subjects.

Aisling wasn't aware that I knew her father had betrayed me to the Brits. Not wanting to embarrass her, I hadn't mentioned that fact to her. What was done was done. Anyway, come to think of it; was she aware of this? I knew Mick hadn't told her.

Despite this, our lovemaking had been fevered and desperate since her personal disasters; so perhaps she didn't know....

But now we could really relax and talk at length. Her face became almost ugly with distaste. "Weed, I cannot believe that we are actually negotiating with these *British animals!*" She spat the words out in disgust. "How can we even trust them to keep their word when they have repeatedly lied to us for hundreds of years?"

So this was only what was concerning her! I was secretly relieved...

I tried to be diplomatic. "Well at least it will give us time to build up again at worst... we were near our absolute limit. And it has given me my freedom, which is a big improvement! Besides, there comes a time when you have to negotiate. The cabinet is discussing a treaty negotiating team for our side to go to London at the moment. Dev will probably go, an' he'll wear 'em down with his never ending verbiage and papers."

Her eyes were steely. "It must be an *all* Ireland treaty, the *whole, complete damned island!* Nothing *less!* The murderous treatment Catholics are getting now in Ulster *must* cease."

I agreed with her and left it at that. I discussed our current predicament and what we should do. She was no longer working with Mick. Finally she was about to graduate with her Trinity College degree in Music.

I would contact Mick or members of our movement to try and find some employment. I must see if I could stay at my old home with Aunt Biddy. From what I had managed to learn, the neighbours were not blaming me for the fires and loss of property they had suffered.

I had not brought up the subject of marriage with Aisling. Sadly somehow, it didn't seem to fit the current state of our relationship.

We finally kissed and parted. Her intensity continued to worry me as I walked away; the clouds above suddenly seemed more shapeless and ill-defined to me at that moment....

Song

 I felt restless and unsettled as I left Weed and walked the two miles to my place. I saw little of my surroundings, the busy streets and shoppers became colourless and insignificant as I mused.

The bond and music of our love was still there, but the sound was quieter. I didn't like to admit it to myself, but he had changed in some way; life on the run had made him more careful and even conciliatory at times. I used to find his sometimes reckless immaturity of old a particularly attractive male quality. But now? He seemed willing to make compromises these days.

Of course I had changed too....the loss of our unborn baby was hauntingly ever present in my mind and Weed had also been devastated. Part of our closeness had died with the unknown creature. Weed hadn't mentioned marriage since my miscarriage and this lack hurt me, lessening my self belief, and irritating me even more…

Mick had not wanted me working for him after my father's death. And that was another thing; I was present at the time of his execution and had heard why the sentence of death had been passed. Dad had betrayed Weed to the British. Was my love aware of this fact? I didn't even feel I could discuss this with him; I was so humiliated and ashamed of this betrayal. Had Mick ordered the hit? That would be why he did not want me working for the organization now…

On reflection, I didn't feel my father's death as much as I should have. His funeral was a rather grand affair that he would have approved of; but I only went through the motions. I could *not* forgive his betrayal. Nora didn't like *that* at all.

Mother had responded to the loss by immersing herself in religion even more. The family businesses were being run by my uncles and aunts…so she had little else to do. Rory and I were away and the estate essentially ran itself.

I sighed to myself deeply; how had my life changed so suddenly? I felt heavy and listless, but anger was swelling in my very being… why had life conspired against me so unfairly? I felt resentful and bitter at all and sundry…

Nora would have none of it! Her face and eyes were impatient and scornful.

"*Silly* colleen, what's t matter with ye now? Y've still got y' *love,* an' *food* aplenty on y' table…an' ye' still athinkin' y' hard done by! Hmmph! Life can be a lot worse, believe me… I'll be ashowin' ye, f'sure… T' squirrels, bless their lil souls tasted *ver'* g'd! Much better than t' rats we caught by t' privy….'s all we c'ld get tho'. But then theys w's gone too…rats need food as well; t'was none around…"

I nearly vomited at the thought; eating rats caught near an outside toilet! But Nora obviously knew nothing of germs and modern hygiene. If I was starving to death would I do the same? I asked myself shuddering at the very notion.

"Several other families on t' estate is died. Also many deafs on other lands that Mister Morrison… didn't 'fect. But he made it reach us sooner, *t'devil:* I loaths tha' man! We'se spent some o' t' rent money on food; very *'spensive* now, but me dad said, we'se not b' needin' a home an' farm if wese all *dead*! Other families 'as rellies in other countries whose sends 'em money; wese not sos lucky…an' *we* don' 'ave enuff money for t' family t' go overseas, likes some. Wese trapped 'ere!"

From my reading of the period I knew that in the 17th and 18th centuries the penal laws in Ireland forbade Catholics, about eighty percent of the population, from owning or leasing land, gaining an education or joining a profession… even living in a town was discouraged! Low level tenant farming was all that was left for most folk and the famine situation I was witnessing had grown out of this unfair, entrenched discrimination.

The history had told me that at this time, in the midst of the biggest famine, an average of forty to fifty ships of food, mainly grains and livestock, were leaving Ireland each day, often under armed guard in the worst affected areas, to stop starving Irish from trying to access it.

The British Government tended to think that the Irish always exaggerated problems in the country and therefore were slow to act. Also, because of the Corn Laws, taxes that made food expensive; grains of any kind couldn't be economically imported. The British Government did not lessen these tariffs significantly until the May 1846 "repeal" of these. It was to be three more years after that before they were completely removed; too late for the hundreds of thousands of victims of the famine......possibly over a million; the total number is still in dispute.

Ireland was ruled from London; a local parliament would have acted decisively. My poor friend Nora had only a limited understanding of the causes of the turmoil she was immersed in; but she knew of the effects at first hand....

69

Sky

For some weeks, our relationship continued to idle along; still neither of us brought up the subject of marriage. We were still close, but things were somehow different. I can't remember when the wispy cloud of doubt first appeared in my mind… her love was almost too total I suddenly reasoned to myself… there was an air of desperation about it; not that I minded… but it was an increasing concern. Was it normal to be so intense? I began to notice her political views likewise were growing in a blind fanatical way… no mere shade of grey was allowed to soften her outlook; yet I still loved the creature fiercely.

The variation in her moods began to concern me. She would slide from deep fury to placid calm in an instant. It was all very worrying….

Negotiations had taken place in England. Dev had refused to go in the end, so Mick had gone in his place. After much argument and dissention a treaty had been finally signed; it was less than perfect, but it would mean peace for us, now. The six counties of Ulster had been left out, there would be an Irish Free State of twenty six counties, but there were other annoying conditions, some merely symbolic.

A vote was taken in the Dail on acceptance of the treaty. The result was close, 64 votes in favour, 57 against. A walkout of Dev and his followers had been a shattering event. As Mick said in his speech during the debate, "the Treaty gives us a chance of freedom to obtain freedom in time."

Yet, in some quarters, Mick and Arthur Ashe were being vilified for signing the document, Dev was particularly venomous in his criticism of his former comrades. Politcal stability in the country appeared elusive….

I was a true patriot locked into the movement and striving for our success; hell, I'd killed for it after all; but like Mick I was a realist… flexibility and cunning yes, but ultimately compromise was needed if the movement was to succeed in gaining our independence as a country. I had grown rapidly older and wiser as our struggle against the British had progressed. I realised how near a thing it had been when the truce had been called. Our outnumbered forces had been tired, at the very limit of all our resources; arms, and physical wellbeing. We'd also become emotionally depleted.

But Aisling was so staunch and fixed so intensely on the idea of the mythical Republic that I again began to wonder if this transcended normality. Despite her great house and wealth she followed that line; her family's beginnings had been low but somehow they'd dragged themselves out of that perennial Irish morass of poverty.

Aisling's bloody-mindedness was a very Irish quality after all, but still she worried me. She was backing Dev and those fanatical republicans…

The auburn hair quivered and glowed with anger. Her usually pristine face was intense and even strange; distorted and grotesque with emotion, her green eyes stormy. She spat out: "How the hell could Mick agree to this *"Free"* State nonsense? Even agreeing to accept using the bloody British king as nominal head of our state….. what sort of freedom is *that*? Not to mention the northern counties not being included. It's giving in to the enemy…that's what it is!"

I didn't answer her immediately; something that annoyed her, I was sure; usually I loved the spontaneous banter, humour and arguments we regularly had. It was a big part of our relaxed warm togetherness, the creature our love had become. But here I was worn out with the pressure of events and hesitating, trying to select my words carefully. She didn't like that at all.

"As Mick has said the treaty is only a stepping stone to full independence and the cursed Brits themselves know full well that we don't mean to fulfil the allegiance to the king nonsense; it was only a face-saving clause put in by them to compensate for the fact that they'd given away so much…"

Aisling jammed her face in mine and spat at me in disgust. "Go to hell you dammed *traitor*!"

Her hot spittle cooled as it ran down my face. I was so surprised at this ugly, strange being that had suddenly materialised from the one I most worshipped in my world, I flinched as she spun round and stalked off… it was the end of our togetherness. Stunned and empty hearted, I sadly watched her leave me…

The sky of life is forever blending and flowing; change is the norm and in my long experience, the clear settled blue seldom stays long; fleeting ephemeral visits are more her style. A slight dullness and lack of clarity usually herald deteriorating weather. So it was with my love; the crystal aching warmth was still there all right, but a slight hint of doubt had levered its sneaky way into my mind....

Mick had said at the end of the Treaty negotiations that he had "signed his death warrant" when he agreed to the terms. That turned out to be true, in more ways than he had predicted, -it had also been the death warrant for Aisling's and my relationship...

Song

Losing Weed was bad, but knowing I had been the cause of that loss made it worse; the pain in his eyes haunted me. Even though he lingered in my thoughts every waking moment, the music in my head was quieter, but it was *still* present. But I would *not* back down!. In my saddest, emptiest moment, I knew in my heart I still loved him; and that I, too, still dwelt in *his* mind, no matter what! But my future days would now be empty....

Nora frowned when she came to me. Incomprehension and impatience were etched on her young, wasted face. As usual, she brushed her hair back from her tearful eyes; my breakup with Weed had astounded and puzzled her. She opened her mouth to speak several times, but saw the defiant look on my face as I braced myself for a well deserved dose of down to earth criticism. But after a long silence she merely mumbled:

"I'm athinkin' seein' m' worse days'll help yer get fings in real 'spective Aisling. There's nuffin' else I'll b' asayin' t' ye, 'cept, sadly; wese is more alike than ye think! My *biggest* secret, 't is! Your t' firs' person Ise ever tol' ! "

The ragged teenager stumbled down the dirt road clutching a gnarly walking stick, an empty sack on her bony shoulder ... her rough brown shawl was wrapped tightly around her head, which searched from side to side for anything to eat as she went along. She found nothing; too many of the starving had come this way.

The evening was cold; the western sky contained a long low streak of setting sun, a wild orange and red fading beauty which Nora didn't see. Above, the cloudy sky was sombre; tomorrow it might rain. In the black distance were some faint lights; buildings of some kind. Sly tendrils of damp chilling fog slid off the estuary and began to soften the scene and muffle the noises of the night: the soft murmur of the wind in the trees, an owl call, and the distant lapping of waters. Her scraping laboured steps seemed loud in the gloom.

Nora came upon a large brown cowpat in the middle of the dirt road. I couldn't believe it when she hitched up her skirt and buried both her bare feet deep into the brown mound, a look of rapture on her haggard face.

"Swarm 'n wonderful an' nice 'n squelchy!" She breathed. "T' road's chilly t'nigh; me toes is *achin'*." She paused for a full minute before regretfully resuming her grimly determined walk.

The tiny stone church was simple and plain, its crucifix tipped spire seemed to tower above the small bent figure. It was closed. Nora looked over the wall at the little graveyard around it. Even in the darkness it was possible to see that there had been much activity there, the muddy soil was disturbed and several gaping graves were awaiting more victims of the hunger. Nora shuddered, blessed herself hurriedly and moved on.

"I knows I shouldn't b' athinkin' this way Aisling, but I wonders a bit 'bout God these days…g'd folks is dyin', rich folks 'ave lots of food; 'snot fair at all!'"

Next to the church was a house with light shining through the curtained windows. Two horses, were tied up to a rail behind, munching on some hay.

"S' priest's house, no dogs 'ere, Ise ahopin' !" she whispered reverently as she quietly let herself through the gate and crept up to the lighted window. She pressed her covered head against the wall and listened intently…

"Ah, *He's* here…. talkin' wit t' Father! Ortho' I don' unnerstan' why a man of t' church would be atalkin' t' *im!* They's not eatin', jus' drinkin'. *Good!*" She added rather cryptically.

Nora came away and set out at a faster pace down the road through the village towards the Big House. Her breathing became laboured as she forced herself along. She spoke to me through gasps…

"Ise an idea t'save m' family, at least fors a while… G'd rest m' soul!" she said with grim single mindedness, voice grating with emotion.

She sneaked up to a sizeable house just inside the entrance. Its windows were lit behind the curtains.

"Ise been 'ere twice before t' pay t' rent when Mister Morrison was sick….. 'ees got no dogs either, bu' up at t' Big House theys really *giant* ones!" Nora shivered at the thought.

After pressing her ear against the front door, she quietly tried the handle and the unlocked door opened. She stealthily entered the dark hall, silently closing the door behind her and went through into the parlour. Cooking noises could be heard from the kitchen at the back of the house, but it was the cooking smells that stole her attention…*food!* Nora got herself under control and eased the door to, behind her.

"This is 'is parlour. He eats in 'ere, I'se seen t'grand table afore. 'Ee's so *rich!!* S'lovely 'n warm in 'ere, too"

Knowing how simply she lived, I could understand why she would be so impressed….

Nora warily warmed her hands then her feet by the fire of coal that was glowing red and white in a small fireplace. She picked up a shiny black lump. "Ooh, I've heard of this!" She explained knowledgeably. "Dis mus' b' coal; lots 'n lots 'o heat in a small amount of stuff, but *really* 'spensive, an' messy!" She looked at her blackened hand, and wiped it clean on her skirt.

Nora shook herself as if remembering she had things to do. There was a small table covered with a white linen table cloth, gleaming silver cutlery and a single candlestick which flickered, throwing grotesque shadows of my friend onto the walls and curtains of the room.

An empty crystal wineglass and bottle of uncorked red wine stood beside it. Nora looked around and listened; low noises were continuing to come from the kitchen. She quickly took out of a skirt pocket a tiny bottle, wrinkling her nose as she poured a little pale liquid into the glass. It had a sharp parsnip-like smell, so she added some of the red wine from the bottle … and sniffed it.

"Tha's better…… 'ee won't notice it now, I'ma 'oping…"

There was the sound of a horse pulling up outside. Nora dived behind the full length window curtain behind the table and froze, holding her breath with a pounding heart.

The front door banged open and large heavy steps came down the hall.

"My meal now, Mrs Houlahan!" Mr. Morrison called out rudely down the hall as he entered the room, discarding his coat and leather satchel on to the couch. He then sat down and pulled off his long boots. His housekeeper entered with a plate of roast beef and vegetables, which she placed carefully on the table, between the knife and fork. He wrinkled his nose in distaste.

"Good, now put these boots outside will you, they stink, an clean 'em tomorrow morning; I must have trodden in some cow muck somewhere, the whole damn room reeks of it!"

Nora hiding behind the curtain…looked down at her grubby feet; it was *she* he was smelling!

"I will do so Mister Morrison…" The housekeeper's old grey face was wary.

"After that, off you go for the night…. *Hold it!*" He looked at the table. "How many times must I tell ye? Just uncork the bottle and let the wine get to room temperature. Why've y' put some in the glass woman?"

Out of sight Nora cringed in fear…..

"I *didn't* sir!" his housekeeper indignantly tried to reply.

"Damned Irish, the most feckless, *unreliable* race on earth…. No doubt been helping y'self to it …." He reached out for the bottle and held it up to the candle… and then looked at the glass; deciding that probably none had been taken. "Mmm, maybe not. Get off home, *now!*"

Mrs. Houlahan moved with alacrity, as she picked up the boots and left the room. A minute later, the back door opened and closed as she left for the night.

He smelt the bottle, relaxed and put it down on the table. He drained the whole glass in one gulp, refilled it again and tucked into his meal. On his second mouthful of food he gasped and gagged; he was having some difficulty breathing… his limbs trembled and then froze.

In my head Nora's voice was counting. When she reached sixty she came out from behind the curtain and went to the couch, ignoring the Land Agent, who seemed unable to move; only his strangely dilated eyes followed her in impotent horror. He tried to open his mouth to scream, but couldn't…

Nora unfastened his satchel and took out the hated leather bound rent record book, and the receipt booklet. Opening them she looked at page after page of neat figures and copperplate writing; but upside down. Of course, why hadn't I clicked before? My friend and distant relation was *illiterate!*

She spoke: "So much work 'n pain is 'n 'ere Aisling; all t'em needy families! T' rent wuz t' devil's curse, fr us poor folks!"

Making sure Morrison could see her; Nora put the books into the fire, her face lit up with smiling satisfaction as it flared. She stirred it with the poker till nothing remained She felt into the satchel again and came up with the rent purse…it was quite heavy with coins. She took a third of them, pocketed these and then carefully put the purse back in the satchel, closed it and replaced it on the couch. She went over to the frozen figure and spoke to him. His strange eyes followed her…

"Ise t' oldest Missa Morrison, an' I love m' family; m' job's t'look after 'em; they's sick with hunger now!

"You's tried t' *poison* us.... So's, *Ise* poisoned *you!* Y' won't be abullying cottage folk again.....you's *dead* soon! Hemlock n' deadly nightshade yous drunk.....but theys wont find a trace, once I wash t' glass an' put wine fr t' bottle in it. See's, I've bin cunning... t' bottle is clean; t' poison was only in t'glass an' you drunk it 'n one go!"

She went with the glass to the kitchen rinsed it carefully, returned to the parlour and added some wine to it, till it was only half full, leaving it near his frozen right hand.

Nora ate a third of the food on his plate...her eyes closed in delight. "I c'n feel d' yummy henergy aflowin' in me!" she gushed, regretfully leaving the remainder.

"Like t' money Missa Morrison. Got t' look natural like! Den no-one'll suspec'...apoisinin' or arobbin'. Y' 'ousekeeper didn' put wine in yer glass, *I* did........ Yous wrong Missa, Irish folks is clever an' cunning....an' very 'liable! But Ise hopes, y' go t' *'ell, y' devil!*"

Avoiding the temptation to strike her helpless victim, she left him, after carefully checking to make sure everything looked undisturbed. She added more coal to the fire. Her voice spoke to me.

"That'll lessen me stink in t' parlour, Aisling. Now, I mus' find some more food fr me family."

She went down the hall to the kitchen...

In the well stocked larder she helped herself to a small amount of food and placed it all in the sack, along with a small paper bag of flour taken from the back of a pile of them. It shouldn't be missed for a while. She left the kitchen, exactly as she'd found it. As Nora walked down the hall, she saw a bedroom door, partially open and couldn't resist the urge to look in... as she swung the door open, she was confronted by a dark figure peering back at her! Nora nearly shrieked but then realised she was seeing herself in a gigantic looking glass! She froze for a minute quite shamed, tears streaming down her cheeks. She lowered her shawl from her head, and peered at herself.

"I'se looks so dirty, skinny an' 'orrible.....no' pretty at all! An now Ise a *murderer* an' *thief* too."

She had to drag her eyes off the image, gather herself together and check the parlour. Mister Morrison was dead; his head hung sideways, his eyes lifeless. His tongue was protruding from his open mouth. She closed his eyelids then left the house stealthily. No one was around, good! She moved into some shrubs and paused, listening to the night.

"Ma an' me granma tol' me about t 'emlock an' nightshade...hows theys was poisonous an' everythin'. Wese always learnin' about all t' plants in our lil' forest...

"Anyways, Ise is 'opin' we'll get a month or two more o' livin', now." She felt the weight of the sack....and touched the coins in her pocket; "tho' I needs even *more* food... " Her voice had a ruthless, desperate quality I'd not heard before.

She started as she heard a horse and cart coming down the road. It looked like a delivery van of some kind, with two men riding at the front. It was near midnight, so why at this hour?

Nora knew... "Ise heard, theys is deliverin' t' food fr t' Big Houses late a' night now, deres so many desprit starving folk on t' road! Scared o' us stealin' it. No' very *Christian,* dese greedys rich folk!"

She followed the cart, hugging the dark vegetation at the side of the drive, blending into the shadows....

"Thos' monster dogs is *terrifyin'*..... I hopes theirs kennels is in the same place as las' time I was 'ere. I must get more for t' family..." Nora told me as she bravely crept towards the Big House. She gripped her heavy stick in case she needed to use it as a weapon to protect herself. The cart went to the back of the building following the drive. Nora looked at the smoking chimneys, saw which way the wind was blowing then crept around the other side. Sneaking across the lawn, from shrub to shrub in the darkness, she peered round the corner. There was a burst of loud deep barking and the crash of heavy chains, as the dogs reacted to the food van. The horse whinnied loudly; he was spooked by the dogs too. Nora flinched in fear; but the two Irish wolfhounds were chained up.

"G"d. They's thinkin' it's t' horse an' t'men is 'sturbin t' dogs."

She saw the two men get down, joined by someone from the house, who yelled at the dogs to settle down. It seemed to have little effect; the barking continued. The men started to unload boxes of food, one up on the back, one taking the boxes inside through the back door. Downwind, Nora put her sack and stick down then crept as close as she dared.... her heart pounding. She took in a really deep breath...waiting for a chance.

Then some whole cloth-covered sides of mutton and pork were unloaded. One big bundle was so heavy; both men had to carry it to the house and through the door....

As quick as she could, Nora dashed out of the darkness, quickly leapt up onto the van, grabbed a small cloth bundle from the back, jumped down and ran back into the darkness carrying her heavy prize. The dogs erupted anew....*they'd seen or smelt her!* The men had returned and would have spotted the flying dark figure, but the hounds violently crashing their chains and barking distracted them; they were afraid of the beasts too....

Nora picked up her stick and put the white cloth bundle into her sack; it was now satisfyingly heavy. She was shivery and exhausted, but triumphant as she sneaked off into the darkness. The food she'd eaten at the land agent's house had given her "*henergy*" as she'd called it, all right!

"T'night's Aisling Ise is brave as can be!! Lots o' food for t' family....I'ma thinkin' t'big one is pork. Wese'll b' eaten like rich folks fr a day or two! " She grimaced. " Bu' me toes is still achin' ! "

She made good time, the mist had settled cold and thick on the land, but Nora was gleeful and warmed by her success, though still watchful as she made her way through the darkness. The world seemed empty....no-one had seen her! She felt clever.....though she didn't cross herself as she passed the church....instead she looked guiltily away from it.....which was her undoing...

Without any warning, a dark male figure loomed up from behind the wall of the graveyard; she just caught a glimpse before his swinging staff hit her hard on the back of the head. A shower of stars and Nora crashed heavily, facedown on the road...

She gained consciousness, alone, just before daybreak, her head splitting. Everything, the food sack, coins, and even the poison bottle were all gone. Sobbing at her failure.... She staggered her way back home to her family, her tearful face contorted with self-pity.

"Ise done m' best Aisling....*really* tried s' hard. But t' Lor' 'elp us all now.... an' cos' of all this, Ise is goin' t' *'ell for murder an atheivin'! An'* t' find t' money an' poison bottle, 'ee must 'ave been *agropin'* around in me skirt, while I was out to it!" She shivered at the very thought....

I knew that the famine had dramatically changed the social climate in Ireland; overwhelming hunger had driven desperate people to extremes. The roads were full of starving families, who had nothing to lose and all to gain by petty crime. Desperation clung to the very landscape with a rigid grip.

As the scene faded Nora's voice said calmly:

"Nex' time I'll b atellin' ye somethin' more 'bou' this, Aisling...."

71

Sky

Inside me was this nagging emptiness; Aisling's love for me had been obliterated by misfortune and her fanatical, unrealistic views. Her father's assassination had been a complete surprise for me too; although I was in two minds about that. But no, she always held her views with a blind, rather irrational passion. I'd learned to admire that aspect of her character, extremes; all or nothing was her way of seeing the world.

I was surprised to learn through the grapevine that she was doing some medical training. Why this sudden interest?

I waited outside a Dublin hospital one day where I'd heard she was attending courses and caught a glimpse of her as she left. My heart leapt but I didn't try to speak to her, knowing it would be hopeless. My attachment to her still dominated me, but my skies seemed empty; full of shapeless grey overcast…

Meanwhile, I had gone back to work with Mick again as he tried to bring the new country into life. Going back to a humdrum, clerical job after my exciting wartime existence did not appeal.

To begin with we were a rather makeshift force, quite under armed. Our new green uniforms heralded the arrival of a new order. We Irish were at last running the majority of our counties. The British had handed Dublin Castle over to us and were vacating most of their bases throughout the south. But our government was split into many factions, to a surprising degree.

Arguments, name calling, posturing; former strong allies in a brutal struggle were falling out… and fragmentation weakened the government and slowed the pace of recovery.

Most of the Irish population just wanted to get on with their lives in peace… and couldn't work out what the hell was going on. They found the situation annoying.

The walkout of my love had been similarly crushing; a realignment of my emotional universe.

Some weeks later, I heard indefinite rumours that Aisling had gone out west and had joined the rebel Anti-Treaty side in Kerry; then, nothing. She had just vanished....

Song

 My heart broken and without the love of my life, the music in my very being faded to an indistinct, unhappy murmur, shrouded by my towering anger. Was it normal to be so *bloody-minded* I briefly asked myself? But I smothered that doubt, in relentless, monumental determination. I *would* fight for the Republic! But how could I do this? Women would only have typically secondary roles in the fight. There had been one recent exception; the Countess Markievicz, who had fought on the side of the rebels in the 1916 uprising. I *would* do the same, even if it killed me…

Michael Collins no longer wanted or needed me; my father's treachery had guaranteed that. Anyway, he was now working setting up and running the new government in Dublin, forming the New State Army. Could I ever work again for the people who were forming a *quasi British* government in my land?

Starting with the truce, there had been an uneasy peace in Ireland, after years of bitter turmoil; intelligence was a backwater at the moment. Although, I heard somewhere that the IRA were continuing to bring in weapons from the US, and from any other place it could obtain them. It seemed at least they might fight on; so that was where I must go!

Mick had signed the damned treaty agreement that had sold out the republican ideal to the Brits, even eventually accepting the idea of us swearing allegiance to their cursed king….. what a colossal, traitorous *sell-out*! Then there was the loss of the north eastern counties, including Belfast, where terrible atrocities by the protestant majority were taking place daily against us Catholics. I was incensed and wrathful; bitterness welled up within me.

Another upset was my stupid younger brother Rory, who was in favour of the Treaty. I had discovered that he had been a member of the "Squad", Mick's paid professional assassination team for several years and was one of the 'Big Man's' many loyal followers. No wonder he'd toughened up…

I decided the only way I could initially enter the fight would be by the traditional route. I had completed my music studies at Trinity College and was free.

I undertook first aid and nursing courses and in my usual way became proficient quite quickly. When I worked at a hospital voluntarily, I found the sight of blood, broken bones and injuries did not upset me at all. In fact I rather enjoyed the work. One day as I left the hospital I experienced a sudden burst of music. I looked around me but couldn't see Weed anywhere.....

While I was learning on the medical front, the Provisional Government did nothing for some weeks when anti-treaty rebels took over the Four Courts in Dublin as a protest.

I left for West Cork and Kerry, areas which were staunchly anti-treaty. I eventually tracked down an IRA column near Tralee, the small town I'd visited to see that doctor. I offered them my services in the coming conflict. I was taken to the commandant, a short man, dressed in a tweed coat and cap that was pulled down, partially obscuring his features. His manner was doubtful and wary. His organization was taking over courts, barracks and outposts in the county, in conflict with the Treatyites, but so far little real bloodshed had occurred, horrendous verbal spats and occasional blows were traded regularly as the two sides argued and postured for control.

The Commandant doubtfully eyed my dark sensible skirt, jacket and walking shoes, then frowned

"So you'll be atinkin' there's a fight comin' now then?" He thoughtfully stroked his unshaven chin and looked at me suspiciously with flinty eyes. He didn't like the fact that I was taller than him, *and* a woman. I sensed I'd have to be careful and a little diplomatic here.

"I do!"

"Notin' much 'as been ahappenin' yet… so why?"

"*They* won't give up the damned Treaty and we won't give up the Republic or make concessions! I know for a fact that Collins is under great pressure from the Brits to attack the IRA in the Four Courts. They'll use heavy artillery too, there and at the other buildings he knows you'll occupy. It will be 1916 all over again in a few days, but this time it'll be the Irish themselves doing it. Mick's held off, trying to come to some reconciliation with you boys; but that won't come; both sides are too far apart."

The suspicious eyes watching me intently narrowed "Y' seem *too* well informed for a *woman*. What the hell would y'be knowin' about Michael Collins then?"

It was hard to break a promised oath of confidence, but my old boss had sold out on the Republican ideal, and knowing our chief enemy well might help me. "I worked with him closely for many years on the intelligence side. I could be of value to you there. But where I could really help your cause is as your medical officer, sir. I have even brought some supplies with me." I indicated my second suitcase.

There was a pause as he thought.

"All very well; but could you be akeepin' up with us? We move fast, and cover great distances on foot, up mountains at times and in all weathers. We'll not be awantin' a blasted *woman* to slow us down.... "

"I wont be a hindrance, I promise! I'll dress in men's clothes and I'm not short of courage. I'll look after m'self. "

He paused, "Mmm, I'll think about it. Stay at Regan's Hotel, 'til I get back to ye…"

The very next day, news came from Dublin. Exactly as I had predicted, the civil war had finally broken out, artillery had been used and the whole situation had deteriorated. Already fighting between the two sides was occurring throughout the country. Arguments and squabbles had abruptly turned into a shooting war.

The knock on my door was hurried. When I opened it a young messenger told me to get my things together and come immediately. I was to join the flying column! He had an empty khaki knapsack that I quickly loaded my supplies and clothing into. I also changed into trousers, jacket and a cap that I stuffed my long hair under. We left at a rush.

Things moved quickly as we went to ground in some southern mountains. First, on the way in a dramatic isolated glen, I, with a few other newcomers had to swear the IRA oath. It was a very dramatic, solemn occasion. As a woman in a group of men I tried to keep to myself. Eventually I was more or less accepted, although I think they moderated their language somewhat in my presence. I didn't encourage any gallantry, but a few of the men tried.

To protect me I was given a medical officer's status; which also helped set me apart a bit. To begin with I found trousers quite a pain to wear in warm weather. My legs always felt too hot and constricted! In the cold however they were a godsend! My one concession to femininity was my hair which I'd let grow long again. Washing it whenever I could was a nuisance, drying it afterwards always seemed to take forever. But I would *not* cut it. I kept it in a tight bun.

Nora ignored my current activity. Her confiding face was again tearful. "Ise was goin' t' tell ye Aisling, I was ahearin' a few 'ungry days later, tha' t' man what 'it me by t' church, was caught that night by t' constables b'fore 'ee got t' food t' *'is* family....theys found t' money *an'* t'poison.

When Mista Morrison was found suddenly dead, theys linked it t' 'emlock in t' little bottle.... He also 'ad t' food stolen from t' Land Agent's larder.... so theys hung *'im* for t' murder! So Ise two deaths on m' soul now. Yous is t' only person t' know all this horrible stuff 'bout me.....I aint tol' *anyone* else, friend."

She left me feeling for her, the sheer weight of her guilt was overwhelming; the poor creature, yet in the end, it had all been for nothing.

73

Sky

Mick was stressed. I was working alongside him in the same way as I had in the past. His job had changed; with Arthur Griffith he was now almost working full time on the political side, trying to mould factions into a workable government. Former comrades had turned against him… Dev being the most prominent and he was very influential. Mick could achieve nothing there.

The worst time came when the Republicans or Anti-Treatyites, as we now called them, occupied several buildings in Dublin, including the Four Courts, armed to the teeth. For weeks, despite monumental pressure from the British, and less patient factions on our side, Mick tried to negotiate a peaceful settlement, to no avail. He was loath to attack former comrades… but eventually had to do so, when he realized that Irish independence was on the line. Characteristically, once he did, he went all the way.

On the 28th of June 1922 Michael Collins gave the orders and the Civil War started. The Free State forces used heavy weapons, 28pounder field guns, machine guns and armoured cars to attack rebel or Anti Treatyite positions. The Four Courts were heavily shelled……it was 1916 all over again, except that it was Irish fighting Irish! It went on for some days…. We couldn't believe how few casualties there were considering how much shelling and gunfire there had been. The Republicans had suffered; eleven or so killed, our side had lost just six. In total, there were seventy people killed and two hundred and seventy four wounded; again civilians had suffered the most. The battle for Dublin was over, the streets and many buildings were badly damaged, some completely destroyed. Now the fighting would move to other cities in the country. Limerick would be next and then Cork…

Mick was worn out; he confided in me…… "Superior weaponry did it for us Weed; nothing else. Our new Nationalist Army has a hell of a long way to go! It shouldn't have taken us so long to do the job here in the city. Now I've got some funerals t' go to….even one or two for old comrades on the other side. Let's face it, their own lot can't show their faces at the services or we'd bag 'em, and damned quick at that! Someone should turn up for them!" He did have a sense of loyalty to those he'd fought alongside against the British. He never mentioned the fact that he would be at great risk of assassination himself during these ceremonies. "God preserve us Weed; this is really going to be vicious, so be very careful!"

His warning was timely…. Should I continue to stay with my Aunt Biddy while there were still enemy elements in Dublin?

Amy and her Mum had bravely offered to put me up….. but people in the lane would notice and talk. No I must find accommodation elsewhere. I couldn't put these people at risk again. Our movement; I should now say the new *Government*, would help me out.

Song

It was our column's first real skirmish with the provisional government's pro-treaty troops. At sunrise we'd been caught mining a road, to stop the enemy's troops travelling in the area. A firefight had erupted; bullets were flying around everywhere. Ned, a new young recruit lying prone in front of me, got hit in the shoulder. As guerrilla fighters we tried not to become involved in prolonged actions, hit and run was our style of warfare. The signal for a withdrawal was given but I would not leave my wounded comrade behind, despite the whining bullets around us. Seeing me staying behind, two others also came back and helped me drag Ned back to shelter in some trees, where I quickly stemmed the blood flow and applied a dressing. We then managed to get him back into the forest.

Commandant Kelly was angry that the withdrawal had been temporarily ignored, but I had proved myself under fire and my care turned out to be successful; Ned's wound healed quite quickly, and one of our doctors later approved of my treatment. In the past we had sometimes been forced to leave wounded to the enemy's mercy. The other members of the crew began to see me as a real asset.

A lot of our time was spent training with our weapons and learning tactics as we roamed around our territory. I started to show an interest in this. As I told our chief I should be armed in battle. There was always a perennial shortage of weapons, rifles I found too long and heavy, I simply wasn't strong enough to hold one steady, but a pistol I learnt how to use, though I was not a good shot. I couldn't really practice as we were always short of ammunition. After several actions an extra revolver was captured and this became mine.

Then one red letter day, with some other conventional weapons we were given a small wooden box that had come from America with a brand new Thompson machine gun in it. This was reverently lifted out, and inspected minutely by the men. When I finally managed to get a chance to touch it, I found it surprising light and handy, its short length and front grip seemed perfectly natural to hold, despite the fact it fired quite large 45 calibre bullets. With the lighter, smaller 100 round magazine fitted I felt I could handle it with confidence. Of course only our top marksman would be allowed to use it in battle, but anyway, I got its guardian Keeley to show me how everything worked, how blockages were dealt with…he was quite prepared to show off to a woman! I reasoned that as the stock could be removed, making it even smaller to carry, I would be able to secretly carry one under a skirt! But of course I could never hope to fire it. A brief trial firing by Keeley was very impressive, a staccato rattle, harsh music to our ears. Short bursts at a time were the way it was to be used. The magazine could empty in just a few seconds otherwise!

The war became more heated and nasty. We kept moving, striking then abruptly covering great distances, rarely staying in one place for any length of time. Being unpredictable was vital and kept us alive and viable as a fighting unit. Things had been more straightforward when we'd fought the British; lines had been clearly drawn then. But here we were fighting our former comrades who knew us and our methods and hiding places well; vicious reprisals and hatred flared everywhere, and a resentful segment of the population would inform on our activities and whereabouts to the new government in Dublin. That pillar of the nation, the Irish family, was under threat as members within, took opposing sides. As in fact had happened in mine; my *stupid* brother Rory was fighting for the other side… the Dublin Government was using the Squad against us out here in the west; incorporating these killers into the Dublin Guard Regiment.

As the medical officer I was always kept in the background during any action… but things had got more heated and confused as the enemy had increased their presence here in Kerry. They were even employing some exBritish Army officers and troops, a point which our side used to great effect in our propaganda. This proved perfectly how traitorous their green uniformed army was. Hatred simmered and boiled within me continually…suppressing those persistent thoughts of Weed that would arise from time to time.

Just like the British had done, the Dublin Government's troops were concentrated in fortified "islands" from which they would sally forth to find us.

Even the Catholic Church had come out against us Republicans and had declared from the pulpit, that the Government in Dublin was legitimate…and we were sinners who could be excommunicated from the church for carrying on the fight. Some of our men still worshipped when they could, risking being denounced from the pulpit. Some priests were on our side however and would secretly help us.

It happened about six weeks after I joined our column. We had decided rather unusually to attack one of the Free State army's barracks, breaking the basic tenet of guerrilla warfare. We needed the weapons and ammunition and above all the food stored within the fort. Our anti-transport campaign had been almost *too* successful, Kerry was suffering a small famine, all arms of the rail system had been affected. To stop the enemy getting food and supplies, we had targeted bridges and infrastructure which meant farmers could not get their produce to towns or to their traditional markets, a fact that did little to make us popular with some locals.

Undetected we had managed to actually mine one wall of the building, just under a radio aerial. Setting this off would start our attack. Hopefully the explosion would stop the enemy from seeking help by radio. We always cut the phone lines before an operation.

We didn't have enough men to surround the structure properly but would concentrate the attack on the breach. Two men would cover the main entrance at the front... trying to make us look like a bigger raiding party.

Commandant Kelly was very wary about the operation; this was going to be only one of several similar coordinated actions planned by our HQ throughout County Kerry. Hopefully, the enemy should not expect such a sudden assault just as day was starting to break.

He allowed me to be near to our troops this time; any wounded would be close to the action. The heavy khaki rucksack had become part of me over the last few weeks; I'd ceased to notice its weight. I was supremely fit. My revolver with the safety catch off was in my hand...

Light was just beginning to soften the night to the East; a cool breeze was blowing through the bare winter trees as we crept to within a hundred yards of the high wall of the fort. Aside from a distant lonely birdcall, all was quiet... good! My heartbeat was pounding and shaking my body...

We all sheltered on the ground, low dark shadows. Kelly signed us all to block our ears as the heavy battery we'd carried forward was hooked up to the wires we'd left behind the day before. A quick check and a switch was pressed...

The flash and explosion stunned us as we were pelted with rocks and debris, choking dust and explosive fumes made us cough as we rose up and charged the twelve foot wide gap that had appeared in the wall; the mine had worked perfectly!

Keely was in the forefront of our charge, his Tommy gun held ready. Suddenly, he fell, causing me to also crash onto the ground, knocking off my hat. My long hair came down as I regained my footing. One or two bullets were already starting to whine around us from the fort. Unnoticed by anyone in our party, Keeley was just lying there, a bruise on his forehead; he'd knocked himself out somehow, perhaps when he'd fallen!

I put my precious pistol in my pocket and snatched up the Tommy gun, feeling for the safety catch on the left hand side; it was off. As Keeley had told me, I fired several quick short bursts between my comrades who were sprinting in front of me, at figures with rifles aiming out at us; they collapsed out of sight. The flickering light from the Tommy gun muzzle lit the scene garishly, when firing the weapon danced and jerked in my hands; its noise seemed horrendous. I had never felt such power!

Gunfire ceased, a waved white rag, weapons clattered as they were dropped, arms were raised in surrender; our small force had overcome a much larger group of the enemy, twenty five in total. Most had been rudely roused from slumber and were still only wearing nightwear. The raid had been a great success; complete surprise had been our greatest ally. Three of their men were lying dead, the sentries who we'd surprised. When we checked, we found my shooting had been surprisingly accurate: 45 calibre bullets had killed all three.

"Be Jaysus, it was a *woman* with the machinegun! Mother of Mary what are we coming to?" Wide eyes stared at me in horror and amazement.

I ignored them. I had killed three… *traitors,* as far as I was concerned. So what? In a tiny corner of my mind, my complete lack of remorse surprised and concerned me… but I suppressed this with action.

I handed the machine gun to Kelly and checked; our party were unhurt, apart from a few bruises and scratches, which I quickly dressed.

While all the enemy soldiers were being carefully tied up, and checked for hostage value, I went back outside to Keeley and spoke to him. He was now sitting up, but his speech was slurred and he seemed to be in a daze; concussion I judged. He had a large lump on his head, probably caused by a piece of falling masonry dislodged by our mine. There was little I could do for him. He had a splitting headache and his eyes were dilated; we would need to get him to a hospital.

Our trusty Ford truck puttered up to the main entrance, and the loading of weapons and food supplies began. I helped Keeley up into the cab.

An hour and a half later as the day brightened, we were twenty seven miles away at a favourite hiding place in the mountains to the south east. Keeley had been dropped off on our way with a doctor sympathetic to our cause. Because his injury was not a gunshot wound, he could be placed in a proper hospital. The authorities checked all medical institutions, especially after an action in an area, looking for wounded enemy…especially gunshot injuries.

"Good thing y' saw Keeley, an' grabbed t'weapon; did well too! Y' can have it on our next op, but the gun's so valuable when attackin' we'll have two guys behind you, in case y' hit. Gotta save the thing if y'go down. Turned out t' be a great action, all round!"

My spirits rose, this was a real honour… although I suspected that Kelly was using some cunning here. Every man in the column wanted to have our sole machine gun; giving it to the only woman present should stop all arguments….. anyway I had been the key to our success! Rifles were almost useless in close attacking situations and pistols lacked power. Our enemy didn't have truly portable machine guns… but our side did have a few!

Triumphant martial music flooded my mind accompanying my success… I was finding it hard to sleep after the day's excitement.

As I restlessly tossed and turned that evening, a sad eyed Nora came to me.

"Well, that'd be a turn f'r t' books! Since y'can't sleep, I'll be atakin' y' back to my times again……"

75

Garden

The little fields looked unkempt; weeds were now dotted here and there, only the garden beside the cottage seemed cared for. Some young plants were growing in the little enclosure: carrots, a few sprigs of parsley, and some bean plants looked healthy, but were too small to eat, as yet.

A tiny wisp of smoke was visible above the low chimney. There was the sound of coughing and moaning coming from inside.

"I'd b' abracin' mesel' Aisling, if I wuz you! T' unnerstan' me, y' got t' see what was ahappenin' t' me a' t' end….'*orrible* y' agoin' t' find it, I'ma sure. Dad an' me ma is *really* sick, an Tom an' Katie 'ave t' fevers. Danny an' me is t' only *well* ones; wese is so lucky, an' dunno why! Come inside now."

It was a grey day outside. As I bent my head to enter through the low door, a wave of stench hit me in the fetid air; a mixture of diarrhoea, urine, vomit and sweat, I was permanently on the verge of gagging myself. It was gloomy, gone was the simple but cheerful interior of my former visits.

I knew from my reading that starvation in itself killed few, weakened resistance to diseases, cholera and especially dysentery, which dehydrated victims, were the most common killers…

Nora's parents wasted bodies lay together on a bed. Her father coughed at regular intervals; Mother was moaning quietly and grasping her stomach, under the coarse home spun blanket. Her face was skeletal and shiny with sweat. With an effort she opened her watery eyes and saw Nora there…for a second or two she didn't recognise her oldest daughter, but then gave her a weak smile. Her lank dark hair was in disarray; her voice weak.

"Danny an' t' others Nora?"

Nora dipped a cloth in a saucer of water and tried to cool her mother's brow. Her father turned over and looked fondly at his oldest child. With a supreme effort in his weakened state he reached out and touched her face lightly, love in his eyes. He was too weak to even speak… though he tried. His lips trembled. Nora lightly kissed his hot forehead.

"Tommy an' Katie 've got t' fever, real bad Ma, but Danny is strong. Ise is so tired an hexhausted…all t' time now…"

Her mother looked at her husband beside her and tenderly held his hand.

"Send Danny t' fetch Father Scully, Nora love; we'se is both adyin' now. I'm athinkin' t' water in t' well is bad.. try an' use only t' rain water off t' roof." She closed her eyes. Nora didn't tell her the rain barrel had been used up days ago and was empty; the well was now the only source of the essential, precious liquid.

As she went to the door to summon Danny, I was shocked at how slowly my friend Nora was now moving; almost trancelike and her call wasn't strong. Eight year old Danny came, carrying a few twigs of firewood he'd gathered together from their little forest. Though thin, he appeared stronger and was the only one of the family to have some colour in his face. When told, he seemed to be glad to go…

Nora's voice in my head was bitter: "Wese don't need *church* an' *prayer* n' *stuff*; wese only need *food*! Me Ma n' Pa still 'ave t' faith….Ise is not s' sure 'bout that anymore; theys wan' t'go t' heaven; after what Ise done…. *'ell* is more like it f' me, Ise afraid…"

Thirteen year old Katie was thrashing noisily around on the bed… delirious and moaning. Beside her, Tom was limp and still but, breathing jerkily. On all their bony faces starvation was etched.

Nora went out to the well with a wooden bucket; the fresh air was welcome.

"Water s' *heavy*," she moaned to me. "Ise seems t' be doin' this, day an' night, now!" Lifting the water took an age. She took some cloths smelling of vomit and defecation and slowly washed these, before pegging them onto a washing line to dry.

She explained to me that all four weren't strong enough to make their own way to the privy, so soiled themselves in their beds. "I'se is acleanin' up t'mess all t' time Aisling," she wrinkled her thin nose distastefully before doing so. "Ise try an' keep 'em clean, an' give 'em drinks of water; theys very thirsty all t' time! Har' work f' me, but they's m' family, an' Ise loves 'em!"

An hour and a half later, a cart with two men and Danny on the back pulled up, followed by the priest on his horse, Father Scully, the one who had come that day the Sullivans had been evicted. Nora was livid; the men, and especially the priest, and even *worse*, the *horses*, appeared *well fed!*

The priest blessed Nora and asked about her sick parents. Nora told him the situation; but when the Father tried to enter the cottage, the stench battered him back. With a distasteful look he said in a severe tone to her: "Bring your parents out here child. You really *must* keep the place cleaner Nora Kinnane; it's unChristian to have your home in this condition. You men, help her bring them out."

Tears of rage at this unfair insult streamed down Nora's face; she was killing herself caring for her family as best she could while weak with extreme hunger. Hatred boiled within her…. she could feel this emotion using up even more of her precious reserves of energy. She bit her tongue for her parent's sake… but her mother and father didn't react at all to the sunlight and fresh air; they had *both* passed away. Danny hurled himself sobbing at his eldest sister and Nora held him as tight as her weakened arms could.

The priest moved upwind then blessed the mortal remains, mumbling incantations in Latin. Nora was incensed that she'd had no final words with her parents, the only consolation was her mother and father had died close together as they would have wished. The priest didn't seem very sympathetic or empathetic; so many had already died in his parish.

"Sadly, your parents, God rest their souls, did not get a chance for a final confession before facing their maker. I would advise you and your young brother here to have that holy sacrament now…."

Nora's tearful voice came to me, echoing a statement I was to make about sixty years later: "I will *not* confess to *that* man! Ise is not agoin' t' tell 'im what Ise done…" His comment about her housekeeping still stung; she knew this chubby, rosy cheeked man had servants to keep *his* house.

Back in those days, a parish priest had so much power over his flock… he was never criticised or had his behaviour questioned by his parishioners in any way; this pillar of the community was always assumed to know better.

So when Nora started doing so in front of the men, loading the bodies of her parents onto the cart, Fr. Scully was completely nonplussed! Nora pulled down her shawl, disrespectfully baring her undernourished face and head. Her voice was harsh and scornful:

"Father, why weren't y' after abringin' us some food, eh? Even y' 'orse is well fed! 'S not very *Christian*! How could ye not help those adyin' of hunger? Yous was fren's wiv that devil Mr. Morrrison, who tried t'kill us! Yous is guilty as *sin* an' will be agoin' t' *HELL* you *greedy,* stupid man!"

The shocked men listening to this tirade in front of the priest were embarrassed, although the short one seemed to be enjoying the priest's discomfit and growing anger at this unimaginable situation.

"Cos yous is rich an' can b' eatin' when y' want.... Y' no' thinkin' right: *FOOD* is what wese all aneedin', not *prayers* an' *blessin's* an' *confessions!* Yous is *murdren* us, jus' like Morrison! Read y' bible, its asayin' ye sh'd b' 'elpin' t' poor." Her accusing young eyes bored into the priest's.

Father Scully regained his composure with great difficulty, trying to ignore her look. His admonishing voice was low and emphatic:

"Nora Kinnane, even allowing for the fact you have just lost your parents in terrible circumstances, such an unChristian outburst against God's church and its representative, will be punished severely. I will pray for your poor soul…"

"No doubt whilst eatin' a big meal. *Ell* is where y'r agoin' Fr. Scully, an' I'll b' thinking; a *g'd thing too!*"

The enraged priest slapped Nora's face so hard she fell over, taking young Danny with her. He then realised he'd gone too far. He spoke down to her lying on the ground. "When you finally come to your senses Nora Kinnane, visit the church for confession and forgiveness."

Shaking his head at such naked insolence, he climbed up on his horse, signalled the men in the cart to follow and rode off, just as it started to rain. The short man made sure the angry priest was not looking back, then reached under his seat, and threw a paper bag at Nora, for a second it seemed as though he might say something, but then thought better of it; he had his own soul to think of, after all.

Nora regained her feet; the paper bag contained a *small loaf of bread and an apple!* She nodded her thanks to their benefactor. They smelt the bread…and then the apple, mesmerised, but tears welled up, this manna might have kept her parents alive longer; but now they had left their children behind; she *must* keep her brothers and sister alive.

They were so poor that they couldn't afford a funeral service for their parents, there was not even a penny left to put towards one. She couldn't even witness their burial as she must stay and care for her siblings. Her heart was torn apart; as well now, she'd upset the priest! Her head was splitting from that slap, but also from that other heavy blow on the head she'd received some days back. Everything was getting on top of her; but she *must* pull herself together.

Nora got Danny to bring their parent's blankets in from out of the rain. The cottage seemed empty and sad without their parents. Tom and Katie were sleeping, quite unaware of what had happened. She decided to let them both sleep peacefully on. Katie was quietly snoring.

Nora placed the apple and the loaf on a chopping board. She cut the small apple carefully into four equal pieces, and gave one to ravenous Danny whose eyes had followed her every move intently. He quickly wolfed down his quarter; Nora decided to eat her share later when her brother and sister woke up. She looked forward to slowly savouring the sharp, slightly tart taste. She then cut four thin slices off the loaf; she'd keep her slice till later too. The lad again ate his slice quickly, as they listened to the rain on the roof....

"If wese careful, this food should keep us agoin' f' a few more days! Oh, Ise is forgettin'..... *quick*, put t' containers out t' catch t' rain Danny." She told him what their mother had said about the well water.

While he was doing so, she put the remaining shares of food safe into the earthenware jar with the lid on by the fire...this was ratproof, though there were none of those creatures around these days!

Nora then lit a small fire, tipped a small amount of rainwater into a little metal crock she hung over it, went out into the rain, unpegged the cloths from the line that she'd washed earlier and put them inside the door. She plucked a few tiny sprigs of parsley, and after some thought, pulled up two precious immature carrot plants from the garden; with these she'd try and make a little soup for them all to add to the bread and apple. That should cheer everyone up a bit! Then she spotted a spot of yellow gold some distance from the house; It was a dandelion! Every part of this plant was edible; she would add it to her "soup". All this effort on top of everything that had happened today exhausted her; she moved deliberately, almost in slow motion.

When she re-entered the cottage, Danny was squatting on the floor hugging his bony knees, rocking back and forth, gazing into the flames. Nora kissed his forehead as she passed him, but unusually, he squirmed at her touch and wouldn't look her in the eye...

Suddenly, it *bludgeoned* Nora, she lifted the lid off the jar, it was *empty*; the apple, loaf and bread slices *were gone!* Not a crumb remained!

The betrayal, as much as anything, stung her... "How c'ld ye be adoin' that Danny Kinnane? Stealin' fr' y' own *starvin'* family?"

The sullen little face and glittering eyes looked blankly at her. Suddenly he charged his sister, knocking her backwards smashing her head on the table corner, as he snatched the carrots, parsley and dandelion from her, and ran out into the rain. Nora passed out, vaguely aware that Katie and Tom had been woken by his actions....

When she came to, it was dark...her head was aching and she felt too weak to stand up. The fire had died out, she dully noticed. There was no sign of Danny.

Nora eventually crawled painfully to the open door; light rain was still falling... then she saw that every plant in her precious garden had been ripped out and was gone! Shattered, she crawled back to her feverish brother and sister, reaching up from the floor to touch them, then her arms slipped down and as she curled up, her heart stopped; the earthen floor was cold on her cheek.

Her voice came to me: "Twas like softly adriftin' t' other side Aisling, 'snice thin' was me tum stopped arumblin'; *I wasn't hungry*!

"Katie an' Tom was sick an' 'elirious....an' I could see em alyin' there. T' nex' day that man on the cart came wiv 'is wife an' a little food, an' they looked after them. I sees 'em carry my body out t' the cart, an' carrys me to t' graveyard. Some days later he carved m' name on t' stone y' found,. Tom and Katie lasted only a week or so more, theys was so sick...

"Your granddad Danny never came back; 'ee was tough an survived somehow, an' lived to quite an ol' age in t' end. Ise really hated 'im for what he done t' us, 'is family......... but over t' years, Ise comes t' *love* 'im again; 'cos he brought m' *you*, m' *bes' preshus* frien' ever!!"

She faded and was gone. I was left thinking... I knew that at that time, not all priests had been so uncharitable and distant. Many tried to help their flocks as best they could....

What a story! I had descended from such a turbulent, bitter time; and here I was today involved in yet another....

76

Song

The flames clawed their way up into the cold night darkness, our grotesque silhouettes defiantly danced in an orange frenzy on the white walls of the outhouses we were also setting alight. Surprising how quickly such a big structure could succumb to fire: a gallon of petrol splashed around, one flaring match and instantly, family history would be obliterated. There was something almost gleeful and naughty-boyish in the manner of my comrades during this exercise....

The Big House would not last long; it would be a visual flaring shriek to the Nationalist Treatyite troops who had lookout posts miles away in the hills around; they'd come for sure.

Fire was an ancient Irish weapon; the whole landscape was littered with blackened skeletons of former dwellings, large and small. This had often been a punishment for passing information to the other side. The Brits had also indulged in the practice during the recent war of independence and now the Nationalists were doing the same; we all did it. Normally the informers were shot if we could capture them, but the burnings would punish the families left behind... bitterness flourished in this harsh political climate.

The owners of this Big House had left County Kerry, before we'd made the roads and rail links almost completely impassable. This time it was not that they were alien settlers in our land, as the well to do Irish owners were Catholic, but it was just the fact that their large home would make a perfect major fortified winter base for our enemy, in their war against us. We couldn't allow that.

I was sadly aware that we were losing the battle for the hearts and minds in the county for our cause. The lack of enthusiasm we experienced when we landed on a farm had grown more evident, even open hostility was visible at times; but we were heavily armed... and very reluctantly we'd be fed. But to achieve our mythical Republic, we had to be harsh. Our cause became ever more hopeless...

Since we'd crippled the transport system in this rugged area, roads and rail had been made impassable so enemy troop movements were difficult. But this also meant that farmers couldn't get their produce to markets. Towns and villages suffered and accordingly unemployment had risen dramatically. Even the safety valve of emigration was shut off, travel had become almost impossible. Blaming we Republicans for this economic shutdown had been a propaganda coup for Dublin.

It had been my idea to await the enemy's rushed arrival at this scene. As guerrilla fighters, us Republicans would usually just melt away into the darkness immediately after such an arson attack, but tonight we would be waiting and unexpectedly ambush them! There were only two routes to the scene, and each had wonderful spots for an ambush, little forested tight corners on the two access roads, where the enemy would have to slow down. Our large column had split, and both groups were in place. We'd managed to mine the best one as well…

As we withdrew, the acrid stench of burning assailed us, my clothes and especially my long hair would stink of it for days, how the hell could I wash it out? I even asked myself if a woman should be here in this column, but kept my real thoughts from the rest of our party.

It turned out to be a big success for us! Normally the night was ours, we slinking figures in the shadows, but this time the Green and Tans, as we'd cruelly labelled the green uniformed government troops, had carelessly rushed to the fire in the darkness. The mine explosion had been set off perfectly, throwing the leading vehicle, a Crossley armoured car, onto its side. It caught fire, illuminating the scene further, blocking the road completely. The stalled troops were easy to pick off with rifle fire from the darkness under the trees. One short burst from my Thompson machine gun clattered, my bullets sparked off the vehicles. The few enemy survivors surrendered, a grubby white handkerchief was waved, and the firing subsided.

We emerged cautiously, fearing a trap, but it was real; they'd thrown down their weapons and had given up. There were four dead including their two officers, and five wounded; two of them badly, these we'd leave behind. I'd be dealing with the three living casualties.

We'd sustained no damage whatsoever and had gained weapons and ammunition. Those green uniforms might also come in handy in the future…

To me, one tall, slightly wounded captive stood out: indecently good looking, he was not in the least bit put out by his circumstances. His companions looked dejected and terrified as well they might. Their army and ours were in an escalating cycle of reprisal; prisoner execution was becoming more common. Both sides also used captives as human shields; the Treatyites to protect road and rail repair parties and the lorries and trains delivering much needed food. We on the other hand also sometimes used civilians in this way.

This fellow joked and smiled broadly, trying to cheer his comrades up. He spoke in English: "Well now, we've come a bit of a cropper lads, but what the hell, I say!" He gripped his left bloodied sleeve. I put down the machine gun and went to him and rolled it up, a flesh wound was visible.

His dark blue eyes twinkled at me in surprise, "A *woman, my God! And* particularly easy on me eye. Well, I'd be achangin' sides for a vision such as y'self, sweet colleen. *The* girl with the machine gun! We'd heard rumours of ye, of course, but I for one didn't believe them. Well, I'll be *damned!*"

Ignoring his banter, I rolled up his sleeve none too gently and started to dress his wound, after checking that there was no bullet to dig out. It had passed right through his arm and out the other side, luckily missing nerves and arteries as far as I could tell; just deep flesh wounds. He reached out with his other hand and tried to stroke my hair. I knocked his arm away; his eyes glinted. I pointedly ignored him, but was aware out the corner of my eye that he was watching me, and felt a bit vulnerable.

The captives were kept apart but under armed guard. They were tied together on one of our trucks. Lights off, we puttered through the darkness, our arms at the ready. Our CO didn't seem interested in the prisoners at all, which I thought was rather unusual. Since we relied on our mobility, prisoners were a liability… yet it seemed we were taking these three with us. Why? I wondered. We hadn't interrogated them in any way as yet. We warily drove on back roads, hoping to avoid further Nationalist reinforcements rushing to the scene of the fire and our ambushes.

If we had been up against the Brits it would have been easy, but our own people not only knew all these secret byways, but also how and when we might use them. This time their attack was rather amateurish, one of the enemy fired prematurely at us, which warned us. The gunflash told us where to aim for. I let of a short burst with the Thompson in that direction. We stopped, then backed up quickly. A flare sailed up into the air… lighting the scene garishly, dazzling us for a second or two, then I realised that our prisoners had somehow freed themselves and were desperately escaping, running and zig-zagging as they went. It was a reflex action I suppose; without thinking I gave them a short burst; all three collapsed, the tall, goodlooking one with the wounded arm cartwheeled as my bullets hit him. The flare above us dimmed and went out; but with bullets whistling around us we successfully withdrew....

If they'd waited until we were well into the tree lined valley, we would have been wiped out! It had been a perfect trap... and couldn't believe that we'd escaped with just a few bullet holes in our vehicles!

Next morning, in safety, our chief came up to speak to me with a look of hatred on his face, but turned and went away without saying a word. What could I have done wrong?

One of the other members of our group told me, I had shot and had almost certainly killed the CO's only brother! I didn't know what to do; this Civil War pitted family members against each other; I really kept my head down after that.

Song

Over the weeks I learnt how to use my power and status. I had a series of astonishing insights, but as usual kept these to myself. There had been many skirmishes yet my column seemed to come through comparatively unscathed.

The men began to think me as lucky; a sort of Joan of Arc figure... "The woman with the Tommy gun" had become famous and gave an aura and status to my group. My comrades enjoyed that aspect of it! I deliberately let my long hair down when in battle. I arrogantly thought my visible presence distracted the enemy, spoiling their accuracy, and also that men would not aim deliberately at a woman, even one with a machine gun! I may have been correct; bullets often whistled around me, yet I was never hit.

On one occasion, when Commandant Kelly had called for a withdrawal, I said to hell with that and single-handedly charged. My comrades had hesitated, then not wanting to appear weak in front of a woman, they'd protectively followed me. We carried the day, and had won, but I had disobeyed orders... and put members of my group at risk. I had made our commanding officer almost appear weak; a very big mistake.

We used to have political IRA intelligence officers visit us at intervals. They told us what was happening to the units on our side, how we were doing, what the enemy was up to, and the mood of the general population. They also sought insights from all of us as to how we could do better. These visits helped me understand how most of our fighters were unsophisticated farm or village boys; brave as lions when required to be, but not really educated in the ways of the world. Some of them swallowed simplistic ideas; hook line and sinker! Although one lad suggested that: "Every column should have a fightin' lady doc like we have, 'n' we'd b' getting' the Republic for sure!" A comment that was loudly supported by the rest of our troops. They all looked at me, and to their delight, I flushed with embarrassment and turned away.

We were told the Dublin government was using Red Cross vans as transport for arms and troops, so they were now considered to be legitimate targets by our side. This was just one example of the conflict deteriorating into further viciousness. Legally, the IRA had signed no international conventions or agreements so therefore this was OK for us to do, we were told. Treatment of prisoners was another area of concern. Anyone of us captured could expect torture and even execution, and we should treat our prisoners the same way… normally of course because we were so mobile we couldn't be encumbered by them, unless they had particular value for a hostage exchange, then we might drag them along with us.

It was one of those scrappy, messy engagements where confusion reigned. We had ambushed an enemy convoy of trucks carrying troops. We had shot up a Red Cross van and wrecked it, along with some trucks. Our unit had just received some rifle grenades, rather dangerous weapons that fired little bombs, but these sometimes exploded prematurely and anyway, weren't very accurate. The enemy had withdrawn leaving the badly damaged vehicles behind. When we inspected the ambulance we found four dead, already wounded young soldiers, a young woman and a baby; but no weapons at all! A very quiet, thoughtful column retreated from the scene. We had been lied to and four souls had died. The retaliation from the enemy would obviously continue to escalate….

Weed floated into my mind….. no, that wasn't true; if I was *really* honest with myself he was stubbornly and annoyingly there all the time in the background! It could have been him. When I faced up to things; God how I missed him! But then I would allow my disgust at his support for the Truce to smother my longing and I would feel harder, tougher and more determined to win the Republic; even though there was a sneaking realization that my side would not win; too much was against us, and as time went on fewer of the locals were supporting us, no matter what the intelligence men said. I rammed these negative thoughts to the back of my mind. Harsh music clashed there; I steeled my spirit, we *must* fight on!

It was the place that brought about the big change. We regarded this isolated glen, and the cave we used, as our safest refuge, once our sentries were posted. It was high in some craggy mountains

As well, the weather was deteriorating; a cold wind was coming off the Atlantic and was busily roaring through the trees. Weed would have described the misty clouds as clambering desperately up the peaks or some such description; fairly apt I thought as I watched them. Funny how I couldn't forget his obsession…

We were all tired and hungry and needed a rest after weeks of unrelenting pressure. This place was perfect for recharging our batteries. A wood fire was smoking, the food cooking smelt mouth wateringly good! We were also trying to dry the clothes we'd washed in the rocky stream by draping them over some low bushes. I kept my washing some distance apart from the men's. The sun was shining only intermittently.

I was alone in the open space down by the bank, where, hoping for a bit of privacy, I washed my hair in the stream. I was just beginning to dry it when there was an urgent scream from Kelly: *"COVER!"*

Just as I grabbed my Tommy gun, there was a sudden explosion of sound: with a roar a biplane painted green burst over a ridge and bouncing in the turbulent air currents, passed by a hundred feet or so overhead. I distinctly noticed it was trailing a long wire out the back. As I desperately ran for cover, I put my foot in a rabbit burrow, wrenching and twisting my ankle; the pain was so horrific I nearly passed out. I lay still on the peaty ground, sweat pouring off me in shock. I'd never known such pain! The plane motored on over the next ridge, dropped down and disappeared; it had all taken only a few seconds it seemed…. Surely we hadn't been seen in such a brief pass! Only the wind could be heard again.

I lifted myself upright and found I could just painfully hobble towards the trees; everyone else was already under cover. I was only half way to shelter when again with that sudden roar, the plane reappeared over the lower ridge; I flattened myself. This time I was certain we had been spotted, as a Mills bomb was dropped from the craft. It arced down and exploded harmlessly with a muffled thump in the stream behind me. While lying on my back, I whipped the safety catch off my Tommy gun and fired the whole magazine at the craft, a full eight second burst; aiming slightly ahead to allow for its speed. I saw lots of bullet strikes along the fuselage and wings. I tried to hit the pilot and observer. Then, trailing a little blue white smoke, it shot over the hill line to the north and was gone. The sound of the wind and my hot gun, creaking as it cooled could be heard above the quiet murmur of the stream. The engagement had only taken a few seconds, yet I had fired one hundred rounds of our precious ammunition!

The aeroplane never came back. I got up and painfully limped over to my comrades, my wet hair in disarray. I was exhausted and the pain in my left ankle was horrendous, it was already swollen to twice its normal size; I was crippled. I tried wrapping swathes of bandages around the swelling.

After all the close calls and skirmishes of the last few months it seemed unfair for me to be disabled by a *damned rabbit hole!* I was going to be a millstone to my column now......

Cloud and mist descended as we packed up.

"Not jus' you Doc, they saw the fire and a few of us on the first pass. Damn it, we can't be a usin' this glen again… we'll be aneedin t' find another hidey-hole now. Did ya see the trailin' wire on the plane? The bastards had radio on board n' could tell their base we were here. The enemy could be on their way to us, even now…. *Move!*"

Commandant Kelly turned to me. "Now you Doc, you're out of the battle, f' a few weeks at least. There's a place I might be able t' leave y' at…."

All the gear and weapons were packed and lugged two miles down the track to the hidden trucks. Tired resigned faces told us another haven would have to be found as quickly as possible, of necessity far from here.

I had to be carried; much to my disgust. In my current state I was a major handicap, holding my column up.

Thank God I had trained one of the sergeants, Ernie Hennessey, in all the areas of first aid, just in case I'd been hit or killed. He'd become quite proficient and had a cool head; so first aid should be catered for. I had to give up my machinegun, of course; that proved more of a problem, as every man in the platoon wanted to be in charge of that! It was strange how being parted from a mere piece of metal depressed me; it had somehow formed my personality, given me a status…

78

Sky

I found myself at one of the Free State strongpoints in the south east of the country at that large ancient fort I had noticed on my first visit to Kinsale, when Aisling's father had sent the blue limousine to pick me up. The British had used this complex as their main military centre for several hundred years and now the new Irish Government was doing the same.

King Charles fort was a vast complex of stone walls and buildings and grassy parade grounds that overlooked and dominated the narrow entrance to Kinsale harbour. From a favourite spot on the ramparts near my cramped office, I would view the morning mists on the still water, see them fade and die in sunlight, watch the clouds on the horizon out to sea and back the other way the sky and haze mantled green hills to the west… the beauty would often sadden me, somehow reminding me of my emptiness.

Fishing boats were always coming and going, the occasional small freighter passed through the channel. My office had a small window looking out on this view.

I'd had doubts, especially when Michael Collins had responded to British pressure and had attacked the IRA occupiers of the Four Courts in Dublin. Our old enemy had supplied arms for him to do so; thereby starting the civil war. Mick hadn't wanted to attack old comrades and had held off as long as he could, but eventually he'd been forced to act.

Instead of joining the army where I would have to sign on for years, I had become a civilian Intelligence Officer. Despite my complete lack of formal training, Mick had backed my application and he pretty well *was* the government these days, so here I was, doing mainly humdrum work, keeping our eyes on those who did not want the new order to succeed. I suppose I was the Irish Government equivalent of a G man!

As was common, the IRA had been divided in this part of the country. Most had adopted Mick's view that the Treaty was a major step on the road to Irish freedom and had joined the new government. Countrywide elections had clearly shown that a majority of the general population thought that way too. This had made my mind up for me. But there were still a few diehards who wanted the Republic now or nothing… and were prepared to do anything to get it. Dev was making these noises and was now on the run…at times near here, rumour had it. We would love to have captured him as he was a focal point for the extremists.

In the little port I would go past the Girl's School that Aisling had attended that she'd once pointed out to me. That damned woman was still in my thoughts even months after parting…

One morning while admiring the restful view as usual, I smiled to myself as some new recruits were being drilled on the parade ground below me. They were bad; one man in particular had three left feet and got everything wrong! I sympathised with the poor fellow as a sergeant screamed abuse at him. I was just turning away, when a group of officers standing below me caught my eye… some looked British despite their new green uniforms, one in particular seemed almost familiar….

Then it clicked….. *it was that English officer who'd brutally tortured the baker Sean Quinn at Kenmare!* I almost collapsed in shock.

This was an aspect of the new government I hated; we'd employed, on a short term basis, some British officers, to fight against the rebels. We needed military expertise to win this new Civil War. Times were tough in Great Britain and work was scarce, so there was no shortage of out of work soldiers to recruit.

Knowing that some had a history over here, our new powers that be even allowed them to pick what area of the country they could work in, which annoyed the rest of us who had no choice in the matter. We checked all candidates and of course avoided anyone known to have committed atrocities. Perhaps there was no real record of his past here….

I must make sure it was him! I'd access all the army records of those stationed here… and find his name.

It didn't take me long to go through the current officer's list, I found him! He'd just arrived, so wouldn't yet know I was here. My name didn't appear on any army lists, but my fame might work against me, if someone discussed me. However, the British officers tended to spend most of their free time together.

I copied all his details and his photo matched. He definitely was the violent Auxie I'd seen in action that morning, all right. Captain James Edwards, 41 years of age, from Chatham in England, married with two grown children, a boy and a girl. I also discovered he was going out on a patrol of the South Coast in the next few days; I would have to move quickly.

Now what would I do? He'd got away scot-free so far….. and who knew what other crimes he had committed against our people? To my mind came that scent of burning, melting flesh again mixed in with that odour of baking… and I could hear that arrogant casual drawl as he spoke, mocking a great patriot before brutally attacking the helpless man.

I *would* avenge the Quinn family! But before he died, he must know why he was being killed. My relentless anger was tempered by careful calculation. Murder in the courts of the new country of Ireland was treated harshly as the new government was desperate to achieve public order and stability. Edwards must not see me; he'd remember me for sure. But I must act fast…

That very afternoon nature came to my aid; fog rolled in off the sea, grey, dense and clingy. The fort was soon obscured in mist; the shouted orders on the parade grounds below me became muffled.

I knew where the officer's mess was located… through the partially open door I saw he was drinking at the bar facing away from me. I walked quietly away, thinking.

At my favourite lookout on the ramparts, I knew there was a sheer drop of forty feet or so to a narrow grassy ledge that fell away down to the shore of the channel. In this fog it should be easy to push him off the wall, if I could just get him to come alone. Then it came to me! I could go and knock on the officer's mess calling out that there was a toll call from Chatham in England for a Captain Edwards. That'd do the trick, especially if I used an English accent… I could then say the phone was in a small office, "this way sir…" and get him to follow me to the place; he wouldn't see my face…. A sudden turn, a blow on the head…a massive shove; it'd be easy!!

But then a little burst of unusual maturity stopped me in my tracks. If Ireland was going to become of age, this score settling, murder and mayhem must stop. The rule of law should deal with all these cases…. Personal vendettas must not be encouraged….

Damn! I suddenly made up my mind….I would leave immediately before this violent criminal spotted me. I'd go to Dublin tonight!

79

Song

The solemn grey eyes looked up at me calmly out of a glowing pink face, topped by wispy blonde hair. What was the tiny creature actually thinking? Was there trust in there somewhere, I wondered? Perhaps it was as simple as the fact I was wearing her mother's clothes that made her feel at peace; but no, that look *meant* more, I was sure! I couldn't help but smile at wee Katie McGorram; she seemed to like me.

But a remnant of sadness seeped into my mind along with a hinting echo of that soft tune heard when I had been pregnant. Would my lost child have looked at me in this way, if it had been born? Then Weed inevitably pressed his way back in yet again. I resolutely pushed him aside, my past was lost… my world *had* changed.

This warmth for an infant was such a different emotion for me to feel after living as a guerrilla fighter, permanently moving from skirmish to skirmish, witnessing and taking part in death, injury and atrocities, resolutely hiding my emotions, never wanting to appear weak in front of the men.

Babies were thankfully unaware of the conflicts and complexities of life. Her nine year old brother Liam, who was regarding me with large worried eyes and six year old sister Mary were more reserved but very anxious; I drew them to me and gave them a long hug, which seemed to help all of us. I suddenly realised how exhausted I was from the strain and the continual turmoil of my life in the column.

The children's father had been killed here in front of them in their own home by the British, before this civil war had erupted. I'd spent three days with this family, learning what was required of me, before their ma had left to go to her mother who was dying in Cork. She would be away for ten days or so. As the farm was very marginal and the transport situation chaotic she couldn't afford to take her children with her. I would take her place, while my injured ankle would hopefully mend. As far as the jobs and caring for the children went, I thought I would cope, despite my privileged background. In a way I was looking forward to these two weeks of change...

My long hair was hidden in a bun. It was so distinctive I knew I should have cut it short, but I suppose it was vanity yet again. I covered it by a scarf. Wearing women's clothes again, I was surprised to find, was a pleasant experience. On the road with the column, I'd left behind so much of my essential being....

I had to pass as a widow mother of three, singlehandedly running a small, poor limited holding at the end of an isolated track. The two neighbouring farms were supporters of our side and would protect me as much as they could. My biggest problem would be my accent; the second I opened my mouth I betrayed the fact I was a foreigner in these parts. Having been for weeks with Kerrymen I could adopt only a reasonable approximation of the local brogue. But my Irish also had an accent. The trouble with this civil war was that the enemy had local soldiers who could instantly pick up any inconsistencies and who sometimes knew the area and the people intimately. When we'd fought against the Brits things had tended to be much simpler, much more clear-cut. I must say as little as possible if put on the spot. Anyway, it was not expected that in this out of the way holding I'd come into any contact with the enemy.

Having become famous as "the woman with the machine gun" I was being sought everywhere throughout Kerry by government forces; my capture would be a big deal for our enemy. Mind you, they'd expect me to be on the move with my column... I felt quite vulnerable without that Tommy gun, I had been ordered to have no arms at all, but had brought a pistol and a few rounds of ammunition with me. I had sewn an extra large pocket into the rough skirt I was wearing... just in case.

The Dublin government had passed a law that having a weapon on one's person or even a single bullet was a capital offence; although as yet the law had been inconsistently applied, long imprisonment seemed to be the minimum punishment for this crime.

I had been dropped off to stay here and recuperate from my ankle injury, which was still swathed in bandages. It was a typical low farmhouse; one end of the building had been burnt by the Brits, and had not been repaired as yet. The sharp smell of the scorched timber hovered defiantly over the poor buildings. A few stunted trees grew around the structures.

It was astounding how much work was required to run the little farm, family, gardening, cooking, washing clothes, cleaning; it went on from dawn to dusk...

the baby usually on my hip. But it was strangely satisfying, as each task was done and as the days went busily by, my ankle seemed to gain strength, and I felt more at peace.

The older two also started to relax. Liam and Mary had told me that their Ma always sang as she worked, so I did too. Evening story telling was always a high point! I tried to remember the tales of my childhood, which seemed so long ago to me now. So much had happened in the intervening years. Regardless, the kids loved every yarn; especially tales about Ireland's past. The hugs, the tucking in, the quiet goodnight kiss, the candle blown out, my return to the peatfire warmed kitchen, a quick check on baby Katie, the sound of the autumnal wind sighing around the damaged house; I would then be at peace, but thoughts of a similar life shared with Weed would inevitably arise, and hints of loneliness would invade my defensive, resistant mind...... but I did miss him so much.

Last thing at night, Nora would come to me, her little face hard, voice firm: "Now then Aisling, this is the livin' y' *should* b' adoin', not that fightin' carry-on. I ask ye, a woman needs t' settle down! You n' Weed together.....s'way it should be! Kids, swarmth and peace, *not* Guns, n'killin', causin' famine and shortages for the ordinary folk! There's no end to it....s'far as I can see. Mother Mary, you've got enough food, s' what more would ye want? Eh? *Stupid woman!*" And she would indignantly disappear in a huff, leaving me doubting my warlike life.

Indeed, to be honest, I was not looking forward to the end of this idyllic rest period. My ankle was getting stronger. After the first week I had removed the bandages, although I still limped a little.

Each day Liam would milk the cow twice and bring the pail of milk back to the kitchen. Our few pigs and scrawny chickens he would feed with our scraps. The lad seemed to enjoy the responsibility. He'd then fetch fuel for the kitchen range, from the blocks of peat that were drying out on the south side of the wall. Thank God it was the school holidays.... otherwise it would have been almost impossible to keep my presence more or less secret from the community. As far as the kids were concerned, I was Aunty Ada, who was just visiting. Mind you they were firmly instructed to call me Ma if any strange visitors should come…

80

Sky

That night I passed through Cork, which had only recently been taken from the Republicans and arrived in Dublin in the morning. The new flag was flying everywhere around the city which seemed to have a positive air about it, though the damage caused by the rebels was visible and quite extensive, especially in the Four Courts area and opposite the GPO and Gresham Hotel in Sackville St. The disturbing scenes of damage and loss were strangely reminiscent of the 1916 uprising against the British.

I made my way through the traffic to my own outfit's HQ and tried to contact Mick. By phone I finally managed to get through to Joe O'Reilly, Mick's general dogsbody and personal assistant. The Commander in Chief of the Free State Army was in Limerick, but was returning in a few hours. I told Joe it was vital I saw him without saying why. He said he'd try and arrange something. I left instructions as to how I could be contacted.

I stayed with my Aunt Biddy, who warmly welcomed me again, despite the loss of her husband, which she could have blamed me for; after all, it had been myself the Tans were looking for that day they'd come. She still didn't know that I'd shot and killed him myself; no one did. My heroic fame caused by our side's propaganda after the fight and fire in the lane meant I was looked up to by most.

The burnt out house had been rebuilt; she told me that Mick had arranged the finance to do so… the rest of the lane was also more or less repaired, and the neighbours also welcomed me back.

Blind Amy was especially affected and clung to me, as she sobbed. When she asked, I told her Aisling and I had parted and now I didn't know where her friend was….. just out west somewhere, possibly fighting with the irregulars against peace and the Treaty. Her face was contorted with sadness. Her wispy blonde hair shook with emotion. Those strange but warm eyes glowed.

"Ah, I was always atellin' er t' follow her heart not her head. She was so kind t' me; now I can earn money wiv me new harp an' singin', thanks t'her…" She touched my face. "I c'n feel y'r heart's abreakin', Aidan; but her's is too, I c'n *feel* it!" Her face took on that distant timeless look, the voice became softly haunting. "But she *will* afind a great peace of a kind, an' the wall of ideas between yous…. will melt thr' the years….but oh s' slow!"

Tearfully, she felt her way out the door and back to her place. She'd aged a lot in the last few years; to be blind during that raid must have been terrifying: what with the noise, the fire and gunshots. I noticed a greater air of confidence about her however and her body had filled out somewhat. But why did I somehow feel closer to Aisling when I spoke to her? Fey Amy O'Driscoll seemed to understand and see the world as it *really* was.

When I entered the restored little parlour, I had tears in my eyes, hearing in my mind that gritty voice and cough, and sensing Shamus the loyal beagle on my uncle's lap…yet really it was now cold and silent, smelling of the sterile new paint, another crucifix and only one or two photos on the wall that Aunt Biddy had managed to replace. Those books were gone, and the mantelpiece was empty. This plain room had helped turn me into the man I had become over the years.

Through the small window I could just hear Amy playing and singing sadly from across the way…

That afternoon I learnt that Arthur Griffith, a major co-negotiator with Mick and the others in London and now the Prime Minister of the Free State of Ireland, had died suddenly. This was a devastating blow to the new country and our side in general; just when we needed stability most…

Many of Mick's old comrades like Harry Boland and Cathal Brugha had also died in the anti-treaty rebel uprising, he'd had to suppress; I'd heard he was bereft at this loss of many of the people who had fought for and had helped achieve the independence of the southern provinces of Ireland. The North still remained an intractable problem. Catholics were in a small minority there and their treatment by the majority of Protestants was an ongoing area for concern. The deaths and persecution were forcing many to abandon Ulster and head south into the Free State.

There was a pressured knock on the door at 6.30 the next morning. A messenger gave me a piece of paper with a time and place scrawled on it written in Mick's writing. I hurriedly dressed and rushed off before even having any breakfast. Aunt Biddy appeared in her dressing gown, rubbing her eyes; she kissed me as I left.

81

Song

My ninth day at the farm had started like any other; the morning drizzly but the sun had eventually broken through the wan clouds and the land looked less rocky and almost productive. I'd just fed the baby and put her to sleep, and had gone outside to work in the vegetable garden with young Mary when a distant movement down the track caught my eye. At first I thought it was my column returning, but no; the green uniforms told me it was a Free State Government force stopping at one of the farms down the track! My heart leapt with fear… but really, I was lucky because I had some time to prepare. I hoped and prayed they would have no one local with them.

The children were frantic. The last time an armed force had come here the British had killed their father and had set fire to their home. I consoled them as best as I could and reminded them to call me Ma. Without them seeing, I took the pistol from its hiding place, loaded it and put it in the secret pocket of my skirt. It was a better hiding place as I was unlikely to have my person searched, but if it was found on me it could be a death sentence. I then went to pick up baby Katie, who was grumpy at being woken up. A crying infant would be a convincing prop and looking after her would mean I would have to speak less. I had grown to love the little creature, so my care would be no act…

I checked my headscarf in the small mirror, I must bend my back to appear shorter, my face looked too white, some dust and dirt smudged on helped there, my hands needed as Nora had often told me: "some good honest mud t' sort y'r ideas out, woman…"

I went out into the garden with the children and started weeding again, watching the two trucks puttering up our track out of the corner of my eye… the Dublin Government's traitorous tricolour flag fluttering on them. As they came into the yard I straightened up a bit, Liam and Mary clinging to me terrified, the baby crying.

The rear vehicle stopped and disgorged some troops. Orders were given and the soldiers immediately started searching the outhouses and lean-tos; looking I supposed for any IRA caches of weapons. I hoped there were none around that I didn't know about! No, surely my unit wouldn't have put me at risk.

The front truck stopped near us, it was painted green, and stencilled in yellow letters on the door, *The Dublin Brigade* I was horrified to read. This was *the* elite Freestate Army column staffed by the Mick's Squad members, the assassins. They were famed for their brutality! Well at least they weren't local I told myself, trying to be positive. How would I play this? I must naturally be a bit indignant at the intrusion, but not too much… I must not annoy them. Even at a time like this, I tried to see what weapons they were equipped with; only Webley pistols and Lee Enfield rifles as far as I could see, with one large clumsy Lewis machine gun. Mmm, I thought, my nimble little Tommy could have been handy here! I buried the thought and my hatred. The soldiers climbed down.

An officer, a captain came to me from the lead truck, politely enough. His uniform was quite smart, his leather boots gleamed. Tired steely eyes raked me, and the three children, then took in the scene, the washing flapping on the line. He seemed to relax a bit then consulted a clipboard. "Mrs. McGorram, we wish to search your holding for any weapons, explosives or fugitives."

Baby Katie cried loudly, the dark figure upsetting her.

"Far as I can see, y'r *already* doin' so!" I snapped as I tried to settle the baby down. "Scarin' m' kids; twas the damned Brits las' time…" I nodded at the burnt end of the house. Little Mary buried her face in my skirt. On the other side I could feel the hard pistol and the clip of ammo pressing against my thigh…

"I'm sorry Ma'am, but we must search everything. Please stay here," he ordered.

I snorted and bent back to weeding as the officer went off to supervise his men. I and the children began to relax as we worked. After ten minutes, he came back.

"Mrs. McGorram, all seems to be in order, you're free to enter y'r house but my lieutenant and three of our men are going to stay and check y'r fields. Arms are often buried in these parts. Thank you for your cooperation."

He climbed back into one truck, the motor was cranked and it noisily started; the vehicle bumped its way down the uneven track. I was relieved and went back in the kitchen; the house had been turned upside down, all the furniture had been moved as they looked for secret hiding places, every drawer pulled open. Thank God I'd put the pistol in the skirt I was wearing; it would certainly have been discovered otherwise. Through the window, I could see the remaining troops scouring the six stony acres… it was beginning to look like I had escaped detection.

To calm my nerves, I made a cup of tea, and a few minutes later was sitting at the kitchen table, Liam and Mary playing on the floor, Katie asleep in my arms, when the open door darkened, it was the Lieutenant from remaining searching soldiers. He knocked on the door before entering.

"We'll be going now Ma'am, all seems to be in…." he stopped, eyes large in complete surprise. I dropped my cup on the floor with a crash, tea spilling everywhere, the china shattering. The children began to wail…

It was my brother Rory! He recognised me instantly…in my mind flashed memories of our childhood, how I'd protected him from our now dead Father…. but he was wearing that hated uniform. I slyly slid my hand into my skirt pocket ready to whip out the pistol as we eyed each other.

"You….. *Aisling*…!" He was even more astounded than I was…would he betray me? He looked older and harder, a grown man. Why hadn't I thought of the possibility, he had been in the Squad back in Dublin after all.

A soldier appeared beside him. "Finished the search, sir. Nothin' at all, the place is clean as a whistle."

Rory looked at him. "Get your men back to the truck Sergeant. I want to talk to Mrs. McGorram here alone; you soldiers will spook these kids even more. Be there in a jiff. "

"Very good sir," and off he marched.

Rory stared at me…. I didn't know what to say to him. And then a look of realization came on by brother's face.

"*You* are the famous lady with the Tommy gun….. aren't you? She is tall, has an educated voice, long auburn hair and green eyes….damn near shot down one of our planes a week or so back; killed the observer, only twenty miles from here, too. Fanatical fighter we hear; hell why didn't I think of it before? Yes, it's *got* to be you! I heard you'd come here, out to the west."

I had baby Katie on my left hip, my right hand was on the pistol in my skirt pocket; I slid off the safety catch. There was no point in denying anything. In a choked voice, I managed only to say, "Oh Rory…!"

"Quick, I don't have much time. Listen, I've always wanted to tell you I'd nothing to do with Father's death. Someone up very high ordered it…and a southern group did the job; the silly old bastard thought he could buy his way out of trouble, and he *had* informed the Brits on your guy Weed which put us all at risk, even you. He didn't realize how good our side's intelligence was and that the world had changed."

He frowned and spoke intensley "I only have one sister.... Survive this war Aisling, it's nearly over and my side will win, daily we grow stronger. Your side doesn't stand a hope in hell, you've even lost almost all local support these days. Nearly everyone in the south of Ireland is sick of the war and destruction! Get out somehow before people find out who you are....you'll be executed if my lot ever catch you!" He came to me and gave me an awkward hug....Katie cried, Liam and Mary looked up at him.

"Funny seeing you all maternal; strangely enough, sister, it sort of suits you! Now, you wouldn't have used that pistol on me, would you?" he looked around. "Sorry about the mess. I must go." He smiled and twinkled at the kids, gave me one last, firm searching look, turned and went out the door.

A minute later the second truck puttered away and the farm was quiet again, though my heart was still thumping loudly and my legs quivered so much, I could barely stand. After a rest I tiredly started to get things tidied up.

That night rain lashed the roof and the wind wailed and shook the building so hard, I couldn't sleep even though I felt weak and exhausted.

Nora came to me speaking in her most impatient tone: "Aisling, fings 've come t' a pretty pass, when y'r even atinking of *shootin' y'r own brother* now....The good Lord! What's got inta ye woman? Strikes me, he's tried to talk some sense inta ye! Not that ye'll listen of course....y'r a sad creature at best, m'friend..."

She vanished, leaving me unhappy and doubting myself. Rory probably was right. I had been beginning to think the same way; but...

82

Sky

Michael Collins had aged although he was only thirty-two; his face had thickened with sallow unhealthy skin, dark rings were under his eyes; unrelenting pressure had taken its toll. He'd also put on weight since I'd last met him. He had a cold and frequently coughed into a clean handkerchief that he extracted from the breast pocket of his smart Commander in Chief of the Free State Army uniform.

I'd been thoroughly searched for weapons by people I'd worked with in the past, before I'd been finally ushered into his office. No one, even friends, were trusted, it seemed. Trust between friends became the first casualty in a civil war. It was a time of strange alliances and bizarre turns…

"*Mess,* Weed! *Christ,* what a shambles from top to bottom; I tried but the whole country was unravelling. Example: in a twenty day period at the beginning of April, the idiots robbed more than 320 Post Offices, for the damned Republic they said……then in the Parliament they actually admitted some of the proceeds went on their booze! Jaysus! There's so many weapons floatin' around out there, with lots of clowns willing to use 'em. And I'm the one who brought most o' 'em in, to fight the Brits!

"Had t' do it and attack the silly bastards, before everything was lost……the 16th of June election, which they tried t' stop takin' place clearly told 'em what the whole damn country wanted: Peace an' the Treaty; but they just wouldn't listen! Things 'ave come to a pretty pass when *I'm* the voice of moderation!" he laughed ruefully. "If this continues, watch yersel' Weed. I've firebrands on my side, I can barely control.

"Now Arthur Griffith is gone…at what a time! Funeral in a few days here in Dublin, I'll be at the head of it all… which is risky, but has to be done. A lot of the old gang blame me alone for achievin' the Truce….sellin' out they call it, they'd love t' top me!" He sighed.

"Now, what'd ye want ter tell me that was so urgent?" His large desk was covered with a large number of files stacked neatly; trays were full of letters and documents. He reached for a pen.

He frowned as I told him about Kenmare and what had happened, Captain Edwards and his whereabouts. I was also open about the way I'd come close to disposing of him myself, but explained why I didn't. He frowned at me then scribbled down some notes....

"I'm athinkin' Mick, we could use the trial of Edwards as a unifying reminder to both sides as to what we fought for, since Kerry is the big hold out for the irregulars. Quinn was a Kenmare Republican ... yet *we* are punishing his tormentor. I'd be a witness, and see if the wife survived... she could be as well, perhaps even the oldest kid, although we wouldn't wanta remind young Orla Quinn of it all. It would be a sort of an example of bi-partisan cooperation, which would go down well; lots of publicity, possibly international; for once not entirely related to our Civil War.

"Only problem is, we hired the bastard ourselves! But if we nab him quickly, we can say we just brought 'im back here to punish him! The court case would have to be perfect in a legal sense, evidence presented etc. so even the Brits, who'll of course object to one of their nationals bein' charged at all! But once the facts of his behaviour come out... they'll want it over an' done with and out of the headlines as soon as is possible! The Free State must be seen t' be usin' the process of law; gives our new government legitimacy!"

Mick looked at me in silence for several seconds as he thought deeply.... I should have been flattered to have the complete attention of the most important person in the country. Eventually he spoke.

"See yer haven't changed Weed! I'll get a team onto it. He's on the South Coast huh? We'll get 'im. Write down everything yer remember from that day. Now you stay here in Dublin. We may have a change of job fer you...in the near future. I'll see you at the funeral!"

"Got it all here ready for you Mick, with his personal details. There's some suggestions about the process too." I handed the packed large envelope to him.

"Good! Now, before yer go; have you heard anything from Aisling?" I shook my head.

"Have you been hearing of the legendary "Lady with the Tommygun" out in Kerry? We don't have a name for her at all, but the description fits Aisling to a T, except it's rumoured that's she's a doctor. The damned woman has killed a lot of our troops, even came bloody close to downing one of our aircraft a fortnight ago! I sort of wondered if it might be her. I noticed when we worked together she could be fanatical. Since her father was killed by us, we lost track of her. Check an' see if she obtained any medical training anywhere… I'd like to know. Now, I've got to a mountain of business to do…"

I left his office, passing a string of people waiting to see him. As most were non-military figures, I gained the distinct impression he'd taken over many of the functions of the new government since the Prime Minister's passing.

I of course knew that Aisling *had* done some first aid courses and had obtained some medical supplies before disappearing. She *must* be the Joan of Arc figure!

While I looked up at a sky of streaky grey clouds foreboding drizzle, I decided not to tell Mick. I did not want my love to be targeted in any way. For the millionth time I wondered where she was and what was happening to her….

83

SONG

Mrs McGorram returned to her small holding and her children, relieved everything had gone so well. She told me how difficult travel had become as so much rail and road infrastructure had been damaged and destroyed by our side.

Her mother had passed away two days after she'd arrived in Cork, so she was there at the end. After the funeral she'd been able to tidy all the family affairs up.

She was absolutely horrified to hear of the Free State Army visit and search, but didn't say *why* she was so upset. I wondered if the property might have arms hidden on it somewhere, after all!

Although the children were overjoyed to see her back, they were sad I would be leaving. This interlude of domestic peace had destroyed my iron resolve. My brother Rory had only reinforced my growing perception that the cause, though just, was lost. The Republican fire had left me, only stubborn embers remained. What would I do now?

I went for a last evening walk around the stony fields of the holding by myself, thinking. I must get to Killarney somehow, then perhaps catch a train to Mallow first, then another south to Cork or even Cobh if I was lucky. Yes I would abandon the fight and return to the East and my mother. I hadn't been able to keep in contact with her as it was impossible to send off any letters, since I didn't want the irregulars to know who I was and where I came from. This would protect my family from any reprisal.

Desertion was a capital punishment offence in the IRA, but no one in the movement out here knew my real name, so I might get away with it. Also being a woman might help me treatment wise, if I was arrested by either side. The thought crossed my mind that much as I complained about the treatment of women, I was ready to use this when I could to my advantage. Was that really reasonable? I asked myself...

My appearance was the main problem; my long hair would have to be cut off. Mrs McGorram mustn't know about it; I didn't want my side to learn how I'd changed my appearance. Thank God I'd secretly kept those plain glass spectacles from when Weed had become a hunted figure. I would wear my simple dark skirt. I had enough money left for the trip. In the field everything was supplied or just stolen as the column went along, so there was little opportunity to spend money.

Because of my accent, I'd never pass as a local so I'd pretend to be a school teacher from Dublin returning home. I gave my host a bit of money for some of her son's schoolbooks to carry with me. I returned to the house. The children were sleeping, when I told Mrs. McGorram I'd be leaving early in the morning, giving her the impression I'd be rejoining the column again. But I didn't want to carry the pistol in the current climate, so offered it to her; warning her about the new law. She took it willingly, saying she had the perfect hiding place for it

She wished me luck, with tears in her eyes. I was touched. I kissed baby Katie, Liam and Mary, their sleeping faces angelic......and retired.

Nora came to me her pinched face showing relief. "Some sense at last; tho late I'd be atinkin'! The good Lord, Mary an' all the Saints protect ye Aisling!" and she was gone before I could answer her.

Sleep is always a problem when fighting in a war; with the column I'd taught myself to wake at an early hour when necessary. So just before sunrise, I quietly let myself out the door into the chilly morning air and walked briskly down the track. I didn't dare look back at the holding, where true peace had gently touched me, and my blind ugly patriotism had withered ....

84

Sky

 The funeral for Prime Minister Arthur Griffith was a large solemn affair. Dublin really was in mourning. The columns of soldiers and marching pipers were watched by large subdued crowds lining Sackville St. as the coffin made its way to Glasnevin Cemetery. Sad tension was in the air; the loss of one of the founding fathers of the fledgling nation; what would it mean for the future?

At the head of the parade was Michael Collins resplendent in his Commander in Chief's uniform of the Free State Army in tall shining boots, with General Mulcahy walking beside him.

This was the first time I really understood how highly Mick was thought of by the general populace; as an excited hum and even comments of admiration accompanied Mick down the street as people pointed him out to one another, as he marched along. The crowds seemed to be almost in awe of this legendary figure.

I was worried for his safety; after all, a desperate civil war was in progress and now Mick would be *the* prime target for the extremists. He was brave all right, casually ignoring the risk! Upright and apparently unconcerned, he looked every inch the hero. I peered around at the onlookers, but saw no signs of danger. Perhaps even the enemy realised that a major state funeral was not the place for an attack…

That very evening I got a message from Mick to come immediately. Typically, even on the day of a major occasion he was working. I had to go to an office in Dublin Castle which was going to be completely handed over to the new government, the very next day.

"Right Weed, the Edwards thing is in process, we've arrested him, we'll get that trial underway soon; you'll be contacted when the time comes." He sneezed, his cold seemed worse; he looked even less well.

"Now main thing, I want yer t'head the Police Intelligence Department of Public Security here in Dublin. The cabinet have agreed. S'more status 'n position rather than income; tho' it'll pay better than yer've bin used to….but not that much more mind; the government's skint and will be fer a decade or so; what wiv makin' good the damage these damned hotheads are causin' t' the country. We need leaders who aren't locked into colonial ways and quite frankly we're sick of bureaucrats infighting. Clean young broom, you'll sort em out! They don't understan' that this is a new world; but you really get it. Well, what d' y' think ?"

I was amazed and a bit overwhelmed. "What about qualifications Mick? You know I haven't been t' university… they'd not like a newcomer. And I'm not even thirty yet."

"Tough! I haven't been there either, and look where I am! Anyway you're famous…that gives y' status. Just *take* the job, 'n y'start early tomorrow, before the bastards know what's hit em!"

I thought rapidly, it was an unbelievable offer for a poor Dublin boy. There really *had* been a revolution in Ireland! "OK Mick, I'll do it! Thanks," I eventually managed to get out.

He grinned at me tiredly and pushed some documents and a file across his desk to me. "Thought yer would, contracts and warrant filled out here already! Sign 'em now. Just give it y' best shot, this file'll tell y' what the job's about. You're goin' to have to dress a bit better. Now I'm off t' Cork an' the south in the next few days… it'll be good to be back in me home territory again!"

"F' Christ sakes be careful Mick. And thanks for all this…"

For a second or two I thought he might have forgotten, what with everything he was dealing with, but no, Michael Collins never forgot *any* detail, no matter how small. As I turned to go, he asked casually, watching me closely: "did y' find out anything about Aisling on the medical training front?"

"No," I immediately lied, shaking my head.

"Doubt if y'd tell me anyway! Mind you, this mysterious "lady with the Tommy Gun" hasn't been seen for some weeks now; might have been a casualty. Things are really hotting up in Kerry; some on our side want blanket reprisals against the rogue IRA and all their supporters…I can barely hold 'em back.

"Well, good luck Weed; you've got one of the key jobs in the country!" He shook my hand, and I left him, somewhat stunned by everything that had come to pass.

Could he be right? Was Aisling really that woman? If so, was she be a casualty of some kind? *Hell,* what would my side do to her if she was captured? She was reputed to have killed many of our people…

That evening back in Aunt Biddy's parlour, I leafed through the file, with growing excitement. The new department I was head of would have access to any information I might need.….

Song

The trip had been a nightmare of delays, but as a woman teacher, I'd managed to easily pass through the Free State checkpoints. There were none on our side... which showed we must be losing. Then again, we'd have spies and informers everywhere, watching everyone. I tried to keep my face empty and vacant; I did not want to be recognized, by either side. The papers the column had given me were only glanced at casually.

Then came a surprising sign of the times. At one of the Free State railway station checkpoints I was thoroughly frisked by a woman who was with the soldiers, even my hair and hat were checked! She would have easily found the pistol if I'd kept it. Thank God I'd got rid of the damned thing! Ultimately however it made sense, Mick and the IRA had often used women to carry messages and occasionally weapons in the fight against the Brits... of course both sides now knew that.

The vast amount of damage done to rail lines and roads surprised even me, and I'd been involved in some of it! The most spectacular was the Mallow Viaduct; a whole section of the seventy foot high structure had been blown up. It would take years and a fortune to repair. That rail line would be unusable until then.

It reinforced my realization that our war was lost, though a newspaper I found in a train carriage reported on continuing atrocities against Catholics in Ulster; many had been murdered by the Unionist Protestant majority there. Our fight had been for a unified Ireland, including these north eastern counties.

As I idly watched Ireland slide slowly past the train's windows, I realized how much I loved my home country in all its guises; the well-churched smoky towns and cities, the soft greens, the gently rolling countryside, the villages and farmhouses dotted on rich farmland, the windy roads, rivers and streams, the little forests, the boggy lowlands, the rounded hills and rugged mountains, the rocky, barren uplands, the bays, inlets and offshore islands, all blessed by the seasons: the cheerful bright spring buds and blooms, the mild warmth of summer, the cooling golds of windblown autumn, the chill darker world of winter; all adorned by the clouds and mists constantly veiling the land with soothing gentle rains and damp persistent drizzle. Such an achingly beautiful world it was! The people of this land somehow mirrored this landscape; hardworking, religious and superstitious, argumentative but amusing, exasperating but always musical! I warmly felt part of them: this feeling was all beyond shallow politics.....

Weed would have approved of my poetic thoughts. And *that* was a point.... he'd actually slipped from my mind these last few days, even though I was heading east towards where he was living! This should have concerned me but my mind was somehow more amorphous in thought and form; tension had finally left me, specifics required far too much *effort*. Even my hatred for the Free Staters had thawed. I am sure this casual, relaxed vacancy got me through the checkpoints...

I was seeing everything in a new way. While with the column the land had been a source of danger or advantage; fighting distorted one's perception of the immediate world... but that was now behind me....

With the very last of my money, I caught a taxi from Kinsale to my home. The landscape was much as I remembered it, calming me further. With my short hair and glasses, I was sure no one local would recognize me. I felt a sudden surge of tearful emotion when we passed the corner where my father had been murdered in front of me. As we proceeded onwards past the church and little school on the banks of the estuary, I tried to get my emotions under control.

I didn't want the folk in the small gatehouse on our sweeping drive to see me, so I got the driver to drop me off at a small forest on the north border of the estate; there was a favourite track there that led to the Big House. My mother would be pleased and very relieved to see me; perhaps her prayers *had* made a difference, I'd come through unscarred, after all! My experiences out west had made me much more independent and confident; I was no longer a spoilt rich girl expecting everything to be done for me. I was looking forward so much to being reunited with my beautiful harp that I'd sent home from Dublin, just before heading west. A lovely deep hot bath would be absolute heaven!

I set off happily, quietly humming, walking through the cool beautiful trees that were wearing autumn colours, carrying my small suitcase. I laughed when I surprised a family of rabbits who gaped at me for a second before frantically sprinting for cover, their tails bobbing! Some red squirrels in the sycamores above scolded me as I made my way. The birds in the trees called out sweetly and I could hear the cattle and sheep in the nearby fields. The path was a little weedy and unkempt in places; that must be seen to! I was really looking forward to that first sighting of my home where I had happily grown up.... I turned a corner and out of the forest...squinting in the bright sunlight.

The view slammed me in the stomach... *low blackened ruins with twisted charred timbers* were all that remained of the house, stables and sheds! Everything had been burnt...it must have been done some weeks ago; weeds were already sprouting up in places.

I doubled up with pain. It seemed to me that my youth had somehow gone up in flames with it. Was this divine punishment for my actions out west, where arson had been one of our major weapons? I'd taken part in several of those actions, justifying them in turn by strategic necessity... to gain the Republic.

The IRA and its many factions had burnt many of the Big Houses all over the country, as much an anti-wealth stance as a political or religious statement. The well armed perpetrators would stop any fire brigade from trying to fight the flames so the damage was often absolute.

Tears pouring down my cheeks, I dropped my case and staggered towards the cold reeking remains. Had my mother died in the conflagration? There was no sign at all.

In the ruins below where my room had been I found the metal tensioners from my harp, the beautiful frame and gut strings were no more. A piece of shiny white porcelain caught my eye; it was part of my Titanic saucer, and a foot away I found the engraved brass nameplate that had adorned my large doll's house... so many memories gone!

I felt so alone and bereft in this world, an empty swirl of emotion tumbling and rumbling in my mind. A cacophony of discordant sounds was overwhelming me; I desperately needed a friend....without looking back I staggered away, past the now neglected gardens, the overgrown drive, the empty, also burnt gatehouse and out onto the road. I somehow knew where I must go....

86

Sky

Aunt Biddy fussed over me proudly as I dressed in my new suit, collar and tie, and shiny brown shoes. I left very early in the morning to start my new job. I reasoned that if I got to the office first, and was working when the others arrived, my appointment would seem more natural despite the fact I was only twenty five years old! I would immediately request some files from records, and would hit the ground running in effect. I would be nominally friendly but keep some distance from my staff… but I would pick up the nuances and personalities and use these to my advantage.

Working with Mick had taught me a lot, although I doubted if I would ever approach his level of output! I would need to be really organized from the word go….

Our work was vital to the Free State Government… the information we held was needed by all the new departments. Mmm; that was another thing; my organization would be a perfect target for the anti-treaty rebel IRA. I must do an immediate review of security, especially in the records and files area. I carried a small loaded pistol with me; once it was known I was heading the outfit, I would of course also be a major target.

Having a multifaceted plan of immediate action cheered me up and gave me confidence. I looked up at the sky for an omen…. comforting rounded clouds lit by the early glow of dawn blessed the dark blue above… yes, I *would* succeed.

When I arrived at work I dived into the staff files, many of my team were in their fifties and several had been doing this work for decades. Remembering Policeman George's concern, I mentioned the magic word pension to them; how I would work hard to protect their rights in this new, changed world…. This calmed them down and they worked with a will.

I was young but so much had happened to me over the last few years, I was much tougher and older inside, where it counted. Anyway, 'me stubborn' was up…. I told myself again; yes, I *would* succeed!

I had been on the job for a week. Things had gone well on balance….the staff was busy and I'd been accepted as the new boss, despite my youth, without too much fuss. My calm demeanour and poker face routine was working a treat… they were never sure what I was thinking, but my quiet assurance gave the impression that I knew exactly what I was about! Sudden requests for information got me through any awkward moment! I kept a number of these standing by in my mind for just this purpose.

I was mastering the intricacies of our system quite well, and had come to the conclusion that we were taking too long to process requests for information. I instigated a streamlined system that effectively halved the time it took to action a request and get it to the interested party. I was beginning to understand that the position I had somehow fallen into was very powerful in the nation's scheme of things….

As always Aisling had not been far from my mind. In a request for files on people, I slipped in one for the Kinnanes. It made interesting reading. As I'd suspected her father had been involved in racketeering as well as in legitimate business. I turned the pages with interest: Rory was now a Lieutenant in the Free State Army. There was an earlier coded reference which confirmed to me he had been part of the assassination team, 'The Squad', much as I'd suspected all along.

I turned to the next leaf in the file and there it was! *The letter that Aisling's father Eammon Kinnane had used to betray me to the authorities!* This harmless looking bit of paper had torn my life to pieces and had been indirectly responsible for many deaths. I then looked at the notes on the killing of her father, and then a final entry, which was a fortnight old note on the burning of the Kinnane Big House. A southern IRA irregular group, barely under central HQ control was suspected… but nothing had been proved. This was a problem for us throughout the country.

Poor Aisling, her home burned….just like mine had been. I wondered if she knew, and again where she might be….

In my corner office I suddenly heard a swelling buzz of consternation on the main floor; raised anxious voices. What the hell could have happened? I was reaching in my desk drawer for my pistol when my office door burst open; there was no polite knock this time.

My second in command Kileen had large frightened eyes, his words burst forth: "Mr Duffey, Mick Collins is *dead!* They shot him west of Cork, ambushed at a place called Beal na Blath, headwound … his body is being brought back to Dublin by steamship from Cork. God, what'll happen t' the country now?"

I collapsed back in my swivel chair, completely shattered. I turned around and faced my window, not wanting Kileen to see the tears in my eyes. Images flashed through my mind: that first meeting in the library so long ago, all those close calls and successes, the risks he'd taken when fighting the Brits, his flaws and good humour, his pigheaded deviousness, his support for the disadvantaged, his bloody mindedness when it came to finance, his brutality on occasion, and then even backing my appointment for this job. He'd changed me in every way: there was almost *too* much for me to remember....

More importantly for the new country, this changed everything. In the end his had been the most important voice of moderation and compromise…in our increasingly bitter and brutal civil war. The 'Big Man' was gone, and at only thirty-two years of age....

But I must carry on, I had a department to run, life had to go on. Now I would have to pull myself together and address my upset staff…

"Mr Kileen, please make sure our building flag is flying at half mast. Then arrange for all our staff to assemble in the big room, I will address them there."

It was a sombre occasion. They knew I was an acquaintance of the slain leader. My words were brief but to the point, I mentioned how much Ireland had changed for the better because of Mick's actions over recent years. I then gave them a lecture on security and how our department could become a target for extremists. We must be aware of this at all times. I contacted the Free State Army and arranged for some permanent armed guards to be stationed at our main and rear entrances.

But now the state funeral for the 'Big Man' was to be held. The country without him seemed a more uncertain and dangerous place....

Song

I saw nothing as I stumbled along, ragged haunting music pummelled my mind relentlessly; the dusty uneven road seemed to wind across the empty countryside forever. My breathing came in gasps as I fought for air; my very being had been shattered by all that had befallen me. I blindly *refused* to admit any liability for all my misfortune; fate alone was to blame! I longed for mental peace and something told me I would find it down this route. I didn't really know where I was going; but go, I *must!*

Without thought I selected several turns… and after some time I came to a tiny old abandoned church around which was a simple grave yard, all very isolated. I just felt I *knew* this place and someone here, but couldn't for the life of me remember who… it was all rather distant and strange. As I lay face down on a mound of earth there, a vaguely familiar but concerned young face flickered into my mind. The young girl's lips were moving; she was trying to speak to me I was sure, but the music in my consciousness was too loud for me to hear her… then a man's face wearing glasses pushed her aside stayed briefly, and then he too left me, lying limp and heavy on the grass….

I just lay there, vaguely aware of the cool darkness of night and the glowing warmth of the morning sun…perhaps I slept; I'm not sure. A misty rain started wetting my clothes… but I lay nestled shivering in my little musical haven, my cheeks touching the grassy earth of the mound…the wind sighing about me gently. I thought I heard someone speak out loud; surprised tones, but then silence returned.

Much later I was surprised by strange voices, strong arms lifted me against my will, of course I struggled against them, but to no avail. I was carried off in horse and trap accompanied by a priest, black cassock and white collar, a policeman and a nun… all trying to console me for some reason. I was beyond all caring and wouldn't speak.

They didn't know who I was; actually *I wasn't so sure myself!* Then I heard a *Nora Kinnane* mentioned; now, *that* name sounded vaguely familiar, in a misty, mindful sort of way....

I dozed off, my limp head swaying in my lap as the cart turned corners. Time had left my world, suspended in a morass of faded forgotten recollections; but I couldn't have cared less....

88

Sky

It was the largest funeral in Irish history. I was stunned by the immensity of the crowds; the sea of people dressed respectfully in their best, filling the streets and packing the squares, even hundreds were on the roofs of office buildings lining the route of the funeral cortege. And this was only a fortnight after the Arthur Griffith funeral where Mick himself had given the oration. It was so shocking.

Newspapers suggested that five hundred thousand had come to honour the young man who had captured the public's admiration, and was seen now as *the* key figure who had gained a measure of home rule and independence for Southern Ireland by way of the Truce and Treaty. Dying at the age of only thirty two at the hands of extremist rebels added to his martyr status and the myths around him in the public mind.

I had gone to pay my respects to Mick in the chapel of St. Vincents Hospital where he had been laid out in his Commander in Chief's uniform, a white bandage on his head, lighted candles at his head and feet with four solemn soldiers guarding him. His pale lifeless face seemed to me empty and waxlike. I felt a smart pinstripe suit would have been a more fitting, final clothing statement for him.

That bounding enthusiasm and quick fire flood of conversation and concentrated activity that always accompanied the 'Big Man' were eerily absent… the chapel was quiet except for the weeping of those who had come to mourn and the soft shuffling steps of those filing past the coffin. Memories brought tears to my eyes; how so many times we'd come close to disaster! That larger than life personality had always got us through, however. But now?

The body was taken later to City Hall for a public lying in state. Thousands of people of all ages filed respectfully past. Then Mick was taken eventually to the Pro Cathedral where a packed Requiem Mass was held.

I took Aunt Biddy, blind Amy O'Driscoll and her mother to the Cathedral. I was recognised and we were ushered to a section at the front of the mourners.

I saw many of the key figures in the movement there, including a very upset Joe O' Reilly who'd been Mick's faithful right hand man for so many years.

Amy seemed to feel the occasion most powerfully; tears dwelt permanently in the corners of her pale eyes. I squeezed her hand consolingly. After the fire in our lane Mick had helped everyone there financially to repair the damage; and he'd briefly spoken to Amy at the time in an encouraging way. Once he'd learnt of her loss, he'd also obtained a replacement harp for her.

After the service the coffin was carried on a gun carriage, towed by six black horses; also to Glasnevin Cemetery. As the cortege moved along the tricolour Irish flag it was draped in swelled and flapped in the wind…telling us something I fancied; perhaps the spirit of peace and freedom escaping from the casket..

This death had brought all sides together in grief. If only this unity could have lasted longer, perhaps the Civil War could have been brought to an end sooner, saving so many lives. Sadly it was not to be….

I then left the ladies and walked behind the cortege with dignitaries and others who had known Mick, all six miles to the cemetery. The last post was played on bugles, the touching funeral oration given by General Richard MulCahy, raised rifles fired a salute and the coffin was lowered into the grave. The 'Big Man' had touched so many lives on all sides of the Irish equation. I was sad; this signalled the end of an era. I wondered how my position might be affected now, since my getting the job had been Mick's idea…

I was called to the group running the service. The General, who I'd only briefly met once or twice in the past, beckoned me over. I was surprised as he was very much in charge of things in general and the war in particular; I felt quite honoured he'd even remember who I was. He looked worn out.

"Sad day, Duffey. As y' know, Mick always got so much done. He's goin' to be really missed, an' that's the truth. But we must keep on with the good work; speakin' of which, your department is functioning especially well since y' took over: the whole damn Cabinet have noticed the improvement! When Mick suggested y'd be the man, we argued, especially 'bout y'r age….an' you havin' to deal with older entrenched bureaucrats but, as usual, he wore us down in the end! He was right; so keep up the good work. Anything y'need?" He sighed and added: "mind you, things are tight at the moment, as usual…"

I mentioned the need for extra security as the department would be a prime target for the rebels… in exactly the same way the British version had been the focus of our efforts for some years. He agreed to help out in this respect and went back to his party.

Alone again, I looked a grey Dublin sky thinking again of Mick and how he'd unwittingly brought Aisling and I together. His grave was now covered with layer upon layer of flowers; there must be hundreds of wreaths! My Aisling would have loved the scented display. Where was she now? How would she take the news of Mick's passing?

The smartly turned out officers in the honour guard saluted, turned and then dispersed. One Lieutenant suddenly came towards me. It was Aisling's brother Rory! I nodded a greeting. He looked older and sharper than I remembered. Of course, as a member of Mick Collins' assassination squad, he was now in the Dublin Brigade which was fighting the Republicans out west. He shook my hand with a firm grasp.

"Heard you'd gone up in the world Duffey. Never ever got to thank you for saving me at the checkpoint that day… put it down to arrogant youth; my apologies! Seems a century ago now, so much has happened since.

"Now, some news about Aisling; just between us, of course. I met her out west, in a farmhouse a few weeks back: didn't let on to my lot. I think she was taking a break from fighting; she was limping, only an ankle injury I think. When I saw her she was masquerading as a farmer's widow and mother, on a poor isolated holding. There were three kids there too, one a baby! Not hers of course. Strangely enough the setup seemed to suit her. I do believe she is the famous woman with the Tommy Gun! She never denied it…looked thin, but as fit as a fiddle, and as hard as nails!"

Normally I was never very forthcoming but this was different. I was learning about my love and Rory was protective of his only sister. We had a shared interest in the woman.

"Mick thought that might be the case too; your sister fitted the description except for the rumours about her being a doctor. He asked me to check, but I already knew that she had done some first aid courses, before she went west. To protect her, I didn't tell Mick."

Rory looked at me sadly. "Well, she's completely disappeared; the last action she was seen in was a fortnight before I came across her. On that occasion she damn near shot down one of our aircraft and killed the observer on board. Since then, not a whisper!

"Y'know, I've a strong suspicion that even the IRA column she's with, don't know her real name… which might protect her a bit. They can't win; it's just a matter of time. Their current Commander in Chief, Liam Lynch, is just so bloody minded and refuses to negotiate in any way, even though he must realize it's hopeless!

"Fanatical as hell, my sister! If she comes back, there are going to be some big shocks for her. As well as our stupid father assassinated in front of her, now our Big House has been burnt down; with almost every other building on the estate. Our mother, who has heard nothing from Aisling for months has withdrawn completely from life and entered a nunnery. Everything has gone to hell!

"Meanwhile, I'm fighting out west, where things are getting nastier by the day, innocent civilians being caught up in the fight and killed by both sides; hell of a mess! Only Mick could have calmed down the extremists on our side, but now he's gone. God help us….

"Listen if you hear anything about Aisling please let me know…you're in a key position to find anything out first. I know you'll have the sense to keep quiet about it for her sake. Keep me posted if anything should turn up. A letter to the brigade will get to me, wherever I am stationed."

"I heard about the house burning, terrible for you too no doubt." I told him. He nodded regretfully, we shook hands again and Rory rejoined his group.

Yes, the burning would be yet another big shock in her tumultuous life. I must try and find out more about Aisling, but in a low key way.

I looked above the city of the living, the mourning crowds, the flowers and the blanket of wholesale grief which lay over the cemetery, the grey rain clouds being bullied along by a persistent easterly.

My life seemed somehow emptier without that towering, bounding personality. I trudged home reflectively; my thoughts lonely and longing. Also, what could I tell Amy about Aisling? The blind girl would sense instantly if I tried to hold anything back. She always asked me if I'd heard anything about her friend…

Song

The tones of the white coats were hushed and shocked…. nurses even cried quietly in the background. It was disturbing; apparently someone important in Ireland had died, shot in an ambush. The name I think I'd heard somewhere before; a certain… Michael Collins…. but no, I couldn't think where or if I had ever known this person, whoever he was; though I tried *really* hard to remember. Worry blanketed the institution; but it was all beyond me…

I hummed happily to myself as I looked out of the window from my locked room at an iridescent rainbow that arced across a cloudy sky; such beautiful colours triggered a cascade of music in my mind!

My world was now one of jangling keys, quiet acceptance, and lots of frowns and big words, which I didn't understand. So many questions….confusion jangled within these light green walls. But my soul was untouched by anything here.

The thin faced girl who came to me from time to time with such sad desperate eyes…..always speaking to me, but I couldn't *hear* her at all. Rather curious how she appeared, without keys or opening doors; but no worry!

Otherwise, day followed day, meals, words and restful interludes slid past, warm sheets and blankets melted me into a neutral comforting haze.

Ah, so detached I was….

90

Sky

 I should have taken the hint; it definitely was an omen. The low Dublin sky was a uniform dark grey and rain was teeming down; even my umbrella was little use in such a windy deluge. My suit was soaking when I entered the entrance to the special court that been specifically convened to try Captain James Edwards of the former occupying British Army of excess brutality during what was now being called the Irish War of Independence.

As I had predicted, Press interest in the case was high; many reporters from Britain, Europe and the US crowded the media section of the seating. The new Free State Government was on show to the world; and although a jury had been dispensed with, no less than five high court judges would decide the case. Justice must be seen to be done fairly by the world's newest country.

There was also a packed public gallery; people had come from all over the country to witness a former occupying enemy soldier being hopefully brought to justice… so many citizens had suffered at the hands of Black and Tans and the Auxilliary Officers that the British had employed to suppress opposition, they were relishing this chance to see history being done. Normally such a trial would have taken place close to the scene of the crime, but Kenmare was in the staunchest rebel area of the current Civil War, so the trial was being held here in the capital.

Things began innocuously enough; the accused gave his full name rank and number. Edwards looked every inch the British Army officer, and answered the court officer in a clear and confident voice; I noticed that his arrogant drawl had disappeared completely. He looked around the court quite unfazed that he was the centre of attention. He portrayed an air of puzzlement as to why he was in this position. After the charges were read out, he pleaded not guilty in an emphatic tone that rang around the court above the rattle of heavy rain on skylights above.

I was going to be the prime witness for the prosecution. Since I was now a civil servant heading an important government department, it was thought by our side that I should be an anonymous witness throughout the trial; "witness X." Of course, Edwards would know who I was, but legal concessions were given to his side in exchange for him not revealing my name. His legal team was top notch and we suspected the British Government were paying a big bill for it! Joe O'Neill headed the defence team, an innocuous, harmless looking character who I'd been warned about. Low key questions leading to a viper like attack on any inconsistencies was how he operated; and then watch out!

I'd begun to regret my restraint those weeks back and now felt uneasy about this whole business; though 'me stubborn' was still up. In my mind I wanted to keep my mental promise to Sean Quinn, that I would avenge his treatment; anyway I was now committed to this course of action. Quinn's melted face and bravery haunted me still. I was in the visitor's gallery, watching proceedings, just a normal member of the public as far as everyone was concerned at this stage of proceedings.

The Kenmare baker had died; how was in debate, since his body had never been found. His wife Sinead had survived a period of incarceration and had been reunited with her children. She would be the prosecution's second witness. Young Orla now eleven years old, was with her mother and was going to be our first.

Orla hadn't lost any of her dignity, and was determined to avenge the brutality her father had suffered. A small figure in the box, she took the oath and when asked, told what she had witnessed that morning in her father's bakery and home. She spoke well; her small voice clear, her accent charming.

In his cross-examination O'Neill asked her a few questions in a gentle, sympathetic tone. It was quickly ascertained that she hadn't actually *witnessed* any brutality, but had only seen the terrible injuries her father had sustained. The young girl was stood down.

Her dark haired mother was also in the same position, except that she had seen her husband's left hand jammed on the hot stove by Edwards and burned, but she'd then fainted and also hadn't seen how her husband's face had been injured. Only when she'd come to, had she seen his terrible injuries.

O'Neill was much more emphatic with an adult. He took her back to the beginning of her arrest and got Sinead to relate what had happened then: the punch to the face she had received, her bleeding lip and the other injuries sustained. Sinead didn't hold back at all in her description of what had happened; O'Neill let her describe her terror and distress at seeing her husband hit with a rifle in the face. This turned out to be the key. Having got her to say how extremely distressed she had been, he then questioned her again and again about how her husband's left hand had been burnt…who was on what side of her husband etc. Eventually the stressed witness's report varied and he pounced. Under pressure Sinead finally wavered… She was stood down, a slight doubt hanging over her testimony.

The head judge looked at the wall clock, conferred with his learned colleagues, and declared that recess would be taken. The court would reconvene at 2pm.

I met the prosecution team at one for a final briefing. We only had three witnesses for our side, the main one would be me. Things had not gone well on balance. It was felt that O'Neill had been restrained so far and I might be in for a difficult time. I would be in place behind a screen before the court opened to the public. I would only be visible to the judges, the prosecutor and defence lawyer during my testimony.

As I sat rather tense behind the screen listening to everyone filing in and taking their seats, I was bracing myself for an ordeal. I rather wished Mick had been there… his overwhelmingly confident outlook and cleverness were needed here.

I took the oath and the Prosecutor got me to tell my story. In a firm, reasoned voice I related everything that had happened that day, from the time I had crossed the bridge and had entered the town up to my arrest in the bakery and how I had been taken off to the barracks afterwards. Out of the corner of my eye I could see O'Neill taking notes. When I discussed Quinn's treatment there was an angry murmur from the public gallery; the subsequent lack of any medical treatment, and possible torture at the barracks caused a further stir.

Then the defence lawyer cross examined me. Was I not armed with a pistol at the time? Was the weapon loaded? I answered yes to both questions. O'Neill stated that the violence used then in the situation by the Crown, was therefore justified, at least to a certain extent. I pointed out that the soldiers outnumbered us and were, of course, much better armed! The partisan audience approved of my comment… O'Neill let that go.

He asked me details about how I had been restrained in the bakery. Had I struggled with the four Tans holding me? Had they experienced difficulty trying to do so? I said they *certainly* had! The gallery laughed at that one. I naively felt things were going my way. Strangely, he then asked me if I was a large man, er, bigger than the baker Sean Quinn. I said I wasn't, in fact I was shorter and much lighter in comparison.

O'Neill paused for effect, then asked me, if four soldiers were barely able to control me, the two restraining Quinn, a much larger, stronger man, must have found it near impossible to control the baker, I thought back to that day and stated that he'd had a rifle smashed in his face, and lost at least one tooth, and was no doubt concussed and unsteady anyway. O'Neill smiled at me for a second.

He stated that I had been arrested, because at that time I was a wanted man for violent crimes -er murder in Ireland. He couldn't go any further without revealing my identity. Was this true however? After an electric pause I admitted that was so.

He then asked me if I hated the British authorities at this time; I quickly agreed that I did, and when I tried to explain why, he cut me short, by just asking me to just answer the question; yes or no. I went ahead anyway, giving examples of the brutality, stating that my elderly, sick uncle had been executed by these forces (which wasn't quite accurate!). Immediately I received a rebuke from the judge who threatened me with a Contempt of Court charge. I stopped, suddenly aware that I'd overdone things.

O'Neill got me to tell the court what it was I alleged to have seen; how Quinn's hand and then face had been burnt on the stove top. I told them word for word what had been said, by Edwards and the baker. The public gallery was stunned silent at my description at first, then, angry murmurs arose there. The head judge called for silence, stating that he would clear the gallery if need be. I was pleased that at least the world now knew of Quinn's suffering and bravery.

O'Neill moved onto my escape on the way to Mallow railway station. I stated how I had been rescued. He wanted to know what had happened to the six men escorting me. I told him they had been shot. Then I fudged my testimony again; and said as far as I knew, they were all dead. I had been trussed up and was lying face down on the truck, with the soldier's boots resting on my body. So many bullets had been flying around; I had thought that I would be a goner too! At least that part was true.

The lawyer asked me what had happened to the men's bodies? Lying, I said I didn't know. He asked me if it worried me at all, that there were six families in Great Britain who did not know where their sons were. I replied, you mean like the Quinn family here and countless other Irish families? The gallery briefly erupted, but was suddenly silent again as the judge glared that way. O'Neill stated that my hatred for the British Army, coloured my recollection, and must therefore make me an unreliable witness whose testimony should be taken with a large dose of salt. I vehemently denied this...

O'Neill stated that that was the end of his cross-examination of me.

The judges adjourned the court until the next day. Our side felt things could have gone better on balance, but our case could have been worse. The whole case was resting almost entirely on my evidence. What was O'Neill up to? Tomorrow the defence's case would be presented.

It was still raining lightly when the court was convened on the second day. I rejoined the public in the gallery.

Edwards was the only witness for their case. He was calm and serious, answering questions put to him in a thoughtful, measured tone. Only when explaining how the Baker had burnt his hand that morning did he depart from the truth; Quinn, a big strong man, he said, had wrestled with the two soldiers holding him, and being unsteady, perhaps concussed, just as witness X had suggested, had fallen and his left hand landed on the top the stove burning it. Under no circumstance had he put the man's hand on the element! The wrestling match had intensified after this injury and then the hapless baker had fallen again, but face down this time. The soldiers had lifted his head up as quickly as possible to try and minimize damage, but Quinn's face had been terribly disfigured, just as his wife and daughter had said.

I found it hard to contain myself at these lies; using *my* comments to support his evidence! I was livid with rage....

Edwards stuck to his version of events when cross examined by my team. If his soldiers were so concerned, what medical care had been obtained for the victim? He was asked. At the barracks, a medical orderly had looked after Quinn, he informed us. What about the torture at the barracks as described by Witness X? There was *no* torture, Witness X had admitted not seeing anything as he was in a cell, but the Baker *had* screamed in pain continually from his injuries, for quite some time. They had not been able to find any morphia to give to him as their doctor was away to the south at the time.....

He was so damned *convincing*; Edwards was getting completely away with a war crime! We had failed! I was numb with disappointment...

This whole business had been a rude reminder to me of my youth and inexperience; I had been getting too cocky. For an uneducated, twenty-five year old, I had done brilliantly in life with Mick's help, but I now realised I was still shallow and had a hell of a lot to learn about life....

At this point, my side received a note handed down from the public seats by a short nondescript type dressed in working class clothes. The court clerk who received it wasn't sure for a moment as to which legal team it should go to, and looked up. The fellow emphatically pointed to the prosecution side. He looked a bit familiar, but where I'd seen him, I couldn't recall.

My legal team huddled together discussing the note and glancing up at the man who had passed it to them. The main prosecutor then asked the judge and O'Neill if the prosecution could call another witness to the stand: a certain Mr. William Jones. The judges glanced at O'Neill, who gave his assent, quite certain that the case was in his bag anyway. Unseen by him, Edwards looked suddenly worried.

William Peter Jones was called to the stand. He took the oath. Edwards had slumped in the defendant's box, head down. Gone was the polished veneer and confidence.

When asked by my side, he explained in a cockney accent that he had been a private in the British Army, stationed in Kenmare at that time, and had been present in the Kenmare bakery that morning. He stated categorically that everything *I* had said was accurate; that Sean Quinn had been brutally tortured by Captain Edwards, who after deliberately burning the baker's left hand had pressed and held his face down on the hot stovetop.

The court erupted into an uproar that took a whole minute to die down. When asked by my side why he had come forward voluntarily, he answered that he was ashamed that such lengths had been gone to; Quinn had been a brave man. The kids appearing afterwards, seeing their grossly disfigured father, had disturbed him deeply. Even though it was a dirty war there had to be limits on behaviour. Not all British people behaved in this fashion…

O'Neill then cross-examined Jones, but he doggedly held to his account of events. Getting nowhere on that tack, the defence lawyer then questioned whether Jones *had* actually been present during this episode. There were no records to place him there; the British had removed everything when they had withdrawn. Jones was asked if he had any actual proof that he was there.

For a moment Jones looked nonplussed at this turn of events …then a sly hint of a smile appeared on his face; this jogged my memory; of course! Witness X had mentioned an unusual skill he had that would identify him at Kenmare. I guessed what was coming…..

O'Neill was annoyed with this fellow who had severely weakened his case and snapped at the witness, asking what this might be. Jones cleared his throat, and gave a perfect series of warning dog barks, that echoed around the chamber. The whole court was stunned for a second; some people even began to applaud! The judge struck his gavel for silence... very annoyed at the change in mood; after all this was a serious occasion.

Beaten, O' Neill stated he had no further questions and Jones was stood down.

After a lunch break both sides presented their summing up and the court was adjourned for two days while the judges reached their decision, the defendant Edwards being remanded in custody until then.

The trial made the headlines; here in Ireland and overseas, much as I had hoped. The new Free State legal system was on display and almost all reports were favourable, things had so far been fair and even handed as far as anyone could tell. The barking witness had brought an element of humour to the situation!

But then came a big surprise....perhaps O'Neill realised his case was lost and had advised his client accordingly. Captain James Edwards changed his plea to guilty! This might lessen his sentence in the long run... and so it proved. The change of plea also made the headlines.

The judges however, presented the reasoning behind the whole case so the world could see how the witnesses and evidence had been evaluated and decisions arrived at. With the late guilty plea, the sentence was reduced to four and a half years imprisonment, then deportation from Ireland. An unusual condition was that The Free State also undertook to protect Edwards from other inmates during his incarceration.

Overall, things had gone well. Punishment was seen to be done fairly; revenge had been taken out of the equation. The sentence was not excessive, but the public admission of guilt and the fact that the whole world now knew of his shameful actions, was a life sentence in effect. The case also reminded the world of the brutality that Ireland had been subjected to by the British. On balance I was pleased!

Private Jones told us where Quinn's body and some others had been secretly buried near Kenmare by the occupying force: tidying up another loose end...

That evening I learnt that Aisling had been institutionalised somewhere, and was undergoing treatment of some kind. Where, even I couldn't find out... but I would in time. Her family would be ashamed of the fact. The good news was, she had somehow survived the fighting out west! The rebels were finally being decimated by the Free State forces...surely a ceasefire and end to the conflict couldn't be far away?

Song

 Strange how the great calm wafted into the maelstrom my life had become. Looking back there had been one or two brief advance episodes over the last few weeks, before this final enduring act set in.

Others had noticed and remarked on my state and my sudden lack of any reaction to their comments. That had surprised them. To me these occasions seemed entirely natural and were accompanied by a low pleasant murmur of music that stayed permanently in my mind.

The best part for me was how I would forget during them. A soothing sense of pleasant fatigue, total relaxation…was gently lowered onto me, making me smile, sliding me into a vast symphony of restful non-involvement. I quite happily did nothing: people, friends, places, clothes, food, happenings…...-nothing mattered at all!

Time ceased to exist or matter in my silky world of tranquillity; limits meant nought….

I was only vaguely aware of what was going on around me, but couldn't be bothered responding to what was happening: low concerned voices, locking doors, white coats, rustling uniforms, antiseptic scents… being dressed by others, my long hair washed and combed. There were occasional vague hints of embarrassment; but they meant nothing to me; Aisling an Irish Princess in a court of placid, enduring peace….

Once there were wires, a sudden shriek of music in my head, a cascading convulsion of stars falling…then fading as the serenity returned. Distant raised voices… an argument of some kind between the white coats… but I didn't care.

Soon after, there was a final trip by car; a procession of scenes sliding past, trees villages and countryside flowed as I was shifted to a big quiet place. Here there was a difference, the rustling uniforms were grey topped by white and accompanied by rattling beads, the voices softer, the air warmer. Occasionally beautiful hymn singing would echo and soar in the building.

Years slipped by languidly in my dark varnished room, with a curtained window, the source of sunlight, colours and dark at which I would gaze from my comfortable scarlet velvet throne. One soft caring voice and shape became my world of years; I didn't like it when that voice was absent or there was a change…

Ah, then there was the emaciated young face with large tearful blue eyes framed in untidy black hair that would float into my mind at times, accompanied by a sad traditional air. The girl's lips were always saying something…what, I never knew. My condition seemed to upset her. This concerned creature would dim and fade, leaving me a little perplexed for only a second or two; then that restful, uncaring calm would return to me…

Very rarely, there would be another visitor of some kind to my haven; before this arrival, the music in my head would be louder and clearer in some way. The visitor had a darker form, a deeper, almost familiar voice; yet somehow still caring in tone. At times the words seemed full of despair. Why, I couldn't work out at all. My hand would be gently held by a warm large one…

After a time, the face would lightly kiss me, sometimes it was wet with tears, then I'd be alone again in my kingdom…and the music would recede gently to the normal background level. I was left wondering of distant dreams and times, all of which were lost somewhere in the outer regions of my mind. That deep voice and scent… where and when had I known them? I never could recall…

But sleepy peace would come back and lower itself upon me again and I would cease to be concerned. The music of my life would resume…

One day, the mind music seemed to explode and for a flashing second I *remembered* the only man I'd ever really loved! Weed, had been coming to see me forever, even though I hadn't made the effort to recognize him and *I* had been the cause of our parting…over something as silly as politics. I still loved him and actually said so. I also recalled my ragged young friend Nora from times long past! I could see her faintly, beckoning me to her.

Then a final crescendo overwhelmed me and I was drifting far from life, deep into a comforting ocean of harmonic sound and all-seeing light….

Sky

Secretly I just had to. Why did I continue to put myself through it? 'Me stubborn' was up again I suppose! I never told anyone where I was going, hinting only slyly that there was some secret business I had to attend to… which was true in effect. From the year 1924 when I discovered her whereabouts by chance, onwards four times a year for nearly forty years I would make the effort and visit my past. I couldn't stop what became the habit of decades. Aisling and I had been enmeshed in a togetherness world of love and I could *not* leave her; even now when she didn't know me.

Dressed in my best I'd set forth, my mind an untidy jumble of emotion; sadness, anticipation tinged with a smidgeon of the dull acceptance of fate.

The winding oak-lined road leading to the impressive buildings of the expensive institution framed the seasons of my life; autumn being my favourite. Crunchy russet windblown leaves mellowing and layering the land matched my wistful mood best.

I would always have a last look at the sky before pressing the bell button and entering the building through the great doors. The place was cool, echoey and very orderly, an air of numbing efficiency pervaded the place, it seemed to me. Nuns quietly scurried about their work; occasionally a patient could be heard.

I was always greeted politely by the sisters running the home, and was surprised how quickly they came to know me, despite my four monthly spaced visits, until one of the younger ones, a rather sad eyed Sister Catherine, quietly informed me that I was the *only* visitor that Aisling received, which distressed and embittered me greatly. Apparently her family paid the bills, but that was all. One year I checked up on them and found their businesses were steadily flourishing despite Eire's fluctuating economy. Her brother Rory had been killed in Kerry on the very last day of the Civil War…

From a modern perspective, looking into Aisling's green eyes had been like peering into the depths from a narrow aircraft window high in the stratosphere; seeing a vast scene: first the blue, cool clear upper air of confidence, then the grey cloud layers of doubt, a wispy strata of fear, the white billowy clouds of the stubbornness and loyalty, the purple thunderheads of anger and jealousy, and sometimes, for a fleeting instant, the green land of limitless warmth that glowed far below, only to vanish in the haze and ever moving mists of time. Such was her Celtic soul; or so it seemed to me …

Now, however, the lively animation and the green eyes sparkling with life had faded -no gone, to be replaced by placid, vacant orbs; she saw me I'm sure, but I didn't really register. The face to me was still beautiful in a marble statue sort of way, but the cloud of auburn hair was now cared for by the staff and somehow lacked vibrancy or life of any kind.

I'd sit by her; hold her hand and try and talk but would get little response. Sometimes my cheeks would be wet with tears for a past lost to time, feelings smothered by the years. Once, at just such a time, she squeezed my hand and said "There there, dearie!" But this trace of consoling warmth faded as quickly as it had appeared.

I suppose over the decades she grew old, grey and wrinkly, I know I certainly did! But with Aisling I never noticed: her old essence and spirit remained young in my mind all those years.….

The caring Sister Catherine told me she was a model patient, never getting upset; but I loathed Aisling's lack of emotion above all. I wanted the woman to scream, react in some way….. *anything* at all; tear the whole show to pieces! Her unnatural, persistent calm was unnerving, especially to one who had known her former fieriness. Likewise her room upset me, so clinically neat and tidy. A crucifix and a picture of Mother Mary looked down on us from above her bed. There were no photos of her family, or me for that matter. She'd not been particularly religious when we'd been together; the Republic had been her real passion and religion when I thought about it. And *that* had become the cause of our parting.

The high point of my visits was in the mid '30s. On one occasion I was in a similarly tearful state and walked to the window of her room to compose myself by looking at the sky, as is my way, when a soft alluring voice spoke behind me. "Ah, what a time we had, my Love…..!"

I spun eagerly around, but already, she was drifting away again into her murky ocean of indifference.

As I left, the door would close behind me shutting out my old dreams as I tiredly rejoined the cold and somehow emptier world outside …

The telegram from the home came at the end of July 1958. Aisling had had a sudden stroke. I left from my southern home immediately but it was too late. When I arrived thirty hours later, she had passed away. That should have been an ending of sorts, but it wasn't.…

The home's chapel was small and intimate, which somehow accentuated the shameful absence of mourners. I and one other man, a representative of her family, perhaps a retainer of some sort, were it, although some of the staff attended, including Sister Catherine who was most upset, God bless her. Someone else should join me in my grief…

The soft colours of the stained glass windows played on the white coffin and the vestments of the priest. I remembered back all those years ago to when my stepbrother Padraig had drowned in my childhood and how he'd looked so small in his coffin, Aisling also looked almost tiny, pale but with a serene face; perhaps *real* peace had come to her at last, she'd finally escaped her memoryless, emotionless world of perpetual detachment. Yes, perhaps it *was* a release for her.

And me? I felt vacant and empty but it was not a Fin du Siècle moment. My love could not be dissolved and obliterated so easily; my stubborn sky of feeling was too unbounded…

There was a little hidden cemetery I'd never noticed before near the oaks along the drive and Aisling was buried there. The other man glanced at me curiously and spoke to the Mother Superior, possibly finding out who I might be, but left before Aisling was interred, a further insult I reasoned. I never had a chance to speak to him. I threw the first clod of earth down onto the coffin and turned away, looking at the cloud filled sky, hearing the coarse dull thud of soil burying the love of my life. The rattle of rosary beads and the rustle of a nun's habit intruded on my empty musings. I turned back.

Sister Catherine's tear-streaked face appeared surprisingly old and lined to me as she spoke in a low voice. "Aisling passed away without pain, she was at peace. But at the end she was suddenly quite lucid." The sister glanced nervously at the Mother Superior; nuns were not supposed to converse with men after all. But her eyes were watching me very closely.

"Listen Mr. Duffey, she made a rather strange comment to me. At the very end, she looked around with animated eyes and said: "Weed will always stay in my heart *forever*. I was always *the* cloud in his sky, and he in mine. He was the only one I ever loved, despite everything. He *must* know!"

Then Aisling spoke as if she was actually seeing someone. "Nora, I'm joining you…" and she softly floated off to eternity. Those were her very last words. I'm sure she said *Weed*; strange name, though I suppose it could have been something else. The cloud comment too. Does it make sense to you? Did you know this Nora?"

The nun's face betrayed an almost desperate eagerness to be close to any vestige of romance and warmth that her chosen way of life denied her. The look on my face gave away that I must be the Weed in question….and she knew that I must have loved her patient; after all, for decades I had visited her despite a complete lack of response. My answer brought a deluge of tears.

"Perfect sense, sister! It really does, thank you! Except I do not know of any Nora…" But my heart leapt, after all these years Aisling had felt the same despite her vacant condition!

Sister Catherine had been the agent, bringing a final clarion call to a great love. I was glad that this meant so much to her; the poor kind creature deserved her own love story…

I returned to my home in the far south on my beloved Beara Peninsula, in a sad but warmer frame of mind.

My wife was waiting for me….. she searchingly touched my face. "Aisling's dead Aidan? So sorry I am my love… the y'rs had blessed her wiv ye loyalty, an' her not knowin' ye. No one could be expectin' more.."

"You *knew* it was her I was seein' all these years Amy? You never said anything and ye didn't mind?"

The face smiled.

" 'Course I *knew*; an' didn't mind. Aisling helped make ye who ye are, and she changed me greatly. Yer loyalty melts me heart…twas what firs' attracted me to ye! Sides, I sort of knew ye'd end up bein' mine! A man of secrets ye t'ink y' are my Aidan D'…. but *I* touch y'r heart an' mind, wiv more than my music alone. *I'm* the mother of y'r children, an' *I* warm yer bed an' mind at night, *I* dwell in y'r sky of life…blessed ye be in love my husband."

She smiled and kissed me. I clung to her, her soft cheek warming my heart. I *had* been so lucky in life!

Y'know, the way I see it, love is a limitless sky that most of us just aimlessly float around in, and even then we are lucky; some seem to miss out all together. A rare few soar heavenwards and stay emotionally aloft, gliding effortlessly from year to year, the feeling a warm backdrop as they face the storm clouds of life. I luckily had been one of those.

Oh God! There I'm going off once again, with those clouds of fancy…

93

Sky

 A few times over the years, I visited Mick's grave at Dublin's Glasnevin Cemetery and couldn't believe how, even now, so long after his death crowds still visit it reverently…..

Daily bouquets of fresh flowers still appear magically. Some wag told me that he wondered if the local council hadn't helped keep a good thing going to fire up the tourists, but no: the orders for the blooms come from all over the world, day and night, certainly helped by the Neil Jordan film which only scraped the surface of the guy's personality and work ethic, not to mention the whole damn complexity of it all. In true Hollywood style; accuracy mustn't get in the way of a great yarn. On my last visit there I saw what has apparently often happened since the film; A card with flowers to Michael Collins and *Julia Roberts!* Mick would have roared with laughter at that, probably even more so as Julia is still alive and well.…

Dev is also buried there in an unremarkable family plot like any other Irishman. It is hard to find and seems to be of little interest to the public, yet, over the years, he had been an important national figure.

His refusal to go to London during treaty negotiations left Mick in a position to seize the reins of power. Dev was a great political survivor, but he completely underestimated Mick. Once assassinated at a young 32 while fighting for peace, he became a saint-like martyr who did no wrong; even more of a legendary figure.

Also at that time Dev went against the wishes of the people who were more than ready for peace at the end of the brutal, punishing fight with the Brits. Perhaps some remembered his arrogant response to a clear cut election result in favour of peace and the Treaty: "The majority do not have the right to be wrong!" or words to that effect.

Mick's comment that the treaty "gives us the freedom to eventually achieve freedom," made more sense to people. Even taking all of this into account history seems to have dealt with Dev quite harshly.

Dev led many Irish governments over the decades and eventually became President of the Republic, and was the oldest head of state in the world at the end of his long career.

I did meet him once a few years before his death. An old, tall but bent figure, now hard of hearing, but still respected as *the* old man of Irish politics. The tired old eyes flicked over the group I was with as he was speaking to someone and then started as he recognised me, I was sure…

He moved as if to come over to me, but then thought better of it. I did not respond, the Dail walkout and the subsequent Civil War, he helped cause by initially being a figurehead the rebels could coalesce around, still saddened me. Although, as the struggle progressed, Dev was sidelined and became less important; but the subsequent death of Mick still affected me. Indirectly too Aisling's life had been smashed by these events….

I should learn to forgive more; tho' tis a bit late for me to start trying to, now…

For sure, the decades have swept past almost unnoticed; the early free governments, the depression, the second Great War, the initial slow modernization of the nation, then that lusty Celtic tiger. The latter really upsets me. Cell phone clutching, property value obsessed yuppies, the extravagant lifestyles. Pure greed is all it is; was this really what we'd strived, fought and died for? It won't last, time herself is only briefly generous, then her impatience reasserts itself, as a sunny open sky invariably fades and storms arise…

94

Sky

Ah, but old I be getting now. I can't fathom it all, or be bothered much to try. Old age showers us with a great cavalcade of shattered illusions yet I cling somehow to a positive view of the past; we all took part as best we could; we were there as fate decreed; she treated us as she willed....

A filigree duvet of haze covers the land of my mind with shadow. Cloud children of the Atlantic, lilting mountains of mist that sing to the winds, lulling me into a state of peace and well-being. The modern young laugh and mumble to themselves about dementia... but their minds have been drowned brutally, bludgeoned by a tsunami of modern information, so how would they know what is really important? I'd be askin' ye...eh?

History lowered a poisonous cloud of dissension and insoluble conflict, warfare and stupidity upon us here in Ireland; the bitterness of it all is with us even now, some seven decades later. I peer back to those far off events through the tarnished, blurry telescope of time; me thoughts all a jumbled. A hell of a mess it was for sure..... but I'm proud to have been there and done my bit.

Who was right in the Civil War? I'm now inclined t' think *all* sides were...each fought for what it fervently believed in at that time: bravery, family dissension, and bitter loss were shared by *all* factions; these were perhaps the birth pains of the proud independent nation of Ireland that lives on today. The problem was the *lengths* both sides went to, in the fight. But the passing years cover one in a warm mantle of mellowing acceptance and tolerance....perceptions soften.

Surprisingly, my thoughts for old mother church are also kinder. I miss her overbearing, busybody tentacles enmeshing our society, wriggling into every personal crevice; but nonetheless bringing some moral stability and a more predictable order to things in general, qualities that have faded somewhat these last few decades. Yet the abuse that has destroyed her can't be ignored; terrible it has been for so many....

I now spend all my days in the tiny cottage by the lake, to others alone, but to me the cramped interior is packed with those I knew. Light now hurts me ancient eyes so the curtains are pulled in daytime. But the gloom inside is aglow for me with memories and past friendships as I slowly go about the comforting little rituals of life. The tiny building fairly swells and breathes of long ago life…

The ancient land around it has known so many events over the millennia. But its spirit endures majestic and unruffled by mere humans. The tired, worn stone peaks and hills seem resigned to suffer on; sensuous clouds fondling their tops, and damply caressing and clinging to the valleys.

I shuffle out only at sunset when the gentle Irish air and soft glowing landscape soothes my mind. Mysterious shiny ripples born of cool wandering Atlantic winds melt and glide on the dark waters, quietly kissing the reeds beside the old wooden boat landing, where in my mind I watch the evening clouds forget the orange sun, grow old and die, fading into darkness; just as *we* must.

Clouds are free vaporous spirits untroubled by poverty, politics and petty laws; even gravity seemingly cannot touch them… but the winds of change do move them; and so it is with us humans.

Yes, I'm *still* rambling on….!

As I said at the beginning of this account, we *are* all just clouds. We come and go, most of us easily forgotten; grey, hazy and indistinct; a persistent misty film obscuring the deep blue and dulling the sun. But a rare few of these vaporous creatures stand solid, proud and memorable, sharply defined against the heavens, playing with the light, swelling, lifting our souls and whispering to us of great things to come, inspiring thoughts and emotions. Aisling, Amy and the great Michael Collins too; abilities, faults and all… were three of those… and they've never left me even for an instant, in all these years; The real monuments we leave behind us are the vibrant memories held by those who lived, loved and lingered in our sky of life.

And me? I was a dull, featureless low lying vapour, packing a surprising punch and unexpectedly sticking around; forever and ever…

Yes, I'm *still* here. I've outlasted almost the whole bloody lot: the fearless hard men, the patriots, the cowards, the informers, the indecisive, the anxious, the frightened and especially, the desperately uninvolved; the whole damned *Irish* crock of them!

So, after all, the mirror *was* wrong. I was tougher and more enduring than *all* of them. Then again, weeds are always hard to get rid of! Thank God we're a nation of them!

To be sure, God *did* move in 'sterious ways!

And now, I fancy, a vaster sky is upon me, where several towering clouds await…

About the Author

Don McGregor is an ex-international school principal, now writing full time. He is from New Zealand but has worked and lived in China for almost seven years, also in the South Pacific and in the Middle East. Don enjoys travelling, reading history, playing his guitars, music in general and offshore solo yachting in his spare time. A former pilot he is interested in all aspects of aviation. He lives on a beautiful island off the coast of his home country.

Aisling's Cloud is his fifth published novel.

His other titles are:
Merran
A Wistful Legacy
Phin
Billionaire Phin

(All titles are also available worldwide in ebook form in a several formats: Kindle, Kobo, Barnes and Noble… etc.)

Printed books available from www.copypress.co.nz.